Michelle lay there, the covers over her, barely breathing. Her eyes closed, her heart racing. She'd heard something. Nick turned over, his hand brushing her shoulder accidentally. Her eyes shot open. There... there it was again. She lay still, stopped breathing. She didn't want to look; it would go away. It was a way of keeping it at bay, whatever was out there, whatever was lurking around outside, beyond this room, somewhere out there in the deserted countryside. But it didn't work. The sound was still there. Some branches scraped against one of the windows. She froze, rigid. There it was; it happened again.

THERE WAS SOMETHING OUT THERE...

SIGNALS

DEBORAH DEUTSCHMAN

PLAYBOY PRESS
PAPERBACKS

Published simultaneously in the United States and Canada by
Playboy Press Paperbacks, New York, New York. Printed in the
United States of America. Library of Congress Catalog Card Num-
ber: 79-89966. Reprinted by arrangement with Seaview Books.

Books are available at quantity discounts for promotional and industrial use. For further information, write our sales promotion
agency: Ventura Associates, 40 East 49th Street, New York, New
York 10017.

ISBN: 0-872-16604-X

First Playboy Press Paperbacks printing March 1980.

Part I

THE FOUNDATION

That suspension of disbelief that comes at unexpected times in one's life—Nick Schrader thought he was prepared for almost anything that summer after his wife, Carole, left him, less than a year after they had moved out West, to Sonora Pines, California, where he had been offered a job with the Foundation for the Study and Research of Contemporary Sciences.

The summer after she left me, he said to himself as if he were talking to someone else. Not that the seasons really existed here. He felt so distant, he thought he might as well be watching a never-ending movie about himself. Except for the Foundation, his twice-a-week sessions with Dr. Richardson, his life had no structure. He drifted. His time was his own. He went through the days by habit, coping by rote. He was too well conditioned not to. But in the evenings and at night he was on his own, at a loss.

Often at night he found himself walking on the beach or driving around, sometimes stopping off at the ball park where the Mexican kids played softball. He would stand outside his car, beyond the streetlights, and watch the kids there on the dried-out grass, going through their ritualized motions, totally unaware of his presence.

Or he would drive through the dark downtown streets, the sections that constituted this town's version of slums, along the bumpy roads full of potholes. It was all unlit. Rows of pickups or old cars, a couple of wrecks parked at the curb. Past the closed Mexican food stores with their broken neon signs of TACOS TO GO flashing on only half the letters, the junky body-paint shops, several lumber-yards, small factories, an army depot behind barbed wire, intervals of noise from a jukebox or TV from the few late bars still open, glaring lights on in the dirty windows of a curtainless diner, a softly lit soul-record shop with a small group of blacks inside.

5

Nick drove on, slowly, past a shopping center, a twenty-four-hour liquor store, a crowded Laundromat, a twenty-four-hour falafel drive-in, back, past the endless lawn of a high school, up one of the winding roads of this hilly town, onto Main Street and up its length— three miles of lit, empty sidewalks, shops, restaurants, banks, lit windows of furniture, mannequins, signs.

Or he would stare at the same scene for hours on end from a window or from the sun deck of his beach house: the sand, waves, clouds, the night sky graying, the visual hallucination of dawn. Or he would listen half the night, lying on top of his unmade bed, to the sound of the waves breaking outside on the beach, in this half-sleep.

He walked through the sparsely furnished rooms. The house was much larger than their previous one in George-town—when they had moved in last year they had not even had the time to buy new furniture. Carole had kept putting it off, though she had driven down to Los Angeles several times a week (supposedly to look for furniture) right after they moved in. She had taken Johanna with her. Johanna rode in the back with her toys. They stayed for the day, returning late at night, Carole carrying Johanna, who was usually asleep by that time, straight into bed. Carole had gotten a whole list of names of people from friends and friends of friends to look up in Los Angeles. One of them had been Mike Gallagher.

It was July now. The days had simply transformed themselves into weeks, months. The house was unbearable. He tried to stay out as much as possible. He made the rounds of the local bars, cocktail lounges, and sat there, drinking, just to be around people, so that he would not have to go back to the house, be alone. No one ever really bothered him, intruded on his solitude, even seemed aware of his presence there at one of those side tables or in a corner. He thought of himself as the observer: recording the low-key dramas, the boring, mundane series of events —they all seemed the same. And that's what he liked about these places, the dark, the sickly dim lights, the plastic booths, tacky decor. Nothing different, nothing un-expected, could really happen. These places were inter-changeable. Entering them, he felt all that spring and early summer that he was back in his own element, as if he could breathe again, as if these places were like some sort of life-sustaining transfusion. He sat there, recording (in time he came to feel like a camera) the scenes, the bland events that occurred. The ultimate detachment, he told himself. The observer as a human camera. The self as mechanical—an emotional machine. It was a game he was playing. He didn't take it that seriously, felt it was a phase, passing . . . but he let it continue.

In the beginning some of the girls (in the places where there were girls) tried to get into conversation with him, lingered over the change, hovered close by, attentive to his glances, smiling. One of the young cocktail waitresses (probably a student at the university, he thought) sat down. She asked what he was drinking. He motioned to the bartender for two of the same (gin and tonic). The girl had a flower in her hair. He was trying to figure out what it was—a rose, a gardenia? He couldn't tell. It was too dark. It bothered him. He wanted to know what it was. The girl smiled, leaned over for the peanuts, brushing against him—she had on some sort of awful perfume. "You seem different," she said. "You know, most of the guys around here—well, just look at them." She pointed to the bar. "I mean, you're not lecherous."

He ordered two more gins. They talked about the different bars in town. She wasn't at the university, but she was going to beauty school. She was going to be a manicurist. He felt something under the table. It happened again. Her foot. He stared at her. She didn't change her expression at all, went on talking. Hypoallergenic, soaking hands, false nails. Her leg wrapped itself around his; still she went on talking, her expression unchanged. Her hand moved along his crotch. He almost gagged on his drink. But she didn't even seem aware. He nodded to what she was saying. She'd always wanted to be a beautician, maybe it wasn't very profound to him, but that's what she liked doing; why, she'd be happy doing that all day, almost. . . . "I get out of here at eleven. I can meet you outside, we can go someplace, your place if you want." He nodded. "OK." He thought, What the hell am I doing here? She could almost be my daughter. How did I ever get myself into this? He made up some excuse—just remembered some appointment. He never went back to that bar.

Another time, he took a girl (a cocktail waitress from the Blue Paradise Cove) back to the house, only because she reminded him of a girl he'd once known. He kept the lights off so he wouldn't have to see she was someone else. And he didn't want her to see the mess the place was in. She'd think he was strange. But she left the light on in the bathroom, looked at the bedroom, the clothes over the furniture, everything turned inside out. "You live here?" she asked. "You OK? It looks like it's been burglarized or something." She looked at him strangely. But he managed to change the subject, distract her— make her think he was normal. She kept moving around, squirming underneath him. Finally he pushed himself into her. He concentrated on the strands of her hair, peroxide blond. Then it was over. She seemed to be asleep. But she wasn't. She wanted to start over again. He told her he was too tired, and suddenly he was, exhausted, and he just wanted to sleep, alone. He didn't want her there. He had to get rid of her, get her out. He said he was hungry; why didn't they go out, get something to eat. She looked at him strangely again. They got into his car; he took her home. He eliminated that bar, too.

Nick stood in the bedroom. It was still night, but the gray light that leaked through the closed window screens could have been either moonlight or dawn. He stood in the middle of the room; slants of gray light cut up the room in strips, as if it were made up of different panels of tarnished light. He was suddenly so tired he almost didn't know where he was, and he'd had too much to drink. He felt himself swaying slightly; he closed his eyes. He let himself sway. The sheets looked as if they were silk in this light, swirls. Beckoning, as if they were waves. He sank down onto the unmade bed. He sighed deeply, in weariness, defeat. Tomorrow, he thought, tomorrow I'll get up. . . . All this has got to stop, he said to himself as he had too many times over the last few months.

When he awake, it was light—unmistakably morning. Someone was hammering outside on the beach. He heard a car start up from the house across the road. He raised his arm to check his watch. But it had stopped. Ten after seven. It must be later than that. He looked over at the rumpled sheets, the clothes on the floor, the general mess.

In his stockinged feet, he made his way across the puddles of dirty clothes into the bathroom. He took off his clothes, let them drop on the white hexagonal tiles. He showered, shaved, ripped open a plastic package of new underpants, took the pins and stays out of a new light blue shirt, peeled off the sticker on a new pair of black socks—he'd been buying new clothes almost every time he ran out of clean ones. He slipped into a worn pair of jeans; standing in front of the mirror, he brushed back his medium-length hair so that it looked shorter. He went out into the living room. The curtains were open, inundating the room with light. Newspapers on the coffee table, dead flowers in vases on the stereo speakers, paper plates with dried globs of colors—palettes of leftover food on top of the records, on the bookshelves, on the mantel—mounds of ash in the fireplace, books arranged in different piles across the parquet. He found the shoes he was looking for under a laundry bag next to the unpacked carton of Jordanos' groceries—Tide, Comet, bottles of 7-Up, ginger ale, tonic, a giant bag of potato chips, cans of Campbell's soup. Into the kitchen—dirty dishes, pots, glasses tottering on top of each other on the white Formica counter, in the stainless-steel sink, on the butcher-block table.

He took two Sunkist oranges out of the refrigerator, rinsed off a knife. He put up some water from the tank of Sparkletts water. He sat down in one of the four chairs at the butcher-block table, cut the oranges in quarters, and ate them. The water started to boil. He looked up as if he'd just been reminded of something but for a moment couldn't quite remember what it was. He rinsed out a spoon, a mug, measured out some Spice Islands instant coffee.

He went back out into the living room, stood in the powerful light in front of the wall-to-wall window. The glare blocked out the narrow sun deck, the beach, the ocean. He stared at the sliding glass door, which had turned into a panel of light. The light hurt his eyes. The door blurred. He moved back, out of the blinding light, into the room, until the sun deck, the beach, came back into focus. He pushed open the door, stepped out onto the sun deck; he stood there inhaling the soft summer air. He took a sip of coffee. He leaned over farther—someone down on the beach, next door, at the Walkers', was ham-. mering some planks of wood together, building some sort of crate. Someone he'd never seen before. A tanned kid in swimming trunks. He stopped hammering. He started sawing off the uneven end of one of the planks. It must be the Walkers' new gardener, Nick thought. (There was a large turnover of gardeners—usually college kids.) The beach was private. No one seemed to be up at the Walkers' yet. The curtains were all drawn. The kid went on hammering, sawing, whatever he was doing.

Nick stared at the ocean—a colorless expanse, scintillating, an endless mass of light. The waves landed quietly, careening in small white fountains, tugging against the sand, leaving slick wet shadows as they moved out again. Some sandpipers stood at the edge, waiting. A gull dipped down. Nick went back inside, locked the sliding door. He threw the rest of his coffee into the kitchen sink. He noticed the clock next to the juicer. Fifteen after ten. He went back into the living room. His wallet, car keys, a small note pad, a ballpoint pen were on the cocktail table. He stuffed them into the pockets of his jeans, went into the bedroom for a sweater. On his way out he saw the clock on the living-room mantel had stopped. Three-twenty-five. What the hell, he thought. What a life. What's the use? He pushed in the door lock and let the door slam behind him. On his way across the gravel to the garage, he heard the electric saw again. He got into the '73 Chevrolet, turned the motor on. He stared at the car clock. Suddenly he remembered—how could he have forgotten? The Walkers had left for Europe last week. They spent half the year there: They had a house in Marbella. How could he have forgotten that? Every time he saw Bob Walker on the beach or ran into him in the grocery store, he kept saying they were only waiting for July 14, to leave. That kid must be their house-sitter. Nick waited a full minute for the car to warm up. He drove slowly through the winding country roads, down Mission Ridge, into Valinda, Cerritos, all the way down the length of Pine Cliff, Westview, and into Silver Springs Road.

Situated in the lush secluded southern California countryside below the Santa Ynez Mountains, overlooking the sloping expanse of the town and the ocean below, the Foundation for the Study and Research of Contemporary Sciences had originally been only another one of the indistinguishable estates with which Sonora Pines had once been synonymous. From the end of last century it had been the winter residence of rich New Englanders and Midwesterners; with its ideal year-round climate that never varied more than twenty degrees, the water, the mountains, it was a natural resort area. Less than a hundred miles north of Los Angeles, it was protected from the influx of urban developments that was to plague most of the rest of the southern California coast. The city of Sonora Pines had been almost entirely rebuilt after the earthquake in 1925; since this was the heart of one of the most conservative areas in the country, strict zoning had been maintained throughout the years and the original landscape had been preserved insofar as it was possible. Hidden from view by dense foliage, in the more select areas, a large percentage of new houses and condominiums blended into the scenery, or were built directly into the rugged, terraced hills that made up most of the topography. There were no billboards, no advertisements; only a single discreet flashing neon sign announced the presence of the numerous motels—which were all to be found, for the most part, on the side streets off the waterfront and off Main Street. Light industry had been relegated to the outskirts of town, as had the university, the airport, an army base. Outside of town could also be found what was left of the lemon and orange groves, an exclusive residential park of expensive new homes that resembled a cemetery, a showground, the drive-ins, the country's largest reservoir. . . .

But driving through the placid Sonora Pines countryside, one was totally unaware of what lay beyond. It was as if nothing did. Lulled by the sylvan atmosphere, one could feel oneself almost drawn, as if in a trance, into the green whirlpool of nature, shot full of light, the earthly paradise as it might have been imagined by the French philosophers of the eighteenth century. There was that sense of removal, of distance, that one feels watching oneself in a dream: the lanes of eucalyptuses lining the roads; oaks, pines, sycamores, trimmed shrubs, flowers year round; fields adjacent to perfect lawns, ivy-camouflaged stone walls, private roads, recessed grounds—and the estates beyond.

Silver Spings Road was one of several roads that led off Westview. One could have easily driven down it without noticing the Foundation for the Study and Research of Contemporary Sciences. There was no sign, no indication of its existence, nothing to distinguish it from the other estates.

Nick pulled into the driveway, past the weathered mythological statues, the fountains filled with branches and leaves, the endless acres of unmowed lawn. (Priorities in the already-accounted-for funds were on research, not "aesthetic distractions"—the Foundation had been having trouble meeting its expenses in the last few years, since the retirement of Dr. Tynner. The new president, Dr. Rodney Osmond, had inherited all of his predecessor's problems without any of his apparent ability to circumvent them—the circumventing had simply been a series of evasive tactics: Nearly twenty years of bookkeeping fell into Dr. Osmond's hands or, rather, onto his head.)

The parking lot was full, the number of bicycles and speedbikes the same as that of cars. Nick pulled up to the side of the main building next to the scum-covered swimming pool, which had not been cleaned in months. Chestnut trees surrounded the pool and blossoms floated down onto its surface. A slight whir of machines, identifiable as typewriters, emanated from the open windows. Nick went in a side door, down a sunlit hallway—antiques (Directoire chairs, Regency sideboards, Louis XV commodes), easily recognizable paintings (a small Watteau, a Bellini Madonna and Child, an early Picasso, one of de Kooning's women, a small Matisse, a Seurat that had never really been completely authenticated—it remained propped up on a table), tapestries on the walls (Louis XIV Gobelins, Heriz silk prayer rugs, Kashan pictorial rugs, Flemish seventeenth-century rugs), sculptures (casts of

Rodin, Brancusi, Arp, Giacometti, Moore), shelves of relics (Netsilik Eskimo amulets, Aztec carvings, New Kingdom Egyptian papyri, Ming porcelains, Shang bronzes, early Amida Buddhas). A water cooler in an alcove was the only giveaway that this was not a private residence.

Several of the wood-paneled doors were open: blonde, suntanned California girls (from Central Casting) at IBMs; a long-haired boy with his sneakered feet up on his desk; an elderly scarecrow in a white lab coat standing at a window in a white room full of chemistry equipment; a football-player build, stripped down to his tennis shorts and socks, doing push-ups on the marble floor of his office. Nick opened the last door on the right: a bare desk, an intercom, a phone, a small electric clock, a desk calendar, a revolving desk lamp, a swivel chair, two French windows, a bookcase brimming with books and periodicals, a standard typewriter on a typing table, a file cabinet, a 20-10 Xerox copier, two modern easy chairs, a coffee table, more books, piles of periodicals on the floor. Nick threw his sweater over one of the easy chairs.

He sat down in the swivel chair at his desk. He stared at the closed door facing him; at the ceiling; at the wavering path of sunlight along the white marble floor. He sighed. He turned the key in the lock of the top drawer of the desk. He took photographs out of a white envelope. He dealt them out on the desk as if they were cards. They were of Johanna, his four-year-old daughter. He had taken some of the photographs himself last spring. Carole had sent him the others last week, from Cape Cod. He stared at the photographs he'd taken: Johanna, grinning, petulant, mischievous, in white underpants on the beach in front of the house. It was April, he said to himself. I had her for the weekend. That was right after Carole had taken that apartment down in Los Angeles; she was getting ready to open up that boutique of occult junk. What an idiot. What a fool I was. I should have known better. I really believed her. I thought it really would make her feel less constrained, more independent—being on her own. It was coming out here—that was the mistake. If we'd stayed in Washington or gone back to New York. . . .

A statistic, he said to himself, that's what I am. A statistic of modern life.

He looked at the small framed calendar of 1974 on his desk: Thursday, July 18. She'll be back the end of next week. I have the weekend of the twenty-sixth. I've got to have that place cleaned. I've got . . .

He put the photographs away, locked the drawer. He opened the drawer below, took out several thick folders (all marked IN THE MACHINE AGE: WORK AND ALIENATION); the irony of the title seemed so fitting, in the last few months, that it almost never escaped him each time he started to work on it. He put the folders on his desk, opened one subtitled CITY. He skimmed through a few of the Xeroxed pages. He wrote in the margins: "These problems were especially pronounced in areas of population pressure . . . for instance, in the '60s, thought forms and symbols as consensus-making devices . . . the ephemeral notion of personal authenticity aggravated in the framework (lack of rigidity indicated) of a postautomated society . . . the scale was in the ratio of 2:3 . . . crowds revolving through mirrors reflecting mirrors: symbolic alienation . . ."

There was a knock at the door. Nick looked up. Another knock. He didn't answer, hoping whoever it was would go away. But the handle turned, the door opened. A spare, elderly man in chinos and a tweed jacket who looked as if he might be having gastric problems stood in the doorway. It was Conrad Tynner. "Ah, you're here. Have you seen Osmond?"

Nick shook his head.

"Just wanted to check. I lent him my copy of the *Times*."

Nick didn't respond.

"The New York *Times*."

"Oh." Nick nodded. What a comment on his place, he thought. The former president going from office to office looking for his New York *Times*.

"Well, if you see him tell him."

Nick nodded again.

"Thanks." Tynner closed the door behind him. Nick turned his chair toward the French windows, through which hazy reels of sunlight, spliced by the oak foliage across the way, were projected onto the walls. The windows had not been cleaned since before the rain last winter. The room had not been cleaned either, but that was different. The standing order was that no office was to be cleaned without special (written) instructions. Nick had simply never gotten around to giving anyone any special instructions. In retrospect, he thought it fitted in with the general genteel decay of the place.

Ten of two. He picked up another one of the folders from the top of the desk, opened it, and started making some more notes in the margins of the pages.

The afternoon passed. He got up once to use the men's room across the hall. He felt dizzy. For a moment he was afraid he was going to lose his balance, pass out right there, hit his head on the sink or the tiles. He returned to his office and leaned back in his chair. He heard something outside. He swung around to the windows. But nothing was there, only the weakening strains of sunlight.

He continued working—circling words, underlining sentences, making notes on the sides of the Xeroxed pages. The intercom buzzed twice, but he didn't want to be bothered.

He was about to take a break, take out the photographs of Johanna again, when there was another knock at the door.

Susan, one of the Central Casting California girls, tanned, in a minimal tennis dress, with a mane of blond silk, came in. "Oh, hi, Nick. I don't want to disturb you. I wasn't even sure you were here."

"What is it?" Nick was annoyed because he'd almost been caught sitting at his desk, absorbed in Johanna's photographs.

"Do you want anything typed up before I leave?"

Nick shook his head, frowning, impatient.

"Transcribed? Anything?" Susan smiled blithely, quizzically, mock flirtatiously. "See you tomorrow."

Nick looked at the closed door, tilted back in his chair. Four-thirty. He picked up another batch of the Xeroxes.

The rest of the afternoon passed. The light began to shrink slowly from the walls, withdrawing in slow motion. He could hear the cars pulling out of the driveway, the typewriters calming down, one by one. Footsteps, voices phasing out. He tabulated the progress of silence, of evening.

He started working on another folder.

It grew dark. Finally he switched on his desk light. He stood up, stretched, felt dizzy again; he realized he hadn't eaten all day. He went down the dimly lit hallway, out the side door. There was another car in the parking lot, an old convertible. George Macdavitt's.

He drove into town, to the Store, a twenty-four-hour health-food place. He bought two no. 5 sandwiches (sprouts, cheese, and tomato on whole wheat) and a banana-nut shake. He took them back to the Foundation.

There were some lights on in the north wing. Macdavitt's car was still in the parking lot. He must be working late, Nick thought. He unlocked the side door, went back into his office. He sat down at the coffee table, and ate. It was twenty of ten.

He worked for a few hours. Around one, he decided he might as well spend the night in his office. That way he could get an early start in the morning. He switched off the light. He pulled the two easy chairs together, settled back in one, and put his legs up on the other.

Then suddenly he woke up with a jolt, thought he'd heard something. Some voices. Some people in the hall outside. I must have been drifting, he thought, getting my dreams confused. He listened. He heard the water cooler gurgle, once, twice, the heavy sound of water burping down. I'll have to remember to tell Dr. Richardson I'm hearing things now, he thought half facetiously. He heard the water cooler again. The same sound. He listened. But there was no interruption in the flat monotone of silence this time. Even if there had been, he wouldn't have heard it. He was asleep again within seconds.

Sonora Pines, like other exclusive residential communities on the southern coast of California, was patrolled at night by the local police patrol. There were signs to this effect outside most of the estates and the tree-enclosed large houses recessed off the deserted roads. The four men who got out of the Sedan de Ville green or blue Cadillac (it was difficult to tell—there was not much of a moon) in the middle of that night of July 18–19 in that year, 1974, were either unaware of this fact and didn't care if the car was seen or not, or had taken it into consideration and had timed themselves accordingly, as it was less than fifteen minutes since the last check and the patrolman would not be around again for at least several hours.

The Cadillac was left there, in the open, parked alongside the edge of the road, against the high shrubs outside the Fairfield estate on Westview. The four men seemed to know exactly where they were; off Westview, they turned a few yards away, left into Silver Springs Road. They moved on, almost soundlessly, it seemed. The faint audio registered in the background; some bird or owl calling out, the fluttering mobiles, responses of branches, muted wind chimes of foliage set in motion, troubled by a sudden shift of breeze, a trickle of pebbles skidding down onto the macadam, something snapping, a dulled brittle crack of some twigs underfoot, the loose summer night casting its spell, fragments of some sort of slow-motion hallucination.

The four men slipped through an opening in some bushes, across the uncut lawn of the Foundation for the Study and Research of Contemporary Sciences. The grounds were unlit; there was no light from any of the windows. They passed the rows of Greek and Roman statues, several fountains, down the gravel path toward the main building. All four were wearing sneakers. One of the men—almost a boy, with a red bandanna around his head—stopped short, annoyed. He frowned, cocking his head, indicating the two cars in the parking lot.

The man in the dark turtleneck barely blinked, bored. "It's OK. I told you no one's here. Sometimes they leave their cars, drive back with each other for a drink, go to each other's house. It's OK."

They went down some side steps; the parking lot was now in full view. There were several bicycles in the bicycle stands. The boy stopped again, cocked his head. The man in the turtleneck motioned for him to move on.

"Naw. I don't like it. I don't like it. Naw. Not one bit!"

"Shh! Shut up!" the man in the turtleneck growled, letting his hand cut through the air in a karate-chop pantomime.

They stopped at the side door. The one in the turtleneck nodded. "OK. Now." He took something out of his pants pocket. He pulled on a pair of surgical gloves. The other three did the same. He looked them over. He seemed satisfied. He took a key out of his pocket. The door opened onto the dimly lit hallway—antiques, paintings, tapestries, sculpture. The man in the turtleneck stood still. He listened, nodding his head up and down several times as if following some sort of silent musical rhythm, then he beat out time with his hand. He nodded once more, decisively.

They went down the hallway, past a number of closed doors, through a small gallery filled with glass display cases of Chinese statues and vases. There was another hallway on one side, and on the other, a French window that opened out onto a small lit courtyard with a fountain and some more Greek gods. They went down the hallway, the man in the turtleneck leading the group. They stopped in front of the only door that had a band of light at the bottom. The man in the turtleneck turned the handle. They went in.

An overweight, middle-aged man, in a white shirt with the sleeves rolled up, was smoking a pipe, listening to a static-filled conversation on a Sony cassette recorder, one elbow on the desk, supporting his head, taking notes with his free hand on a 5 x 8 yellow memo pad with a Bic pen. His eyes magnified through his horn-rimmed glasses; the pen dropped. He coughed; his pipe shot out of his mouth, struck the desk. He jumped up, both hands grasping the desk. "What the hell . . ."

"OK, Macdavitt. Where's the files?" The man in the turtleneck didn't change his expression. "Grab him."

"Are you nuts or something?" The fright had turned to disgust. "Breaking in here like this, with whoever these people are."

"Grab him."

"Is this some sort of sick prank, hmmn?" Macdavitt was surrounded, pinned from behind, both arms wrenched around. "Hey, you're hurting me!" Sweat glistened on his forehead, his receding hairline.

"Did you do as I said? What I told you to do? Did you leave the files in the Plymouth parked on Armona?"

Macdavitt nodded, stunned.

"Then why aren't they there?"

Macdavitt didn't answer. The man in the turtleneck gestured to the cassette.

A man's faint voice could be heard through the static on the tape: ". . . East of Station. It hovered in the air alongside of us . . . before it went off the radar . . . heading almost due west at a speed given as 2,000 to 4,000 miles per hour. It wasn't like anything either of us had ever seen. We didn't . . ."

The man in the turtleneck flipped the cassette out, put it in his pocket.

"Hey!" Macdavitt protested.

The man in the turtleneck cocked his head. The boy threw his arm around Macdavitt in a bear hug. The man in the turtleneck, looking morose, nodded slowly. The grip tightened; color came into Macdavitt's face.

The man in the turtleneck watched. Macdavitt grew more flushed. "That's enough!" the man suddenly said, as if he'd had a lapse and had just realized what was happening. "OK."

The one with a beady-eyed, sharp, wise look, and a diminutive build like a bowlegged jockey's, pulled out a wrench from his shrunken jean jacket pocket.

The man in the turtleneck opened the drawers of the desk, the drawers of the two file cabinets. He rifled through the file dividers and folders.

Macdavitt glared, fish-eyed. The silence was taut for a moment, reduced to slow motion. Then it snapped. Macdavitt started to struggle, squirming in the hold. In accelerated motion there was a scuffle, but Macdavitt didn't have a chance. Fists were shoved into Macdavitt, the wrench rammed into his stomach.

The man in the turtleneck nodded and the fourth man, a heavyweight in a suit, pounced. And it was over. The man in the turtleneck cocked his head toward the window closest to the desk. Macdavitt was led out. The man in the turtleneck flipped the cassette lid back down, took the note pad, brushed the loose ash into the ashtray, tapped out the pipe, and slipped it into his pocket. He turned off the lights, closed the door behind him, and followed the others down the hallway.

They walked Macdavitt across the terrace, up the two

steps, across the grass, to the swimming pool. The man in
the turtleneck stood to the side, away from them, under
the open umbrella of a garden table. The heavyweight
and the boy restrained Macdavitt. The jockey put his hand
over Macdavitt's mouth. The man in the turtleneck stared
at one of the statues that lined the far side of the pool.
Macdavitt slumped over, a deadweight. They dragged him
by the underarms to the diving board. The heavyweight
grabbed Macdavitt's head as if it were a ball and swung
it, smashing the diving board. The springs of the board
sent off a series of quivering tremors. Blood sprang out
from Macdavitt's head, shooting out in a thick spray. The
jockey made a clawing motion with his fingers; the boy
took out Macdavitt's wallet, car keys, and handed them
to the jockey. The man in the turtleneck cocked his head
toward a large stone sundial partially draped under some
bushes. The jockey gripped the sides; the sundial tilted
over. The heavyweight let Macdavitt's head drop on the
flagstones. The man in the turtleneck kept his flashlight
on the sundial. The jockey and the heavyweight slowly
carried it closer to the pool. They heaved Macdavitt's
body onto the sundial. The jockey opened his jean jacket,
unwound the bulge of ropes around his waist. Macdavitt's body was tied to the sundial. The man in the
turtleneck scanned the ropes with his flashlight. Macdavitt's body, slouched and rigid, was pinned across the
sundial. The man in the turtleneck nodded. The jockey
and the heavyweight awkwardly dragged it toward the
edge. They pushed it over, into the pool. The scum-
covered surface of the pool erupted, opening up. They
waited until it closed.

The jockey hosed down the diving board, the flagstones,
and wound the hose back exactly as it had been over the
faucet, the nozzle resting on a deck chair. The heavyweight brought over a garden chair to cover the gaping
earth at the side of the lawn where the sundial had been.
The area was checked out several times with flashlights.

"I'll drive his car out." The man in the turtleneck extended his cupped hand. The jockey threw over the car
keys. The man in the turtleneck got into the Ford convertible and without turning on the lights drove it out the

open front gate. The headlights came on for a second, flickering through the hedges, and then went out again.

The other three went back out the same way they had come, across the terrace, up the driveway, across the lawn, through the bushes at the side entrance and out onto the road, up to Westview, where the car was parked.

Nick, asleep in his office, again thought he heard something. He shifted around in his chair. He had a strange dream, something involving some men breaking into some offices, rubber gloves, guns, a car pulling out of a parking lot resembling the Foundation parking lot. Too much Watergate, he said to himself in his dream. I'll have to remember to tell Dr. Richardson that one. . . .

Nick woke up with a start early the next morning, cramped and stiff from his makeshift sleeping arrangement. For a moment he thought it was still night, still evening, still yesterday. He'd overslept. He turned to the windows. Bars of bright gleaming gold light, that newly minted luster, the dead giveaway of dawn.

Disgusted with himself, or, rather, with the vicious cycle of another bad night's sleep, and already feeling raw and jumpy, and knowing it would be another wasted day, he pushed back the second chair with his stockinged feet and stared at the floor.

He put on his shoes, went out into the hall, switching off the lights. Macdavitt must have forgotten to turn them off. He went into the men's room.

He went out the side door, into the unrelenting glare, the overpowering scents of summer; the silence broken only by the birds.

His car was the only one in the parking lot. He drove into town and had a large breakfast at Sambo's.

He picked up a copy of the Los Angeles *Times* from the vending machine outside, thought about going back to the house to shave, but decided he'd do it later, get some work done first, leave early. Really because he couldn't bear the idea of facing the mess the house was in. He felt the bacon he'd just eaten coming up on him.

The Foundation parking lot was still empty. It wasn't even eight yet. He went into his office, closed the door be-

hind him, sat at his desk, and started working on the
work-and-alienation files again.

Slowly, he noticed at intervals the background rhythm
picking up. A throbbing presence—voices, steps, the pace
of typewriters. The place was coming back to life.

Later in the morning, when he took a break and went
out onto the terrace outside the French window, he saw
the police car in the parking lot. He didn't think much of
it, figured it was probably one of the patrolmen coming
by to check the alarm system.

He went back inside. Dennis Cavanaugh, the political
scientist who had the office next to his, was in the doorway. "Hiya, Nick. Sorry for the interference, but there's
some police guy wants to talk to everybody."

Nick followed Cavanaugh into the main lobby. A police
officer was writing something in a steno pad, using the unoccupied receptionist's desk for support. A patrolman
stood by his side, handcuffs dangling from his belt, a gun
in his holster.

The officer looked up, let his eyes rest a moment on
Nick's unshaven face. "Dr. Schrader? Hope we're not disturbing you, but one of the patrolmen who was on duty
noticed your car in the parking lot last night. The tan
Chevrolet, license plate 916 LYS?"

"That's my car."

"We just wanted to check that out." The officer scrib-
bled something down. "You spend the night here last
night?"

"I slept in my office. I was working late."

The officer wrote something else down. "Now, by any
chance—I hope this doesn't sound too strange to you—
but do you remember hearing anything last night? You
know, a car, some people's voices maybe?"

"Did somebody break in?" Nick felt strange—he remembered his dream.

"No. We don't think so. It doesn't look like it, at least.
Let me explain. Dr. George Macdavitt—he works in that
wing over there?"

"That's right."

"Apparently he didn't come home last night. His wife
phoned here early this morning, but he wasn't in his office.
His secretary, Miss"—the officer paused to check his notes

—"Miss Jameson looked around, but he wasn't here, and neither was his car. Now, the thing is, one of the patrolmen noticed Dr. Macdavitt's car last night until around one in the morning in the parking lot beside your car. There were only two cars. . . . Well, you see, now, the thing is—why we're even here in the first place, what makes this kind of strange, is that Dr. Macdavitt was going to pick up some houseguests at the airport this morning. Now, Mrs. Macdavitt spoke to him"—the officer looked down again—"around eleven-thirty last night, and he said he was on his way back, would be home in a little while. When he didn't come back, she thought he'd probably decided to work all night, as he sometimes does." The officer waited.

"That is kind of strange," Nick said.

"That's why we wanted to know if you heard anything. You know, even anybody walking around?"

"Have you checked the airport?" Nick asked. "Maybe he went straight out there this morning?"

"Mrs. Macdavitt had to go and pick up the houseguests herself."

"No, that doesn't sound in George's character, does it?" Nick asked Dennis Cavanaugh.

"No, it sure doesn't."

Later, around lunchtime, the intercom buzzed. "Oh, Nick. This is Rodney. Why don't you come and have some lunch in my office?"

Rodney Osmond's office was in the Chinese gallery in the north wing—off an atrium with some trees, a small pool, three unoccupied desks. The secretaries were out to lunch and Nick heard several voices inside. He knocked on the door and went in. Dr. Rodney Osmond, a tall, disconcertingly boyish middle-aged man in his early sixties with a shock of white hair—boyish in the sense that he looked as if he'd been aged overnight—got up from behind his desk. The officer was seated in a Louis XVI chair, pulled up close to the desk, his steno pad open in front of him. The patrolman, at the long Regency side table against the wall, was on the phone.

"Hi, Nick. I gather you've already met." He motioned to the two policemen.

The patrolman got off the phone. "No. Still nothing."

The room was silent for a moment. Rodney Osmond's bushy eyebrows went up. "Sherry?"

"No. I'm fine, thank you," Nick said.

There was a knock. A frail middle-aged Mexican in a butler's outfit, balancing a crowded silver tray on his shoulder, crossed the waxed parquet.

"Thank you, José. Why don't we move over?" Rodney Osmond indicated the conference table with its four place mats, settings. They sat down. José served. Vitello tonnato. There was a muted exchange between the two policemen. The patrolman tried to cough discreetly. "I'm afraid I'm not much for fish. . . ."

"José, perhaps you could fix the officer a sandwich. Nick, we have some fine Cabernet rosé from Anjou."

They started to eat. The bread was passed, the butter. There was another knock. José took the silver lid off the patrolman's plate. The patrolman studied the pink slices of cold steak.

Rodney waited until José had gone out. "Let me explain." He paused—his mouth pursed, head tilted, the points of his fingers pressed together, forming an arc. "George—Dr. Macdavitt," he clarified for the two policemen, "is one of the truly great physicists of the age. The only reason he has not received the Nobel prize so far is purely political. Which is usually the case. His work is right alongside Oppenheimer's, Teller's, Fermi's. Let me say immediately, Nick, that Washington has agreed that these two gentlemen should be informed of the situation. They might be able to help. And believe me, we need all the help we can get. Yes . . ." Rodney paused again and then went on, seemingly oblivious of the expressions on the two policemen's faces, adding as an afterthought, "And of course, you've been cleared—you were cleared —because of your background in the State Department. What I'm going to tell you is all in strictest confidence, you understand. Among the four of us."

Nick continued methodically chewing, concentrating on his vitello tonnato, methodically nodding, waiting.

"Now, George—Dr. Macdavitt—has had access for years to all sorts of highly classified top-secret documents —ever since his early work with the government—long before he was at Los Alamos. In other words, he's been involved in a number of highly secret projects. For the last number of years—I really don't know how long— he's been working on his own on some sort of top-secret project. Some people in Washington got wind of it. We got a couple of calls, some visits. You know how these things leak out. And, well, some people in Washington felt word of this might get to the other side. I told him it might be better to lay off for a while, until it cooled off, let it just blow out by itself. Well, you know how stubborn he is. Well, sure enough, they tried to make contact with him."

"The Russians?" the officer asked, obviously wanting to keep things as clear as possible, jotting something else down in his pad.

The patrolman simply snorted, chewing on his third roll —his steak sandwich was untouched—and making a sound like what-do-you-know . . .

"And I guess they set up some meetings—rendezvous. In gas stations, telephone booths, restaurant chains. The whole sordid melodrama. You see, he's really caught in the middle—Washington trying to get him to stop pursuing this project, for his own good, and trying to protect him against his own wishes. They put some security around him. But he's managed to lose them a number of times. And then the Soviets trying to threaten him— bribing him. Apparently, they offered him access to all sorts of information. Documents and files he'd been trying to get hold of for years. Then, this last spring, they started getting suspicious, felt he was playing both sides, trying to gain time. They started threatening him again, trying to blackmail him. He came to me. He was afraid for his life. Of course I got in touch with Washington. His security was increased. But there were still times he managed to get them off his tracks.

"Then, earlier this summer—just a few weeks ago— he told me they'd threatened him, taken out a gun, in some parking lot at night—three men, told him they wanted all his papers, tapes, files. They wanted it all handed over. He gave them some papers, a few more tapes—kept dawdling. He wouldn't give them certain papers, he put some things in a vault. They found out about it, got him into a car with the vault keys, made him go in. Again they had guns. Still he had some documents he was holding off on. I don't know how they got wind of it. Anyhow, last week—last Friday—he told me they'd given him another ten days. That makes the time just about up.

"Now, our problem is we don't know what's happened to him. We don't know if some other branch in Washington has him in safe custody or what—it's such an intricate network there's no way of getting a straight answer from them. Or if he's with the Soviets—and they've decided to take him into some sort of temporary protective safekeeping. I don't believe they'll do anything to him. He's too valuable. Still, it could be unpleasant. But Washington expects the situation to be cleared up in the next few days, and we should have some sort of straight answer as to his whereabouts."

"What about his wife? Has she been threatened? Does she know about any of this?" Nick asked. He didn't know what else to ask. It was the only thing he could think of.

"No. Thank God. His family's been kept out of this. George is at least that much of a government man. No, he never talked about what he was doing, working on. I just hope they—the Soviets—realize that. I think they will, if they have up to now. No, I couldn't even tell you what he was really working on myself—this project of his—any details, anything. He just said he couldn't go into it. . . . We simply told Sally—Mrs. Macdavitt—that he had to make a trip—at the last minute—to Washington. It was top secret."

"The Cadillac," the officer said, putting in a reminder.

"Oh, yes. Nick, one of the patrolmen who was on duty last night, noticed a Cadillac parked on the side of the road outside the Fairfield estate."

"It was unattended," the officer filled in. "We don't know if there's any connection. I didn't want to mention it when I was talking to you earlier—we weren't alone—but did you notice a dark green Cadillac, '74 license plate?" The officer checked his notepad. "189 CTJ? Around midnight?"

"I was working in my office."

The officer jotted something down. "You didn't go out at all last night? For something to eat or anything?"

Nick frowned. "Well, yes, I did, as a matter of fact. I went out around nine, into town to get a sandwich from The Store, the health-food takeout. As a matter of fact, I can tell you exactly what time it was. I noticed that when I was in The Store. Nine-twenty. There's a clock above the counter where the cash register is."

"I guess all this will seem pretty foolish a couple of days from now," Rodney said.

"You didn't mention it before, you see"—the officer smiled politely, self-satisfied, flipped his pad shut—"that you'd gone out. And I wondered about that—that you wouldn't have gone out to get something to eat."

"I just didn't think of it. I was only out a few minutes."

"Well, thank you, Dr. Osmond. Thank you for your time. And the lunch. We'll let you know if we hear anything. Dr. Schrader." The officer stood up.

"Yes. Now, no matter what time. You have my home number."

The officer nodded.

"Doctors." The patrolman's head dipped down. The two policemen went out, closing the door behind them.

"And I just thought George was working on some sort of blueprint—a theoretical outline for the year 2074. That shows what kind of place this is."

Rodney smiled slightly. "The intellectual as isolationist. Let's not get into the philosophical-ethical implications of that. Well, I didn't even really know either. By the way, as you probably gathered, your two years with the State Department gave you a head start in all of this. I thought of you—I brought you into this—because you seemed the least likely, nobody would suspect you, you see. The fact that you were here last night—that coincidence—is only an added benefit . . . nobody could suspect you."

"Well, thanks. I'm not sure how to interpret that."

"You're not even remotely tainted by any sort of interest in the physical sciences," Rodney went on. "A sociologist. Plus the fact that you're such a recent acquisition. You haven't even been with us a year. You see, the logical choices would be Braunheimer, Spaulding, Fishbach. But you . . . Who's going to suspect you?"

"I take it you mean the Soviets?"

Rodney smiled benevolently as if to a somewhat slow learner who was beginning to catch on; he nodded, his head moving up and down a number of times, an avowal of confidence well placed. The expression suddenly switched off. "You understand this is totally in confidence. It's not to be discussed or even mentioned, even in the most veiled terms, to anyone." Rodney smiled again, blithely. "You're classified now, you come under national security or, rather, you will very soon."

Nick went back to his office and tried to work for a few hours. But it was no use. He kept being distracted— looking at a page or the wall, or turning in his chair and facing the window, staring at the window, and then suddenly realizing that he had just been looking at the words on the page, or staring at the smooth texture of the white paint on one of the walls or at the projections of dusty sunlight without being aware that he had been; he would give a slight start, annoyed with himself, almost embarrassed and self-conscious as if he had been caught off guard by someone; he would brusquely go back to work. And then the same thing would happen again . . . and he would be looking, staring. Finally, he gave up. He put the files away.

He drove back to the house, didn't bother checking the mailbox, went straight into the bedroom, collapsed on the bed, and promptly fell asleep. He had a dream. Something involving clouds. The clouds were not at all like real clouds. They were dense, had substance, more like soft boulders. One cloud entered a large empty room through an open window and stayed there, on the parquet, like some sort of huge weight, a presence. . . . Delvaux, Magritte, de Chirico, he said to himself. "You never look at the paintings," said Carole, who was standing beside him. "When we go to museums or galleries you always look at the people." Another point of contention. And then he was floating in the dream, floating; sinking down onto a bed he recognized as this bed. The dream was in soft colors, pastel hues, nebulous. Elusive. There was nothing to hold on to, almost as if there were no gravity. He was moving into another world. He was trying to remember what the dream was about when he was awakened by something; then he heard the phone. He let his hand crawl up onto the night table, feeling over the address book, the plastic bag of almonds, knocking over the pack of illegibly filled index cards, grasping the telephone and clutching the receiver, the long cord bouncing up; he shoved the receiver against his ear. "Hello? Hello?" There was no answer.

He got up, checked the clock on the dressing table. A quarter after four. He went into the living room. He still had over an hour to kill. His appointment wasn't until five-thirty.

He looked at the room. He thought about sorting through the piles of books. Again he thought, I'll do that tomorrow. This weekend. I'll get the house cleaned up. He went back into the bedroom, into the bathroom. He took a long shower, stood with his eyes closed, without moving under the jet of hot water. He shaved, put on some new underpants, socks, a new shirt. Tomorrow. I'll do a wash tomorrow. The phone rang again. He got it before the second ring. "Hello?"

But again, whoever it was didn't answer.

Dr. Richardson's house off Westview, a few minutes from the Foundation. Dr. Richardson was vaguely affiliated with the Foundation. He attended some of the "dialogues," had been a guest lecturer on and off through the years, and had done the research for several projects under its auspices (including his best-selling *Men in Power*—psychiatric profiles of a number of contemporary heads of state—which had been excerpted in the *Reader's Digest*, *Playboy*, and translated into nine languages). Dr. Richardson, an ardent tennis buff—his schedule was arranged so that he had half his days on the court—played tennis regularly with several members of the Foundation; in this select country-club community of golf and/or tennis, his credentials were beyond question. Nick had originally gone to him (gotten into a conversation with him after a game at the Foundation) about Carole. Last spring, when he still thought it could work out, when he still believed what she said—that she wanted to take that apartment in Los Angeles to be by herself, that she needed to be doing something on her own (that was why she was opening that boutique), that she needed the time (to think things out). An evasive tactic to gain time for what was soon evident.

Dr. Richardson's office was in the guest house off the garden in back of the large house. Nick waited outside the paneled oak door with the heavy bronze knocker (a relic from a dig, Dr. Richardson had pointed out to him). He studied the flagstones. He waited until he heard the back door close—Dr. Richardson had two entrances. He went in the front door: a small waiting room, a banquette, two stiff antique chairs, Picasso lithographs on the wall-papered walls (Nick didn't like waiting in there—he could hear the monologue or silence going on inside). The door to the office was open, waiting, like an invitation in a dream or in some sort of trance, the cliché giveaway of what kind of office it was, Nick thought each time. Dr. Richardson, in a white Lacoste sport shirt, white flannel pants, and tennis socks and sneakers, appeared in the doorway. "C'mon in, Nick. Sorry for the outfit, but I didn't have time to really change."

Nick sat down on the leather couch facing Dr. Richardson behind his marble-topped desk, cleared except for a small Mayan statue. Dr. Richardson settled back in his Eames chair, looked at Nick questioningly, and waited.

Nick started off with Johanna, the photographs. "You understand, it's become like an obsession. . . ."

"Sure, it's the only thing that's left."

"That's what I thought, at first. But that's only the surface. Underneath . . . You know, it's what I told you about . . . oh, it's something much more lurking. It's symbolic in some way. You know, the constant reminder of my own mortality, something as corny as that. Almost the more I see her grow, change, the more I see myself diminish, altered. As if we were opposite vials of life on a lever. I stand at one end, she at the other, tilting slowly in her direction, the inevitable growth process, culminating in my own eventual death. . . . I suppose it's all accentuated because I realize I'll be seeing her so infrequently. She's at that stage now where you can notice changes almost every week—the way she looks at things, the world, her grasp of reality. I suppose it's all an intellectualization of resentment. I resent being away from her. . . . My real hostilities are lodged with Carole. Since I can't face up to that—it's too explosive. We've been through that so many times, and then we just end up saying things we don't really even mean. . . . Since I won't—I mean I can't—come to grips with Carole—she won't let me—I focus all my attention on Johanna. This obsession—almost. I never thought I'd be saying this—as if she'd replaced Carole. A four-year-old child. Whimsical, evasive, distracted, capricious . . . A four-year-old child interpreted by adult standards . . . I suppose—what classical shit—if she didn't bear such an uncanny resemblance to Carole . . . But it really is uncanny. Or, rather, to be more accurate, the way Carole looked as a child—the way I imagined she might have looked—she didn't in the photographs I've seen of her as a child—didn't look at all like Johanna. She had blond hair then. They both have dark hair. No, it's more the aura. I look at Johanna and I see Carole as a child, the child I never knew. And now my own child I'll never really know either, I'll only know by intuition. Stopgaps in the dark. I'll have occasional clues which I'll try to fit together logically. Only there won't be any logic, because the clues will not longer be valid. And before I know it, it'll be over, and I'll be confronted with a stranger . . . the way I suddenly was this last spring with Carole."

The subject shifted to Carole, where it stayed for the remainder of the session. ". . . she'd simply walked back in, Johanna was with her. It was dusk in that one, I remember telling myself in the dream that it was dusk, to try to figure out if it had any significance. The end of something or what . . . Actually she does have a key to the place. She kept it for some reason. But maybe she didn't. Maybe she just forgot about it. I haven't mentioned it to her. It's like the last link—as long as she has a key . . . of course it's a good way of keeping myself worked up, keeping the wounds open, the imagination thriving. I should get that key back from her. It seems kind of strange to mention it after all this time. It'd be kind of awkward. After all, why didn't I mention it before? Then I had another dream. Some woman—it wasn't Carole, I mean it was a substitute figure, but I knew it was Carole anyway. I had it about five-thirty. I became almost semiconscious of the light outside toward the end of the dream, so it was definitely in the last stages of REM, just before waking. This dream took place on Cape Cod. Her parents have a summer house there, and we used to go up there sometimes in the fall and winter for weekends by ourselves the first year we were living in New York. The house was right off the water. We used to go for long—"

"I'm sorry, Nick, but the time is just about up."

"Just as well. It was more or less a repeat of the first dream."

Dr. Richardson walked him to the door. "By the way, how are things at the Foundation? Heard you had some trouble. Somebody tried to break in, the police were over?"

"Oh, not really. It was just the police patrol, checking out the alarm system or something."

"Heard it on the courts. Dennis Cavanaugh."

"Word sure gets about quickly around here."

"It's a small community. How's the project?"

"I'm getting back into it. I should finish the transcripts soon, next week. Then the real work . . ."

"Tuesday, then." Dr. Richardson waved his hand placatingly.

When Nick got back to the house, he went over to close the living room curtains. Something caught his eye, something on the beach. It looked like the same boy from the other morning—the Walkers' house sitter. He was standing at the edge of the water.

Nick pulled the curtains shut. He turned on the lights, went into the kitchen. He heated some canned soup. He read for a while in his study.

Later, in the bad light at the close of dusk, he went out for a walk on the beach. The boy was still there. He was just standing there, down at the other end, past the cove, beyond the Walkers'.

The next morning, Saturday, Nick was up early. Something felt different to him; even the light looked different, sharper, as if it had been slightly off focus before. The bedroom looked different, more like a set, as if he had suddenly become a character in some book or movie. What dramatics, he thought.

After he'd showered and shaved, he put on some trunks

and went out onto the beach. There was no one. In the innocent light, the beach stretched for miles like an apparition of an undiscovered world, and the water was like a field in a dream—the waves, white herds, breaking in vigorous rhythms onto the clean sand as if in a renewal of energy—the whole scene was like a dream, the abstract, the symbolic made visual. A young world untouched.

Walking out onto the beach, Nick felt as if he had walked out onto another planet. He watched the water at his feet spread in and out like a shadow. Some sandpipers scurried along. He started to jog. When he was a few yards away, he turned around to look. But there was no sign of the boy, of anyone. He broke out into a run. He kept running, in and out of the wet demarcation line where the water had been, weaving in and out of the obstacle course of the surf. He kept running until he collapsed, kneeling on the cool sand—he was surprised at how cool the sand was against his bare legs.

He had run almost to the other side of the bluff, a mile away. Here the private houses gave way to condominiums and apartment houses. But the beach was still deserted, it was too early. The volleyball nets were up but there were no players. He sat down and watched the sunlight detonate soundlessly, in slow motion, a line of flames across the wrinkled foil of the calm water; the fronds of the palms fluttering like paper decorations in the breeze, which was slapping in a halfhearted, bored sort of way against the shore. Across the grass, next to the road, a man covered with newspapers was asleep under a picnic table. Nick watched the light catch and then flare in the apartment-house windows.

He folded his legs in position, closed his eyes, and tried to censor all sounds, concentrating, until he was aware only of his own breath, his heartbeat, the nervous sputter of cells on the gray-lit network of his closed eyelids; and then, until he was aware of nothing, or what he interpreted as nothing.

He stayed that way, without moving, breathing slowly, for what seemed to be an indeterminate period of time. Then, gradually, he became conscious of lapses in this withdrawal: the monotonous wash of the water moving into the foreground, the raucous barking of some gulls, the panicked flapping of wings overhead, and the steady source of heat increasing, as if it were being filtered in through this invisible dome of air that enclosed the space where he was sitting; the dry odor of the sand was now noticeable. He had trouble breathing for a moment. The beach seemed suddenly suffocating, as if the final volumes of air were about to give way, to be compressed into heat—as if the innocuous scene of this clean early-morning beach had suddenly metamorphosed into a desert in the hallucinatory midday sun.

He sprang up and ran all the way back to the house.

He sank down onto the living-room couch and waited until he had caught his breath. He couldn't stand the sight of the mess the house was in; it always looked worse in the daylight. He put on a pair of jeans, a shirt. He drove into town and had breakfast at Sambo's.

Afterward (not wanting to go back to the house and not quite sure what to do, and feeling guilty for not taking advantage of the weather) he went for a walk along the water, along Vizcaino Boulevard, with its grass, its picnic tables, its palm trees.

He walked out toward the fishing nets spread out on display on the almost-white sand, toward the harbor; the clutter of docked boats in the distance. The water there was smooth and dense, like endless layers of glass, the color of seaweed, as if the seaweed had run and dyed the water. The sky was flawless, a coast of cloudless blue air.

He kept walking.

The figure in the weaving haze of light moving toward him in the distance appeared, at first, silhouetted against the fragmented levels of the sloping beach—a delusion of perspective—to be moving away from him. But as he kept walking the figure came nearer.

The young woman, blonde, suntanned, in a tight white tank top, jeans, seemed bent on ignoring him. She kept her eyes on the water, on the fountains of foam of some waves that were just starting to break. It was obvious she didn't want to be distracted. Nick, about to pass her, started to walk faster. Just at that moment she looked up, her eyes settling slowly on him as if he'd just come into her field of vision and she was adjusting her gaze to put him into focus. She smiled. Nick, taken aback, smiled more by reflex than anything else. He was still smiling after he had passed. The young woman tossed back her golden mane— as if she were shaking herself free—a nervous motion. A gold chain swung down on her tight tank top.

Nick walked to the end of the beach, to the public recreation building, the volleyball nets, and then back. An old man was picking up the litter from the grass beneath the rows of palm trees with a pick; two other men in white uniforms were going along the length of Vizcaino Boulevard emptying the garbage cans. Some gulls stood watch, hopping from one area of the grass to another, their beady eyes scanning in search of prey.

The young woman was standing at the edge of the water, apparently intent on watching the mirage of sailboats, a cluster of translucent silver dots slipping away from the harbor in the clear morning light. He was not sure she had even seen him, but she turned around. "Hi. Since we both seem to be going in the same direction, mind if I join you?" he asked.

"Sure. Why not?" she said. She walked alongside, in step with him, but kept her eyes averted, on the water. They walked for several minutes without speaking. "You're from the East, aren't you?" she asked.

It wasn't what he had expected her to say. "What makes you say that?"

"Something in your gait."

"Seriously?"

"Seriously . . . no, you're not used to talking to strangers."

"Is that what people in the West do? Talk to strangers?"

"Did you just move out here?"

"I haven't even said where I come from, but already you've decided I'm not from the West. What makes you so sure?"

"I know."

"OK. What else do you know?"

"You really want to know?"

"Gee, I don't know. Maybe not. Seriously, how did you guess I was from the East?"

"You would have talked to me back there." She motioned with her head. "You wouldn't have been so uptight trying to decide. You would have just gone ahead."

"You were looking at the water, you didn't seem to want to be disturbed."

"See, that's it right there." She tapped her forehead and then pointed to his. He saw she had on a man's watch, a gold Omega covering most of her wrist. "You should stop that."

"Ah! A true woman of the West."

"You're putting me on?" She seemed puzzled.

"Who's doing it now?"

She laughed. "You come from New York?"

"And what's behind that one? What makes you think that?"

"The repartee."

"And where do you come from? Oklahoma City?"

She shook her head, grinning.

"Des Moines? Las Vegas? Eureka, Kansas?"

"Is there a Eureka, Kansas?"

"Thirty-five hundred seventy-six inhabitants. You won't give me any help, huh?"

"It makes it more interesting that way."

"More interesting?"

"For you. Not for me. I already know all about you."

"Like?"

"Like, you're some kind of surveyor, you have something to do with numbers." She pretended to study his face. "No, maybe more a scientist . . ."

"You've seen me before?"

She shook her head.

"At a party? At the Foundation? You've come to some of the dialogues . . . in the back of the room. You always sit in the back, right?"

She kept shaking her head. "Are you with the Foundation?"

"In a way . . . I'm not an organization person."

"I was close enough. A scientist."

"What do you do?"

"What do you think I do?"

"Do you do this often?"

"Do what?"

"Pick up strange men on beaches?"

"The line follows, are you strange?"

"I might be."

"No." She appraised him again. "No, I don't think you are."

"Then you'll have coffee with me?"

"I don't even know your name."

"Nick. And you're?"

"Michelle. Michelle Worthington."

"Nick Schrader. How about the wharf?"

"I'll follow you in my car." She got into an old white Datsun parked at the curb, outside the beach parking lot.

The wharf was really no more than that. One of the few authentic remaining ones on the southern coast: a live-fish tank, a live-bait shack, a fishermen's collective, a run-down fishing-equipment store, and a luncheonette— fresh-fish place—Neptune's Den, a favorite with the tourists and usually crowded except for off-hours.

The menu—the day's fresh catch—was written on a blackboard above the jukebox. There was a horseshoe counter, around which some morose-looking local single men sat, heads lowered to their doughnuts and coffee cups or bowls of chowder, and a row of worn banquettes overlooking the water and the harbor.

Since this was an off-hour, they had their pick. They sat down at one of the banquettes. Michelle lit a cigarette —Marlboro filters. She had her coffee black. Nick had a bowl of chowder. Sunlight permeated the windows. She put on her sunglasses. Nick could barely make out her eyes. There was something about her. He was convinced he had seen her before, but where? She must have been at the Foundation. . . . Where had he seen her before? He almost had it . . . he had even spoken to her, someone had introduced them. But he was too distracted trying to make conversation. (She smiled but didn't hold up her end.) "What is that?" he asked, pointing to the amulet dangling at the end of the gold chain that dipped down between her breasts. She wasn't wearing a bra.

"What? This?" she asked, holding the amulet up. "It's an Egyptian scarab. To ward off the evil spirits, I suppose. Some guy I slept with last year a couple of times gave it to me. I should have given it back to him but I like the shape, the way it feels." She finally acknowledged his expression. "I don't believe in hypocrisy. I guess I'm part of the modern generation."

"Is there such a thing?"

She nodded. "It's a new age."

"So we're told, at least. . . . The new woman. Does she exist? I don't believe things have changed that much."

"Things? What things? You mean going to bed. You can tell you haven't been to any encounter groups. A real easterner!"

"Why do you keep saying that?"

"Because you're a hypocrite. Unless you're just part of the old double-standard routine."

"I happen to consider myself very emancipated."

"Hmm, that's the worst kind."

He grinned. "You're right."

He found out that she had been married—"It was suffocating"—that she was not divorced from her husband but separated. They didn't see the need for divorce—"That's like giving some credence to the marriage." They were still on friendly terms; he'd gone on a camping trip with her and their two children this last spring. She'd been a chemist with a large pharmaceutical company in San Francisco, and had been laid off along with several hundred other people last year when the budget was halved because of the recession. She'd come down south then (because she'd wanted a change); she decided on Sonora Pines because of the university. It was better than U.C. at Los Angeles. She'd been brought up in Los Angeles, "During the drought of the fifties." Besides, her parents were there. She was going for her Ph.D. in psychology, a subject she'd always been interested in. She and her kids lived in a nice little house up in the hills. It was a good life. Simple. But she needed that—"For a while, for the time being, at least. When I get too bored I'll pack the kids up and head on down to Yucatán or something. I've always wanted to go there. Camp on the beach, fish . . . the natural life. Until then . . . I can't complain. I'm happy . . . relatively, you know. I mean, at least I'm not miserable the way most people I know . . ."

"Where have I seen you before?" Nick asked more to himself than to her.

"Are you going to start that one again?"

In spite of himself, he grinned sheepishly.

"How the hell should I know where you've seen me?" She lit another cigarette, exhaled dramatically. "Where do you shop?"

"That's it! No, no, that's not . . . I just know I've seen you." He kept shaking his head.

"In your dreams," she suggested.

"Why not? Who knows? In my dreams . . . maybe—the power of suggestion." He smiled.

"The girl from the West."

"Yes . . . the Golden Girl."

"My hair's streaked."

She suggested they go to her place for lunch. She'd fix some sandwiches. She was a fast driver and Nick had trouble following her; with each sharp new incline of the road, he became more unsettled and apprehensive. She hadn't given him her address and he was afraid he'd lose her. She stopped so abruptly, he thought she was going to make another turn. But it was a dead end, a curved gravel driveway. Her house, one of those modern stone and wood contraptions with lots of glass walls out of *Architectural Forum*, was built on an incline overlooking the town and the water below. He parked beside her, outside the garage. She led the way up some side steps onto a sun deck and in through the sliding glass door of the combination living room–dining room–kitchen. The furniture was minimal—a couch, a table, director's chairs, oversized colorful pillows on the floor—the casualness trying to mask the economical factor but only accentuating it all the more.

She told him to look around if he wanted to. But he didn't. He followed her into the kitchen, an open area behind a bar counter at the other end of the room. She had him cut up some tomatoes and avocados in slices (they were grown outside in the garden). She put up some drip coffee.

She stuffed everything onto a tray. They sat at the picnic table on the sun deck and ate the sandwiches she had made: alfalfa sprouts, lettuce, tomato, avocado, cheddar cheese on homemade bread (her husband, she said, supplied her with fresh homemade bread every week—he found it therapeutic).

She lay down on the bench, her coffee cup tilted on her navel, her eyes closed to the sun. "Hmm. This is so soothing. I could almost fall asleep."

Nick tried to keep the flies away. Finally he piled everything onto the tray and took it into the kitchen.

When he came back out she was lying on her stomach on the floorboards of the sundeck, her top off. "I'm not trying to seduce you, I'm just trying to get rid of my bikini-top marks."

"Why should I think you're trying to seduce me? Where would I get an idea like that?"

She laughed. "I'm more subtle than that."

"I believe you . . . I'm getting the idea that you just might be." He leaned over. She pushed him away in mock-earnestness, but he kept his hand on hers. Her eyes lowered, their two heads came together. They kissed once, chastely, smiling with relief, almost like children. The phone rang, but she let it ring.

Suddenly she jumped up (she had put her top back on), looked at her watch. Ten after two. Shit. She had promised some friends to go sailing. She was supposed to meet them at two. They had to get down to the harbor immediately. Nick asked why didn't she just phone. They didn't have a phone. They lived on the boat. Nick let her race on down ahead. He saw her car in the harbor parking lot. He hurried out to the wharf. She waved, motioning him not to bother to walk out to the end of the wharf. But he wasn't sure if that's what she was saying. He kept on. She motioned him away again. She was talking to someone. Some kid, bare-chested in cutoff jeans. It was too far away to tell, but he looked like the one on the beach. The Walkers' house-sitter. Nick wondered why he was talking to her. He waited.

She came toward him. "Boy! Was he zonked out!"

"You didn't find your friends?"

". . . kids today . . . God knows what that one was on. But now he'll probably take his board and blithely go surfing. He'll be in the proper state of mind expansion to appreciate the waves. I guess that's California for you. . . . Naw, they left."

They went for another walk on the beach, sat down on

the sand. The few swimmers started to leave. A faint
breeze was now perceptible. She asked him if he'd like to
go to a party with her tonight. They could leave if it got
too boring. Nick felt as if he were in a dream, all this
was totally unreal.

They went by his place. She wanted to see his house.
She went through the rooms. "This says everything. You
sure you didn't make this mess, throw everything around,
books on the floor, on purpose? Don't you ever throw
bags out? What are all these paper bags . . . newspapers?
Haven't you heard about recycling?"

"I'm kind of embarrassed. I didn't want you to see it
like this."

"Oh, don't be. You should never be."

"OK." Nick considered it, saw she was serious. "I
won't be."

"Well, I won't spend a night here with you. It's haunted
by your wife."

They stopped off at her place (the house where the
party was going to be was up in the hills anyway) so that
she could change. This change involved another top—a
tie-dyed shirt—some eye makeup, lipstick. She took a
sweater along. They went in her car.

Rock music, an almost auditory hallucinatory whir and
beat, pulsated out of the darkness surrounding the ram-
shackle house (it was built on several different levels).
Michelle explained the owner was an architect during the
weekdays. They followed the din to its source, into the
hypnotized dark, past the guideposts of stationary people.
Overpowering wafts of incense mingled with the pot. A
few figures were dancing, that is, doing some sort of im-
provised solitary form of gymnastics. The place was throbbing, in the trance of the music; crazed reflectors sped
past, the walls seemed to be revolving, a swirl of dis-
solving forms—light, smoke, and the steady beat holding
sway. Michelle took Nick's arm and led him into another
room.

"Michelle!" A huge, bearish man pounced on her, his
paws smacking down on her back. Trapped in his grip,
she swayed back and forth with him. He whispered something in her ear. She laughed, her head lodged against his
chest. Still laughing, she slipped out of his hold.

She took Nick's arm again. "He's crazy . . ." But she didn't follow up to explain.

There were several more encounters, displays of physical familiarity, seemingly charged exchanges. Nick wondered what he was doing here, what he was doing here with this girl he'd picked up on the beach.

"Let's get out of here," she suddenly announced, as if she'd read his thoughts. "I don't know any of these people. I hate people coming up to me like that."

They went outside, into the dark. Nick felt this was all unreal, as if all day he had been in some sort of dream state. He was simply not the sort of person these kinds of things happened to; even as he thought that he smiled. "Things," as she had said. It was unreal and because it was unreal it didn't matter, it didn't count. But somehow he knew already that it did. He felt comfortable with her. She didn't make demands, didn't ask for anything. If she had in any way he would have picked it up immediately—he was at that stage, he knew, that emotional convalescence, where any sort of demand would be rebuffed, any sort of attachment muffled. But she didn't, didn't do any of the predictable things. That was it. She didn't do anything predictable, so he was already hooked, wondering what she would do next.

They finally found her car. "Why did I drag you here? I shouldn't have dragged you here. You must have been bored."

"No. But that noise . . ."

"They'll all end up deaf. A deaf generation."

"There have been tests. Symptomatic of a greater disease . . . the morality of the times."

"It makes me nervous to be around drugs. You know, around here the police have nothing better to do. It's the kids I feel sorry for. You know, like that guy who came up to me. He sells the stuff. Ever since he lost his job . . . I'm afraid my drug days are over . . . not that they ever were . . ."

They sped through the dark countryside. Nick felt at peace for the first time in months, didn't feel a need to speak. She pulled into her driveway. "Let's take it slowly," she said.

She didn't ask him in. And Nick didn't feel like pushing

her—he wanted to give her enough rope. And yet he was surprised at how let down he felt. He was suddenly cold; it was dark; there were no lights around anywhere.

"I'd ask you in, but I really have to be up early to do some work. I have a class Monday morning. Why don't you come over tomorrow? For brunch. You can meet my kids. Tony'll be here, too, but he won't stay long. Then we can have the rest of the day to ourselves. How about twelve?"

He was awakened by the phone. "Nick, did I wake you? Rodney. Listen, something seems to have come up. Would you mind dropping by? I know it's Sunday. . . ."

Nick saw the police car in the parking lot beside Osmond's Cadillac. He went through the deserted halls straight to Osmond's office. He knocked. "Come in, Nick." Rodney Osmond was seated on top of his desk, close to the officer, who was in the chair that he'd sat on the other day, writing in his pad. The patrolman was looking out one of the French windows. "I guess we don't need any introductions. There's no point in beating around, Nick. We finally got word. Mrs. Macdavitt got a call early this morning. At eight-fifteen."

The officer nodded.

"Someone—she didn't know the voice—told her her husband was safe and everything would be all right if we just did as we were told, then George was put on. She said he sounded strange, not at all like himself, but you know he probably had someone telling him what to say. She said it sounded almost like a recording. This is just what I was hoping wouldn't happen—getting her mixed up in this. Well, at least we have something to go on now. God knows where it will lead, though."

"What do they want?" Nick asked.

"That's just it. We can't tell yet. Oh, obviously it's all related to the project—getting him to hand over all his papers. Apparently he'd already done that, according to Washington. Of course the papers were all pretty much altered—and I would imagine they've figured out as much by now. It was a way of stalling. I just hope he's not another runner-up for the casualty list in the 'cold war.'"

"What happens next?"

"We just have to wait. We should hear pretty soon."

"And in the meantime?"

"There's some security officers from Washington with Mrs. Macdavitt," the officer put in.

"What have you told her?"

"Well, of course she knows it has something to do with what he was working on."

"Doesn't George have a heart condition?"

"Yes." Rodney Osmond closed his eyes and nodded. "That's what's really getting her upset, I think."

"They have some kids, don't they?"

"Two sons."

"What've they been told?"

"One's in Europe for the summer, the other—the oldest one—was sailing with some people from here—a group— to somewhere in the South Pacific, I think."

"So we just wait around?" Nick said.

"Yes. That's just about it." Rodney Osmond nodded absentmindedly.

"We're going to head on over"—the officer motioned with his head—"to the Macdavitt place. We'll let you know."

"I'll be here all day. I have some work to do anyway. . . . Well, Nick, there's no point in you sticking around."

There was a VW bus beside the Datsun in Michelle's driveway. Nick went up the side steps to the entrance. He was about to knock when Michelle opened the door. "I heard your car. I just tried you a little while ago. I thought maybe you'd overslept . . . after last night. I was beginning to wonder."

"I had to go to the Foundation. . . . Yeah, I overslept." He grinned.

"We went ahead, but I'll make you some eggs or something, if you want." She rolled her eyes, made an expression of disgust toward the sun deck. They went out. Tanned, with a trim beard, in a shirt casually unbuttoned, patched jeans, espadrilles, her husband was solicitously leaning over a suntanned blonde little girl who was resignedly evaluating the items left on her plate. He was cutting up her meat for her. "Nick, this is Tony," Michelle said without much enthusiasm. Tony continued cutting up the hamburger with a fork. "There we are! Hello, Nick. How are you?" He put out his hand. Nick and he shook hands.

"I don't want any more hamburger. I've already had my protein."

"You're supposed to say hello. So people'll think you might have some manners," Michelle said.

The child made a face and slipped under the table.

"Well, that was Heather." Tony laughed, unperturbed. "Now, c'mon, Heather, we have to finish—"

"Peter! Peter!" Michelle called out. "He's in the bedroom watching the Angels. Peter!"

Peter, in baggy jeans and a baggy T-shirt, reluctantly came out holding his plate.

"No, I didn't ask you to bring out your plate. I want you to meet Nick. Honestly, you don't hear a thing, do you?"

"Hello, Peter," Nick said.

Peter looked down at his sneakers. "Hello. Can I go back now, Mom?"

Nick found it incongruous that anyone should call Michelle Mom. Peter put his plate with an untouched taco on the table, took the bowl of nuts and raisins, and went back inside.

"What can I get you? As you see, around here we eat different cuisines. You have your choice."

"What are you having?"

"Eggs. Bacon, sausages. I'm the one having brunch."

"Fine."

Heather's head popped up. "Mommy, why does Daddy eat eggs if he's a vegetarian?"

"Because I'm a lacto-vegetarian. That means—"

"Shall I make you some eggs, then?" Michelle asked Nick with an edge of sarcasm, and disappeared into the house.

"I've been on the seed diet," Tony told Nick. "It's simply an updated version of the brown-rice diet. Do you know about it?"

Nick wasn't sure if Tony meant the seed or brown-rice diet.

"It's a new thing"—Tony went right on—"really big

down south, L.A. You know, you're regarded as the northern part of the state up here. I really got hooked on it. It's just the natural balance of acids. You know, fruits, to keep the system cleansed out, and of course you've got your natural proteins—nuts, whole grain—you're allowed an unlimited amount. Well, look who's here. Heather, are you going to rejoin the civilized?" Heather's head popped back down. "No. Okay. Michelle tells me you're with those Pinkos? That's the way people think up here. A real stronghold. This is about the last outpost, politically speaking. Roosevelt here is still a dirty name, and I don't mean Franklin. This is the heartland of your not-quite-resuscitated stiffs. The bastion of your local variety. Cadaver county. They play golf, drive around in their Mercedes, polish off their martini highballs, but don't let that fool you, look a little bit closer and you'll notice a strange kind of glow, stage makeup, rouge. They may be parading as suntanned paragons of sun worshipers, but it's just makeup, breathe too close to them and they'll start to flake, disintegrate. They're very dusty. They're really just made up of dust. This is the nightmare of health, of the natural life. But you should know all about that. Michelle says you're in sociology."

Nick nodded. "Yes, that's right."

"I did a short on the Foundation. About six, no, seven years ago. Well, it started out as a full-fledged thing, but we got into a hassle with the producers, the network. You know, you had some guy there working on the Warren Commission Report. It was shown on CBS. You might have seen it. Pretty deleted form, but it had some good work, especially some long shots and long tracking shots showing the place."

"No, I never saw it."

"Well, they dig it up once in a while on the educational channels in the East. But you won't see it out here."

"Yes, it is a pretty conservative area."

"Ha! Reactionary. This is a right-wing paradise. They're practically Birchites here. It's really amazing they've allowed the Foundation to stay around, that they haven't burned it down, stoned you people."

"No, a lot of people in the community come to the dialogues."

"Yeah, but they don't give their money, do they?"

"I think a lot of the funds are from the government . . . but as a matter of fact there have been a number of contributors from around here."

Tony took out a Schimmelpenninck box, raised his eyebrows dubiously, and offered the box. Nick shook his head. Tony struck a match, inhaled, picked off a fleck of tobacco from the tip of his tongue with a grimace of distaste. He looked the other way for a moment, then sighed or, rather, exhaled and poured some more white wine from the jug of Almadén into his glass; he looked inquisitively at Nick.

"That stuff always gives me a headache," Nick said.

Tony nodded, gathered some nuts off his plate, and passed them down to Heather.

Michelle put a plate of eggs, bacon and sausages in front of Nick. She sat on the bench beside him. Tony smiled at Michelle, who stared back at him without any sort of expression at all.

"Well, Heather, are you ready? I want to get some more background scenery," he explained to Michelle. "I think we'll go up toward the cliff." He picked up his heavy Beaulieu.

"I thought you said you wanted to avoid the traffic, you had to get back to have drinks with somebody?"

"Well, this won't take very long. Besides, you've been having such strange weather up here I want to take advantage of today. You know"—he addressed Nick—"summer's the foggy time of year on the Coast."

"So I've heard," Nick said.

Tony nodded. "I think I'll use a medium-yellow filter, Michelle. What do you think?"

Michelle shrugged.

Tony and Heather went off. Tony with the Beaulieu on his shoulder, Heather trekking behind him, clutching the canisters of film. They climbed up a path in back of the house and slipped behind some trees.

"He's just driving me crazy. I wish he'd leave. He said he'd only stay for lunch, he was in such a rush, no, couldn't even wait, had to eat. Oh, you have no idea how he gets on my nerves. . . . Hi." Michelle leaned over toward Nick.

"Hi." He swallowed his eggs, laughing at his nervousness. They kissed.

"How'd you sleep?"

He grinned.

He helped her bring the plates back into the kitchen.

"When he goes maybe we can take the kids for a drive, go down to the beach or something. Meanwhile . . . What do you want to do now?"

He knew what he wanted to do. She pretended to be embarrassed. They went for a walk instead, downhill toward the bluff, which overlooked the town and the water below. The sharp sunlight made everything stand out in relief. They sat down on a patch of grass. Michelle said she often came here to think when she wanted to be alone. They sat with their arms around each other.

It started to get chilly. They headed back to the house. Tony was reading aloud to Heather, the two of them sitting close together on the living-room couch. Tony was reading from a book called *Magpies in the Sky*.

Nick and Michelle went into the kitchen area and sat on the barstools. "What domestic bliss," Michelle whispered. "The parental image. He hardly ever spent time with them when he lived with them. Now look at him." Michelle put up some water for more coffee.

The afternoon passed. And still Tony showed no indication of leaving. Peter rolled the TV into the living room. He wanted his father to see the game. He had to stay at least until the end of the inning. Tony shot apologetic glances at Michelle, who ignored him. "Well, they won," Tony announced.

"Mom! You should've seen Steve Garvey!"

The children went out to the driveway to say good-bye. "How can I say I'm sorry?" Michelle put her arms around Nick's neck. "I had no idea he was going to stay like this. I wouldn't have asked you . . ."

". . . no, I don't think it was so much what she said. Because we didn't really say that much. No soul-searching confessions. It's more what wasn't said. As preposterously cliché as that sounds. An immediate understanding, in quotes. Of couse it's absurd, preposterous. I keep telling myself it's just another figment of my imagination, a fitting finale to this moribund summer. . . . There I was, walking on the beach and, and . . . yes, the Golden Girl of the West. I keep thinking she'll fade away, I'll wake up. It's only another dream, another product of my feverish, over-stimulated brain. I suppose the effects of solitude . . . the last few months. The fantasy life taking control of the alienated subject's psyche . . . the final touch. Well, I should have expected it, known as much, I was suscept-ible, vulnerable . . . open, maybe even, yes, waiting for something like this to happen. Where I wouldn't have to do anything . . . there I would be in this already existent situation, relationship. And that's exactly what it is . . . it's as if she'd seen to everything . . . as if she already knew me."

"Sounds too good to be true," Dr. Richardson said.

Nick raised his eyebrows, couldn't help smiling. "Yes, isn't it? It's as if she were totally attuned to me . . . but, you understand, in a rather uncloying way. Nothing ob-vious. As I said, more a certain attitude . . . in what passes between us. I sound almost like some sort of ad-vertisement, the greeting-card speech from the couch. A maudlin sense of well-being, your common variety of contentment. Dreamlike, almost. I keep having this image of her, I can't explain it, nor do I want to. As if I were in another state, enveloped by her presence . . . everything seems an extension of her. Even her house seems an ex-tension of her. It's a modern house—lots of glass—but that's not the point . . . there are plants everywhere, even in her bathroom . . . light everywhere, a skylight of sorts . . . ferns, vines, climbing lianas. I just stood in there the other morning, my eyes closed . . . then I caught myself in the mirror above the sink. It's really almost been as if I were in a dream. I was totally unprepared for something like this, for this. I guess I've shed my solitude, this stance of detachment . . . without much prompting."

"How does it feel?"

"Wonderful. And then her kids . . . I walked into this perfect setup—it's a ready-made family, not mine, but that's all right. We took the kids down to the wharf for dinner after her husband finally left. I caught some people looking at us, smiling, as if thinking what a happy young family. Maybe I'm fantasizing. But, as we all know, that's the same thing. . . . Now Johanna'll have some kids to play with when she comes up here."

"You have her this week, don't you?"

"For three days. I'm picking her up down in L.A. At the airport tomorrow afternoon. At least those are her latest instructions—they're flying back from New York, and I'm to pick up Johanna at the airport. She and Mike are flying on from there up to Vancouver until Saturday. Something about some rock festival. I couldn't figure it out. Then Saturday I'm to drive her back down to L.A. . . . Poor kid, being shuffled around like this . . ."

That Wednesday Nick got down to the airport early. He walked around for a while. He went into one of the coffee shops and had a Coke. Then he went out into the large antiseptic waiting area and waited. The plane was late. He saw her immediately, suntanned and small. He was always struck, each time, by just how small she really was. She was dragging along a Pan Am flight bag; her teddy bear was stuffed into it. She'd had that bear as a baby. Mike was in a flowery shirt, jeans. Carole's tan seemed even deeper against her white lace shirt, washed-out jeans. She had a silk bandanna around her long dark hair. Mike was holding Johanna's hand. All three were suntanned, distinctly Californians, casual affluent travelers standing out against the rest of the arrivals in seersuckers, summer dresses, Bermuda shorts, with their assortment of cameras, diaper bags, Samsonite hand luggage. Carole's head tilted back as she spotted Nick. Then she smiled. "There he is," she said, standing right in front of him. "Have you been waiting long? We were late taking off."

He bent down to Johanna. "Hiya, Jo-Jo." He kissed her. "How was the flight?"

"Her name is Roger this week. Last week it was Carlos. She won't answer unless you call her Roger," Carole told him.

"I've got the chills. I want my sweater," Johanna said.

"I'm going to wait for her bag," Mike said, leaving them.

"See, Mike's going to get your bag, then you'll have your sweater." Carole knelt down to explain. "It was cold on the plane. The air-conditioning system was going full blast."

Nick nodded.

"How have you been?" Carole asked, taking advantage of their few minutes of privacy.

"OK. And you?"

"The weather was pretty lousy."

"It rained all the time," Johanna pitched in.

"Well, not quite, darling," Carole corrected. "Almost. It probably seemed that way to her."

"You have tans."

"That's from the weekend we were up on the Cape. What a mess that place is. I always forget. . . . She has some sort of poison ivy. There's some medication left but you'll probably have to have it refilled. I'll give you a copy of the prescription."

"Gee. How did you get that, Jo-Jo?"

"Roger," Carole said.

"Roger. I bet it itches, huh? Where is it, on your hands? Can I see?"

"It's all over. We were on some picnic; it was all over the place. She was rolling around with some kids . . . weren't you, Roger?"

Roger nodded.

"Listen, Nick." Carole lowered her voice to a confidential tone. "There's been a change of plans. I didn't want to go over it on the phone with you because I thought it'd get too complicated. But you know the group War Paint & Feathers, well, their lead drummer, Little Joe Shapiro, got busted—some frame-up—and Mike's been on the phone the last two days with the lawyers. They're trying to settle out of court, but he's got to be there. They're down in Acapulco. So we're going to fly down from Vancouver Saturday morning. We're just going to change planes here, at eleven . . . and I thought I'd close up the boutique. You know, just until the middle of next week. I mean, we're not going back to the house, so there'd be no point in your bringing her back there."

"So you want me to drive her back here?" Nick nodded, keeping his voice low so Johanna wouldn't hear him.

"Oh, I knew you would!" Carole threw her arms around him.

"Before eleven o'clock Saturday morning."

Carole was looking the other way. "We'll be back the middle of next week."

"Isn't it kind of hot down there this time of year?"

"There was no heat in the house." Johanna had overheard. "The water was too cold. I don't want to go on that boat again."

"Is Mommy teaching you how to sail?"

"I caught a starfish, but it died. We put it in a box and buried it. Mike is going to get me a rabbit."

"Here we are." Mike had brought over a duffel bag.

"Is that her suitcase?"

"She saw all the hitchers on the road. Listen, we were lucky she wanted only a duffel bag. Her sleeping bag is in there."

"She only sleeps in a sleeping bag now."

"I'm going to get a tent for Christmas."

"We said we'd see."

"You said you promised."

"Now, c'mon. We never said that. You'll just have to wait and see."

"Well, we'll have to see what we can do about that. . . . When's your plane?" Nick said.

"About an hour." Carole seemed uncertain.

"Yeah. I want to go over and check out the tickets."

Nick took the duffel bag; Carole gave him the medication and Johanna's vitamins. Johanna went reluctantly. She wanted to wait until she saw them board the plane.

Nick led her out into the still afternoon. The desertlike heat filtering through all the concrete, all the terminals, modern buildings. Rows of cars. He had trouble finding his car in the parking lot.

He drove straight up along the water to Sonora Pines. Just under two hours. But Johanna was already asleep, in another time zone. Nick carried her into his bedroom, undressed her, put on her pajamas, kissed her on the forehead. He closed the door, went into the living room to call Michelle. He slept on top of the covers that night, next to Johanna.

During the next two days, Nick and Michelle took the children to the beach, gave their full attention to the swimming races, the ball games, the Frisbee contests, the skateboard displays on the sloping road outside Michelle's house. They went on picnics up in the hills, they went to the drive-in (*Planet of the Apes, Benji,* and *Supercat and the Three Tostadas*), they went grunion catching.

Then, Saturday morning, Nick was back at the airport with Johanna.

Saturday afternoon, after he got back, Nick went to the Foundation for a few hours. He was seated at his desk, working on the transcripts. Four o'clock. He was just about to put them away when the intercom sounded. It was Rodney. Could Nick drop by his office? He knew what that meant. There hadn't been a word about Macdavitt since last Sunday.

The door was open. Rodney was on the phone, the same police officer on another. The same patrolman was standing at one of the French windows again, his back to the room, studying the garden. Rodney pointed to the Mr. Coffee on the sideboard. He poured himself a cup. Someone was mowing the lawn outside. From the fragments he could hear, he gathered Rodney was speaking to Macdavitt's wife. The officer spoke too softly for Nick to make out the words; he seemed to be questioning somebody.

"Well, Nick"—Rodney turned with an air of resignation—"it looks like all our fears were justified. Mrs. Macdavitt received a phone call yesterday morning—Friday morning. Two million dollars in unmarked hundred-dollar bills were to be left Saturday morning—this morning—before six A.M. in a brown attaché case in a phone booth off Fairfax Avenue, in the shopping center. Washington arranged for the money. It was left in the phone booth as instructed. But it was never picked up. Now we're all just waiting. Whoever's holding Macdavitt obviously isn't interested in money."

"I don't understand," Nick said.

"We're obviously not meant to." Rodney lowered his voice. "Looks like those boys in Washington have bungled it again. I didn't tell you about this yesterday. There wasn't any point in dragging—"

"Who called his wife?"

"We don't know. All they said was that they wanted

two million dollars in unmarked bills . . . But it was never picked up. So now we're just biding our time. Washington has sent out some more people to be with his wife, and we've got some people watching around here, supposedly."

"What happens now?" Nick heard himself ask.

"We don't have much choice. We just keep waiting."

The officer hung up. "I'm going out to use the car radio. Get some more men over here." He motioned to the patrolman to stay where he was.

Nick slept late the next morning, Sunday. He was on his way to Michelle's when the phone rang. Rodney sounded matter-of-fact. Frowning, Nick pulled into the Foundation parking lot. The police car was there again. There were several other cars, too. On Sunday morning? Nick thought that was strange.

Nick went in, down the empty halls. The door to Rodney's office was open. No one was there. Rodney had probably just walked out for a moment. Nick went over to one of the windows, waited absentmindedly, facing the garden. Where the hell was he? Nick stared at the lawn, the rows of statues lining the driveway, the fountains—the photographs of another age. He heard it again. What was that? A sort of leaden rattle, as if hundreds of coins were being rumbled, but the sound was magnified—the links of an iron chain piling in heaps on top of one another and then being lifted up. Nick ran out the back, into the garden.

A tow truck was stationed at the swimming pool, its iron chain unwinding, crashing down through the lowering film of weeds and scum, clanking against the sides, the bottom. A small group was gathered around the edge: Rodney and some men Nick didn't know.

The body was dragged out, packed onto some sort of stone table—the sundial. A stiff bloated mass of discolored rags, bulging, water spewing out. And this sack, which had once been human, tied to the stone sundial, emptied out slowly, mercilessly, as it was carried across the lush tree-bordered angle of lucid blue sky, leaking water in its wake across the flagstones around the pool, across the bed of bright summer flowers; it hovered for a moment in midair and then, dripping tediously, was dumped like some inept puppet and left to drain on a patch of sunlit lawn.

Nick turned away. He thought he was going to throw up.

Nick went back with Rodney to his office. The three fairly nondescript men in the blurred early stages of middle age or premature defeat, Nick thought, who had been around the pool—black shoes, button-down white shirts, regulation sideburns—accompanied them. Nick never got their names. They never gave them. Rodney made several references to previous statements. Apparently he knew the men.

The one who asked most of the questions never really changed his dour expression or his flat methodical tone of voice. Once in a while he winced; he kept slipping Lifesavers into his mouth. Nick finally realized they were Tums. The man with the Tums. That's too much, Nick thought. The questions were so simpleminded ("Were you aware that Dr. Macdavitt had once had access to top-secret documents?" . . . "What did you know about his past? Did he ever speak—mention in any way—was there even a veiled reference to what he was working on now?" . . . "Has any of this leaked out of this room?" . . . "Are you aware that this involves national security?") that Nick had to control himself. "C'mon," he wanted to say. "Get off it."

". . . I went to school with him. I've known him most of my life," Rodney was saying.

"We realize, Dr. Osmond, that this isn't the most opportune time for such questions," the man with the Tums finally volunteered.

"No," Rodney said. "It certainly isn't the most opportune time."

The other two men wandered around the office, checking the bookcases, behind books, under tables, turning back the Oriental rug, examing the collection of sculpture (the Kamakura period, thirteenth- to fourteenth-century Japan, Rodney informed them). Nick watched them, thinking, You must be pulling our legs. This is a spoof, it's so obvious, you've got to be joking. Straight from Central Casting. A way of trying to get a reaction, a rise. Trying to get one of us angry, unnerve us . . .

The man with the Tums went on with his questioning. (He prefaced everything with "Now, Dr. Osmond or Dr. Schrader . . .") ". . . either one of you is aware—realizes what this involves, what is at stake . . . Please try to remember. Anything that was mentioned. Dr. Macdavitt might have implied something. Please try."

"Looks clean to me," one of the two men announced.

"Nothing here." The other one also seemed satisfied, glanced at his watch, wanting to move on to something else.

The man with the Tums nodded but ignored them, and went on with his monologue. "Now, Dr. Osmond or Dr. Schrader, if you have any questions or should happen to remember anything, run into anything, come across some information, no matter how irrelevant you may think it is, please get in touch with us at once. Of course we'll be keeping in touch with you. We expect further contact to be made, Dr. Osmond, Dr. Schrader. They won't believe there's nothing left. From what we can surmise, they believe Dr. Macdavitt did not give them full access to his papers. They believe there's something—some vital information—being withheld. Of course, that is not the case. There are no such papers. Besides, Dr. Macdavitt was not in possession of as vital information as they thought he was. It's unfortunate, most unfortunate, to say the least, that he was used as a pawn. But this was a matter of national preservation, you understand.

"The death, after the autopsy, will be reported a suicide. Mrs. Macdavitt will corroborate this. That is, that is what she will be told. We don't want to endanger her life in any way. Of course we'll have her watched at all times. We would appreciate, Dr. Osmond, Dr. Schrader, that you would bear in mind Dr. Macdavitt's depressed state, his frequent depressions. A long history of mental instability . . . We will try to keep it as tasteful as possible, naturally.

"And of course, again, if anything comes up—you want to discuss anything, you should happen to remember anything . . . Dr. Osmond, Dr. Schrader . . . No, don't bother seeing us to the door. I think we can find our way out . . . yes. . . . And we'll be briefing the two police officers who so unfortunately got mixed up in all this. They'll be briefed accordingly. You understand this is strictly confidential, a matter of highest—"

Nick caught Rodney's eyes. "I gather your names are also confidential," Nick said.

Tums blushed—the mask of his face reddening to the edge of his modified crew cut. He nodded, his eyes on Rodney. "Dr. Osmond . . . yes . . . I'm afraid they are. However, when and if it becomes a necessity, you will be briefed . . ."

"I know, accordingly," Nick said, finishing for him.

Tums ignored him, went on, ". . . accordingly. . . . And now, let me reiterate this was a tragic accident, a great loss and a terrible blow to all of us. It just signifies that we played too willingly into their hands. I assure you, the repercussions will be felt for quite some time."

Michelle looked up from the disassembled Panasonic cassette recorder. She was seated at the dining table in the living room. Peter stood beside her, elbows on the table supporting his head, absorbed in the insides of the Panasonic. Michelle was using a screwdriver. "Hi. We're trying to get the sand out." Smiling, she added in a singsong voice, "It was left outside overnight. . . . What's the matter?"

"We already tried using a head cleaner, but that didn't work," Peter said.

"Are you OK?" Michelle got up.

Nick held on to the back of one of the barstools at the kitchen counter.

"You look like you're going to pass out." She touched his forehead. "I think you better lie down."

"No. I'll be all right. I just need to get some air." He pulled open the sliding screen door and stumbled out. He leaned over the wood railing that separated the sun deck from the rest of the garden. Michelle followed him out, closing the glass door behind them. Peter, taking the cue, went into another room.

Nick steadied himself on the rail, his eyes closed.

Michelle stood beside him, an expression of total concern on her face reflecting his distress. "You look like you've seen a ghost."

He laughed sardonically at the unintentional aptness.

Then he let out a deep sigh, keeping his eyes averted, focused on some blurred point on the indefinite line of the horizon where the hills merged with the layer of haze that was the ocean. "Well, you might as well know. You'll find out soon enough. George Macdavitt's body was found."

"I don't understand."

"It was dragged out of the pool. Just a little over an hour ago. Suicide."

"George Macdavitt, the physicist?"

He nodded to himself as much as to her—a resigned formality—acknowledging something he couldn't accept.

"He was at Los Alamos. Didn't he get into some sort of controversy with the government? Wasn't he blacklisted from the academic community in the fifties?"

"It was never really clear. Besides, that was a long time ago. He was at Harvard, M.I.T. after that . . . then the Foundation."

"I know. I've read all his books. I used to buy any magazine that had an article by him. I'd watch him on *Scientific Outlook*. He was on at least once a month. He seemed so levelheaded, so objective . . . detached . . . as if he could never be anything but totally unemotional, analytical in his approach. One of those truly scientific souls."

"Yeah," Nick said bitterly.

"Isn't it strange?"

Nick didn't answer.

"Did he leave any note or anything?"

Nick shrugged.

"Who found him? Did his wife find him? She's a well-known scientist."

"No, it was the swimming pool at the Foundation."

"How come you were there?"

"Rodney Osmond called me. He wanted me to go over some things with him."

"And when you got there . . ."

"I guess they found the note."

"Oh, there was a note?"

"To his wife, his two sons."

"When did it happen?"

"You mean when did he kill himself? I don't know. It

was awful. He was all covered in slime, filled with water
. . . it just kept pouring out . . . like a gargoyle. . . . I
guess they'll know more after the autopsy."

"But it was suicide."

"Well, yeah, of course, what else could it be? Besides,
apparently he had a long history of depression. He'd been
seeing doctors for years."

"And he seemed so reasonable. The epitome of a
scientist. You couldn't imagine him doing anything im-
promptu, anything that hadn't been deliberated for years."

"Well, apparently this was. At least it was at the
Foundation. At least his wife didn't find him."

"It's incredible. I just can't get over it. It just shows you
never know . . . you take things for granted, I mean the
way other people act, as if they were automatons. You
just assume what they say is what they feel—that that's
all there is. We can't be bothered to go deeper, to pay
attention. We're too self-centered. We deal in appearances,
in surfaces. George Macdavitt. The great man of science
. . . of our times . . ."

"Yeah."

"And he committed suicide." Michelle shook her head
in disbelief; she made a slight bitter sound verging on disgust. "Just unbelievable."

"Yeah. I know."

"George Macdavitt," she said again.

"Yeah." Nick sighed wearily—a sigh that was open to
a wide range of interpretations.

The official autopsy report on Dr. George Macdavitt
simply stated: Suicide—"concussion of the brain, compound fractures of the skull rendered by contact with
the concrete bottom of the aforementioned swimming
pool . . ."

The announcement was made to the press. UPI, AP relayed the story worldwide. Most radio stations across the
country carried it on the hourly news. There were short
film biographies on all the major networks on the evening
and late-evening news. Further, more lengthy programs
were planned for the coming weekend. A one-hour special
was to be shown on both CBS and NBC.

The New York *Times* obituary started on the bottom of the front page and continued for two full columns in the obituary section:

DR. GEORGE H. MACDAVITT DIES

By Lambert Russell

SONORA PINES, Calif., July 29—Dr. George Hewitt Macdavitt, one of the founders of the Atomic Age, was discovered early Sunday morning in the swimming pool of the Foundation for the Study and Research of Contemporary Sciences in Sonora Pines, California, where he was a Senior Fellow. The death was listed as an apparent suicide. He was 62 years old.

Dr. Macdavitt, an associate of Edward Teller, Enrico Fermi, and J. Robert Oppenheimer at Los Alamos during World War II and a member of the original Los Alamos group in 1942, had been known in recent years to be an ardent opponent of nuclear power. He had written numerous articles and essays on the subject, had appeared on many panels in colleges and unievrsities in this country as well as abroad, and had participated in discussions on radio and television. For several years he had been alternate host on *Scientific Outlook*, an NET weekly program. Several of his later books (most notably the vastly popular *Tools of Science*, *At the Crossroads*, *In the Scientific Eye*, and *The Race for Power*) were turned into television documentary series. Dr. Macdavitt, a pacifist, had also been active in the antiwar movement. He was a favorite speaker with college students.

Dr. Macdavitt had been associated with the Foundation for the Study and Research of Contemporary Sciences since its inception in 1956. However, he did not become a permanent member until 1965. Since that time he had been a senior fellow, contributing to the Foundation such papers as "The Sources of Power: The Government Misuse of Nuclear Energy," "The Coalition of Energy," "Raw Power," "Under

the Politics of Disarmament," "The Wasteland of
the Future," . . . He was at the time of his death
working on the seventh volume of *A Scientist's Notebooks* (his collected essays and papers).

In 1965 he was a professor of physics at M.I.T.
While at M.I.T. he finished the major part of *The
Race for Power*. While there, he also formed the
League Against the War—members of the academic
and intellectual community against the Vietnam War.
His involvement with the student-based peace move-
ment in this country dated from this time.

From 1961 to 1963 he was part of President Kennedy's Science and Energy Commission and an adviser to NASA, then located at Cape Canaveral.
During this time he also worked on a number of
government projects with the Air Force. In the years
1955–61, he was affiliated, in an advisory capacity,
with the scientific end of a number of private business
and industrial organizations. From 1955 until President Kennedy came into office, Dr. Macdavitt was
inactive in government and the political scene as a
whole. He was then working on *The Politics of
Atomic Energy* (an account of his years at Los
Alamos) from the safe and removed vantage of
Harvard, where he taught physics from 1955 until he
left Harvard to join the Kennedy administration.

At the height of the McCarthy period, Dr. Macdavitt was called several times before the House Un-
American Activities Committee (he was then still at
Los Alamos). Dr. Macdavitt, never of a placid nature,
became an open foe of the proceedings, calling them
"Orwellian tactics," "autos-da-fé in a computer-run
society," "Walpurgisnacht bureaucracy." There were
a number of heated exchanges.

Senator McCarthy referred to him publicly in de-
rogatory terms, implying that politically he was un-
sound, "a wolf in sheep's disguise leading the youth
of this country to the other side"—that he was a
Communist.

Dr. Macdavitt and his wife, Dr. Sally Guild, took
their two young sons and left for England, where they
lived in the countryside outside Oxford. Dr. Mac-

davitt remained in this self-imposed exile from 1953
until a public apology was sent from President Eisen-
hower in 1955. During these two years, Dr. Macdavitt worked on *In the Scientific Eye.* He also
lectured at Oxford and was on a number of BBC
programs. . . .

Dr. Macdavitt was at Los Alamos until 1953. . . .

In 1953, after the Oppenheimer hearings, Dr. Macdavitt left Los Alamos, feeling he could not support
the policies of the government. It was at this time,
colleagues say, that his political outlook underwent
a major shift.

He worked closely, in highest secrecy, with J. Robert Oppenheimer, Edward Teller, Enrico Fermi, and
I. I. Rabi at Los Alamos during World War II and
until 1953. . . .

He was part of the original Los Alamos group. . . .

In 1939, for the first time in this country, he dem-
onstrated the release of nuclear energy by fission of
the uranium atom. He invented the gaseous-diffusion
method of separating fissionable U-235 from other
forms of uranium and directed much of the subsequent development of the process. His work contributed to the development of atomic weapons and
modern nuclear power. . . .

Dr. Macdavitt was born on June 27, 1912, in St.
Paul . . . graduated from Harvard in 1932 and received a Ph.D. in physics from there in 1935. From
1935 to 1939 he was professor of physics at Harvard,
where some of the more prominent names in contemporary sciences were among his students.

In 1940 Dr. Macdavitt married Dr. Sally Guild, a
well-known scientist in her own right. Dr. Guild, a
chemist (and the author of *Scientific Adventurers*—
essays on notable contemporary scientists—and *Beneath the Skin*—an account of her work in cell biology), has been acclaimed for her work in chemical
biodynamics and her research in virus-caused cancer
in laboratory cell cultures. She taught for a number
of years at Columbia University and Radcliffe College
as well as at the University of California in Los
Angeles and at Berkeley.

Dr. Macdavitt also leaves two sons, Edward and Lionel.

J. Robert Oppenheimer wrote of George Macdavitt in 1950, "Upon meeting him one is immediately struck by the utter graciousness and civility of his manner. The epitome of the twentieth-century scientist, his sensibilities are more that of the nineteenth century, more that of the artist than of the scientist." Dr. Macdavitt himself said, "The scientist in his laboratory is the true artist of the twentieth century, on the verge of discovering, on the brink of witnessing other worlds—whether it be breaking the genetic code, the atom, or trying to decipher the meaning and consequences of the existence of the multitudes of worlds within worlds beyond this one." Dr. Macdavitt was truly a man of his times, an intellect who grappled with the forces of the future.

In recent years, afflicted by severe depression, Dr. Macdavitt had been under the care of various psychiatrists.

The services will be for the immediate family only. Dr. Macdavitt's body will be cremated, as he had wished.

A memorial service will be held sometime later in the year, it was announced, at Harvard University.

The following week, the schedule at the Foundation was more or less erratic. The daily dialogues were suspended. Reporters, photographers seemed to be everywhere, shooting away, interviewing secretaries, gardeners, wandering around the grounds, by accident into offices, into bathrooms. The driveway was jammed with cars, vans, minibuses equipped with camera cranes, mounted crews. The Foundation members were forced to park down the road and, as the week progressed, often off the main road; they were asked to show their identification at the entrance gate by the numerous plainclothesmen and policemen who patrolled the area.

Nick retreated into his office. He was trying to finish the first part (the interviews with the factory workers) of the transcripts on work and alienation. He locked the door, closed the curtains. No one bothered him except in the men's room. "Just tell them you're one of them," Dennis Cavanaugh told him. ("No, I'm with ABC," Nick told the kid with the beard in the safari outfit, loaded down with canisters of film and equipment. "You are?" He was obviously puzzled. "So am I. Gee. So how come I don't know you? You must be a free-lancer or something, right?" After that Nick switched to "local press.")

Nick slipped in and out, almost unnoticed—though he noticed one of the two men who had been with the Tums man last Sunday when Macdavitt's body had been dragged out. The man seemed to be associated with CBS, at least he had a CBS badge. He had stationed himself (with several other people) at a card table down the hall, outside Nick's office. Every time Nick went into or out of his office the man was there. Nick looked him directly in the eye, but there was no sign of recognition or acknowledgment. Nick almost began to feel maybe he was mistaken, maybe it wasn't the same man, he was only imagining it was, the man bore only a striking resemblance. . . .

By Friday the crowd had trickled out (leaving behind a few strays from the main crews, some vans, yards of black cable snaking across the halls, parts of equipment, metal trunks, and the proliferation of paper bags, sandwich wrappings, Styrofoam cups, plastic glasses, empty liquor bottles, cigarette butts on the carpets, behind statues, under the furniture, tire tracks on the lawns, trampled flower beds, empty film boxes scattered across the terrace, the garden, multiplying around the pool) and the Foundation returned to its former informal schedule.

Nick was standing on the terrace outside his office. He was watching one of the gardeners, an old Mexican, pick up the trash from the lawn—item by item—striking each object with his stick, then unhooking it like a speared fish into the large work bag around his shoulder.

Dennis Cavanaugh was in the parking lot, in his tennis shorts, squatting on his tan muscular haunches, grinning, his racket in one hand, the other holding on to the open door of the green MG belonging to one of the TV reporters, in a tennis dress, her head resting on the wheel, whispering with him—his mocking laugh framing the intervals of this muffled exchange. He suddenly sprang up, slammed the door. The girl revved the motor and raced out past the statues toward the gate. Dennis shook his head. Nick watched him, amused.

"Thought I'd get in an early game," Dennis called out to Nick, as always full of double entendres.

"Dennis, you'll never grow up."

"Doesn't bother me." He grinned. "I'll manage! She wanted to stay here like that," Dennis went on, an excuse to comment on the girl's attributes. "Imagine. She was going to film us in that little dress."

"They would have thought she worked here."

Dennis laughed appreciatively, on cue. "Hey, listen, you're coming to the dialogue, aren't you? We're convening in the garden. They're going to film it . . . in a natural setting. The old man didn't want to do it at first. He's very upset about this, you know. George and he practically grew up together, you know. But he's anxious to get back into the routine, so they didn't have too much trouble persuading him."

The dialogue was held in the garden, in the sunlight under the trees, beside the Roman statues. Card tables and chairs had been set up in front of one of the fountains. The film crew perched on the second-story window ledges or on their revolving platforms, with their cameras and mikes suspended in midair, or holding on like monkeys to the chiseled limbs of the statues. In the crowd of faces, Nick at first didn't see the man from Sunday, the CBS man. It took a while to get started. The cameras were rolling. "Democracy and Industry" was the topic. There, obstructed by the shade cast by one of the statues, the man with the CBS badge was watching.

". . . this form of competition, of course, is just a mirror of the capitalist system, magnifying . . ." Dr. H. R. Lejeune, an adviser to numerous Presidents and administrations dating from Woodrow Wilson, a sprightly elderly gentleman with a bow tie, was interrupted by a noticeable German accent.

"Dear Doctor, you are not making sense. You are forgetting that such enterprise cannot even begin to exist in the Communist countries." Dr. Greta Landsteiner-Schorr, the famous economist daughter of the legendary playwright Friedrich Landsteiner, took him to task. "This has been proven over and over again. Just look at EEC. Disorganized, no planning, no center—chaos. It is all very vell for you to criticize a system vhich breeds only monopolies . . . but a solution to go back to the grass roots! You are talking nonsense! This is cottage industry, very vell for underdeveloped countries vhere democracy is still in its cradle, but here ve are discussing not theoretical imaginings. Ve are concerned vith those governments vhere free-flowing interaction betveen vhat you call monopolies and the state exists. Of course, they are the same. You cannot separate the state from the industry. They are symbiotic."

"You are referring to Communism then, I take it?"

"Communism! Vhat are you talking about! In Communism there is no mutuality . . ."

Rodney Osmond leaned back over Dr. Landsteiner-Schorr, who was seated between him and Nick; his hand tapped Nick's shoulder. Nick gave a start. "Nick," he whispered, "come into my office at lunch."

". . . this is the disease of compartmentalization," and Dr. Landsteiner-Schorr slammed her fist down onto the card table. The card table wobbled. "If ve discuss industry ve are not talking about these rules of thumb."

They broke off for lunch. Nick waited, standing in a group with Dennis, until he saw the CBS man behind the statue turn the other way. He hurried through the crowd, up the steps, out of the garden, down the hall into Rodney's office. Rodney wasn't there yet. The flimsy curtains of the open French windows lifted up in the breeze, blowing in gusts of light. Nick went over and closed the windows. He stared, distractedly, at some of the books on the shelves on the far wall beside the door, barely aware of what he was reading off: Erikson, *Edenic Myth*, *Modernism, Art and Technology, Subversion in the Military, The Aesthetics of William James, Notes Towards the Definition of Culture*, Rieff, Vico, Marcuse, *A History of West Point, The Year 2000, Microbe Warfare, Population Control* . . . Nick looked at the door, for some reason. The handle started to turn slowly. The door opened slightly, almost in slow motion, opened wider. Nick, without thinking or knowing why, moved back, pressing against the bookcases. His heart was pounding. The door continued opening, its shadow lengthening across the sunlit parquet. Then, just as suddenly, the door closed. Nick didn't move. His eyes shot back and forth from one end of the room to the other; his ears strained, but he could hear nothing other than the intermittent scraping of some branches outside against the windows.

Then the door flung open. Nick stiffened, a sort of upright cadaver—an image of himself flashed in his mind, pinned like a dissected rat. Letting the door close behind him, Rodney went straight to his desk. Nick felt his shoulders practically drop. Rodney swung around. "Oh, it's you! I thought I heard something. What are you doing standing there? Why don't you sit down?"

"I wasn't sure it was you."

"What do you mean you weren't sure it was me? Who else is it going to be?"

"Someone came in here."

"Really? Who?"

"I don't know. The door opened, someone looked in."

"Probaby just looking for the john. Those people have made a mess of this place."

"No, I think it was someone trying to get in here."

"That's because of everything that's been happening. Our three stooges. You're letting your imagination—"

"No, somebody came in here."

Rodney looked him straight in the eye, assessingly. His mouth pursed, he motioned with his head. "Sit down."

Nick sat down in the chair closest to the desk. Still standing, Rodney leaned back against the desk, feet crossed. He appeared to be studying his shoes or a spot in the Persian rug.

"One of the men who was here last Sunday has been here every day this week," Nick said.

"Really? I didn't notice. That's strange. Hmm. I wonder why. Are you sure?"

"He's been eying me like a hawk, follows every move I make. Every time I go to the men's room, there he is, down the hall, staring."

"Hmm. Did he see you come in here?"

"I don't think so. It was probably him opening the door, though."

"Hmm. I'll check that out. Maybe I'll give Richard

Castle a call. The one who was doing all the talking the other day. Find out what it's all about."

"Richard Castle? The one with the Tums?"

"Yes, he does seem to like them, doesn't he? If that's his name. Listen, I'm used to them. They've been hanging around this place for years. I think they probably still think we're a bunch of Communists going to do God knows what. They used to come around in the middle of the night, snooping around, with flashlights, cameras—imagine that! I don't know what they thought they were going to find! I was scared to death. One time I was working late, one of them tripped down the terrace steps, broke his ankle. That was back in the fifties. I thought they'd stopped all that nonsense. They did. For a while. But then George . . . You know I grew up with him, our families lived on the same street. We went to school together."

There was a sound, some sort of minor crash, something dropping.

"What the hell was that?" Rodney put out his hand as if to ward off whatever it was.

Nick saw that his hand was shaking. "Someone probably dropped a camera."

"More likely a sculpture. I wish they'd go already. They've just turned this place upside down."

"Well, most of them have. CBS is the only one—"

"Nick. I've been thinking, the last couple of days. I'm not sure how best to broach this, so I'll get straight to the point. George, as you've gathered by now, had access to all sorts of secret material. Now, he gave over most of his papers, his research, and so on. I mean they forced him to hand it over. Washington, that is. Don't get me involved in that mess with the Soviets. I never could begin to unravel that one. For all I know, it could have been George's invention, his paranoia, and believe me, he had reason to be paranoid. They hounded him. . . . This whole business with the Soviets . . . Of course, it could have been their own concocting, I mean those people in Washington. I wouldn't put anything past that crew. I'm not going to get myself bogged down in that."

Nick was still trying to figure out why Rodney had wanted to talk to him, if he could have just been anybody. He could see how upset Rodney was, and he wanted to talk to someone, and he, Nick, filled that need. He listened, half attentively, still not convinced that Rodney was really going to say anything. But he also had the feeling there was something else. He nodded, trying to concentrate, but his eyes kept going back to the trees at the window. He was probably reading too much into it: Rodney just needed to talk.

". . . Nick, George left some papers in my custody several months ago, this last spring," Rodney went on, his tone of voice hardly changing, as if all this—even talking about it—was painful but he had no choice. And the only way he could do it, talk about it, was as quickly as possible. "I haven't even looked at them myself. I'm not really even sure exactly what is in them. He was putting together that last volume of his—*A Scientist's Notebooks*—which was to be in the hands of his publisher the end of the summer. The seventh volume of his collected papers . . ." He went behind his desk and sat down in his chair. He was almost looking the other way, at an antique Beshir prayer rug on the wall to Nick's left. "I can't afford to get myself all involved in this. I have this place to think of, people I'm responsible for, other lives at stake here. . . . When George was first working with the government, at Los Alamos . . ."

Still, Nick couldn't help wondering where all this was leading to.

". . . no . . . no, even before that . . . I don't know how, I was never sure, I mean he wouldn't go into it . . . he came across some Air Force files." Rodney sighed. The light flared through the trees in back of him. Nick kept his eyes on him, trying to seem interested. Rodney nodded, as if to emphasize what he was going to say; Nick had the feeling of someone reciting his lines and not being completely convinced of what he was saying. "He was with Project Blue Book with the Air Force from the beginning—that is, until they realized what he was about to do."

"Project Blue Book? Wasn't that about UFOs?" Nick could hardly believe what he was hearing. But Rodney was serious.

Rodney sighed again. "Yes."

"UFOs?" Nick had to repeat it, he couldn't believe he was hearing right. "George Macdavitt and UFOs?" He swallowed. He heard his heart beating. He had the feeling he was being pulled into something or, rather, he already was in. He just hadn't realized it until now.

"Yes. All that nonsense. Sheer gibberish. But he had all the facts. I don't deny he had some probably quite valid points. I would be the first . . ." Rodney gestured, lifting his hand off the desk and letting it drop back down. "There are, after all, so many things we don't understand. . . . Well, I saw it over the years," Rodney went on, almost as if he were talking to himself. He heard himself talking. His voice sounded distant even to himself. He had the feeling, almost, that he was talking about a fictional character. Someone he'd known in another world, in the past. And, of course, that was true, now that George . . . He didn't finish his thought.

"It was a madness." His voice cracked slightly. "I mean it was much more than obsession. He collected material everywhere, wherever he went. He was monomaniacal. Questioned everyone, traveled halfway across the world. Thousands of miles. To interview somebody, get a firsthand report. Just to speak to someone for a few minutes, often some poor illiterate who'd witnessed those lights up there or had some strange object following him at night . . . That's all he really did at M.I.T., you know. Had to leave, it was impossible. Then at Oxford, the same thing. The CIA was going to do . . . God knows what. Threatened all sorts of things. The CIA, the KGB. He never really said. Just implied. All sorts of mad things.

"You know, he would travel to Cairo, down the Nile, some remote village. Some mad escapade, some notion about Osiris' body being buried in different parts along the Nile, only the body was really just some sort of ultimate ultracomputer left thousands and thousands of years ago by some advanced space travelers. Yes, the whole science-fiction formula. Might as well have been 2001. But he had all these proofs, all these figures, data. Very intriguing. Who's going to dispute it? Well, apparently the whole government did. No one wanted to hear a word—and more than that. I couldn't believe what I was hearing. It might as well have been a fantasy. And he had a thing about ruins. Was convinced that's where the clues were. He'd camp out in ruins, trek over to India, down the Amazon, across the Sahara, up the Himalayas.

"It was madness. No doubt about it. No. I have no doubts now. He was totally mad." Rodney kept hearing himself, and his voice sounded false, as if he were trying to convince himself. "He wouldn't give up, you know. That was the kind of man he was. And then, of course, it leaked out, you know. Word got around—M.I.T. When he was at Harvard, too. He was totally possessed, mad."

Rodney's tone was one almost of wonder, Nick thought, as if he were speaking about someone who was undeniably quite mad but nevertheless wise; and as if he—Rodney— were fascinated by this madness. But Nick was becoming more and more unsettled. He was troubled by why exactly he was being told all this.

"I'm not quite sure how he gave up most of his papers." Rodney continued. "He had tapes of interviews, Xeroxes of top-secret Air Force documents, films, microfilms, the most highly classified stuff, stashed away everywhere. Apparently under floorboards, inside lamps, in the wainscoting of his house in Cambridge, you name it. The mad scientist . . . I think there was a raid or something. In any case, that was about the time he came here—in 1965 —provided he drop all that nonsense. Those were the conditions we set up, we had to, you understand. He seemed to accept them. I believed him. Tynner believed him. Other people did, too . . . his wife . . . We could never have taken him on otherwise, not with the way it could affect this place. We'd had enough adversity in this community to start with, let alone to get enmeshed with the government again. I thought it was all over, and so did Tynner. I didn't realize at first . . ."

The room seemed unnaturally quiet to Nick. Rodney's voice carried, as if it were much louder than it really was. In reality, he was talking so softly that Nick had to strain to catch all the words. He was aware of the wash of light through the trees behind Rodney. Everything seemed so placid, so civilized, and yet George Macdavitt had been killed.

"Thought he'd really dropped it. It got worse, of course. That's when the CIA got in on the act. Then, in quotes, the Soviets. Then God knows who else. Just further evidence that he was suffering from delusions of persecution. Just further proof of his madness. All this intrigue. After all, you'd think that would be the one issue we'd agree with the Soviets on."

Nick stared at the film of light and foliage through the glass, the branches moving soundlessely. The only sound was Rodney's voice. Nick heard his heart beating faster. Then he realized what it was: Someone could be listening. Outside the window, on the terrace, outside the door.

"But no. According to George, the government felt it was a matter of national prestige that we unravel the mystery of UFOs before the Soviets. Even though it would be kept secret. It had to be kept secret because the government was afraid of national panic. But George was convinced it should be made public. He thought there would be some panic at first but that people would adjust to this new situation pretty readily and without any long-term adverse effects. Besides, they deserved to know. They had a right."

The room looked more and more unreal to Nick. This staid, decorous setting. And what was being said. What he was being drawn into, just by listening. It was science fiction. Some crazy dream he'd gotten into.

"He was quite vehement. The government, however, he said, had conducted numerous lengthy studies on the matter and their findings showed they had reason to believe otherwise. The government was convinced the whole thing could only lead to mass hysteria." Rodney suddenly stopped. He stared out of one of the windows. Panels of foliage swarming with light. He thought of planets, of atoms, of all the hidden, invisible worlds. He looked at Nick; he wondered what was registering. If he hadn't made a mistake. Of course, he had no choice now, it was too late.

He went on again. "George was like a brother to me. I just haven't got the heart to look through these papers. . . . Nick, I want you to look through them. Tell me what you think you can salvage: epigrams, notes, personal markings—whatever. Maybe it'll be enough for a book. It's just too painful for me. I just can't . . . and . . ." he added as an afterthought, "and just forget whatever references you find to those unidentified objects—that nonsense.

"I have a batch here I put together with some that Sally gave me, though I should rephrase that, handed over to me, the other night. Sally gave me some more notes of his, one of his notebooks. He kept notebooks all his life. She wanted me to have his last notebook. . . . I realize this must all seem absurd to you, Nick. And it is. I had to get these papers, this notebook, from inside a toilet tank." Rodney could still hear himself speaking, as if he, too, were now a fictional character recounting this fictional event. He picked up the crystal paperweight Virginia had given him one Christmas. To grasp something real.

Nick watched him pick up the paperweight from his desk and cup it in his hand.

"Virginia and I were over with some other people, a few old friends, but really mostly family, at Sally's last night. Sally came up to me, shoved a plate of sandwiches into my hand. 'There are some papers I want you to have, inside the toilet tank in the hall bathroom.' You know, some of our friends from Washington were among the gathering. I put the plate of sandwiches down on a table, waited—what I thought was an appropriate time. I went into the bathroom. I looked inside the tank. And there they were, wrapped in a green plastic garbage bag inside the tank."

Nick watched him smiling slightly, sardonically. The refined white-haired gentleman catapulted out of his genteel element, into the crude modern world, Nick thought, where amenities were for the birds and unaccountable things like the rumors of violence, poverty, wars one heard about occurred. Like George Macdavitt's death, fishing something out of a toilet tank, his last papers . . . Happened to innocent people.

"I've put them with the other papers he gave me. I want you to see what you think can be used for a book, as I said, or some excerpts for some article in the Foundation magazine. Just see what ideas you have, and just skip any references to those unidentified objects. Don't even bother with that." He felt guilty, for a moment, apprehensive, he didn't want Nick to get more involved than he already was. He almost wished he hadn't taken George's papers; but what could he do now? Everything had seemed to gather its own momentum. But no, he thought. He was making too much out of it. Nick would read the papers. And that would be the end of it.

"George could be very persuasive, you know. I don't want you getting caught up in that. Not that you will. You're much too sensible for that . . . for that nonsense. I know I'm making too many explanations, I guess it's just guilt. Nick, you see, since we've kind of got the noose around our necks right now, I couldn't really give these papers to one of the scientists here—I mean Spaulding, Jim Fishbach, Braunheimer. There'd be no point. That would be too logical." Sighing, he pushed back his chair. He went over to one of the windows.

He seemed to be looking at the garden. Nick watched him, half expecting him to fling open the doors, find someone was outside. But he only turned around again.

"You see, they'd figure if George left any papers with me I'd try to get rid of them. They know I realize it's too treacherous for me. I would never chance the consequences involved, the future of the Foundation. They'd figure I would give them to some physicist here, a chemist, an engineer, maybe. Someone technical. With some background. They would never think I'd give them to someone like you."

"So by default . . ."

"No, not exactly. No. You strike me as pragmatic enough to just scoff at the whole thing, whereas some scientist might start putting these rumors together, and God! His scientific love of puzzles would take over. His bent for mysteries, for clues, would get the best of him. No, you strike me as just the right combination. You're dubious enough, yet you have a grain or two of the philosopher in you." Rodney smiled. "Besides, you might even find it interesting."

"Just so long as I don't find them too interesting?"

"Yes, well, it won't take you very long to read. I don't think there are more than two or three hundred pages, at most, including the notebook." He went over to the bookcases, took out three large books, and pulled out a bulging 10 x 13 manila envelope that had been folded in half. He put back the books. "In here you'll find his last notebook plus the random papers he left with me. Why don't you put them inside your jacket? I don't want anybody to see you walking out of here with these."

Nick tucked the envelope into his waist, took off his belt and tied it around his midriff, where the envelope jutted. He buttoned the lower and middle buttons of his jacket.

"And, Nick, I don't want these circulating, needless to say. I want you to give these back to me after you've read them. Keep them somewhere safe, where no one can find them. I'm sure you'll figure out something. I'll talk to you on Monday."

When Nick got home later in the afternoon he went straight into the bedroom. He slipped the envelope underneath the shelf paper at the back of one of his drawers in his side of the double dresser. It was still early, still warm enough for a swim. Michelle was not coming by for another hour. He put on his trunks.

Dropping his towel on the sand, he ran to the ocean and threw himself into the cold water. He swam out as far as his strength could take him. Then he let himself float, weaving, in an indefinite course, below the unnaturally hot late-afternoon sun in this surrealistic swimming pool, until he felt dizzy. The sun had given him a headache. He swam back in slowly, taking his time.

He dragged himself out of the water, dripping and shivering. The air was cool. He had the chills. He rubbed himself down. He looked over again. It was Michelle. She was talking to someone at the other end of the beach, just before the cove. She waved. He waved back. It was the Walkers' house-sitter.

He wrapped the towel around his shoulders. And waited. Slowly she came closer, into focus. She was beaming. She started to run, awkwardly, self-deprecatingly, her arms flapping. In spite of himself he grinned. She threw her arms around him, rubbing the towel against his back vigorously. Her head rested a moment on his towel-covered chest. "You look freezing! C'mon." She pushed him toward the house.

"No. I'm all right. Why don't we take a walk down there

and back?" He pointed to some rocks a few hundred feet away.

"OK. I was going to surprise you. I'm early. Did you just get back?"

"No, I swam for a while."

"Feel better?"

He nodded absentmindedly without looking at her.

"How did the dialogue go?"

"They seemed to think fine. They're going to reshoot a couple of parts on Monday."

"You mean they haven't left yet? Osmond must be climbing the walls."

"Hmm."

"What's the matter? You seem distracted. Did you have a bad day? . . . Talk! C'mon, you can tell me." She smiled, rolled her eyes coyly, mock-seductively.

"Who was that you were talking to?"

"Oh!" She laughed, annoyed. "So that's it! The Walkers' house-sitter."

"I know . . . but how come you were speaking to him?"

"You know? So why are you asking?"

"How come you were speaking to him?"

"Oh, c'mon, Nick. He's just some kid. I could almost be his mother."

"Not quite. How come you were speaking to him?"

"Well, if you want to know the truth, I was walking on the beach . . ."

"And you just struck up a conversation?"

She sighed. "Well, if you want to know the truth, no. I've seen him before. In the supermarket. In Jordanos', if you really want to know. In the vegetable and fruit aisle. OK? He was picking up a romaine, I was trying to decide on apricots or peaches . . ."

"And he helped you decide?"

"Exactly! You figured it out!"

"What were you talking about?"

Her eyes widened, incredulously. "What was I talking about!"

"Were you talking about the weather?"

She didn't answer.

"Don't sulk," he finally said. "I'm sorry. Don't take it

seriously. It's just I think there's something strange about him. Something wrong . . ."

"What do you mean?"

"He's always on the beach."

She laughed. "He's trying to get rid of all the kelp from the storm."

"No. Often he just sits there."

"Maybe he's meditating."

"Maybe . . . but I don't think so. There's something strange about him. He's always here—on the beach. Before I leave for work in the morning, early—I mean even at seven—there he is. Late in the afternoons, early evenings, sometimes even after it's dark. I remember one night a couple of weeks ago I was walking on the beach . . . and there he was, waiting."

"Well, if I may say so, you haven't exactly spent that much time here to really see that."

"That's just it. Whenever I am here, the odd times, odd hours, when I come back here to shave in the morning or get some clothes . . ."

"Those are probably just the times he is here. He probably has an odd schedule, like you."

"Hmm. Maybe."

"After all, he is house-sitting. He's just probably trying to do a good job, trying to get rid of that kelp, and you're making a mystery out of it. Why don't we go back and take a shower?"

The skin on Michelle's fingers was starting to crease. She got out of the shower. Nick stayed in. He left the glass door open, watching her. She wrapped a towel around herself, blew him a kiss. "I'll be back in." Nick closed the door. He stood, without moving, under the soothing jet of hot water. He turned the hot water on higher. Several minutes passed. Ten minutes. Where the hell is she? he almost said aloud to himself. Leaving the shower on, he slowly slid open the glass door and climbed out of the tub. He opened the bathroom door and crept out. Michelle was at the dresser. She saw him in the mirror and flung around, her mouth dropped. Then she smiled. It was only a split second. Nick frowned, something struck him as odd. "I was looking for a shirt of yours to put on," she explained.

"They're in the top drawer on the other side," Nick reminded her. "You're looking in Carole's side."

"No wonder it was empty." She laughed. But Nick felt it was an effort for her to laugh. Still smiling, she took off the towel and moved toward him.

They went back into the shower.

Later in the evening, when they were back at her house and he was sitting at the kitchen counter with the children watching her cook dinner (zucchini and shrimp and rice), he remembered the expression on her face when he had come out of the bathroom. . . . She was smiling at him. He lowered his eyes, embarrassed. He felt guilty for not trusting her.

When they were in bed he caught himself watching her, feeling remote, with that sense of distance he had not felt these last couple of weeks, since they had gotten involved. He was feeling detached again. Inside her, watching her; she continued moving. She stopped. She ran her hand over his face, touching him as if she were blind. "Where are you?" He was disgusted with himself. Disgusted because he felt it was just a ploy to keep himself safe, to pretend it didn't matter. He told her that. They stayed up most of the night talking. "Of course it's normal," she kept reassuring him. "You've been terribly hurt. Carole just moved out on you. It's understandable. It just takes time . . . it'll be all right." He was won over again. And trusting, in the simplicity of need, he feel asleep in her arms like a child.

That morning, Saturday, Michelle went off to Yosemite with her children for the weekend. She would be back Monday evening. They were going to go camping. She thought it would be a good idea for her to be alone with them; she'd been picking up their resentment, Nick's invasion of their lives. And besides, she felt things were moving too quickly, she wasn't sure where they were going (she was sure, she told Nick, that was just the point, that was the trouble). She wasn't sure she liked where they were going—where she saw they were going. ("Don't look hurt. I mean I'm scared. I wasn't prepared for this either.") She didn't want to get tied down again, not now anyway, not for the time being. Besides, a couple of days away from each other would do them good, might be just what they needed. They'd never been separated more than half a day, hadn't spent a night apart (except for the time with Johanna) in the last two weeks. They needed a breather.

Nick felt strange being back in his own house (he'd been almost living at Michelle's). It was like returning to some old life, one he no longer understood. The house was clean now (Michelle had helped him put it back together) and seemed even emptier than it had after Carole had left. If that was possible. It was, almost. He walked through the rooms; it was like going through a set. It was gray (it had been foggy all day). Gray. The rooms seemed gray. The carpet looked gray (it was tan) in this gray light. He imagined he was leaving footprints behind him in his wake, he imagined shadows of his footprints on the carpet.

He missed Michelle more than he had anticipated. It hadn't been a reality until she was gone. And then she was gone. That was it. He was alone. All he could think was forty-eight hours (she was coming back Monday evening). It amused him at first, that he should miss her like this. Then it annoyed him. He worked (he'd brought the transcripts home with him). He worked most of the day, Saturday.

In the early evening he fixed himself a drink (gin and tonic). He sat on the sun deck and watched the sunset. The pleasures of solitude, he thought (and he toasted his reflection in the glass door), are no longer pleasurable, if they ever were. He felt this was just another scene in a movie he was watching about himself.

He kept putting it off. Finding things to do, to delay (worked on the transcripts). He had dinner. He heated a can of clam chowder, scrambled some eggs (Michelle had been keeping the place stocked). He waited until it was dark. He drew the curtains.

Finally he went into the bedroom. He sighed and, as if with the inevitability of postponement, reluctantly took out the manila envelope.

He opened the notebook first. He started reading. It was handwritten. He skimmed a few pages, he read haltingly, adjusting to the handwriting. It was somewhat slanted, jerky, words were broken up. It was an erratic script, without any real patterns, words sloping left and right, breaking off in the middle. He kept reading. He didn't stop.

Part II

COLLECTING EVIDENCE

To Security 5A200 Washington. 2 August.

Subject was observed leaving Dr. Osmond's office (1348). Subjet, in our opinion, has been elusive all week. He has spent most of his time in his office; whenever he emerged (to go to the men's room, etc.) he glanced around furtively. We have tried to keep as close a watch as possible, which has not been easy. He may even be aware of this. During the filming of the dialogue ("Democracy and Industry" was the topic—the unedited film is available from CBS) Dr. Osmond whispered something to subject. I was too far away to lip-read. (Later reviewing of CBS film confirmed: Dr. Osmond: "Nick, come into my office at lunch." Subject gave a noticeable start at inception of this request.)

I lost subject from sight at breakup of the dialogue (1302). Subject disappeared in the crowd—confirming my suspicion that he was watching—though I was trying to stay out of sight and still keep an eye on the proceedings insofar as this was possible. On a hunch, I quickly made my way to Dr. Osmond's office (I opened the door casually, as if by mistake). But subject was not there.

As there were people around, and Osmond's secretary was seated directly outside, it was impossible to hear anything. I saw subject leave the office at 1348. He was not carrying anything. However, I should note here that subject, who usually dresses casually, to say the least (though this seems to be the rule rather than the exception here), has been wearing suits all week. His jacket was buttoned (lower and middle buttons). He could very possibly have been hiding something. Subject went back to his office (the curtains were drawn). He stayed there until 1632.

At 1635 he got into his car. I followed him back to his house. He went for a swim. (His Friday session with Dr. H. I. Richardson had been canceled. Richardson was on the panel of a symposium on "Psychiatry in Transition" at UCLA this afternoon.) I used my own discretion, I did not enter house at this time. Subsequent exploration failed to reveal anything.

Top-secret cable to Security 5A200 Washington. 3 August.

LOOKS LIKE OUR BOY SCHRADER HAS THE PAPERS STOP PRELIMINARY CONCLUSIVE EVIDENCE POINTS IN THAT DIRECTION STOP VERIFYING STOP PROCEEDING ACCORDINGLY UNTIL FURTHER NOTICE

Report by Agent R. Castle to Security 5A200 Washington. 3 August.

Re Macdavitt: We've exhausted every source. The matter still stands as is: All we can hypothesize for certain is that two or more Russian agents entered the Foundation the night of Thursday–Friday, July 18–19. (There was no sign of a break-in, confirming they must have either had access to a key or received help from the inside.) Also, they were probably known to Macdavitt, as there was no sign of a struggle in his office, and he probably also went off willingly with them. The conclusion seems to be that the agent (or agents) he had been dealing with was among them.

We can still only interpret the brutality of the act as a warning. The fact that they continue to refuse to admit their culpability could simply be further proof of their guilt. Or perhaps a new ploy. We are investigating the latter.

Top-scret cable to Security 5A200 Washington. 4 August.

SUSPICIONS HAVE BEEN VERIFIED AND CONFIRMED STOP SCHRADER IS IN POSSESSION OF MACDAVITT PAPERS

Michelle woke early. Through the blinds of one of the two windows a slight strip of light was projected across the large room of the Yosemite Lodge motel. She looked over to the other double bed, where the children were sleeping. She picked up her Omega watch from on top of the copy

of Muir's *Yosemite and the High Sierra* (which she had
been reading to the children) on her night table. A quarter
after six. Carefully, she got out of bed, trying not to make
any noise. She was wearing one of Nick's shirts. As she
crossed the worn-out red carpet barefoot, the floor
creaked. Peter (who was sleeping with his head at the
foot of the bed, not wanting to be next to Heather)
turned in his twist of sheet—Heather had the blanket.
Michelle waited, but he didn't move again. She went over
to the bureau; she took out some clothes from her BOAC
flight bag—bra, bikini underpants, a yellow tank-top. The
twenty-four-inch color TV on the desk beside the bureau
was bleeping over and over again the soundless picture of
a station's test pattern. She switched it off. She went into
the bathroom and quietly closed the door. She opened
the frosted-glass window to get some natural light. She
took a quick shower, brushed her hair, put on some
makeup.

She put her things away, back into the BOAC bag. She
slipped into her tight jeans, pulled on a bulky cable-knit
cardigan. She went over to the night table for her watch,
picked up her shoulder bag, put on her espadrilles, her
sunglasses, and stepped out into the glaring light, quietly
closing the door behind her. Several of the cars were already gone—the motel doors were open. The windows of
the Datsun were opaque with mist. Michelle walked over
to the phone booth across from the still-closed coffee shop.
Two young bearded hitchhikers, seated on their packs,
were already stationed outside the driveway. The booth
was cold and reeked of stale odors, cigarette smoke, and
the sweat of strangers. She tried to close the door, but it
was stuck. She got out some change from her coin purse,
a pack of Marlboros, some matches. She lit a cigarette
and, facing the sun, waited a minute. Then she turned the
other way, with her back to the open door. She waited
for the dime to register. She dialed a long-distance number. The operator came on, told her how much more to
put in. The number rang, but there was no answer. She
tried again; again there was no answer. She tried a third
time. On the fourth try, someone answered on the first
ring. She spoke for a few minutes, less than three minutes.

The person at the other end never said anything. She hung up. She went back into the room to get the children up for breakfast.

Nick stood at one of the windows in his office, looking out at the high gloss of colors in the garden. He heard the procession of cars pulling in, the beginning of another day. Eight-thirty. He sat down at his desk. The light hadn't come into the room yet. The room looked pale, cold. He shivered involuntarily. He tried to compose himself. He arched his fingers together, sighing. He pressed down on the intercom. Susan came in. He gave her some of the transcripts to retype. He waited another ten minutes. Nine o'clock. Rodney always arrived punctually at eight-thirty.

He knocked. "Yes, I said yes! Come in. It's open! Come in! Oh, Nick, it's you, come on in." Rodney was seated at his desk. "I'm just going over the calls I have to answer. I'll be right—"

"No, I've got to talk to you immediately."

"What's the matter? Don't tell me!" Rodney groaned. "I should have known better. Why did I do it? Why? OK."

"Look, I'm not trying to say I know the technical end of it all, but do you know what's in there? Do you know what he found, the things he's documented? And case after case, not just scientists. He's got secret Air Force files, top-secret classified documents, under-oath testimony . . . the top names in the military."

"I have only myself to blame."

"Rodney, don't you understand?" Nick saw himself standing there, on the Persian rug, in front of Rodney at his antique desk with the semitropical garden in the French windows in back of him. But then he thought of the handwriting on those pieces of paper; and he saw George Macdavitt's body. "Don't you see what was going on?"

"OK. You tell me. What was going on?"

"It's all classified, witnessed. It's all documented! He's got everyone's name . . . documents from the Joint Chiefs of Staff . . . it's incredible, unbelievable, we've got to get it out. Rodney, don't you see? It was a frame-up. They were just trying to get him out of the way."

"Nick. I heard it from him for almost twenty years. Now, I'm not going to hear it from you. Do you understand?" He pushed back his chair, stood up. "I told you I gave you those papers for you to look into, see what could be salvaged for a book. Not to get all caught up in this nonsense. And that's all it is. Grow up. Can't you see he was deranged? A brilliant, brilliant mind gone to pieces. Don't you think other people have investigated all that? His case against the combined superpowers . . .

"I thought, no, you'd have some sense. . . . You scientists are all the same, you can't resist. Any mystery, anything that even resembles a puzzle, and you're all scurrying around, racing against the clock, speeding through that maze to find the solution. Oh, that's why I didn't give them to Jim or Spaulding or Braunheimer, get some physicist all tangled up in those hieroglyphics. But there's nothing to solve here. Can't you see? Pure conjecture. Loopholes everywhere. There isn't one argument, one case that holds water. I've been through it all, Nick. Believe me. I know what I'm talking about."

"Have you read any of this? I just want you to read—"

"You come in here, Monday morning, nine o'clock, your eyes on fire, in a frenzy. A recent convert. Oh, there's nothing worse than that. And believe me, I've been around enough of them to know. . . . I haven't even had my second cup of coffee yet." He looked at Nick with pity. "It's a lost cause, Nick. You're just being naive. I didn't think you would be this naive. I just gave you those papers to read, not to—"

"I just want to ask you, have you even looked at them? I mean, have you even read a few pages?"

"I don't have to! Look I gave you those papers with the single intent and purpose . . . I didn't ask for this nonsense."

"I just want you to look at them, just read a few pages." Nick, unbuttoning his jacket, pulled the manila envelope out from his belt. He took a few pages out. "That's the least you can do. That's the way I first felt. Saturday night, when I started reading this thing. I thought, What the hell . . . then I started reading. I kept reading."

"The convert's description of the holy writ, 'unearthly the vision' . . . 'And out of the sky there came the visitation of golden charioteers of light from the stars such as the prophet had never seen before,'" Rodney recited, with perfect inflection. His poetic fund-raiser's voice that could woo any audience. "'. . . and he fell on the ground and prayed' . . . Ezekiel: 'And I looked, and behold, a whirlwind came out of the north, a great cloud, and a fire infolding itself, and a brightness was about it, and out of the midst thereof as the colour of amber, out of the midst of the fire. Also out of the midst thereof came the likeness of four living creatures. And this was their appearance; they had the likeness of a man. . . . And I heard behind me a voice of a great rushing . . .'"

"No, you've got to read this. I'm not leaving this room—"

"Listen, don't you come barging in here—" The intercom buzzed. "Yes, what is it?"

"I have a call from Geneva from Dr. Bergonzi," a woman's voice said.

"I'm not here!" Rodney's hand flew up from the intercome button.

"I'm going to give you a Xerox of a couple of pages." Nick held the pages out.

"Xerox?"

"I'm going to leave them with you. I want you to read them."

"What do you mean, Xerox? What have you done with the originals? I want those papers back!"

"I'm going to leave you these Xeroxes—"

"Where're the originals?"

"Don't worry. They're safe."

"Where did you make the Xerox? Who saw you?"

"No one. Don't worry. I did it in my office. On the copier. It's legible, though. You'll be able to read it."

Still glaring, Rodney took the papers out of Nick's hand. He sank down in his chair, as if his whole body had suddenly caved in. Looking pained, he skimmed through the pages. "What the hell is this? I know all this. George tried to go over it a million times. This was part of his campaign, to undermine the scientific community, to enlist these idiots. . . . All right, I'll read it for you. Now get out of here. I've got a lot of other things—"

"I want you to call me as soon as you've finished. I

don't want to talk about it—the contents—in either of
our offices."

"What is it now? You're afraid they're bugged? No,
but it's all right to talk as we've been doing, hmm? Where
do you want to talk?"

"The grounds, anywhere. We can walk around the
grounds, go somewhere for lunch."

"You're all hopelessly naive. The credulity of innocence.
I can give you a point-for-point retort, just as documented, just as classified, for everything. For every case,
every reference in here—that's been dug up in here. And
so can the top people."

"I just want you to read it."

"All right . . . I'll drop by your office when I'm finished,
as soon as I have a chance."

Nick closed the door behind him.

Synopsis of surveillance log. 5 August.

At 1116 Schrader returned to Osmond's office. Osmond
and Schrader left Foundation in Osmond's car 1121. We
followed them to the Cove, a local seafood restaurant on
the main boulevard, off the water. They were seated away
from the windows, at a table against the wall. It was
impossible to follow the content of their conversation—
this is a popular eating place and by noon it was filled—
there was no possibility of being seated in their vicinity.

At one point we noticed Osmond banged his fist on the
table. They both drew or wrote something on a note pad
that Osmond took out of his jacket pocket, and also on
their paper napkins. We inspected table and area after
their departure, but they had taken their napkins with
them. The place was still crowded (1415), so we were
well covered. We quickly paid cashier. We followed them
out. They got into Osmond's car. They drove to beach
parking lot, parked there, and talked until 1512. We could
pass only so many times from the road. They returned
to Foundation 1528.

From Security 5A200 files.

Nicholas Farley Schrader (5 ft. 10 in., 148 lbs., hair:
brown, eyes: gray), b. February 5, 1939, in Philadelphia,

to Edward Schrader [1] (b. 1905, Philadelphia) and the former Edith Farley [2] (b. 1912, Lake Forest, Ill.).

There are two brothers: Francis (b. 1937), with father's investment firm; Gerald (b. 1940), an architect; and one sister: Elizabeth (b. 1935), a pediatrician, m. to Richard Hartigan, a psychiatrist. (Files available.)

Detailed background of above available, though subject does not appear to have overly close ties with family (beyond the observance of holidays, anniversaries, birthdays). Check with Bell reveals fifteen calls to his parents since he moved to California ten months ago. He has seen them twice: for a week during Thanksgiving (1973) on Martha's Vineyard, where his parents have a summer house, and for Christmas (1973). Both times with his wife and child.

Subject had usual childhood diseases. (File available.)

Attended Groton School. (File available.) Nothing appears to be out of the ordinary. A fairly routine, uneventful childhood except for high scholastic and intellectual ability. Copies of school reports, tests, etc., available. (Superior IQ. Top 1%. Note for possession of photographic memory possibility.)

There were two grades skipped (eighth and tenth). (File available.)

Entered Harvard 1955 (high frequency of Harvard graduates at the Foundation noted). (File available.)

Graduated 1959. Postgraduate work at Harvard (sociology), M.A. 1961, Ph.D. 1963 (thesis: "Societal Conflicts in the Cultural Adaptation of Minority Groups").

National Institutes of Health: 1963–65.

Rockefeller Foundation: 1965–68.

Columbia University: 1968–71.

Department of State: 1971–73.

Subject has been with the Foundation for the Study and Research of Contemporary Sciences since September 1973.

---

[1] With the investment firm of Barker, Liverwright, Grinhold & Schrader. Semiretired since 1972. Has heart condition. (File available.)

[2] Daughter of land developer James Morrison Farley. (File available.)

Files available of above (including clearance for Department of State).

Subject has published essays and articles in *American Journal of Psychiatry, Psychology Today, Science, American Sociological Review, Journal of Social Issues, Journal of Comparative Psychology, Saturday Review/World, American Journal of Sociology, Journal of Personality and Social Psychology, Journal of Experimental Psychology, Harvard Educational Review, Scientific American,* and others.

Subject has published the following books: *Roots of the Future: An Inquiry into Cybernetics,* 1968; *The Modern Industrial Crisis: Man vs. Machine,* 1971; *The Loss of Power: The Individual in the Modern Military-Industrial Complex,* 1972; *A Study in Alienation: Work and Alienation,* volume 1, 1973 (subject is presently working on volume 2). Subject has contributed to the following anthologies: *The Year 2000, Frozen Lives: The Minority Experience, In the Age of Anxiety: A Compilation of Writings on Contemporary Life,* and *Flower Power: The '60s Revisited.*

Nominated National Book Award 1972 for *The Loss of Power.* Working on presently: *In the Machine Age* (volume 2 of *Work and Alienation*) and "A Report/Survey of Factory Workers," a Foundation project.

For possible investigation: incident in sophomore year at Harvard involving printing and distributing of leftist-oriented political leaflets.

In junior year an affair with Boston University coed resulted in her subsequent pregnancy and an abortion. Coed Joyce Weinstein, leftist, active in early student and anti-war movements (and now in women's movement), may have been factor in subject's political shifts (they made a trip to England together in the summer of 1958—numerous encounters with Socialist and Communist intellectual elite of that country). J. Weinstein: assistant professor of political science at CCNY. Unmarried (as of August 1974). Frequent contributor to leftist and liberal-oriented periodicals (*Partisan Review, Village Voice, The Realist, New York Review of Books, Kenyon Review, Ramparts, Rolling Stone*). Has had no contact with subject since 1965 or 1966 (this could not be ascertained more spe-

cifically in the casual context of an exchange with a
CCNY associate—carrying a copy of subject's *A Study in
Alienation*—in CCNY cafeteria, carried over to faculty
lounge).

Subject active in civil-rights movement. (File available.)
Number of trips south (active participator). Traced
several letters in The New York *Times, The Observer*
(London), *The Christian Science Monitor;* articles (first-
person accounts of trips south) in The New York *Times*
magazine, The Washington *Post*, Washington *Star-News,
Encounter;* name on numerous petitions. (File available.)

Married Carole Eastman [3] January 1970. One child:
Johanna (b. June 1970).

[3] Daughter of landscape painter Curtis Eastman and the former Harriet Sanders (former concert pianist), b. March 12,
1942, New York City. Childhood New York City and Cape
Cod, Massachusetts. Attended Florence Nightingale, Dalton,
and Barnard. Graduated Barnard 1963 (art history). In 1963
came into trust fund ($20,000 yearly) set up by maternal
grandfather (Senator Franklin Sanders of Connecticut). Lived
in Europe (Rome, Paris, Lerici) with Harold Stanford (b.
1935), a writer of fiction (leftist-oriented politics—file available), September 1963–June 1965. Dealt in antiques—in
partnership with Vincenzo di Bramante & Co., antique dealers
in Rome. Returned to this country 1965, lived in Greenwich
Village with fiancé, art dealer–collector James Villiers Beau-
mont (b. 1942), August 1965–November 1966. Had antique
store there on Christopher Street. Returned to Europe with
H. Stanford in November 1966. Lived in Lerici November
1966–May 1967. Returned to New York City. Lived in Phoenix
with Fernando Artiaga (b. 1925), an anthropologist-writer
(from a family of Mexican activists—files available from the
Mexican government), September 1967–May 1968. Lived with
Andrew Lampson (b. 1933), an actor, May 1968–August
1968 in Malibu. Had an abortion in Puerto Rico August 1968.
Returned to New York City, renewed relation with subject
(introduced originally through mutual friends—Sam and
Phyllis Kettering). Lived in subject's apartment 1968–1969.
Married January 1970. Daughter Johanna born June 1970.
Since November 1973 involved with Michael Gallagher (b.
1938), rock-music entrepreneur—head of BWC recording company. (File available.) Resides Beverly Hills (as of April 1974)
with daughter. Opened House of Spirits, a boutique of spiritual/
occult memorabilia, on Melrose Avenue (April 1974). (Fur-

Separated from wife since April 1974 (though no divorce proceedings have been started as of August 1974).

Note: Subject has kept four-bedroom house ($780 month). Receives salary of $25,000 a year from Foundation. Subject has daughter occasional weekends. Subject spends most of his time at Foundation (working on tape transcripts of interviews, etc., for second volume of *Work and Alienation* and "A Report/Survey of Factory Workers," a Foundation project). Under surveillance as of 19 July. Does not appear overly suspicious. But because of close link with Dr. Osmond (he was brought to the Foundation originally by Dr. Osmond) we have taken above precautions. Since the separation from his wife, subject is in twice-weekly psychiatric therapy (Tuesday and Friday, 5:30–6:30) with Dr. H. I. Richardson. However, he appears to be recovering. He has been involved with Michelle Worthington (see file) as of 20 July.

Report by Agent R. Castle to Security 5A200 Washington. 6 August.

Re Macdavitt: There's still no lead or indication of who's behind this. We've made every possible conciliatory attempt to meet with them on common ground in this matter. But they still maintain they know absolutely nothing. (They continue to refuse to acknowledge that Macdavitt had been meeting regularly with one or more of their agents up until two weeks ago. They also refuse to acknowledge that they had received information intermittently over the last number of years that only someone in Macdavitt's position could have had access to.)

We've tried to approach them via Tchernilkov. But they maintain the same. (Even Tchernilkov admitted their network is a closed operation. There is no possibility of such an accident—or misunderstanding in orders—as that of the night of July 18–19 occurring without general knowledge.) This could simply be a way of stalling, biding their time, waiting to see what we do first.

Meanwhile, their position simply continues to be that

---

ther files available.) Surveillance advisable in view of close contact with subject (they are on friendly terms, speak several times a week in regard to daughter, etc.).

they know nothing concerning Macdavitt on the night of July 18–19. They maintain they were as shocked as we, etc.

Michelle didn't return until Tuesday evening. (She'd called Nick on Monday to tell him she was staying over another day.) He wasn't sure if she was trying to tell him something or not; in any case, he was annoyed; it seemed as if she was playing games. He brought it up with Dr. Richardson, even though he felt he was making too much out of it; he was hurt. When she called him to tell him she was home (she said she'd just gotten in), he wasn't sure if he should believe that or not. He drove over there slowly. But as soon as he saw her he felt like a fool. Nothing else mattered. There was something different about her. She was halfway across the room; the only light on was _in_ the kitchen area. She threw her arms around him. "Oh, you don't know how good that feels. You can't imagine."

"Hmm. I think I can." It felt almost unreal to be holding her again. "Where are the—"

"Collapsed." She smiled, pulling away. "They've been up since the crack of dawn. Ha! The crack of dawn _Saturday_. Never again on a weekend! What a mess. It was a real circus. The wilderness throbbing with tourists and rock music!"

He realized what it was: Her hair looked even more golden against her skin, her tan was deeper. "It's a real mess, huh?"

"I should have taken pictures, good for an ecology campaign. But we found a quiet spot."

"You look kind of woozy."

"I am. Oh, those kids!" She laughed. "I don't think they really got any sleep, but they enjoyed it. I'm really glad. Johanna would have loved it. Next time we'll all go . . . but not on a weekend!"

"And not in the summer." He wasn't even really listening to what she was saying.

"Wait until you see what they brought back. We've got a caterpillar invasion in the house, so if you feel something creeping . . . Three days, three days, I can't believe it."

"Almost four."

"Almost." She closed her eyes, smiling slowly. She put her head down on his shoulder. "I just want to hold you, hold you."

He felt almost drugged, as if all his senses were heightened. He could smell the sun on her, in the nape of her neck, summer in the warmth of her skin. "I can smell the sun on you."

They went into the bedroom.

From Security 5A200 Washington. 7 August.

Check out Osmond files again. Is there anything—anything—to recheck? Any clue or possible link—any loose pieces—pressure points. Check out Mrs. Osmond (Dr. Virginia Moray).

R. B. Osmond, 1911– . St. Paul. Family's close ties with the Macdavitts. Osmond autobiography, *An Informal Life.* Re Macdavitt: Get back to all transcripts. Bear down on contributing patrons of Foundation.

Harvard. Politics.

Government. Involvement in WPA.

Security files on Osmond date from August 2, 1937.

Europe 1937—England, France, and Spain. What was exact interest/affiliation vis-à-vis Republicans in Spanish Civil War?

Columbia University 1939—Contact/Get to some of his former students, i.e., those in government.

Wartime years—England. Bletchley Park.

Overseas—rundown on activities. In 1945 transferred to the American military government and took part in the denazification process in Germany. Deputy director and acting head of the division of investigation of cartels and external assets for the American military government in Berlin.

OSS file. CIA file from 1947.

Returned to Columbia University. Harvard.

The McCarthy years—get a separate file on this and see if you can find any more clues as to whether he was compromised.

1955—visiting professor (lecturer), Cambridge, England. List of everyone he knew.

1956—Stevenson campaign.

1956—University of California. Breakdown on all initial funds for Foundation.

1956—Foundation for the Study and Research of Contemporary Sciences (then under Dr. Tynner). Tynner file. Recheck: initial ten visiting fellows, twenty associates, and fifteen consultants (from government, academia, the sciences . . . and update to present). Tynner retired last year (elected as first life fellow). Update on all Foundation conferences, "dialogues," the Foundation's two publications: "The Foundation Journal" (a newsletter) and *Foundation* (a monthly subscription magazine—circulation 120,000).

Recheck files of everyone associated with the Foundation from 1956 to present, August 1974 (every member, guest lecturer, secretary, etc., including kitchen help, gardeners, etc.).

1961–63—Recheck government clearance special assistant to the secretary of state. Department of State. Kennedy—Osmond and wife invited several weekends at Hyannis Port and also frequent guests at White House dinners/evenings. Check.

1964—Did series for NBC on civil rights. Check.

1964—Exact relation and/or support regarding Macdavitt.

1967—Reluctant to take sides on Vietnam—dig under that one.

1968–71—Vietnam / students / Kent State / Cambodia / Ellsberg—recheck Osmond file of those years.

Recheck: publications/articles (*Foreign Affairs, New York Review of Books, Partisan Review, Kenyon Review, Encounter, Saturday Review/World, Political Science Journal, Foreign Policy*, all Foundation publications, papers).

Books: *Observations for Our Times, An Informal Life, Views into the American System of Government, A Study of Democracy* . . .

Travels: England/Western Europe 1937–39—Army 1941–43. England, France 1950. Kenya 1953 (Check). Stockholm 1953 (conference). Geneva 1953 (conference). Cairo 1953 . . . Vietnam 1967 (with special staff/ State Department), 1968 (with representative intellectual group/ writers, etc.). Cambodia 1968. India, Pakistan 1968 . . .

Finances: List of all stocks and securities held up to present—bonds, bank accounts (including wife's). Get income-tax files to present. Addendum: Recheck Mrs. Osmond (Dr. Virginia Moray), b. 1920, London. Graduated Cambridge University 1941. Postgraduate studies Cambridge (zoology). Ichthyologist. Met Osmond 1937, m. 1945. (American citizen.) Taught at Columbia University 1947–49. Radcliffe, Woods Hole. etc. Presently teaches at UC Sonora Pines. In 1972 appointed director of County Museum of Natural History, Los Angeles. See Osmond government clearance files, etc. What did she/does she/ know of Macdavitt, etc.? Foundation—has been on board of Foundation since its inception. Recheck her thoroughly —see if you can get to Osmond (in any way) through her—any marital conflicts.

Children: son—graduate student at UCLA (involved in drug—marijuana—charge, dropped 1968; skirmish with police in demonstrations in 1968/69); daughter—at Swarthmore (living with ex-SDS member, now associate professor of philosophy at University of Pennsylvania). Check.

From Security 5A200 Washington. 7 August.

Get follow-up and update on (whereabouts/present status of all individuals concerned in the following):

Mantell case

Chiles and Whitted

CIA—Admiral Hillenkoetter/1948/Congress (smears on the CIA)

D.C., 1952 (sightings over Andrews Air Force Base, Bowling Air Force Base)

The Utah film, 1952

Bismarck, North Dakota, 1953

The Robertson Panel, 1953

Capella, 1957/leaks CIA-AF/Congress—press

Levelland, Texas, 1957

CIA smear—Senate Armed Services Committee/Senator Richard B. Russell (chairman)

Secret hearings, Washington, 1958

Secret hearings, Washington, 1959

Project Ozma, 1960, 1961/Green Bank, November

1961/National Science Foundation/AF Office of Scientific Research 1961

Ozymandias, 1961–present

Socorro, New Mexico, 1964

Radio Astronomy Institute, Stanford University, 1964 (radio signals)

Kazakhstan, USSR, 1965 (sightings on radar)

Secret hearings, Washington, 1965

The blackout, November 1965 (Niagara-Mohawk plant/ Dam Beck no. 2 plant in Ontario)

Power failures—December—East Texas . . . El Paso to Juarez

Fort Bliss, Holloman AFB, Gray Sands, Biggs AFB, etc.

AF Major Baidukov/double tracking—photographic plates and air and ground radar/Odessa, April 1966

Dexter/Hillsdale, Michigan, 1966

Kislovodsk, USSR, 1967 (sightings—astrophysics station, sighted and tracked)

Mullard Radio Astronomy Observatory, England, 1967 (radio signals)

Secret hearings, Washington, 1969

Blue Book, 1969

NASA, 1969 (Cetus)

Gray Sands

Project Ozma II, 1971

COYNE, 1973

Project Epsilon

Cape Kennedy/NASA/Project Crescent leak

Secret hearings, Washington, 1973

Secret hearings, Washington, 1974

Report by Agent R. Castle to Security 5A200 Washington. 8 August.

Tchernilkov seems to think there might be some lead re Macdavitt within our own organization. He would not identify his source.

Tchernilkov's compliance in our regard cannot be doubted. His position with us is too well secured for that. We have proved ourselves in regard to his welfare as well as that of his family. He knows better than to chance anything at this point. He has never failed or deceived us before; therefore, as puzzling as it may seem, we suggest that we cannot dismiss it and that we further investigate.

Nick was standing with Michelle on the sun deck of his house. It was dusk. It was starting to get chilly.

"Where are you?" Michelle turned to him.

For a moment he'd almost forgotten she was there. "Here."

"You seem so distant, withdrawn. What's the matter?"

Nick kept his eyes on the surf. "Dusk." He smiled. "The more somber elements of my soul take hold."

"No, c'mon." She sounded almost annoyed. "I'm being serious. I mean the last couple of days. I've been trying to find a way . . . I haven't been sure how to bring it up. But you seem like you're not really here . . . the last week or so. Since Macdavitt's death, really."

"No, I've just had a lot of things on my mind." He was taken aback. She hadn't given any indication that she thought anything was different.

"Such as?"

"Oh. I can't go into it."

"Why not? It's not a matter of national security"—she laughed—"is it?"

"What makes you say that?" It seemed such a strange thing for her to say.

"I was only joking. C'mon, you're really jumpy."

"Yeah, I guess you're right." He felt as if his double were standing there beside her. He thought of Macdavitt. He thought of Macdavitt's papers. And she had no awareness of any of it. "I'm just wrapped up in those transcripts."

"You've been a pretty good example of alienation yourself. Lately."

"I'm sorry." He suddenly realized how he must have appeared to her, how distracted he'd been. It was all so unreal. How could he have gotten into this mess? This strange, unreal dream. "I realize—"

"Look at that light! It's like gold . . . the water is so calm."

"It's because of the moon."

"Ah, you did it again!" Her voice sounded too lighthearted to him. She knew something was wrong; he wasn't telling her something. He felt guilty for hurting her.

"Reflex."

"Reflex?" she asked.

"Habit."

"It's hypnotic." She inhaled deeply. "Close your eyes." He watched her standing there beside him with her eyes closed. "You're not closing your eyes," she said. "Listen, you can hardly hear them breaking. It makes you forget everything—the mind-expression drug of nature."

"Michelle . . ." For a moment he had the urge to tell her. About Macdavitt, about the papers, about Macdavitt's death.

"Your eyes aren't closed!"

"I wish I could be more direct with you. I mean I wish I could tell you . . . but you understand I just can't. It's not that I don't want to."

"I understand . . . close your eyes."

He closed his eyes. And the sound of the surf took over, calming him again.

Synopsis of surveillance log. 9 August.

Osmond left on the 10 A.M. flight for San Francisco (he is lecturing and on a panel at Berkeley tonight and tomorrow; returning Sunday A.M.).

Schrader spent the morning in his office. He did not attend dialogue on foreign policy 1948–52. Instead he spent the afternoon in the Foundation library. He took out the following books: *Medical Physics,* vol. 3 (Chicago, 1960); Ernst Opik, *Physics of Meteor Flight in the Atmosphere* (New York, 1958); L. Jacot, *Universal Evolution* (Geneva, 1967); F. Hoyle, *Frontiers of Astronomy* (London, 1961); F. Hoyle, *Of Men and Galaxies* (Seattle, 1964); Brookings Institution, *Report for NASA* (Washington, D.C., 1961); N.J. Berrill, *Biology in Action* (London, 1970); H. P. Blavatsky, *Isis Unveiled* (New York, 1886); I. P. Cory, *Ancient Fragments* (London, 1832); V. Fedinsky, *Meteors* (Moscow, 1959); F. Siegel, *Life in the Universe* (Minsk, 1966); H. Shapely, *Of Stars and Men* (London, 1958); *Beyond the Observatory* (New York, 1967).

These books were left in his car (which he locked) while he was in Dr. Richardson's office (1730–1825).

Synopsis of transcript from Dr. H. I. Richardson's tape of Schrader session. 9 August.

There is no reference to or indication of any of the above. Schrader discussed his dreams, his daughter, fears concerning her (he appears to be obsessed with this—that she could die, be kidnapped), his wife, Michelle Worthington, then back to his dreams.

RICHARDSON [*at the end of the tape*]: He is obsessed with losing Johanna. I try to reassure him, this is not uncommon, can be traced back to guilt, vague guilt that he allowed Carole to leave him, that he is guilty in regard to Johanna, is being irresponsible as a father. I keep telling him this is typical of parents in divorce cases. Guilt, as a cover for his resentment toward Carole, focusing instead on Johanna, where the feelings are less complex. We go over the same ground. In regard to Michelle, he appears to be wavering toward her, wavering in the balance. That is, between moving away or coming closer to her. Vulnerable and afraid of being hurt, the stakes too high, but still drawn to her. Some sort of conflict (which he will not or cannot clarify) seems to exist in his mind concerning her or their relationship. His dreams, the motif of the outsider, correspond acutely to his present state.

Recording of tape enclosed for voice analysis.

Edited report to Security 5A200 Washington. 9 August.
Voice analysis. Voice pattern on psychological-stress evaluator: indication of stress. Conflicts, confusion. Definite indication here of unnatural effort. Subject's voice pattern irregular. Definite conscious attempt at concealment.

Report by Agent R. Castle to Security 5A200 Washington. 9 August.
Leak confirmed. Tchernilkov says his source has revealed leak to him re Macdavitt. It concerns one of our own branches of operations. Tchernilkov revealed this branch of the network was involved in the matter of Macdavitt on the night of July 18–19.
We will continue on the above.

From Security 5A200 files.

Michelle Worthington (5 ft. 7 in., 118 lbs., hair: blond, eyes: green), b. October 25, 1941, in Los Angeles, to Richard Worthington (b. 1919, Bakersfield, California), real-estate broker (file available), and the former Frances Brandt (b. 1920, Omaha City, Nebraska, file available).

One brother: William (b. 1939). Geophysicist. Lives in San Mateo. (File available.)

Attended local schools in Los Angeles (duplicates of reports, etc., available). An above-average student—though erratic—with a marked interest in the sciences. Skipped the ninth grade. A member of the debating team. President of her class—twelfth grade—valedictorian, etc. An avid reader (teachers recall her often reading during classes; file available).

There appears to be nothing noteworthy—beyond a certain spirit of rebelliousness. An individualistic flair that could be simply from that particular stage of development (adolescence). Given to skipping classes, hiding out in the locker room reading. A marked problem with authority—smoked on school grounds—yet president of the student body, etc. The common symptoms of adolescent rebellion. The problem with authority seems to have passed with time.

Entered UC Berkeley 1958. Graduated 1962. Chemistry major. (File available.)

In Peace Corps 1962–63 (Tanganyika). Was first approached in Peace Corps. Involved in covert operations in Tanganyika. (Files available.)

Returned Berkeley December 1963. M.A. (chemistry) Berkeley 1965. (Files available.) In covert operations in the Bay area. (Refer to case officer. See files.) Link to the leftist underground 1967. Involved in the early student movements. In SDS 1968. Active in antiwar riots in Bay area. Jailed twice: for disturbing the peace and in antiwar demonstrations (March 1968 and April 1968). Both sentences suspended. Jailed three times in riots: May 1968 (two days), June 1968 (booked and detained overnight), June 1968 (ten days—rest of sentence suspended). On probation. (Refer to case officer. See files.)

Underground link 1968–72. Acted as one of our top links to the leftist underground movement. (Files available.) Continuing activities in antiwar movement and in SDS. (Files available.) Assigned to leftist political organizers. In the Bay area, participated in underground operations. (Refer to case officer. See files.) Taught courses (philosophy, psychology of violence) at Free University, Berkeley, and university extensions (philosophy, courses on Marcuse, Laing—files available). To protect identity and to continue cover, worked for Raynol (pharmaceutical company in San Francisco) January 1969–April 1973. (Files available.)

Married Anthony Coleman (b. 1939, Oakland) in 1965. Independent documentary filmmaker. With ABC 1962–67, NET 1967–73. Taught film courses at Berkeley, now at UCLA. Living in Los Angeles. Affilliated with KABC. (File available.)

Two children: Peter (b. 1966). Worthington separated from Coleman in spring 1968 (child left with her parents). See above previous. Reunited. Heather (b. 1969). Worthington separated from Coleman in spring 1970 for two months. Reunited. Separated in fall of 1970 (two months). See above. (Files available.) Children with her parents at this time. Reunited with Coleman from end of 1970 to beginning of 1971. Frequent separations and reconciliations in marital status have not overtly impaired operational abilities.

Files available of persons involved with previously, 1958–65. See also files of persons involved with Worthington at this time and later in marriage.

Jim Adler (b. 1941), a jazz musician. Involved with Worthington sporadically (1971–March 1974) and lived with her. (File available.)

Separated from Coleman spring 1973. Moved down to Sonora Pines with the two children. Entered UC there in summer 1973. Switched from chemistry to psychology. (File available.)

Operations files available.

Assigned to Macdavitt in February 1974. Reassigned to surveillance of Macdavitt through a Foundation member April–May 1974. Temporarily shelved: The Foundation member involved proved uncooperative and overly suspicious. (File available.)

Assigned to Schrader surveillance as of 20 July.

Worthington strongly endorsed by the division. Refer to chief of division.

From Security 5A200 Washington to Agent R. Castle. 10 August.

A branch of the network confirms on Macdavitt and the night of July 18–19.

Inform Tchernilkov his source was mistaken. The branch in question knows nothing about Macdavitt. Divert Tchernilkov onto some other track.

Re Macdavitt and the night of July 18–19: The branch in question acted as they did to divert attention—leaving the evidence they did re Macdavitt, the natural assumption would be that it was the Russians. The branch then proceeded to cover up all traces within the organization itself.

Continue to inform Tchernilkov we have ultimate proof it was the Russians, as we thought all along, but that we cannot reveal our source of contact to them.

Sunday morning, long after it was light, Rodney Osmond lay in his double bed in his room at the Marriott Inn on the Berkeley Marina. He had left the curtains partially open when he had come back in late last night after his lecture ("The Present State of Foreign Policy: America as Guardian of Democracy?") and the interminable party, held in his honor, at the house of one of the political science professors. Staring at the panel of light, as he had been for an indefinite period, he lost track of time. He knew he should get out of bed, get dressed. But he let himself drift, drift with the monotone of traffic in the background.

He checked the small folding travel clock he had brought with him; it was on the night table beside his gold Patek-Philippe watch, his loose change, his wallet, and the note pad and Bic he always kept with him. It was ten after eight. His appointment with Warren Hammond was at noon. He was having doubts, as he had all along, for the last two days, since he had first phoned Hammond Thursday evening from a pay phone outside a gas station after he had told Virginia he was going out to get an ice cream cone at Baskin-Robbins. A woman had answered. She seemed to hesitate. Then Warren

Hammond got on. He didn't sound surprised to hear
who it was. He explained it was his wife who had answered——he had been in his study, working; she was always reluctant to interrupt him. "Horrible business,"
Warren Hammond said. "Can't say I was surprised,
though."

"He had a long history of depression," Rodney quickly
interjected before Warren Hammond had a chance to say
anything else. The call he had been debating all day now
seemed so easy, so effortless: He had the sinking convic-
tion Hammond's line was bugged.

Hammond informed Rodney that he had sent Macdavitt's wife a note. Rodney said, "You know he had
been seeing doctors for years." There was a pause. Hammond said yes, he had known that. Rodney explained
why he was calling. He was going to lecture at Berkeley
Friday and Saturday nights; he'd be staying over; he'd
like to meet with him if he had the time. The Foundation
was putting together a memorial book on George. They'd
like something of his, some sort of recollection, anything.
There was another pause. Hammond agreed. How about
Sunday noon at the university, in his office?

Rodney now thought maybe he should have arranged to
call back. Hammond had no way of getting hold of him.
He knew, of course, he was just looking for excuses, for a
way of getting out of it. He still had time. He could still
cancel it, could call Hammond, say something had come
up. But he didn't. He just lay there, in bed, watching the
light in the window, on the wall, drifting. As if by doing
nothing he could delay, postpone. The inevitable. After
this, he said to himself, there would be no turning back.
What melodrama. After this. But of course it was already
arranged, had already taken place. He had no choice. He
was only pretending that he did.

Rodney parked outside the university grounds. He
walked up the incline, up the cement path, across the
tree-enclosed grounds, where students lounged in various
poses of study, sleep, contemplation, meditation——an occasional couple, of indeterminate gender, entwined. It was
hot already, a prelude to another day in the low nineties.
Rodney took off his suit jacket. He had on a striped button-down shirt, a narrow tie. He stood out among the

long hair, the beards, the barely dressed tanned kids in their torn, cutoff jeans, shrunken T-shirts, halter tops.

Another bicycle whizzed by. Some dust shimmered in a plane tree overhead, mingled with the sunlight, and settled onto the parched grass. A bell started to chime. It was noon.

Rodney finally found Hammond's office—his name was on the nameplate outside. The door was partially open.

Warren Hammond stood up, pushing back the Windsor chair he had been sitting in, away from the totally bare desk: He had been waiting, there was no pretense. Warren Hammond could only be described as one of those stereotyped small men—owlish, horn-rimmed glasses, a bald pate, a three-piece suit, bow tie, an impish grin. A malevolent sort of baby face, Rodney thought, demure, apologetic in his solicitude, overly polite in an effort to conceal his real motives (whatever they were), perhaps even his hostility. Rodney had never like him, had always felt uncomfortable around him. Warren usually remained detached, abstract, never really spoke up; so one never knew what he really thought, where he really stood. He simply usually smiled, as if agreeing with whatever was being said. But Rodney didn't buy that. He'd always felt George was naive when it came to people.

Hammond put out his hand. Rodney shook it firmly. It was sweaty. Maybe I'm being too hard, too suspicious. I'm overreacting, he thought. . . .

Hammond motioned him to sit down in the other Windsor chair. The office was minimally furnished: a desk, a table, the two chairs, a file cabinet, two curtainless windows, nothing on the walls, no sign of life—as if he had just moved in or were moving out.

"I was just trying to think how long it's been since we last saw each other." Hammond smiled.

"It's been a long time."

"Awful business. Just awful. I can't tell you what a shock it was—I opened the paper that Monday morning at breakfast—but I can't say I was surprised."

"Yes, he was very depressed."

"Well, he'd had a long history—" Hammond repeated, as if he were reassuring himself.

"I wasn't sure you'd see me," Rodney interrupted. "I

didn't think you'd want to be reminded of all that. But I took a chance anyway."

"Well, I'm glad you did." (What else could he say but that, under the circumstances? Rodney thought.) "I was very fond of George. Of course, it was a long time ago. And it's all past. But I'd be glad to be of any help that I can."

"Yes. Yes. Do you mind?" Rodney flicked open his silver cigarette case. Hammond shook his head nervously, almost apoplectically. Rodney flicked the case shut, blew out the match in a decisive manner. Hammond, almost grinning in his eagerness to be attentive, offered an ashtray. "As I mentioned to you on the phone, we want to put out a book, some sort of memorial tribute. Recollections, short essays, you know, that sort of thing . . . and put it together in some sort of chronological form. The different aspects of his life—people from Harvard, M.I.T., those who knew him well . . . working with him . . . Los Alamos, and his work with the Air Force . . ."

"I couldn't help you on that. I was only at Los Alamos a short time. I'm afraid that was all blown out of proportion during the hearings."

"Yes, I know."

"But I'd be glad to write a personal—"

"Well, that's all we want. We want to try to get a number of personal recollections. I just wanted to check it out with you, and since I was going to be up here anyway . . ."

"Yes, I'm sorry I missed your lectures."

"They were very heated. But, then, that's the way kids are . . ." Rodney didn't finish his sentence.

Hammond waited. He didn't say anything. He looked at Rodney questioningly.

"What do you know about Project Blue Book?" Rodney asked matter-of-factly.

Hammond didn't show any reaction. "The UFO study? Nothing."

"Ah, that's too bad. I was hoping you could help me out."

"Sorry. It's not my department. I'm just an ordinary physicist here."

"Yes, but you were on the project. You were working with George."

"That was a long time ago." Beads of perspiration were noticeable on Hammond's elongated forehead.

Rodney watched him for a moment. He let him dangle, floundering at the end of the line, caught. Hammond shifted about in his seat, hands clasped together. He coughed. Rodney nodded. "We wanted to fill in something about his work with the Air Force."

"I wish I could help you. But I just can't."

"I understand."

"Have you had a chance to walk around at all?" Hammond asked. "Have you seen the botanical garden?"

"The botanical garden?" Rodney was puzzled.

"Yes. Here on the grounds. There are some marvelous new additions. Why don't we take a walk? And since I know you're quite a botanist . . ."

On their way out, through the empty halls, across the bike paths, past the flowers, the lawns, Warren Hammond kept up a running commentary on the various buildings they were passing, the various funds behind each one, the trustees, the financial problems. As if he were saying: This is my life now, I've made a life here for myself. I'm part of all this. You can't reach me. Don't try . . . leave me here in this life, don't drag me back. . . . Rodney kept nodding, bored, distracted, not even really listening. He felt like telling Hammond, You don't have to go through this, you've already made your point. No one's going to disturb your life here.

Hammond walked quickly. Rodney was getting winded. But Hammond, his head barely reaching Rodney's shoulder, showed no sign of exertion; he kept up his brisk pace.

At Strawberry Canyon they turned off into the botanical garden. A tour group with the requisite cameras and vacant expressions of robots about to be impressed by nature wandered around absentmindedly, in a daze, staring at the labeled flowers and plants.

Hammond led the way, up a path away from the crowd, past some stagnating flowers (American violets? Rodney wasn't sure), toward a quieter area. "Here we have a fine specimen of the Hawaiian tree fern *Cibotium glaucum,* also referred to as *C. chamissoi,* and next to it the Mexican tree fern, a close relative, but it is rarely found in nurseries. . . . The Tasmanian tree fern, *Dicksonia antarctica* . . ."

Rodney nodded.

"And here"—Hammond pointed—"you will notice, indigenous to this region, the yellow-pink buds—"

"What do you know about Wells?" Rodney asked.

A slight flicker of disturbance or annoyance passed over Hammond's small bespectacled round face for a moment. Then he chose either to ignore it or to pretend that he hadn't understood. He went on. "This cactus is particularly noted—"

"Philip Wells."

". . . for its hardiness. Its buds always open at the same time of the year, almost to the day. Driving through the desert in the spring—"

"C'mon, Warren, don't be so heavy-handed. We haven't got all day. Philip Wells."

"Look, you should be familiar with these. They grow down in your region. Cacti—"

"Ozma. November '61."

"Cacti—"

"Project Ozma."

"I didn't hear you. I can't help you."

"You heard me, Warren, Project Ozma. Green Bank, 1961. Dr. Robert Fleming, Dr. Lawrence Koenig . . . George had it all documented."

"You mean the Green Bank Formula?" Warren Hammond was pretending to have just remembered. He must have realized that he had no choice, that it wasn't going to be dropped. It was finally registering. "Project Ozma. The supposed space signals. Is that what you mean? It was a mistake. An error. Everyone simply jumped to the wrong conclusion. . . ."

"Fleming, Keonig . . . It cost a lot of men their careers. Messages from Tau Ceti were decoded. The Project Ozma team focused on Tau Ceti, one of the nearest suns thought to have planets. Repeated signals in an unmistakably intelligent code were heard. It was about to be made public and then—"

"I told you. It was a mistake. Everybody knows that."

"The Pentagon stepped in and debunked the whole thing by saying that the space signals received were not space signals at all but, rather, had come from a secret military station—so secret that it could not be revealed. But if this were true, if such a military station existed and the space signals had come from there, why was Project Ozma discontinued?"

"There's no connection. I don't see the connection. I just told you. In the excitement, we made a mistake. It was an error."

"At the last moment you pulled back, denounced everything you'd said. What happened? You get pressured, threatened? What did the government threaten you with?"

"I know Macdavitt had a lot to be bitter about. But it blew out very quickly."

"What do you mean? He was ridiculed. His career was in a shambles. His prestige . . ."

"You should know, Rodney, these things happen sometimes in research. You think you're onto something, and it proves to be a mistake."

"A mistake to have it made public?"

"A mistake. The signals were simply not from outer space. Macdavitt just couldn't accept it, that he'd been wrong, we'd been wrong. He was making a fool of himself. I had to do it, before he made himself more of a laughing-stock than he already was."

"You were about to break it to the public, to the media, and at the last moment—"

"I think you've got your facts somewhat confused."

"What about Fleming? Koenig?"

"Fleming's with Westinghouse now, I believe. It wasn't exactly yesterday. It's been a number of years, you know. And Koenig's with IBM."

"And you're snugly fitted in your little space in the UC complex."

"There are written statements they made. You can check it all out. It can all be verified. Their final proofs contradicted all of Macdavitt's theories. And that's what they were. Just theories. Their proofs are backed up all the way."

"All the way to the government, you mean?"

"You're wasting your time." Hammond frowned, shook

his head stubbornly, almost quivering. Now he would not be budged.

"What about Project Ozymandias?"

Hammond pushed his glasses back onto the rim of his nose, cocked his head, and studied Rodney with an expression of mock, dogged patience. "Ozma? There's a Project Ozma II. It was started in 1971."

"I'm not talking about that."

"By two young astronomers from Harvard. They called it Ozma II after Ozma I. They're looking for the same things we were on Ozma I—stars that have the same characteristics as the earth's sun. The idea is that those stars would be most likely to have planetary systems—"

"That's not what I'm talking about. That's completely aboveboard and they don't know anything. They don't know what really went on, what's going on now."

Hammond looked at him as if he had no idea what Rodney was talking about. "Ozymandias?"

"The name that was given to Project Ozma by the scientists who continued working in secret, including George Macdavitt and Philip Wells. And they continued receiving the same sort of space signals, in an unmistakably intelligent code. You see, George left a number of papers, his research. We have a whole network of names," Rodney continued. "In the government, in the Pentagon, the CIA, in NASA, scientists who were going to go with George. Who were going to support him. Including people who had been part of all the various cover-ups. Commanders in the Air Force, generals, the top scientists in the country. People who had worked in line with the CIA during Blue Book, Ozma, the whole debunking. They were going—are going —to corroborate everything George said. Everything that is in his papers. I want you to get to some of these people. You still have your contacts. I want to get to Philip Wells. I also want to get to some of the scientists working with him."

Hammond's eyes narrowed into slits behind the magnified fishbowl lenses of his glasses. "Rodney, I've got a new life now. It wasn't easy, believe me. Don't get me into this. I can't afford it."

"Neither can I."

"All right," Hammond sighed. "But please, I beg you.

I've got a family to think of. I have kids. A boy in school, top of his class at M.I.T."

"Don't start getting maudlin, please."

"Leave me alone after this. It's for your own good."

"I want to talk to Wells and to some of the people working with him. I want you to arrange a meeting."

"All right. I'll see what I can do. Who's that?" Hammond pointed to a straggler from the tour group, who seemed to be coming toward them.

"I don't want you phoning me," Rodney said. "I think my line might—"

"Who is that man?"

"I don't know. He's from that tour group. I'm going to phone you. How about Tuesday afternoon? Here at the university."

"Hmm." Hammond nodded, distracted by the man. "Late Tuesday afternoon. I have a class until five. That man's coming closer."

"Another cactus buff."

The man, fairly young, fairly nondescript, in a seersucker suit, came toward them, his head bent, studying the cacti. Rodney noticed he had a large mole under his left eye.

"Turn around." Hammond, suddenly in full possession of himself, pointed to a cactus. "Now, over here you'll notice one of the finest specimens of its kind in North America. You could cover the whole of the Mojave, and you wouldn't find a truer example of this species. It's a perfect example of its class."

Security 5A200 Washington to Agent R. Castle. 12 August.

The branch in question has relayed that they acted as they did on the night of July 18–19 only because they had conclusive proof Macdavitt was either going to collaborate more overtly or actually go over there, to the other side, to work with them.

The background was relayed: The branch picked up on the leak that Macdavitt had been passing vital information over to the Russians and meeting with one or more of their agents on a regular basis. They proceeded accordingly. Further facts all pointed to Macdavitt. Macdavitt did not heed repeated warnings. As he could no longer be contained, it was at this stage that they decided to take matters into their own hands.

As there was a very real threat of Macdavitt passing further invaluable information to the Russians and of working openly with them at some point in the very near future (this was heavily documented), to forestall any such event, they acted as they did on the night of July 18–19. It was the only solution, considering the great risk involved.

No one knew, at the time, that Macdavitt had withheld some other papers. It was assumed, at the time, that he had been relieved of all papers in his possession. If this had been known, matters would not have been handled as decisively as they were.

Rodney called Warren Hammond at the university. He did not identify himself; Hammond immediately recognized his voice. Rodney said he was calling from a pay phone in Sonora Pines.

Hammond said, "Wells'll see you tomorrow. Tomorrow afternoon. Three o'clock. The Howard Johnson's in the Alameda shopping center. I have some instructions here. Do you want to write them down?"

"I'm listening."

"This took a lot of doing, Rodney. It puts me in an awful position."

"I got the message."

"You'e to park your car in front of El Capitán, a cocktail lounge, and you're to walk across the shopping center to the Howard Johnson's."

"And he'll be there? Wells'll be there?"

"Three o'clock."

"And what about some of the others?"

"The Howard Johnson's in Alameda."

"How am I to recognize him?"

But Hammond had already hung up.

Security 5A200 Washington. 14 August.

It would seem, at this point, the best way to get to Schrader would be either through Worthington or through his daughter. There is always, of course, his wife. But his

feelings there do not seem to be as clear-cut as they are
about the other two. We can be more certain of his reactions in their cases. We have not achieved the results we
had hoped to through Worthington. We cannot tell if
Worthington is totally responsible for that or not.

To coerce him through his daughter is a fairly routine
matter. The child would be kidnapped. We suggest, however, we hold off on that.

Suggest instead that we continue, as we have been,
through Worthington. It seems, perhaps, she has not been
persuaded directly enough in this matter. Suggest we make
the situation clearer to her in regard to her position, in
regard to her own welfare.

Rodney did as he was told, parked his Cadillac in front
of El Capitán. The gold lamé curtains sparking off irides-
cent in the sunlight, the neon signs turned off—the hollow
filigree outline of the ornate script, an unlit advertisement
for the suburban nightlife.

He crossed the huge shopping center, past a twenty-four-
hour Martinizing, the hot morbit odor of clothes being
pressed floating out the open door; Pet World, a dim interior crowded with caged pets and pet toys; Pizza Hut,
regurgitated tangy spices mingling with the cooking grease
from a taco takeout next door; Kayser's Nutrition Center;
several real-estate niches; the large letters on a windowless
building, DR. SYDNEY BLYTHE, CREDIT DENTIST; another
twenty-four-hour Martinizing; across a parking lot, past
Sears, JACK LA LANNE HEALTH SPA, down a shopping mall.
He felt out of place, one of the few men with all these
women, these kids. A Gourmet Delicacies, Pickwick's
Bookstore, Florsheim, an outdoor postal outlet, Howard
Johnson's.

He went into the overly air-conditioned imitation-wood-
paneled and red leather atmosphere. An assortment of
mostly women, a few elderly couples, some mooning kids
at the counter sharing a milk shake—only the long hair on
the boys, the skimpy natural look on the girls, indicating
it was the present decade. There were three men seated in
an isolated center booth. Rodney was taken aback, though
he gave no sign. Of course, he thought. I should have
known. I should have known they would have already

closed in. One of the men, middle-aged, fairly nondescript, stood up. His short haircut and general blandness could have just as easily suggested the camouflage of Middle America as of the military.

Rodney looked at the other two men: both probably in their late thirties, medium mod suits, slightly longer hair, indistinguishable from the perfect model for businessmen. Why must they all look the same? Rodney thought. Why must they all be so bland?

"Why don't you sit down, Dr. Osmond," said the one who had stood up. "I'm afraid Dr. Wells is not in the country at this time. He's on a dig in the Yucatán, I believe."

"Yes, I see.

The man motioned to him to sit down. The other two moved over.

Rodney sat down. A sunburned teenage waitress came toward them.

"Another Coke." The man smiled pleasantly at the waitress. The smile immediately switched off. "We're not going to beat around the bush, Dr. Osmond, since I trust you know why we're here. You have gotten yourself involved in something that I don't think you quite understand. I don't think you understand the complexities. At least, that is what we would like to believe. We're prepared to be reasonable, I assure you." The smile came on again.

Rodney nodded. There was not much to say.

"We're willing to close our eyes to your involvement in all this. After you've turned over Dr. Macdavitt's papers to us."

"You have all his papers. You sent someone from Washington to collect them from his office two weeks ago," Rodney said.

"Ha-ha. Yes. All his papers, you say? Of course." He pretended to be amused. "But let's go over that, please. You say someone . . ."

"Yes, someone from Washington. He identified himself, said he was with the Central Intelligence Agency. He showed his card. He went through all of Dr. Macdavitt's papers—whatever was left in the files in his office. He took them with him." Rodney was beginning to feel even more uneasy.

The man nodded to one of the other two, who wrote something down on a note pad.

"It was when all the TV people were at the Foundation."

The waitress put down the large glass of Coke. "Do you want a straw, sir?"

Rodney smiled, shaking his head. "Is anything wrong?"

The man hesitated. "No." He looked puzzled, as if he didn't quite understand what Rodney was talking about, or, Rodney thought, perhaps he just wanted him to think that. "Now. What about the other papers?"

"There are no other papers. I just told you. Whatever was left in Dr. Macdavitt's office . . ." Rodney didn't finish.

"Go on."

"There were only the papers in his office. They couldn't have been of interest to anyone. They were mostly notes —of a personal nature."

"You went through these notes, then?"

"I just told you that."

"Of a personal nature?" The man lowered his voice, his eyes narrowed into beady points. Rodney thought of one of those lifelike sculptures, the sculpture of a man, planted here, at this table, against the Howard Johnson's decor. Only it was real. The whole lifelike representation had come to life. Rodney was aware again of the people in the background: voices, the noise of dishes, silverware. "And there are no other papers. Only these papers that were in his office. You went through these papers."

"I just told you. We wanted to put together—"

But the man didn't let him finish. "Dr. Osmond. Please. I'm going to be as straight as possible with you. There are certain issues involved here, certain factors . . . I don't think you have any choice, you see. You simply must co-operate more with us." The smile came on. "Now. For in-stance, we know about your financial problems at the Foundation. We have access to most of the members of your board, your participating trustees, your backers."

"Are you trying to blackmail me?"

"Isn't the word 'advise'?"

"You're not serious." Rodney turned to the other two men, who simply stared blankly.

"Let's just say we're calling your bluff." The smile came on again.

"It's no bluff."

The man nodded. "No, it isn't. That's why we want you to come to Washington."

"To Washington?"

"Tomorrow. Can you fly out for the day? We'll have you back by Friday morning. It's rhetorical, Dr. Osmond. I'm merely going through the formalities. We'll take care of the details. Just pack a bag and we'll meet you at the airport here tomorrow morning at a quarter to seven."

"I have some people from Heidelberg coming to the Foundation tomorrow for lunch."

"Well, you'll have to make other arrangements, won't you? Dr. Tynner can take care of them, can't he?" The man smiled politely, in a detached, bored sort of way.

Rodney frowned. "Yes, I'll . . ."

"You'll just say you had to fly down to Los Angeles for a meeting with some trustees," the man filled in for him.

Security 5A200 Washington. 15 August.
From the report on Dr. R. B. Osmond.

Dr. Osmond was most cooperative, did not need to be persuaded, though there are still several loopholes in the story: He still maintains—as he did yesterday when we contacted him in the Howard Johnson's Restaurant in Sonora Pines, California—that MacDavitt left no papers of interest beyond the personal; that is what he and Schrader are trying to put together; that is the sole reason for his contacting Hammond (Hammond, as you know, had been at Los Alamos and on several Air Force/government projects—including Blue Book and the two "O" projects—with Macdavitt). Osmond thought Hammond might be able to contribute some sort of short memoir or profile of Macdavitt at that time. (Hammond was in contact with Macdavitt intermittently until late 1972; Osmond was not aware of that.)

We tried to keep the session as informal as possible. We brought up several pertinent subjects (see Osmond file). We also impressed upon him the consequences of all this —should he continue to ally himself with Schrader—in regard not only to his own welfare but to that of his family, as well as the financial backing of the Foundation. Though we could not detect the immediate effect of all this—he did not volunteer any additional information (Osmond is either a clever actor and is deceiving us or is genuinely in the dark)—still, we believe there will be a noticeable change in his attitude. And we hope this will rub off onto Schrader.

1. His knowledge of the "O" projects is sketchy, at best. (He says that Macdavitt had some vague references to the two projects in these personal papers of his.)

2. He says he doesn't know where the papers are. The papers in question—according to him—were simply personal papers of Macdavitt's that Macdavitt had in his office. (However, this is very doubtful, as the last search of Macdavitt's office, shortly before his death, failed to reveal any such papers.)

3. Osmond still also maintains someone from the Agency came to the Foundation last week to collect Macdavitt's remaining papers. We have checked this out thoroughly and, of course, it does not hold. No one was ever sent out for that purpose.

We will keep checking this. And we'll put a tracer on it. It may simply be a lack of communication in some division or, of course, the file could have just simply gotten lost, though this seems unlikely.

Voice analysis of Osmond checks out except on Schrader/ Macdavitt papers.

Lying with her clothes on in the dark, beside him on her large double bed, Michelle waited until she was sure Nick was asleep. Picking up her knit Greek shoulder bag from the top of the dresser, she carefully closed the bedroom door. It was cold in the living room. She saw that the glass door was open; the pale floor-length curtains swayed in the cold night breeze. She slid the door shut, locked it.

She locked the front door behind her. She got into her car, backed out slowly, past Nick's car, brushing against some hedges, past the mailbox with WORTHINGTON stamped on the nameplate, which was vibrating in the gusts of night air. She didn't turn on her lights until she was past the curve, on the main road, several hundred yards away.

She drove toward the lights, into town, toward the

water. There were hardly any other cars out. It was ten of twelve on the car clock. She fiddled with the AM-FM dial. The news came on. She switched off the radio, adjusted the clock to twelve.

She pulled into the almost empty parking lot of the twenty-four-hour Jordanos'. The bright fluorescent lights almost blinded her. Muzak was playing, and the air-conditioning system was on too high. She hurried past the rows of perfect fruits and vegetables. She went to the takeout counter, picked up a carton of Marlboros. An elderly couple were buying dozens of packages of chicken parts. In the glare of lights, seeing the darkness outside beyond the automatic glass doors, Michelle felt as removed as if she had landed on another planet. She felt almost bodiless, as if she were only a spirit, had been traveling in the endless night worlds of outer space and had just reentered, had docked—this was a space station. She smiled to herself, thinking of Nick. He would say her reaction was a perfect example of contemporary alienation—and the twenty-four-hour supermarkets of California, presages of the future.

The elderly couple looked unreal, synthetic. The model of someone's idea of an elderly couple. The woman was in a housecoat, the man in Bermuda shorts. They were both pale; Michelle noticed their toenails were long and uncut, yellow, sticking out of their sandals, like the claws on the chicken legs of the parts they were buying. The young clerk also looked unreal, a human robot. Michelle glided out. Everything seemed unreal, as if she were in a dream. She got back into the car. Her lights projected onto the signs plastered on the brick walls of the supermarket: PEACHES 35¢ LB. APRICOTS 39¢ LB. CHERRIES 29¢ LB. CHICKEN PARTS—WEDS., THURS., FRI. ONLY—39¢ LB.

She pulled out of the deserted shopping center, onto the deserted runway of the avenue, speeding down to the ocean.

She parked at the wharf. She opened the carton and lit a cigarette. She sat down on a bench not far from the car. She watched the gradations of dark—the dark water, identifiable only by the recurrent monotone of the surf, the dark overcast sky with its rags of clouds, the dark backdrop of the boulevard with its procession of palm trees and lampposts, the dark of the landscape, of the night all around her, surrounding her.

She didn't hear the footsteps. She was looking down. Sneakers—Adidas. He smiled apologetically, disarmingly. It was the Walkers' house-sitter.

"What the hell are you doing here? Are you following me around again?"

"Hmm. It's a nice night, isn't it? I see we had the same idea." He put one Levi's corduroy leg up on the bench, his elbow down onto his flexed knee, his hand supporting his chin. He pretended to be studying the dark bench. Michelle looked disgusted, annoyed.

"I hope I'm not bothering you," he said, smiling, as if it had just occurred to him. "I wouldn't want to infringe on your privacy. Do you mind if I sit down?" He didn't wait for an answer: He sat down. "I really don't mean to annoy you."

"Yeah, well, you are."

"I'm really bothering you, huh?"

"Look, you just can't follow me around like this. Do you understand? What do I have to do to make you understand?"

"I thought it'd be a good time to talk. Nice and quiet." He grinned.

"Look, I'm just going to scream." She raised her voice. *"Leave me alone—alone.* I came out here to think, to be alone . . . oh, look what you've done now."

A patrol car pulled up at the curb. A policeman came toward them, his flashlight on, lighting up the grass. "Everything all right?"

Michelle nodded.

The policeman waited a moment, his flashlight still on. "We just came here to talk," Michelle said.

The policeman switched off his long flashlight. He seemed to hesitate. "Just checking," he said. "I saw two cars . . ."

"No, it's all right. Thank you."

The policeman nodded and walked back to the patrol car. He said something to the other policeman in the car. He turned around again, waited. "See what you've done now?" Michelle said. "I told you I didn't want to be seen with you." She wrapped her arms around him and kissed him. She waited until the patrol car pulled away.

"Wow! Wow! All I can say . . ."

Michelle glared at him.

"He's going away."

"Yeah, but he saw us."

"So what? What difference does it make? They see dozens of people at night like this."

Michelle didn't seem convinced. "I just hope you're right."

"What do you think he's going to do?"

"I just don't like it, that's all. He could make a connection at some point in the future."

"You're not serious! Too much! Too much!" The boy shook his head disbelievingly.

"You'd be surprised, my friend. Are you going to leave me alone now? Or do you want to wait for another one to come along?"

"OK. OK." The boy did a rapid succession of mock bows. "But you've got to tell me when we can talk. I've really got to talk to you."

"All right, I'll see you tomorrow on the beach. At eleven. He's going over to Osmond's then. So we can talk. Now go. Please. Go! Do you hear me?"

He winked and waved good-bye, walking away backward.

Saturday, for the sceond morning in a row, a small group of men met in a windowless, soundproof office in the Air Technical Intelligence Center in Washington. They were seated at one end of a long table. The allegiances were clearly delineated in the seating arrangements. Senator Russell Burger—the jovial septuagenarian southerner whose façade of gentility and general solicitousness masked the brand of conservatism and preservation of the way of life that had ceased to exist about the time of the Civil War—was more or less in the center between Richard Reed of the CIA, who was presiding, and Wing Commander Wayne Stockton of ATIC. Skipping the space of three chairs, on the other side, Senator William P. Harrington, the liberal New Englander for whom every social exchange was simply an opportunity to demonstrate the natural superiority of a classical education; seated next to him, the two unbiased scientific voices, Dr. Edward Logan, the NASA representative, and next to him, Dr. Friedrich Karp, the well-known physicist.

"Now, as you all know," Senator Burger said, "we're going to pick up where we all left off yesterday. I believe we're all here. You all want to have a vote of hands?"

"No, Senator." Richard Reed tried to smile. "I think we can go ahead. Wayne?"

Commander Stockton nodded. "Might as well."

"Yes." Richard Reed gestured. "Well, then, why don't we just start?"

"Gentlemen." Senator Burger pointed to the large tape recorder in front of the three empty chairs. "Any discussion, you all know, is going to be on that machine again."

Senator Harrington shifted slightly in his seat. "I must admit I'm still somewhat perplexed. It seems to me just somewhat paralogical. I would simply like you to answer me, why are we so afraid? Can you just answer me that?"

"Senator." Commander Stockton caught himself. "We went over this with you yesterday. This is simply the government's position on this matter."

Senator Harrington nodded. His lips curled. His expression could be interpreted as either amusement or pitying contempt. *"Nullum est jam dictum quod non dictum sit primus.* 'Nothing is said which has not been said before,'" he added. "But if these hypothetical UFOs have not done anything for all these thousands of years . . ."

"Yes, but whatever's out there could, after all, be readying itself now to do God knows what kind of damage to us and our way of life." Senator Burger's eyes seemed magnified behind his thick lenses.

"And that is the reason for the secrecy? *Spargere voces in vulgum ambiguas.* 'To spread deceptive reports among the people,'" he added, translating. "But it just doesn't make sense. Surely, if they have not done anything for thousands—"

"Senator." Richard Reed sighed, exasperated. "There've been conclusive studies."

"All right. Let's try another." Senator Harrington picked up one of the two pencils in front of him and kept it moving in his hand. "Now. I have two arguments here pointed out to me by the Rand Study Group, who, as you know, came out in favor of ending the secrecy. One. The risk of accidental war. We could mistake the UFO formation for a Soviet attack. Two. The possibility that the Soviet government could falsely claim that the UFOs are secret Russian weapons against which we would be helpless to defend ourselves. Do you have any comment on this?"

"First of all"—Richard Reed's tone of voice was controlled, as if he were talking to a child—"that study was inconclusive. There was a substantial amount of data missing, whereas the studies we've conducted—the CIA and the Air Force—have had access to a great deal of data of the most top-secret nature."

"But I still can't understand what we are so afraid of. Now, look." Senator Harrington was still trying to be reasonable. "If these UFOs have not done anything harmful all these thousands of years . . . then why would they suddenly do something now?"

"You have to understand, Senator." Reed paused for emphasis. "The government's in a most sensitive position in this matter. After all, with reason. We went over the substantial data with you yesterday."

"You're saying there would be widespread panic. Perhaps even panic on a national scale. And I'm saying, is this really so? That's all I'm asking." Senator Harrington gave his disarming smile.

"Senator." Reed paused again. "When we first entered into these discussions, it was not for the purpose of defending the policies we've held in this matter. It was simply to try to clarify to you, and to Senator Burger," he added, "whatever areas of confusion might still exist in your minds. But frankly, Senator, since you've been aware of the security surrounding this matter for some time now, I can't understand this sudden change of attitude on your part."

"Quite frankly, I simply have never understood it. And now, in the light of recent events . . ."

"I take it you're referring to Dr. Macdavitt? As I said yesterday, it's most unfortunate that you both found out the way you did—about Dr. Macdavitt's involvement with the Russians. But I would think that that would only make you realize all the more the necessity for just this sort of security. You can see that Senator Burger has had no trouble understanding the situation."

Senator Harrington nodded, wide-eyed. "Yes, but what has always puzzled me is the need for this degree of secrecy. Mass terror?" He shook his head.

"We've told you, Senator, repeatedly. This terror has been substantiated by numerous scientific studies. We've had the top scientific minds in the country on this matter."

Senator Harrington smiled again, showing his palms. "But I still don't understand the reason for terror—on the part of intelligent men like us. As I said before, if these UFOs have not done anything all these thousands—"

"Look." Commander Stockton looked disgusted, as if he couldn't believe what he was hearing: Someone was questioning a matter of national security. "These aliens may have their own reasons for waiting."

"For thousands of years?"

"Senator. Surely, you're aware . . ." Reed paused again. "Thousands of years to these aliens may be comparable to two or three years to us—by our time standards."

Volat hora per orbem. Lucretius. 'Times flies through the world.' " Senator Harrington nodded, his eyes half closed, his lips pursed. "Let's return to the Russians. All right, now, let me get the facts straight. The government feels it's a matter of national prestige for us to unravel the mystery of UFOs before the Russians. Even though this knowledge will be kept secret. It's being kept secret because the government is afraid of national panic."

"That's right," Reed said. "As we said, we've conducted extensive research studies."

"And you're convinced the whole thing is best left undisclosed because it would only lead to mass hysteria. All right, that's one thing. But why this competition with the Russians?"

"Why, think of the prestige." Commander Stockton moved forward slightly in his seat, holding out his cupped hand, as if his hand held, at this moment, this prestige. He put his hand back down on the table. "If we were to make the first contact with extraterrestrials before the Russians."

"But surely"—Senator Harrington smiled—"this must transcend nationalities, ideologies."

"This country's already suffered great setbacks not only economically, but in the scientific domain as well," Commander Stockton went on. "It's of the greatest importance we solve these mysteries before the Russians. Even if it's years from now. Not that we really have any other choice in this matter. Dr. Logan has already explained the magnitude to you."

"Yes, now, for instance"—Dr. Logan took his cue—"in November the first message will be transmitted from the radio telescope at Arecibo. This message will be beamed to a cluster of stars 24,000 light-years away. The message will be in the form of 1,679 dots and dashes, showing the outline of the human form, the DNA molecule, the population of the earth, and its place in the solar system. Now, even if this message were received and immediately responded to, we here on earth would not get an answer for 48,000 years! That is the scope of the problem we are faced with."

"In the interval, all sorts of things could arise." Senator Burger didn't need much prompting. "And one of them may be the threat to the very existence of democracy."

"Hence the competition with the Russians?" Senator Harrington asked.

"We can't take anything the Russians do at face value," Reed said. "You see, though they maintain they're operating on pure theory, they're not about to reject any of the extraterrestrial hypotheses. In their study of the UFOs, they're using their astronomical, meteorological, and geographical observatories, their space rockets and satellite-tracking units, their airport and hyrodmeteorological radar."

"Surely, you must realize what sort of effect this would have on the morale of the country"—Senator Burger spoke so softly, he sounded almost as if he were wheezing—"if it were publicly known that the Russians were making these advances in the field of UFOs—or if they were the first to establish some sort of contact with these extraterrestrials. Or even if they were to, let's say, come up with some nearly conclusive proof before us. Why, think of the consequences. This might just be the final blow—it could lead to a total collapse. And then you would have the anarchists running this country. All your long-haired drug-takers, your morally corrupted. Believers in free love and promiscuity, nudists. Why, there'd be nudist camps, communes all over the country. Food coupons! The whole country'd be on welfare. And then where would we be? You see, we all have to think ahead."

"Well, Russell . . ." Senator Harrington smiled to his invisible audience; and as if waiting for their amusement to subside, he poured some water from the water jug into the glass on the tray in front of him. Still smiling, he put the glass back down. "I've never been one to question your sense of patriotism."

"Can you image how traumatic it would be to the morale of the country"—Reed paused for a moment—"if the Russians were to report the first contact with members of an extraterrestrial civilization?"

"And if the Russians were the first to establish contact," Commander Stockton went on, "then who knows, the extraterrestrials might assume the whole planet is Communist. And you think Russia would deny that? Democracy wouldn't have a chance."

"So I take it, then, that your lemma is the future of democracy. Its survival—how shall we phrase it—at any cost?"

"That's right. Democracy," Commander Stockton repeated.

"Now, as you all know"—Senator Burger had on his full smile, as if a sore point had come up in a campaign discussion and it was best to pretend he hadn't even heard it, to just move on to another issue—"Dr. Karp has been working on a number of government projects over the years. I—well—I don't think I have to certify his credentials. And of course Dr. Logan doesn't need any introducing at all. Now Dr. Karp's going to present us with his departmental group research on the Russians and this matter."

"Gentlemen. As we mentioned yesterday, our Soviet experts have pointed out that since the Russians have called for a full-fledged scientific study of UFOs, it is unlikely they would have announced this unless such a program, in fact, was already in existence." Dr. Karp had a slight trace of a German accent. "We have further been advised that the Russians have developed new cameras to photograph UFOs for the purpose of establishing photographic records. We also know, for example, the Russians have conducted studies showing that sightings increase whenever Mars is closest to Earth. They even have groups of parapsychologists studying UFOs. They've also conducted studies based on ancient and sacred documents, documenting the theory that spacemen landed on Earth thousands of years ago, bringing with them the beginnings of civilzation—'gods from the sky.' And, for example, in this light, the biblical account of the destruction of Sodom and Gomorrah might very well be a nuclear explosion as recounted by a bewildered witness."

"Is this the new theology?" Senator Harrington asked.

"No, these are documented interpretations." Dr. Karp didn't even look in his direction. "But the Russians have not limited their investigations to the Bible. For example, they've made studies of Indian texts. The ancient holy Indian sagas in the *Ramayana* tell of 'two-storied celestial chariots with many windows. They roar like lions, blaze with red flames, and race into the sky until they appear like comets.' The *Mahabharata* and various other books describe these chariots at length—'powered by winged lightning . . . it was a ship that soared into the air, flying to both the solar and stellar regions.' "

"There's also the matter of the records," Reed said.

"Yes, I'm getting to that." Dr. Karp aligned the batch of folders in front of him. "Soviet archaeologists believe the chariots may have left 'records' behind. Our source reveals that the Russians have recently found 716 stone disks in caves in the Bayan Kara Ula Mountain bordering China and Tibet. These records contain traces of metals, have grooves like a modern photograph record and a hole in the center. They're been dated to around 10,000 B.C. The Russians believe they're some form of writing. However, their further research in this matter has not been made available. There are reports, however, that when there disks are scraped free of particles, they vibrate as if carrying an electrical charge—again, as documented by our source."

"We cannot debunk this totally, as the Russian thesis of 'gods from the sky' is upheld by renowned experts in the fields of archaeology, anthropology, physics," Commander Stockton added. "Doctor."

"And then there is the matter of tektites," Dr. Karp continued, "mysterious rocks. But they are not rocks at all. They have no geological or mineralogical affinity to any rock chemistry on Earth. They are composed largely of silica, and they also contain small quantities of various oxides—calcium, sodium, aluminum, iron, so on. They could be of meteoric origin. There is reason to believe that tektites originated on the moon. Or that the tektites were the result of an impact somewhere on Earth or on the moon, since many specimens contain tiny nickel-iron spherules of definite meteoric origin. These tektites are found in various parts of the world, Australia, the Philippines, Lebanon. And then there are microtektites, which have been found in ocean sediments. They're a great puzzle. But the Russian experts believe the tektites were formed under nuclear radiation, and that they are remnants of missiles from outer space."

"All this, naturally, is further concrete evidence of cosmic visitors," Senator Harrington commented.

"Ned." Dr. Karp turned to Dr. Logan. "I'll let you continue."

"Thank you, Fritz. I think we should point out again that the fact remains that a great number of Russian physicists have supposedly seen UFOs themselves. The movements they describe—such as wavy light ripples—attest to our own findings in these matter. The fact they proved to be neither planes, meteorites, nor artificial Sputniks can be conclusively documented by their flights along broken lines with great changes in speed. These cases are all from reports conveyed by our source. We cannot readily dismiss this, considering the expertise of the witnesses involved. We all know that in October of 1967, the Russians formed an unofficial UFO study group whose members were made up of prominent scientists and heroes of the Soviet Union. This society announced itself on their television and then went silent—which in itself is not that unusual. After all, this is only the Soviet pattern. Still, we question what has happened to this group."

"We can cite many more such unofficial as well as so-called official study groups formed over the years," Reed said. "A very good example is that of the Russians repeatedly calling for worldwide research on UFOs."

"Well, we know better than to fall for that one," Senator Harrington commented, again to his invisible audience.

"Exactly. They'll only continue to remain secretive and devious in their pursuit of this phenomenon, as they do in almost all of their other areas of research. Despite their protestations to the contrary," Reed added.

"And we've learned, over the years, to take such protestations rather dubiously, to say the least. *Fronti nulla fides*, as Juvenal said. 'No faith is to be put in outward appearances.' "

"Yes. We've—" Reed was either momentarily distracted or trying to curb his annoyance. "We've been able to assemble a great number of their photographs over the years. These photographs only testify further to their superior knowledge of and research on these phenomena."

"We have a number of photographs that reveal hours' worth of the changing phenomena." Dr. Logan took out some photographs from one of the file folders in front of him. "Such as these here in series B-63—if you'll just pass them on—phenomena of dense, milky formations with a rosy red nucleus. Our source reveals that this cloud in question, in series B-63, paled and disappeared, but this red center over here hovered." He pointed to a part of one of the photographs. "We still have no explanation, and their research on this one—as in so many other such cases—continues to remain unavailable to us, despite repeated attempts."

Dr. Karp held up one of the photographs he'd taken out from one of his files. "Another striking example would be in series C-63. As you can see"—he pointed—"in this one . . . Yes, why don't we just pass them around also. Here we have a bright crescent, and as you can see over there, in this next photograph, the faint luminous ribbons, like some sort of exhaust, follow the horns of the crescent. Then, too, eventually, in this photograph here, the brightness of the crescent fades, and the object appears to be a disk. . . . We have no explanation for this series."

"Correct me if I'm mistaken"—Senator Harrington suddenly looked up from one of the photographs—"but I was under the impression that in March of 1968, the Soviet

Academy of Sciences pronounced that this sort of study of UFOs was antiscientific."

"That's right," Commander Stockton answered cautiously, as if he were not quite sure where this might lead to. "But their continued research is in total contradiction of this official statement. And furthermore, in violation of the secrecy they promised to abolish, with regard to us, in this matter."

"As research stands at the present," Dr. Logan added, "and if the UFOs prove to be extraterrestrial aliens, the Russians stand to get the first intergalactic word."

"That's a big 'if.'" Senator Harrigton nodded, as if he were taking the matter into consideration.

"If the present research continues," Commander Stockton went on, "and there is no indication it will not, and if the UFOs prove to be these extraterrestrial aliens, then the Russians stand to maintain their lead in this area. The effects of all this simply cannot be minimized."

Senator Harrington pressed his pencil to his mouth. "May I just interject a note of sobriety? I've been listening to you . . . gentlemen . . . and it has all been most informative and enlightening. However, this simply does not explain the reasons for secrecy, why the public cannot—"

"Yes." Reed closed his eyes a moment and then gave his subliminal smile. "Well, Senator, I think you're failing to understand the issues here. The issues that are really more in the military sphere. The threat of takeover, of intervention by a superior race. These are issues that boggle the mind."

"That's right," Commander Stockton said. "We simply cannot rule out the military aspects, the possibility not only of takeover by this extraterrestrial race but of annihilation."

"You see"—Reed motioned with both hands, as if he were showing exactly what he was seeing, a small space about eight to ten inches in size between his hands—"we simply don't know enough. We have to go cautiously here, and that means we just cannot afford to involve the public. We don't need mass panic. We would have enough on our hands should this situation arise."

"Fritz, why don't we go over the photographs again," Dr. Logan suggested, "in greater detail."

From Agent R. Castle to Security 5A200 Washington. 17 August.

Re Tim Hawkins: Why were we not informed before this of his connection with the branch re Macdavitt on the night of July 18–19? We had already assigned Hawkins to Schrader surveillance. We had gone to the trouble of removing the young man who was house-sitting in the beach house adjacent to Schrader's and replacing him with Hawkins. Our—as you said at the time—"excessive security," as you can see, more than paid off. However, once again, we question why we were not told.

Nick pulled into the Osmonds' circular driveway in front of the two-story stone house partially covered with ivy—the house was recessed from the road and blended in with the several acres of trees and dense shrubs that surrounded it. Nick used the knocker—an Etruscan stirrup Virginia had found in the Mediterranean. There was no response. He knocked the verdigrised stirrup again against the oak door, this time more forcefully. "Coming," a voice chimed, lilting from some distant part of the house. Virginia opened the door. "Hi, Nick! I was wondering who it was this time of morning! I thought it was too early for the groceries."

"Hi. Is Rodney in?"

"Come on in! You got me just as I was going out, so you can have him all to yourself. He's in the back."

Nick stood in the narrow passageway—the entrance: some gilt-framed oval mirrors, English antique side tables with vases of wildflowers on either side. "In the garden?"

"Hmm, where else? Look, you've got to forgive me but I've really got to run. I'm supposed to be at the museum by one. I don't know how I'll ever get there, even on the inland route. I have to show some people through. For funds."

"Sounds familiar."

"Doesn't it? There's still some coffee left in the kitchen —well, you know the way. . . . He's probably over by the flower beds." She picked up her white Gucci bag from one of the side tables, slipped on her sunglasses, took a last quick look at herself in the mirror (Not bad, Nick thought), waved, and closed the front door behind her.

Nick went down to the end of the hall, past the open doors of the dining room, the library, into the kitchen and out the pantry, which led into the garden. He tried to stay on the flagstones, but the path was partially erased by weeds and moss, preserving the natural setting. The foliage was thick, tangled all around—the gnarled effect of a manicured jungle. The sun was high, but it was cool in the garden; the sun was blocked by the screen of trees. Nick went down some steps, past a clearing—a terraced area of yellowed grass—the sun deck, a modest-sized pool, some canvas deck chairs, a barbecue, a converted tool shed— the dressing room; past some gigantic (almost a caricature of science fiction) cacti, dwarfing everything else, almost comical in their ominous oversized presence; toward the blankets of flowers—a shock of colors—where Rodney was bent over, in a short-sleeved shirt, a pair of scissors hanging around his neck, raking a plot of fresh earth. Nick jumped involuntarily, mistaking the thick black hose for a snake. Rodney looked up, frowned, annoyed, and, squinting in the weak sun, continued raking. He had on an old pair of army pants, espadrilles. Some large clippers were lying on the ground next to him.

"Virginia said you'd probably be here. I know Saturday morning is your gardening time, but I thought it'd be better to talk to you here than at the Foundation."

"I'm not going in today."

"No?"

"No, I'm taking the day off. I'm going to garden all day. At least, I was going to. A nice quiet relaxing day." Rodney looked up. "What do you want? You hounded me all day yesterday."

"I thought it'd be better to talk here rather than at the Foundation."

"You already said that."

"Where were you on Thursday?"

"I told you. I had to go down to Los Angeles to see some trustees. Fenwick Vandemere just came back from his cruise to the Far East. I thought it would be a good idea to get to him when he was still fresh."

"At the last minute?"

Rodney winced. He racked over a miniature area. "Be careful, you're going to step over those seeds."

"What are you planting?"

"Hmm? Begonias. I'm sure you didn't come here to talk about flowers."

"No." Nick laughed. "Nor cacti."

Rodney stopped, leaned on the rake. "Look, Nick . . ." He paused, lips pursed, shaking his head. "No way." He kept shaking his head. "There's no way. Do you understand?"

"Yeah, I understand, all right."

"No. You don't. If you did, you wouldn't be here. You wouldn't be harassing me like this, harassing yourself. You'd let it drop. Don't you understand?"

"What did they do to you, Rodney? What did they threaten you with? They say they'd take away the funds, make it difficult, get to the money people? They try to threaten you? They did, didn't they?"

Rodney looked at him pitying. "Why don't you drop it, Nick? You haven't got a chance. You don't know—you haven't got any idea what you're up against."

"What are you reciting, your lines? Is that what they told you? Can't you see the whole thing's insane—the whole idea of secrecy revolving around the UFOs? Secrecy because of some crazy notion about the threat of danger. Can't you see? It's crazy. The likelihood of danger is so minimal, it's hardly worth mentioning. Hasn't it been proven by this point? If this situation has supposedly been going on all these thousands of years without these UFOs doing anything disastrous to us, what do you think they're waiting for? If they were going to act in a negative way, then wouldn't they have already done so by now? Why wait thousands of years?"

"You've been well steeped in George's theories. But thousands of years to them—if they actually do exist— might be negligible. A few years or maybe even months to us."

"The official stance of the combined government agencies."

"Nick. You're being naive. And beside, even if you got it out, what do you think the consequences would really be? How do you think people would react to this? You'd have mass panic."

"More official double-talk. Don't inform the public because they might panic. And if they panic, the situation will get out of control. Therefore in order not to have panic, we will tell the public the UFOs do not exist. Hence the situation is contained. They fed you their propaganda and you bought it."

"You're getting monotonous, you're repeating yourself. What are you talking about, Nick? Why don't you just drop it? Who's this 'they'?" Rodney sighed, looked down at the combed patch of earth at his feet.

"I'm asking you," Nick said.

"What difference does it make? They're all the same, they're all involved in this."

"Is it the CIA? The CIA is in this, aren't they?"

Rodney sighed again, shaking his head. "It's not that simple."

"Sure it is. That's what they tried to tell you. Look, c'mon, we're talking in circles."

"Nick. You're just going to have to put it out of your mind." Rodney sighed. "I have only myself to blame. I shouldn't have given you those papers. I should have looked at them myself first—emotional cowardice."

"Oh, stop being melodramatic."

"I couldn't bear the idea of going through his papers, and I thought they'd be personal. I thought he'd gotten rid of everything—given them whatever they wanted. Instead, look what happened. I got both of us into this mess. No, you've just got to forget about it."

"What the hell did they do to you? They threatened you with the Foundation, didn't they? They did, didn't they? And you bought it!"

"You're being a fool. You'll never get anywhere. They'll never let you. Drop it now while you still have a chance."

"What are you talking about?"

"I saw what happened in the fifties. During the McCarthy era. And I see it's no different now, we just don't know about it. The subterfuge is more elaborate, more sophisticated methods . . ."

"I can't believe what I'm hearing. I can't believe what you're saying. Do you realize what you're saying? It's laughable, a joke. You expect me to take it seriously? This might as well be some sort of skit we're going through."

"They'll just laugh at you, Nick. They'll never let you get through."

"So you're not going to help me. Is that it? That's all you're really saying, isn't it?"

Rodney gave a long, drawn-out sigh. "Stop now while you still have a chance. You don't know what they're capable of."

"Unbelievable! Who would believe what I'm hearing?"

"Why can't you drop it? They'll be onto you until you won't even be able to move . . . like a trapped animal . . . they'll be following you until you're so trapped you won't even know it. They'll close in on you."

"What are you talking about? Tactics for exercises in the CIA game room? Shit. You'd think you're giving a course on K, on *Amerika* with a neon *k*, on *The Penal Colony*. A totalitarian world. Big Brother . . . What a joke? Cut! Nobody'd believe this scene."

"Why don't you just transcribe George's papers, put them on tape, you can go into my office, use the machine there . . . give them over while you still have a chance."

"I really didn't think they'd get to you like this."

"OK, Nick. So what if you got to the press, got through to the media? So what? What do you think would happen then? They'd just laugh at you. You'd be a laughingstock —the way George was—nobody would believe you."

"You're forgetting. What about all those names . . . all those people, all the people involved?"

"You'll never get through to them. And even if you do, they'll never back you. Don't you understand that? They can't help you . . . even if they wanted to. Can't you see that? Their lives are at stake. Why can't you understand? Why are you being so stubborn, so naive?"

"I saw his body. I saw what they did to him."

"That's right, Nick. They'll do the same to you, too, they'll do it to me."

"You're forgetting one thing: the papers. As long as I have the papers, what can they do? Nothing. There's nothing they can do."

"They'll do other things. Believe me. Why did I give you those . . . why? All right. Let's drop it. Let's go have some coffee . . . talk about something else. I don't want to talk in the house. . . . I wish I could help you, but I just can't."

"You mean won't."

Rodney didn't answer.

"Well, I guess there's nothing more to talk about."

"Nick . . ." Rodney paused and either changed his mind or had nothing really new to say. "You just don't know what you're getting into."

Nick nodded. "See you Monday." And he walked out.

Report by Agent R. Castle to Security 5A200 Washington. 17 August.

Hawkins met with Worthington as he arranged with her last night—we thought it was a good idea to keep close tabs on Worthington. Hawkins relayed that she should begin accelerating proceedings. Worthington asked for more time, believes Schrader is almost at the point of bringing her into his confidence re Macdavitt papers. But she was persuaded.

Worthington has been advised to exercise more subliminal measures on Schrader, i.e., by mentioning at random names of observatories, available data, etc., as a means of triggering a response. He may divulge whereabouts or contents of Macdavitt papers unintentionally. Suggested most effective state would be inebriated. We will take precautionary measures of our own in the event she should not carry out the above in entirety. (Her involvement with Schrader continues to be under question.)

When Nick got back to his house, Michelle's car was already there—she was staying over at his place (her husband had the kids for the weekend).

In her bikini, Michelle was lying on a towel on the beach in front of the house. Nick was about to call out to her from the sun deck, but then he saw the Walkers' housesitter, with a red bandanna around his head, sitting on the steps outside the Walkers', and he didn't. He wanted to be alone for a while, anyway. He went into the bedroom. He sat down on the bed. I won't do anything, he thought. I'll wait until next week. In case they're still watching Rodney; and if they're watching him, they might be watching me.

He put on his trunks and went down to join Michelle. He didn't say anything about the boy.

They had the whole weekend—two days with nothing to do. They lay in the sun, side by side, until they almost fell asleep in the heat. Michelle fixed some sandwiches; they took them into the bedroom and ate in bed. They spent the rest of the afternoon in bed.

Later, they went out and made the rounds of his old bars. Nick got loaded; Michelle wasn't much of a drinker.

Nick was having trouble keeping track of what was happening—if anything was happening. It was all like a dream. He thought Michelle said "Philip Wells." He could swear. But she just laughed. "H. G. Wells," she said. She'd been reading a book about H. G. Wells and Rebecca West. Michelle kissed his neck, breathing softly down into his open shirt collar. She laughed.

He saw a man, a businessman type in a pin-striped suit, come toward them and then suddenly disappear. He looked again. The man was no longer there. He kept staring at the spot where the man should have been. He heard something. A hand flashed out of nowhere, hovered above the table. He looked back down at the glass in front of him. He stared at the slight motion of the liquid surface. No. He shook his head, closed his eyes. He was imagining things. He gulped the drink down. Michelle motioned to the bartender to bring him another gin and tonic. Nick felt his head reeling; it felt as if it had been separated from the rest of his body. The businessman reappeared. Nick laughed softly to himself, relieved. He realized the man had gone behind the pillar into the men's room.

Another drink materialized in front of him. "What are you laughing about?" Michelle nuzzled against him, wanting to share whatever it was that was amusing him so much. But he wouldn't tell her. He saw the neon Schlitz sign behind the bar going on and off, as if it were transmitting some sort of message. He shook his head to try to wake himself. "16, 22, 30, 16, 26, 6, 16, 16, 16, 24, 30, 26, 16, 16." " What are you saying?" he asked incredulously. "I'm watching that light." Michelle pointed to the Schlitz sign. "Those are the seconds between flashes . . . like time lags. Watch: 16, 16, 24, 30, 26, 16, 16." He watched. Those numbers . . . Those were Macdavitt's fig-

ures—those were the signal sequences Macdavitt had recorded last year—the time lags between the signals he had
received. . . . He saw Macdavitt's handwriting: "We calculated the distance of the transmissions received from
the reflecting objects . . . we calculated the distance of
these astronomical bodies . . . but there is no known
asteroid or planet in that orbit. . . ."

Impossible . . . he must be dreaming.

"Frequency or wavelength: 1,420 megahertz. Targets:
Epsilon Eridani and Tau Ceti," Michelle went on. "From
the Gorky University Observatory. Frequency or wavelength: 21 and 30 centimeters. Targets: 12 nearby sunlike
stars . . . from the National Radio Astronomy Observatory
in Green Bank, 1972. Frequency or wavelength: 1,420
megahertz. Targets: 10 nearby stars . . . from the 'Eurasian
Network,' Gorky University and the Institute for Cosmic
Rersearch, 1972 to the present. Frequency or wavelength:
16, 30, and 50 centimeters. Targets: pulsed signals from
entire sky . . . Frequency or wavelength: 1,420 megahertz.
Targets: 600 nearby sunlike stars . . . from the Eurasian
Network and the Institute for Cosmic Research, 1972 to
the present. Frequency or wavelength: several. Targets:
pulsed signals from entire sky . . . the Algonquin Radio
Observatory in Canada, this year. Frequency or wavelength: 22.2 gigahertz Targets: several nearby stars . . ."

Nick closed his eyes. Someone was holding him, leading
him somewhere; he let himself be led. He was cold. He was
standing outside on a street corner, waiting for a car to
pass. It was night. Some kids got out of a Volkswagen bus
laughing. The pavement swerved, disappeared, swam back
into view. Michelle laughed, grabbing his arm. . . . They
were in another bar or another part of the same bar, he
thought—in any case, they had changed places. Now they
were in a booth, that was all he could be certain of.
Michelle kept ordering more drinks or maybe it was only
the same drink that could never be emptied. The idea
struck him, for some reason (he didn't really know why),
as incredibly funny; he burst out laughing. He looked at
Michelle strangely, as if from a great distance. Her eyes
sparkled in the dim light, seemed even larger, more deep
set than they already were. He felt himself sinking, slowly
—he felt himself drawn into her eyes as if toward a

magnet. He couldn't believe what she was saying . . . impossible . . . not possible . . .

"Ozymandias." There. She had said it again. He looked at her, terrified, uncomprehending. Who was she? She burst out laughing, pushed him—he almost lost his balance, almost tottered out of the booth. "Shelley's 'Ozymandias,' " she said. Then suddenly she became very serious, intent, her eyes lowered. " 'I met a traveller from an antique land/Who said: "Two vast and trunkless legs of stone," ' " she recited, " ' "Stand in the desert. Near them, on the sand . . ." ' "

Nick didn't hear the rest. For some reason, tears came into his eyes. Michelle bent down, took his hand, and put it to her mouth. She kissed the open palm of his hand, her tongue flicking out slowly, insinuatingly, in a way he found particularly troubling, disturbing; her hand moved down to his bulging crotch, then back up. Her hand was on his fly, on the zipper, yanked it down. He rolled his eyes, gave a start. The zipper snagged; Michelle slipped his penis out. He felt her straining against him. I must be dreaming, he thought, this is impossible . . . in a bar. His eyes were closed; Michelle was breathing heavily. I better look, he thought. He opened his eyes. They were in bed, in his bedroom. He let himself sink slowly down, as if through layers of clouds.

Synopsis of surveillance log. 17 August.
We followed Schrader and Worthington through the town bars (as prearranged with Worthington). We waited until Schrader appeared inebriated. We passed directly in front of the table on way to men's room and slipped a cube of lysergic acid into Schrader's drink. Results unconfirmed.

The sun woke him up the next morning. He groaned, moving his head from side to side, his hands gingerly touching his head, trying to locate the pain, but it was everywhere. He tried to keep his eyes open, but he couldn't. The room was in double, the bed was in double, Michelle was in double. He tried to focus on her smile, but it kept coming in in double. "My head," he whispered almost inaudibly.

"I bet." She laughed softly. "You must have drunk I

don't know how many—I stopped counting. What a time getting you back here . . ."

"The dreams I had . . . strange . . . dreams . . ."

"You were talking in your sleep."

"Did I say . . . ? What did I say?"

"I couldn't make out anything but you kept me up all night, beast. If that's what alcohol does to you . . ."

"I thought we were, you know, having sex in this bar."

"Yeah. We almost were, if it had been up to you."

"Your hand was on my fly in this bar . . . terribly embarrassing."

"You practically assaulted me—"

"I had this incredible erection and you—"

"—like a wild man."

"Oh, my head."

She took his head and quietly rocked it.

Nick told her his other dreams, how in one she was watching the Schlitz sign above the bar and timing it—time lags, frequencies and wavelengths—and then in another how she started reciting poetry. Michelle made a face, shook her head. She laughed.

They stayed in bed most of the day, sleeping on and off. By the time they were finally dressed and out it was almost nine o'clock. Michelle wanted Chinese food. Even the idea made Nick sick. They settled on the Trade Winds, a local steak house and bar. It was jammed. Sunday was also a big night. The place was ultramodern, a sort of nautical Japanese tea-house decor, but it was too dark to really make out anything—the only light came from the small candles on each table and the orange glow of the charcoal from the open kitchen at the other end of the huge room. A girl in a strapless floor-length diaphanous gown led them to a table, past a blue neon waterfall, through a maze of occupied tables and tall jungle foliage. A waiter—a kid in a beachcomber uniform: torn shorts, T-shirt, and sandals —brought them a large conch on which the menu was inscribed in India ink. To Nick, the place was typically California—though he wasn't exactly sure what he meant by that. It struck him as right. Michelle didn't think it was typically anything—if that's what he meant by California, then maybe he was right, she said. A place with no real identity of its own. Bland, combination of styles: Japanese,

Hawaiian, ultramodern architecture, ersatz New England.

They tried to figure out if the couple next to them—an aging out-of-shape ex-football-player type in a colorful short-sleeved aloha shirt, drinking his Budweiser beer straight from the can, and the frail young girl in the lace nightgown—were father and daughter or not. The food arrived: the proverbial chilled salad plate and fork, the basket of assorted heated breads, the oversized lump of charred meat. Nick stared at his plate. He wasn't very hunrgy. "Oh, shit," he said. "Don't look now, but Dennis —the guy who works next to me—is here. Oh, God. I really don't want to see him." He groaned, lowering himself into his chair.

"Hey, Nick!" Dennis called out in a voice that could not be ignored. "Watcha doing here, you old rascal, son of a gun? I thought you were supposed to be working, huh? Finishing those transcripts?" He slapped Nick on the back. "Or is this work, huh?" He blinked slightly, catching sight of Michelle. "Hi, how are you? How have you been?" His tone of voice was flat. They weren't really questions. He was only observing the amenities.

Michelle smiled the sort of smile that was called for. Impersonal, detached, mysterious. The kind of smile that made any further conversation unnecessary.

"You two . . . ?" Nick raised his eyebrows as a way of finishing the rest of his sentence.

"Yeah. Yeah. We've met," Dennis said absentmindedly; then he caught himself, remembering the girl in the halter top who was standing, waiting, in back of him, smiling, not knowing what else to do. "Here," he said. "I want you to meet Nina. Nina, this is Michelle and Nick."

Nick got up, shook the girl's limp hand—it was a girl. Twenty? Maybe twenty-two at most. Nina didn't shake Michelle's hand nor did Michelle offer hers. Michelle was looking the other way so she wouldn't have to shake anyone's hand. Nina assessed her for a moment, then saw it wasn't necessary—she wasn't even looking at Dennis. "Well, well, what do you know," Dennis said. "I didn't even know you two knew each other."

"Are you going with this party or what?" The teenage hostess in the long evening gown was still waiting in the aisle.

"Do you mind if we join you?" Dennis asked.

"Of course not, don't be silly. C'mon, sit down. I just thought you—"

"Naw," Dennis said. "Don't you worry, we get plenty of time alone."

Nina emitted a slightly shrill laugh.

"I think some other time might be better," Michelle said. "I have some things I have to talk to Nick about alone."

"Oh." Nick thought, What the hell. "Yeah. Dennis, you understand. We'll all get together some other time."

"Yep . . . Yep." Dennis pursed his lips as if it were an effort to remain controlled, cool like this. "Take care, Michelle. Nice seeing you again. See you, Nick."

"Yeah, Dennis . . . in the morning. We'll get together soon."

"Bye-bye." Nina gave a mock wave.

Nick waited until they were outside, in the car. "Where the hell do you know him from? Why the hell didn't you ever mention him before?"

"Oh, c'mon! You can't be serious! I went out with him a *couple* of times. Two, three . . ."

"Well, why the hell didn't you ever mention him before?"

"I don't believe it." Michelle looked out at the dark boulevard with its procession of palm trees along the ocean. She was smiling to herself. "I don't believe it. Here you are questioning me about some guy I went out with maybe three times, somebody I barely even knew."

"I just don't understand why you didn't mention him before, that's all." Nick was confused but felt maybe he'd gone too far.

"What is this, an accusation?"

"I just don't understand it. I must have mentioned Dennis so many times. I mean, he works right next to me —has the office right next to mine—and you never even said anything."

"What did you want me to say? 'You know, I think I know him. Is that the same Dennis who chases everything in sight, you know, curly-haired, boyish, juvenile? Because if it is, then that's the same one I went out with.' Is that what you wanted me to say?"

"Well, you could have said something."

"I didn't think it was important. Is it?"

"No . . . I just don't—"

"You already said that. You're getting repetitious, you know."

"I just don't—"

"Oh, come off it!" She clicked her fingernails on the window panel. "I can't believe what I'm hearing. Is this real? Or is this some cliché-ridden scene that was shelved how many decades ago? You want me to read my next lines, is that it? OK." She changed her voice again. "Do you want an itemized list?"

Nick tried to smile. "I'm sorry. Let's not get into an argument."

Michelle sighed dramatically. She took out a cigarette. Nick pushed in the lighter, but she took out some matches and lit it herself. She kept her face averted, her eyes on the night shore—they were just turning past an open stretch of beach—but since the fog was coming in, there really wasn't much to see.

Early the next morning, Monday, as Nick came into the marble lobby, Dennis loped in from the garden. In his tennis shorts, swinging his racket, a can of balls tucked in his armpit. "Hi! Want to join us? I think we can round up someone else for doubles."

"No, I've got some work to do."

"Say. Listen"—Dennis lowered his voice—"I hope I didn't embarrass you last night."

"No. Of course not."

"Oh, good." Dennis sighed, relieved. A gentleman of the world. "I wouldn't want, you know, anything to get between us. . . . She's quite a girl, isn't she?"

Nick looked wary. He didn't want to hear any more, and yet he was curious.

"Michelle," Dennis specified, thinking perhaps Nick wasn't sure whom he was referring to. He shook his head. "Let me tell you, she's really something. Oh, boy, was I hooked. Listen, you better watch out, you know, she's kind of . . ." He made a motion with his hand.

"Kind of what?"

"You know, kind of on and off. Say, you're not getting offended, are you?"

"No, why should I?"

"Just wanted to make sure. She really had me, you know. I mean, she's really wild. I was practically all set to move in with her. You know it was at the stage where I was close to her kids and everything, then . . ." Dennis snapped his fingers, made a sound with his lips. "Off. She was no longer interested. Can you imagine that? Well, it happens to the best of us, I guess. But let me tell you, I took it pretty hard. You remember this last spring— back in May, remember?—when I was moping around, and you kept saying, 'Old Dennis and his romances . . . you got romantic problems?' Yeah. Well, that's who it was. Oh, wow, she really had me. Let me tell you. Well, I guess it was just as well. In that state God knows what I would have done. Could have landed myself right back in the domestic song and dance. You know, it was really strange, the whole thing. I mean, everything about it . . . about her. She just suddenly appeared . . . out of nowhere, almost . . . at least that's the way it seemed. I guess that's part of her magic. When I think I was playing nursemaid to her two kids . . . Gee, I even had them one weekend, I think, when she went off somewhere else. She had to be by herself. Really strange. Then it'd be the exact opposite . . . you know, attentive, all that—you know the way they get. But I felt it was real with her. Boy, was I conned. I remember I was going to teach her to water-ski. She was interested in everything I was doing—I showed her all around this place. Oh, she was really interested. Asked all sorts of questions. She wanted to get all involved in my life. Yeah. And I fell for it. Pretty hard. And then suddenly it was . . . over. Yeah. You better watch out. You just meet her, huh? What, a couple weeks ago?"

"Yeah." Nick nodded.

"What'd you think of"—Dennis drew an outline of curves with his two forefingers—"Nina, huh?"

Nick shook his head. "You're hopeless, Dennis."

Report by Agent R. Castle to Security 5A200 Washington. 19 August.

Worthington has talked to Cavanaugh. She waited, parked outside his house, until he returned at four from his tennis game. Cavanaugh asked her into the house for a drink. She went in. Worthington then proceeded to tell him how very sorry she was that things had not worked out with them, etc. And that she had only warm feelings for him, and surely he would not want to wreck the relationship with Schrader . . . let alone what it would do to Schrader. He had been upset enough after his wife left him, Worthington said, and he was just beginning to trust her and now . . . Cavanaugh said he would alter what he had told Schrader.

Nick waited. He didn't say anything. Michelle seemed annoyed. She didn't even ask him what was the matter. She didn't have to. He waited until they were in bed. "You know, I saw Dennis today."

"So?"

"He has a different version."

Michelle pulled away. "Yeah, he took it pretty hard— I didn't want to be involved with him—you can imagine he's not used to someone else doing the rejecting."

"He said he was all set to move in with you."

"He did, huh? Well, he's dreaming."

"You said you went out with him a couple of times. He says you were all set to live together. Now, which is it?"

"You sound like a child." Michelle sat up, nude, on the bed. She reached over for her cigarettes and the ashtray. She sat cross-legged, smoking. "OK, since this has obviously turned into a full-fledged interrogation, I'll give you all the facts, OK? I was lonely—it was just after the breakup with Tony—and I was going out with different guys—just going out. I met Dennis out at the university. He was giving a lecture on the long-range effects of Vietnamization. I went up to him afterward with a bunch of other people . . . we ended up all going out to dinner. He moved in on me right away, sat next to me, kept putting his arm around me all during dinner, drove me home—I couldn't get my car started, so I had to leave it outside the Hacienda del Sol all night. The next morning, he was here at the crack of dawn, at the front door, ready to drive me to a garage. Well, he was fun—lightweight—I couldn't really take him seriously, but he got me out of myself, made me laugh . . . and he was good with the kids. I went to bed with him a couple of times. But he never really turned me on. So I didn't see any point in letting it continue. OK? What else do you want to know?"

"I feel like a fool."

"Yeah. You should. Oh, c'mon . . . don't look so sheepish." She stamped out her cigarette and stretched out beside him.

When Nick pulled in, early the next morning, Dennis was waiting in the empty parking lot. Nick didn't particularly want to talk to him, but there was no way to avoid it—he couldn't exactly park in the back now. It would look too obvious.

Dennis had on his nontennis uniform—skintight tailored denims, open shirt, Western silver belt buckle. He pretended to be just getting out of his Alfa, though Nick had the feeling he'd been waiting for a while. "Listen. I tried phoning you last night, but you weren't in." Dennis paused.

Nick nodded but didn't say where he'd been.

"I was thinking about what I told you—you know, about Michelle—and really . . . well, I didn't want you to get the wrong impression. You know, I think I kind of distorted what I told you, I made more out of it than it really was." He shrugged. "I guess I was hurt, you know, probably a blow to my pride, my ego, huh? Well, what I'm really trying to say is we were never really that involved you know, we weren't really involved at all . . . when you come down to it. I guess it was my fantasy. I feel like a real jerk. I mean, I just went out with her a couple of times."

Nick mentioned the conversation to Dr. Richardson—he thought it strange that Dennis should have revised his story, taken back almost everything he'd said. It was so out of character. Something just didn't seem right. But he was probably just being too suspicious; his jealousy was getting the best of him, and that was just a smoke screen, a way to remove himself, withdraw emotionally from Michelle. Why was he doubting her? After all, what did he care what Dennis had to say? Michelle was the one who mattered. No, he had to trust her. He did trust her. He'd just have to drop it. And Dr. Richardson seemed to agree with him (insofar as a mainly nonverbal communication can be interpreted in any way). Yes, it would be better not to mention it to Michelle again. Just let it drop.

Carole kept Johanna on her lap the whole trip up (they were taking Johanna up to Nick's for a couple of days) as a way of distracting herself from Mike's driving —going fifty around the twenty curves after Malibu, eighty, ninety, instead of fifty—"making time," as he said, grinning. She tried to keep her eyes off the speedometer, but she'd pushed her seat back as far as it would go (thinking that way she was safer) and the dashboard of the 450 SL was easily within view. Another curve. She closed her eyes. Johanna shrieked with excitement. Mike accelerated some more. Carole clutched Johanna (who was bouncing up and down). Mike laughed. Then suddenly he slowed down—abruptly dropping speed as if he were about to land; a cop car sped past—Mike seemed to have antennas out for them. Carole couldn't understand how he never got stopped. He smiled as if to say, "See?" She tried to smile back, in vain.

She switched on the radio, but the reception was bad because of the lines overhead. The combination of wind from Mike's open window, lashing out against them as if they were in a storm, and the flood of sunlight blinded her. With his aviator sunglasses, hair blowing around him like a mass of light, shirt swollen with wind, Mike was the archetypal California freeway pilot.

Mike went slowly through Ventura, attentive to all the lights. Carole hoped there would be traffic the rest of the way, but there wasn't—the middle of the week, middle of the morning, everyone was still at work; then, into the last stretch, Mike picked up speed—"gaining"—the blur of rocks, cliffs overlooking the water, the fringe of valleys beyond, freeway signs shuttled past almost subliminally. Carole kept her eyes on the ocean; that way the speed was deceptive.

Mike parked in Nick's yard. There were some other cars there—a Datsun, a VW bus, Nick's car. Carole made a face.

The door was open. Nick was in the kitchen, getting some ice. Johanna, suddenly overcome with shyness, played hide-and-seek behind Mike's legs. "It's just a game," Carole said. "If you ignore it she'll get over it."

Nick gave them some drinks—Tab for Mike, unfiltered apple juice for Carole; Johanna wouldn't say what she wanted. She giggled and pressed her face against Mike's thigh.

They went out through the guest bedroom down to the beach. Carole commented on the fact that Nick had cleaned the place up. Nick introduced everyone: Michelle ("The two Michaels," Mike said to Michelle); Tony, her husband; Tony's girlfriend, Cathy; Michelle's children. Johanna ran off with Peter and Heather.

The adults were left to themselves. Conversation took the expected direction—from the weather, to the children, to politics, where it settled, on Watergate.

Nick and Michelle went in to fix some sandwiches for lunch. Carole, on her way to the bathroom, saw them whispering to each other over the counter, laughing softly. Michelle was peeling an avocado, Nick slicing bread, and then they kissed. Carole stopped short for a moment, then quietly went into the hall bathroom like a guest in this house she had lived in. Her heart was pounding.

The sandwiches were eaten on paper plates on the beach. Michelle, stripped down to her bikini, stretched out on a towel in the sun beside Nick. Carole stayed under the parasol. Tony was in the water with Cathy and the children, who were all shrieking, splashing, having water fights. Mike was on the phone in the bedroom (he'd left the number with his secretary). Carole could hear his voice through the partially opened bedroom window in the distance but she couldn't really make out what he was saying; she didn't try. The sun made her tired. She let herself drift. She remembered other times, when they first moved in—only last year. Mornings they sometimes stayed in bed late—they woke up so early, their sleep interrupted by the surf breaking just outside (it figured in their dreams). And lying there in that timeless world it seemed as if everything would somehow be all right. Johanna sometimes would come in and join them in bed, completing this picture of domestic bliss. They could have been any happy young family. Less than a year ago—not even three seasons. But Carole felt (looking back now) she knew even then, lying in bed, the three of them, that it was temporary, just like this house, just like California, just like this way of life out here—temporary, nothing could be taken seriously, nothing was real.

She watched some gulls on the slick sand, where the tide was draining back. How could you take anything seriously out here? How could anything be real out here? The scenery was too much like a dream, a set, and lives seemed even more like scenarios in endless movies than they did anywhere else. Or maybe it was just a phase she was going through. She wasn't sure. But it didn't matter. She was tired of analyzing everything. She'd analyzed everything, tried to put everything in its place, lived a structured existence, all the time she'd been living with Nick. He jumped up, running after the Frisbee one of the children had thrown. He seemed different, much more relaxed. Something about that annoyed her, as if he were doing it on purpose, to taunt her. Michelle had turned over on her stomach; she had her top off. She seemed to be asleep. Her casualness annoyed Carole—everything about Michelle annoyed her. There was something about her. Carole closed her eyes. The sound of the waves breaking, the monotonous surf, was like a trance. She let herself be drawn in. She could still hear Mike's voice but now as if from a great distance, as if it were fading away, like a memory. She let it fade.

Later, there was a volleyball game, of sorts. The stakes kept tilting, the net sagged. Nick, Tony, Cathy, and Michelle pretended to be playing with the children but they were really playing against one another.

Carole and Mike went for a walk on the beach. But Mike couldn't walk very far; he wasn't used to walking. A true Californian, he never walked anywhere. He took off his cowboy boots and hobbled back.

The volleyball game went on almost to dusk. Then there were more drinks, but since neither Carole nor Mike drank, each was beginning to feel more and more like an intruder—a viewer of these scenes of beach life. Tony seemed to be stoned, or maybe as he was just maudlin to start with. Carole wondered how he'd get home—maybe they'd have to spend the night. The charcoals were lit. The children hovered around, finally the first batch of hamburgers and soya burgers and buns were ready; Carole took it as her cue. Besides, Mike had to be up early in the morning; the truth was she wanted to get back before it was completely dark. She whispered to Nick, but it really wasn't necessary: Johanna wasn't even paying attention.

Nick went out to the car with them. Carole said to say good-bye to Michelle and Tony and Cathy for her, to explain. She was sure they'd understand. Mike nodded, waving as if to convey his good-bye too. Nick seemed to be waiting for something. Carole opened her window. Nick came over. He leaned down. Carole said Michelle was great, really great. Nick said he thought she'd feel that way. Carole waved. Nick waited until the car had disappeared down the road. He stood there. He didn't know why. Several minutes passed. But still he just stood there. A cool breeze sifted through the full trees; shadows were lengthening across the lawn; the pebbles in the driveway took on another tint—that of night. For some reason, he felt sad. He didn't know why. There was no reason. But he did.

Two days later Nick took Johanna back down to Los Angeles, back to Carole. A Day-Glo VW bus was parked in the driveway of Mike's pseudo-Greek-temple house. A couple of scruffy kids were in the mirror-walled ultramodern living room. They were showing Carole a collection of Bedouin desert jewelry they'd brought back from Tangier. Carole explained to Nick that they'd gotten her a number of things for the boutique. The jewels—mostly turquoise and amethysts, mounted in silver and gold—were laid out on the chrome-and-glass cocktail table. Carole introduced Nick as "the father of my child." The kids grinned beatifically—they were hip. Nick waited until Johanna was absorbed with the jewels.

He drove out to the Los Angeles airport. He called Dr. Richardson from a pay phone in the empty lounge outside a men's room. He canceled his appointment. He explained he was staying down with Johanna. Then he called Michelle. He explained he was staying for dinner—Johanna was upset. A cleaning lady came in, started to make noise. He said to Michelle he'd speak to her later.

The one-o'clock flight to San Francisco was almost

empty. Nick sat at the back of the plane, where he could watch everything. He thought someone had been following him—a businessman type in a mod suit—but the man was talking with some mod girl. He had moved over to sit next to her; he kept calling the stewardess over to buy more martinis. The girl had a loud shrill laugh. She kept laughing at what the man was saying. He couldn't have been that funny, Nick thought. But she kept laughing.

They both got off in San Francisco (the plane went on to Portland). Nick stood behind them in the aisle. The man had his hand around the girl's elbow and was guiding her out.

Nick parked outside the university. He had an hour to kill. He walked around through the grounds. He sat on a bench, watched the girls. He watched them absentmindedly. He was too nervous. Besides, they were too young for him. Or else I'm just getting old, he thought. What a cliché. He fragmented them, concentrated on isolated parts of their anatomy—a tight bulge of sweater, tanned legs below torn cutoff jeans, tanned torsos, backs decorated with flimsy bits of material, precarious straps or knots. These tanned nubile bodies, manes of mostly blond hair—the Pepsi generation, the embodiment of California . . . He watched them absentmindedly, out of habit.

Slowly he made his way to Hammond's office. He looked at his watch. It was almost five. He waited in the hall outside Hammond's office, pretending to be studying the bulletin board. The light went off behind the frosted-glass top of the door. A slight, owlish-looking man came out, locked the door behind him, and started walking toward the stairs. He was carrying a briefcase. Nick hurried after him. The man almost swerved around.

"Dr. Hammond?"

"Who are you?" There was an edge in Hammond's voice. Two students passed by just at that moment.

"I'd like to talk to you. Can we talk somewhere?"

"All right." Hammond took it as his cue, not wanting to be embarrassed. "There's a coffee shop across the street."

They walked out through the grounds without speaking. There were still a number of students around. Out past the gray brick walls, down the tree-lined street, across to the Silver Spur. It was between hours; hardly anyone was there. They waited until the waitress brought them their two coffees.

"OK," Hammond said. "What's all this about? Look, you people can keep harassing me like this, following me around, but you're not going to get anything from me because there's nothing to get. I already told you—how many times—I don't know anything. You understand? Nothing. And I don't want to know anything, all right? Look, you can keep phoning me all you want, all night, you can keep waking me up, waking my wife and family up, disturbing us like this, you can phone me every hour, you can follow my wife around, you can sit outside my house in your cars all night, waiting for me to come out, you can wait as long as you want, follow me wherever I go. It's not going to work. You understand? I don't know anything. I'm not going to lead you anywhere because there's nowhere to lead you. I don't know anything. Why can't you accept that? Why can't that get through to you? What do you want me to do? What do you want from me? I don't understand. What do you think—I'm just going to throw out everything I've worked so hard for all these years? What do you want from me? What is it?"

"I think there's been some sort of misunderstanding," Nick said. "I'm with the Foundation for Contemporary Sciences."

"Oh." Hammond closed his eyes wearily, relieved. "I see, I see, yes. What is it? About that book? I already told Rodney . . . Don't you understand?" Hammond started to stutter. "I'm being watched. My phone, for all I know, is tapped."

"That's why I didn't call you," Nick said.

"Look, it's just terrible about Macdavitt. Just horrible . . . there are no words . . . but, look, I've got my own life, too, to think about. My family . . . and I can't get mixed up in this. I can't really help you. If anything, Macdavitt's death should prove that."

"I'm not trying to make anything difficult for you. I realize this puts you under a certain amount of strain."

"Strain! What are you trying to do to me? Don't you realize you're putting me in an impossible situation?"

"I need your help."

"I told you already. I told Rodney. How many times do we have to go over . . . ?" Hammond let his voice trail off as if he'd repeated himself so many times that he knew by now it was hopeless, he'd never get through, but still he was going to try, he didn't know what else to do. "What is it? What do you want?"

"Ozymandias."

Hammond looked at him, as if trying to decide if Nick was serious.

"I want you to corroborate the whole story. In public. I want you to back everything. I want you to back all of Macdavitt's papers, documents. You're the only one left from the original project." Hammond, Nick thought, didn't look convinced. "Do you want him to have died like this, as if there'd been no purpose, as if it had all been useless, for nothing? All his work—"

"I can't help you. I just—"

"They're on to you. Don't you understand? They know you were in touch with Macdavitt until a couple of years ago . . . that you'd been seeing him all these years . . . working with him." Nick felt awful, was squeamish about it, but saw there was no other way. "Look, I can go to Washington. I can tell them everything. I can tell them that you were the one who told me about Ozymandias . . . that you saw Macdavitt only last year. You could say whatever you want. You think they'd believe you, believe a word you'd say? Even for a minute? George Macdavitt was killed. Don't you understand? He was murdered. He was left to rot in a swimming pool, strung up like a piece of meat. Don't you understand? I saw his body being pulled out—"

"I didn't know that. Rodney never said . . ." Hammond looked down at his coffee cup defeatedly. He sighed; he closed his eyes a moment. "All right."

Hammond left the coffee shop first. Nick waited a few minutes before he went out. It was overcast, white. The fog was coming in.

Nick got into his car. Checking the mirror, he thought he saw someone parked in a blue Ford at the corner—the businessman from the plane—pull out behind him. But that was too crazy, impossible. It was just too crazy. He turned another corner, but the Ford didn't follow. He drove straight out to the airport.

It was almost dark by the time he landed in Los Angeles. He got his car out of the parking lot. He drove back up to Sonora Pines in the dark. Dark stretches of empty road, dark cliffs, and the dark to his left, the Pacific.

He went straight to bed. He was awakened—it seemed within minutes—by the phone. "Where the hell have you been?" It was Michelle. "I've been trying you all evening. I thought you were going to call."

He dropped by Michelle's the next morning. Michelle was keeping an eye on the clock. She had a class in half an hour. She was spreading some peanut butter on a slice of whole-grain bread for Heather. Heather had her head down on the counter and was trying to count the number of raisins in her bowl of Granola. Peter was reading "Peanuts" aloud to Heather from the Los Angeles *Times* Nick had brought over.

"What happened yesterday?" Michelle asked casually. She handed Heather the slice of bread. "I thought you were just going to drive her down."

"Snoopy says, 'Good grief! That's not a bone.' "

"Hmm, so did I. But Carole wanted me to stay for lunch and—"

"And so you stayed for dinner?"

"Could it be? Is it possible? Do I detect a note of—yes —jealousy? Ah! What is happening to the free, aloof Ms. Worthington? What time did you phone me last night anyway?"

"It wasn't that late." She grinned.

"You're checking up on me again, huh? What brashness!" Nick put on a mock-English accent. "Insolence! Young snipe! What right do you have? After all, I'm a free man."

"Ha-ha. That's what you think. Oh, shit!" She glanced at the clock on the wall. "I've got to get out of here."

Nick kept going over Macdavitt's list of names in his mind. He finally decided he'd try Thomas Sturgis first. Sturgis was closest. He was at the Watkins Lab in San Diego. Nick could do it in a day—drive down, talk to him, and be back in the evening. He could tell Michelle . . .

something. Nick got Dr. Sturgis's home number from information. Sturgis's wife answered. A young, ebullient voice. Hearing her voice, Nick felt immediately guilty, as if he were bringing bad news, interrupting this happy family: She said he was in the garden with the kids—he was helping them put up a tree house; this openness, admitting a total stranger into the midst of the family, left Nick speechless. He couldn't think of anything to say. He heard Sturgis's wife calling out to him in the background. She came back to the phone to say he would be right in, as soon as he had climbed out of the tree he was in. Sturgis got on, a boyish, out-of-breath voice. "Sorry. My two boys had me up in a tree." Nick identified himself, said he had been working at the Foundation for Contemporary Sciences with George Macdavitt. There was a pause. "Let me get on the phone in my study." There was a shuffle of sounds, steps. Someone put the other phone down. "I was in the kitchen," Sturgis said; he waited. Nick explained about the book on Macdavitt.

Sturgis said he could see him for lunch next Friday. Nick said he'd prefer something sooner; he was going East for a couple of days at the end of the week. Sturgis suggested they meet when he got back. Nick said no, they were trying to put this together as soon as possible. An appointment was set up for Monday afternoon at two o'clock in Sturgis's office at the lab.

The Watkins Research Laboratory, a series of whitewashed complexes on the high craggy bluffs overlooking the Pacific, was located some ten miles north of San Diego. Nick got there early. He walked around. The place was more like an ultramodern campus—sterile, manicured lawns; quiet, not a sign of life.

Sturgis's office was straight out of *Interior Design*. Sturgis—unlike so many other people—actually fitted his voice: boyish, enthusiastic, open. Grinning, he shook Nick's hand, closed the door of his office. He was blond, stolid. He looked more like an actor, an impostor, too healthy, too young to be such a well-known scientist. He looked too perfect, as if he'd been chosen for the part. He was wearing a white coat over his clothes. "This isn't where I do my real work," he said. "My lab's in there."

He pointed to a door. "But I come in here for the view."
He laughed.

"It is quite a view." Nick stared at the wall-length
window tableau of the Pacific. Both men stood admiring
the view.

"So you worked with Macdavitt? Tragedy—a terrible
loss. Physicist?"

"No, I'm a sociologist."

Sturgis made a face. "A sociologist? Aren't you kind of
off base?" Sturgis motioned to one of the Marcel Breuer
chairs. Nick sat down. Sturgis remained standing and
leaned back against his long chrome-and-glass desk. "Now,
what can I do for you?"

"Project Ozymandias." Nick felt foolish, self-conscious,
as if he were reading someone else's stilted lines; that was
it: He felt he was playing a part in some unbelievably
convoluted cliché-ridden story; so it didn't really matter,
he would just have to go on with it.

Sturgis looked at him as if he wasn't sure how to
interpret this. Then he smiled, his perfect set of teeth
flashing in his square jaw, and he started to laugh softly
to himself. He turned sideways, took out a cigarette from
the pack of Winstons on his desk, offered Nick one.
Nick shook his head. Sturgis tapped the cigarette down on
the desk, struck a match, inhaled. "Project Ozymandias?"
He was still grinning. "Ozymandias? Well, I know about
Project Ozma. That was closed a long time ago—1961.
There's even a Project Ozma II, started by a couple of
Harvard guys, really bright. They're more or less picking
up where Project Ozma left off. It's in Virginia, isn't it?
Charlottesville? It was started in 1971. Maybe you should
talk to them."

"You know as well as I do they don't know anything."

"Well, I heard they've picked up some signals on their
radio telescope."

"You know I'm talking about a lot more than that.
After Project Ozma was closed," Nick went on, "a number
of scientists, including Macdavitt, continued the work
they had been doing on project Ozma—focusing on Tau
Ceti, and other stars, in secret. This secret continuation
of Project Ozma was Project Ozymandias."

"Wasn't Project Ozma pretty much dismissed?" Sturgis

asked in mock bewilderment. "That whole business with the space signals from Tau Ceti—that was actually nothing more than some interference from a top-secret military base. It was pretty conclusive."

"Was it? Macdavitt didn't think so."

Sturgis shrugged, and the expression on his face seemed to say, What can you do? Some people . . . "I think I heard that . . . I think I heard something about that. George was what you would call an iconoclast, you know, he always went his own way and was always convinced he was right. Which is a good thing. Gives you the ability to trust yourself, your own instincts. But it depends who you rub the wrong way. George had a knack for doing just that . . . that's why he got into so much trouble."

"But a lot of his theories were proven to be right."

"Where they? Who's to say? Theories are theories. Because one's been validated today doesn't mean anything. One learns to cast a dubious eye, believe me."

"What about the signals that were decoded last year on Project Epsilon?"

"Oh, that! You mean, again from outer space." Sturgis nodded skeptically. "Yeah, that's what happens to rumors. They spread."

"You were on Project Blue Book in 1969, the year it closed, weren't you? When the Air Force announced that there was no evidence that any of the other twelve thousand cases of UFO sightings in their files were extraterrestrial?"

"I thought you came here to talk to me about that book on Macdavitt?" Sturgis grinned, throwing the ball back.

"What about the UFO files that were never revealed? What about the signed testimonies from the top names in the Air Force, the government, the Pentagon? The close-up shots taken by Sky Lab II, by the Apollo crews, Gemini—"

"I'm afraid I'm not following you. I think I lost you somewhere."

"General Latimer, Commander Francis, Commander Smith Beauford III, Vice Admiral Stevenson, General Fletcher."

"That sounds like a roster of national heroes."

"What about the file Index 3-5-9 of the photographs, the

films, the radio transmissions of UFOs . . . the hundreds of files that were not even available to the top-secret category? All the files of UFOs in Project Blue Book and Project Capella and Project Cetus, Project Crescent and all the other secret government projects—all the files that mysteriously disappeared?"

Sturgis blinked, squinted, and studied his cigarette a moment. Then he nodded. "You may have some valid points. Who's to deny that? But I'm afraid I just can't . . ." He put out his cigarette in the large crystal ashtray on his desk.

"What about Ceres?"

Sturgis looked up, his face blank, then he smiled again, continued stamping out his cigarette, which was already out. "You know, this is all pretty much common knowledge, I'm afraid. You're simply talking about secret government projects. But anyone with any access—"

"No, you see, I have some of Macdavitt's papers."

"Didn't he give them over? Wasn't he forced—"

"No, there were some he held back . . . held out on."

"I don't see the connection."

"Macdavitt had proof. He knew who was behind all this—who was keeping it from the public. He was about to throw it open. That's why he was killed."

"Killed? Oh, c'mon." Sturgis threw back his head, laughing. "You're letting your imagination get the best of you."

"I saw his body. The autopsy report was falsified."

Sturgis laughed uncomfortably, uncertainly. "But the newspapers said—"

"I'm telling you. He didn't kill himself. I was there when his body was dragged out."

"Look, Macdavitt's death was horrible, a tragedy. But to try to imply that the CIA, or whoever you're trying to suggest, is behind this is something else. Look, I've worked with them. They were on Project Blue Book, they followed us all around. Sure. But it was a game. We knew they knew we knew that they—you know. Who takes it seriously? In these kinds of cases they wouldn't know their ass from their elbow, so I can tell you right off, just forget it. They're about as capable of killing off someone—one of this country's top scientists, a Nobel-prize candidate— as you or me. I'm making certain assumptions about you."

Sturgis grinned. "Besides, this isn't even in their domain."

"I don't know who's behind this. I didn't say it was only the CIA. That's why I want you to help me. I'm not at all sure who it is."

"But you're going to find out, right? And what do you want me to do? Why are you telling me? After all, I might squeal on you. What makes you so sure I won't squeal on you?"

"I don't think so. After all, you're here. You're not at NASA anymore."

"It could be my cover."

"No." Nick shook his head. "Besides, you're curious."

"Curious. So you think I'm going to help you because I'm curious?"

"You want to know what happened on Project Epsilon last year, don't you? And those landings in New Mexico, Arizona, the cases that were just suddenly dropped in the middle. And the signals in Australia last winter and Newfoundland in May and the Mojave last month."

Sturgis frowned, nodded several times, and gave out a long sigh. He went over to the window, his back to Nick; he stood that way several minutes—a figure in a long white coat standing like a cutout against the distilled wash of sunlight: the sky, the ocean, the bluffs; only a faint outline of barely visible lines, a sort of pale X ray of the scenery, was left.

Sturgis turned around again. Nick could not quite make out the expression, if any, on his face in the strong light. Sturgis nodded, or at least he seemed to—of course it might have just been a movement of the head, an almost involuntary gesture to detract from his voice, to confirm what the tone of his voice might otherwise leave in doubt. "OK," he said. It sounded more like a question. "OK." Sturgis leaned across his desk. He started to dial a number. "Can you stay over for dinner?" he asked Nick.

Nick nodded.

Sturgis spoke to what sounded like a secretary. Then: "Hi, Lloyd? Tom. Listen, how about coming over to the house tonight? Yeah. About six. I've got someone I want you to talk to. Yeah. OK. Fine." Sturgis dialed another number. Another secretary. Then: "Jim. Tom. There's someone here who wants to meet you. No"—Sturgis laughed unconvincingly—"no, it's not another relative of a relative who wants your autograph. You're really living off ancient history. Can we drop by your office for a few minutes?"

Sturgis led Nick down several halls. The place was more like a hospital: white, off-white, cork ceilings, subdued, quiet, a tepid hum of machines in the background. Sturgis showed Nick into several laboratories. "This is where the X5II was built. This is just its prototype here, but it'll be going to the Smithsonian soon. Next month, isn't it, Nancy? Dr. Mayer, Dr. Schrader."

The tanned young woman in the white coat holding a tray crammed with containers of different tints, maybe in her mid-twenties, at most, put out her hand to shake Nick's hand. "Yes. Right after Labor Day. Are you a physicist, too?"

"No. Not quite."

"He's a sociologist."

"Oh, are you doing a study of life in the laboratory?"

"You could say that. In a way, yes, that's true. Human life being a huge laboratory, or not so huge, depending on which angle you're looking at it from."

"How is it going?" Sturgis indicated the tray. "They're compounds for cryogenic tests," he explained.

"It isn't. Someone forgot to take this batch out last night. So it looks like we're going to have to start all over again."

"See, we've got our problems, too," Sturgis said. "Dr. Schrader's with the Foundation for Contemporary Sciences in Sonora Pines."

They went into another laboratory, a large dome-shaped room that resembled an operating room. Several people in white coats were studying a number of moving mechanical parts. "You can't imagine the number of times these are tested, pretested, retested before we even start to really test them, check them out. This is—everything you see here," Sturgis added, "is vibration and environment test equipment, production, processing—the FLIR module fabrication and the TOW detector."

They went into a lobby filled with display cases. "This is our museum. It's open to the public—that is, special visitors. My kids actually quiet down here. These are duplicates of the Canopus sensor, which provided mid-course guidance for the seven Surveyor spacecraft moon landings." They moved over to another display case. "These are identical instruments to those flown to Mars, Venus, Mercury, and Jupiter, sending back information from six hundred twenty million miles. And this is a photopolarimeter that sent back key color photos of Jupiter."

"And these radiometers over here measured the thermal balance of Jupiter and the polar ice cap on Mars," Nick said.

"Well, you must have been reading up."

"I have," Nick said. "Is it always this quiet? Everybody stays in his own office or laboratory, huh?"

"It's a nice place to work, nobody ever bothers you. Well, you should know, it's like the Foundation in that respect."

"How long have you been here?"

"Since I left NASA. Over three years ago. And Jim, of course, has been here more or less since the beginning. It'll be five years in October. And here we are."

There was a young, decorous secretary—the prerequisite California type—in the outside office. They went in. Jim Ingels was shorter than he appeared to be on TV or in photos, much less prepossessing, a sort of casual lean slouch of muscles honed down to the bones, almost frail. The reality in contrast to the deceptive image the media had created. Sturgis introduced them. Jim Ingels gripped Nick's hand. There were photographs of Ingels all around, on the desk, on the walls: Ingels on the moon, with the other astronauts, with several Presidents. "Nick here came to talk to me about George Macdavitt."

"Tragic. Just tragic."

"He's with the Foundation for Contemporary Sciences. It seems George left some papers dealing with some of the lesser-known government projects, the less publicized aspects of Blue Book, Capella, Epsilon, the others. Nick's had access to these papers, dealing with, among other things, from what I can gather, the space signals. It seems that George left a number of—what should I say?—theoretical proofs?"

"That's what you think." Jim Ingels made a sound that was not completely a laugh. "It's happened too many times to fall into the category of theory, or the imaginary, or visual hallucination, or mistakes, coincidences. Believe me, I've been up there too many times." He pointed to the ceiling. "I should know. I've taken too many photographs." The intercom buzzed. "Excuse me." Ingels had an exchange with his secretary. He picked up his phone. "Yes, I'm still holding on . . . I'm waiting."

"Well, we won't keep you any longer. I wanted to ask you over to the house tonight for dinner. Nick's coming over. And Lloyd'll be there, too."

Ingels nodded. He put his hand over the mouthpiece. "When do you want me to come over? It's the chairman of the Aeronautics . . . Oh, hello. Yes! Fine, fine, yes . . ."

"Six," Sturgis said.

Ingels nodded, made an OK with his thumb and forefinger. "No, we won't be able to. No way, it's impossible. The board would never put up with it. It just wouldn't fit our image. No . . . Yes, I did speak to them about it. . . . I don't care what you tell him. It's not my problem."

Sturgis gave Nick the directions for getting to his house. He apologized, he had to get back to work. Nick got onto the freeway and went into San Diego. He drove around awhile, parked outside the marina, and walked around. To keep himself distracted, he read off the names of the boats, watched the girls, out of habit more than anything else.

He got back onto the freeway. Sturgis's street was easy to find. He circled around a couple of times and then finally just parked and sat in the car—the only occupied parked car in this deserted upper-middle-class suburban compound. Several people passed him in their cars and stared at him oddly. A police car slowed down, then went on. Five-thirty. He felt like walking, wanted to get out of the car. He was beginning to feel stiff, cramped. But he thought if he did walk around, and the police car passed him again, he might be stopped, might be brought to the police station for questioning. It happened sometimes: He had read of such instances in the Sonora Pines paper. Another cliché of the California life-style that was only too true.

The Sturgis house was immediately identifiable—a modern wood structure with lots of glass, it stood out from the other pseudo-Tudor stone-manor suburban houses. It belonged more to the East and looked out of place here with the palms on the sidewalk and the orange and lemon trees bordering the front lawn. Nick rang. Chimes. A baby was crying. A deeply tanned young woman in a very short white tennis dress opened the front door. "You must be Nick Schrader. I'm Tina Sturgis. Come on in. They're in the back. Just go on straight through. I'm going to go up and see what's wrong with her." She pointed upstairs, where the sound of the baby was coming from. "I'll be right down."

Nick went through the ultramodern interior: It might as well have been an extension of Sturgis's office—no walls, the living room merged into the dining room into the kitchen, where all the equipment was recessed, into a screened-in porch of sorts. A lightweight tennis racket in its press was on one of the deck chairs. Nick went out into the garden—enclosed by trees, it appeared to be much larger than it really was. Tom Sturgis, in jeans and a T-shirt, was dousing the charcoals. He cocked his head, acknowledging Nick's presence. "Jim's up there somewhere." He pointed to a tree. There was screeching, children laughing. Jim jumped down, a gymnastic display, followed by two small boys, about four and five, who skidded down, lost their balance, gave out a series of shrieks of combined exhilaration and fright, tumbled down onto the grass, and sprang straight back to their feet. "Tommy and Douglas. This is Dr. Schrader. Say hello."

An inarticulate grumbling; they both scampered away, disappearing behind some bushes. Jim studied the tree. "You really should get some ropes. One of these days one of those kids is really going to hurt himself."

"Naw. Those kids?" Tom grinned. "They're indestructible."

Tina Sturgis came back out carrying a small baby in Doctor Denton pajamas. She bounced the baby up and down. The baby had stopped crying and was gurgling now.

"Why we had her, God knows." Tom put his face down against the baby's stomach. He made some cooing sounds; the baby laughed. "Just as we were getting readjusted to life."

"We? Ha! Who gets up at night? Every night? I'd forgotten the crying."

"She was an accident." Tom winked.

"Some accident." Tina jostled him in the ribs with her free hand.

Jim went in to fix some drinks. Tom blew on the coals. The boys came out of hiding, tried to coax their father into a game of catch. Tina gathered them together, excused herself. She had a class at seven. Tom explained that she'd gone back to school. She was working for her M.A. in Early Baroque music. Jim came out with the drinks on a tray, on which were also some mustard, ketchup, a plate of sliced onion, relish. Nick had a gin and tonic; Tom, a Dos Equis beer; Jim, a Coors. Sitting there in the garden, stretched out in a deck chair, Jim looked like an advertisement for himself: the ex-astronaut as a regular, all-around American beer drinker. They talked about Watergate.

Tina ran out to say good-bye. She had changed to jeans, a work shirt, and was carrying a load of books. She could have been any typical college student. Tom walked out with her to her car. Nick and Jim talked about the California coast. Jim said it had changed so much in the last ten years it was unrecognizable. He came from California. He'd been born here. He was a conservationist. They had a number of different groups around the state; of course he didn't have much time. He was kept pretty busy at the lab. Still, he was thinking of running for office. A lot of people wanted him to.

Tom came back out at that moment with a wiry middle-aged man in tan chinos, loafers, a button-down shirt. Lloyd Parker. He had also been at NASA. He had a rum and Coke. He now taught nuclear engineering at UC in San Diego. Jim went in to get another Coors.

Lloyd didn't seem very talkative.

Tom served the hamburgers and buns on paper plates. As they sat there in the garden, Nick kept thinking it could have been any suburban garden in the summer dusk. A man drinking Coors, another not talking, one chain-smoking, the fourth waiting.

Tom lit another cigarette, finally explained to Lloyd who Nick was, what he wanted, and that he had access to some of George Macdavitt's papers. Lloyd nodded. He didn't seem particularly interested. The problems of foundations were discussed, the adverse economy, the increasingly reluctant contributors. The thin line a foundation such as the

Foundation for Contemporary Sciences had to tread in a reactionary community such as Sonora Pines. "The last bastion of the Birchites," Lloyd commented. He had not spoken until then.

"But you're in the heart of Orange County here," Nick said. "All the Nixon men who made their way up the government ladder via Walt Disney—you know, when they were at J. Walter Thompson most of them were on the Disney account. Fantasy land maybe, or was it future land? Disney people running the country."

Tom laughed softly. "Don't joke. It's not funny. Jim was offered a big job there a couple of years ago."

"The Blue Bonnet account or something. I thought it over. I just didn't think it was suitable to my image. As an astronaut who had walked on the moon. No, somehow . . . I formed POLO—Preserve Our Lands and Oceans—instead."

"As you probably might have already guessed, I didn't ask you both over here this evening to"—Tom paused— "discuss the state of the country, the economy, or the problems faced by foundations or laboratories in regard to financial support in the community, or Orange County or ecology . . ."

"Or Disneyland," Jim added.

"No, nor Disneyland," Tom echoed in a flat voice, as if to say, You're guessing right.

"I think I got the message." Lloyd was getting irritated.

"OK," Tom said. "I'll get straight to the point. Nick wants to make the whole UFO cover-up public. He wants to reveal to the public what was really going on—what *is* really going on. He has a number of George Macdavitt's papers. He has a lot of names. Generals Palmer and Fletcher, Commander Beauford, Vice Admiral Stevenson. Macdavitt had collected signed testimonies from a number of people in the Air Force, NASA, the government. Nick thinks he can get it through to the public. If he can get enough of these people to back him up. He wants us to help him."

"Why should we help him?" Lloyd asked, addressing Nick in the third person. "Why should we believe him? Besides, what does he think we know? Maybe he's some sort of plant. Why should we trust him?"

"Because you three worked with Macdavitt," Nick said, "because Macdavitt had signed testimonies from all three of you when you were with NASA, and on Capella, and Cetus, and the other secret government projects. And Ozymandias. Testimony regarding top-secret information you had access to."

"Ozymandias, Capella, the so-called secret projects. Hundreds of people in the government knew about them." Lloyd shrugged. "Just scratch the surface a bit, ask around, get a couple of leaks. Get wind of some secret files and you can concoct anything."

"Macdavitt had testimony on Ozymandias last year—the signals detected on November second, to be exact."

"Who is this guy?" Lloyd asked.

"Macdavitt left some papers that the government didn't even know about, that no one knew about. He had hundreds of names."

"OK. Give me some names," Lloyd said.

"Emerson, Fulton, Goodal," Nick recited, "Senator Irving. Senator Garlock, Senator Blaser, Senators Williams, Sperry, Lasseter . . . General Martin, General Kinnan, Commander Richard Garrison, Hendricks, Porter, Moore, Zimmer, Hillborough, Whitford, Goldberg, Kaleuwesky, and Smith of NASA."

"Can I speak to you alone a moment?" Lloyd asked Tom. They went inside the house.

"He had some troubles with the government a while back," Jim explained. "You know, words like 'self-interest,' 'personal gain,' 'detrimental to NASA,' 'not in keeping with its image.' It left its marks, but don't take it seriously."

"He seems almost hostile."

"Nah. Don't pay any attention. He's just sort of an intellectual. Don't forget he's a theoretician, known for his cool. He got us out of a lot of tight spots, both in practice and for real. A couple of times right on TV, with all those cameras on, on the Apollo flights."

The two men came back.

"I just wanted it cleared up why Tom was suddenly getting himself reinvolved in all this. He told me about Macdavitt—he was murdered. And it was covered up as suicide. I gather he already told you."

Jim nodded. "This afternoon."

"Give me some more names."

"Commander Jackson, Vice Admiral Porterfield, Larsborough, Commander Johnson, Sarguis."

"Give me a couple of cases and their proofs—why they were kept top secret. In other words, why they were suspicious."

"Reade, in Oklahoma, 1973. Oxidation traces. Baxter in Arizona, also '73. Propellant residue in some burned bushes . . . nor could the distance between pod marks be explained. In the Mojave last month, soil tests could not be explained . . . in New Mexico this last spring, samples of sap proved conclusively that the vehicle marks were not from a lunar test module, as had originally been thought. There was no explanation other than—"

"OK. OK. OK. Now, these are from the National Security files, you understand, which are not accessible even to those cleared for top-secret information—from the 1948 top-secret conclusion. Macdavitt knew the names, the cases, what was involved—the lab reports, the details . . . a few of us in NASA—the three of us here, a few others—some top government scientists, some people in the Pentagon, the Air Force . . . a handful of people in the whole country. OK. Now, we're going to try to help you. We'll try to put you in touch with whoever you want to get in touch with—within reason. But we can't have any association with you, it can't even be known that we've even heard of you, until the actual public broadcast. When we go before the public. And we don't know when that will be. How long it will take. When we have enough support and backing. But until then, any kind of leak, and"—Lloyd made a noncommittal gesture—"just as they say in the movies, you'll have to forget us. You don't know us, we don't know you. OK?"

"I think it's best if he has his contact through Tom," Jim said. "After all, Tom's been the least involved in this whole thing. Well, he's the youngest, so it stands to reason he has the shortest record. His file must be pretty skimpy, a pretty routine dossier. After all, he's never been cross-examined, never been before any of the subcommittees or at congressional hearings, never been called to appear at any of the private hearings, and the media certainly never really got wind of him."

"And he doesn't have a political future to protect," Lloyd added.

"So I'm the scapegoat."

"If anything goes wrong, we don't know him, so what can possibly happen?" Jim said.

"I want to be able to talk to some of the people who've had encounters, that is, certified government people, in the Air Force, the Army. People from the top-secret files who've actually seen UFOs that could not be dismissed as anything else," Nick said.

"Well, you don't have to go too far. For a start, right here," Jim said.

"There's always the question of doubt, illusion," Lloyd said. "It's a very illusory thing by its very nature. An optical illusion or an illusory phenomenon. You can puncture anyone's statement full of holes.

"Try to convince someone you've sighted an extremely rare or even an unnamed species of bird. Imagine trying to prove to someone that you went for a walk in the woods or the mountains and you sighted a California condor," Jim said.

"There's ample room for mistakes." Lloyd nodded. "The sightings of pilots were all mostly on routine flights—always circumstantial evidence—fatigue, distraction, boredom, and so on. And the same applies to observatories."

"Just look up there." Tom pointed to the empty expanse of deepening blue sky. The evening star seemed to flicker on and off. "Nothing. But you stare long enough . . . and who knows what you can convince yourself of . . . and who knows if you're right? And does it really matter? Now, for instance, I know in the northeast there's a weather satellite. It's scheduled to appear at nine-thirty-two to nine-thirty-seven. Now, what if it appears before that or after? Who's to say whether it's the same satellite or not? Or if it isn't something altogether different?"

Jim went in to get another Coors.

" 'No noise, no turbulence. It passed us on the left side,' " Nick recited. " 'Its speed was about twelve hundred miles an hour. It was about a thousand feet long, shaped like a cigar . . . two rows of windows, an upper and lower, that were large and square . . . from inside a very bright light glowing . . . the underside of the ship had a blue glow like a fluorescent light. And as it passed us, it pulled up and into some broken clouds—and was lost from view.' "

"Farley and Howell, 1952," Lloyd said. "They were both pilots, captain and first officer with Eastern Airlines."

"What about the abnormal radiation recorded by those two Air Force pilots in 1964? Kirkland and Macdonald. They made extensive Geiger-counter readings in the desert —in Arizona," Jim said, overhearing, returning with his can of Coors. "They found all sorts of 'hot'—radioactive— areas all over the northern part of the state. Hadn't they been with Eastern, too? Weren't they the ones who testified before the subcommittee about the numerous sightings they'd witnessed on commercial flights, something like twenty, twenty-two different times? On occasion, too—on these commercial flights—had nearly collided? Didn't they get into a whole thing with Eastern about it? First they were backed, then they weren't."

"Among hundreds of other such cases," Nick said. He went on: " 'It was a clear moonlit night, visibility was excellent. . . . This strange object had a stream of red fire coming from its tail and I could see it was much larger than anything I had seen or read about.' "

"Porter, 1953," Lloyd said.

" 'No wings visible,' " Nick continued, " 'black fuselage, blue glow under fuselage, red flame trailing about thirty to fifty feet. Estimated one hundred feet in length . . . radar confirmation . . . the reply was that that particular quadrant of the sky was blanked out on the radar at that time.' Barrett, 1954. Among hundreds of other cases reported by pilots with commercial lines. Farley and Howell, Porter, Barrett. They all disappeared. Among dozens of other. They were too vocal—too convinced, too convincing; had the scientific backgrounds. They all had accidents of one kind or another. Macdavitt also had that on paper, testimony from witnesses, other people involved . . . proof of falsified autopsies. The expected cover-ups—there were car accidents, heart attacks, drownings, fires, plane crashes, suicides."

"And who are you trying to suggest is behind this?" Lloyd asked. "Because I can tell you who it isn't. It sure in hell's name isn't the CIA."

"I didn't say it was, did I?" Nick said.

"Well, because it just isn't. Take my word for it. We've been through this before," Lloyd said. "Everybody's trying to pin something on them. It's open season, and they're an easy target. But it's not them—not the way they do things."

"Too scrupulous, huh?" Nick asked.

"And so the mystery remains a mystery," Tom said.

"Not so mysterious," Lloyd said. "What's so mysterious? Macdavitt may have been killed, but that certainly doesn't mean all those other people were. I just don't buy it. To pick a few cases, cite a few examples of coincidences. A few people died. It happens. Even to the best of us, you know. And besides, all these people died more or less of natural causes, illnesses, car crashes, plane crashes.

"Macdavitt. That was something else. There are people who would want him out of the way. I can buy that. He was getting too vocal, that's all. And he was warned— repeatedly. I know that for a fact. But on this scale. All these other people. No. But Macdavitt got it into his head that these were not accidents.

"Well, Macdavitt was always a little bit, you know. And it got worse over the years. Well, I could tell you some stories. I won't—don't worry. He was a great man, a truly great mind. One of the greatest scientists of our age. In his field, in physics, in nuclear science. But when it came to this thing, well, the man was obsessed, deranged. I'm sure Dr. Osmond can confirm that to you. A lot of people can tell you. But you know it was hushed up, kept quiet because of who he was. 'One of the founders of the Nuclear Age.' As I said, he was warned over the years, repeatedly told . . . but no, he wouldn't listen, never listened to anybody.

"He came to see me early this year—wanted me to go to Washington with him to talk to some people about these imaginary files of missing people, these accidents, coincidences he had assembled. What's up there is one thing." Lloyd pointed to the sky. "I'll listen to that. But to start concocting these preposterous things about missing people. Well, I won't even listen to that. So you can count me out on that one. I don't want any part of that angle. Isn't it bad enough that Macdavitt was killed? Isn't that enough?

And you don't even know who killed him. You don't have the proof."

"When did Macdavitt come to see you?" Nick asked.

"Last winter. January. He came to see me at the university. I told him to lay off—he was going to get into trouble. Not that I believed a word he said about his latest findings, his latest discovery—of perpetrated cover-ups. But I thought if I acted as if I did and told him he should really lay off because it was going to get him in a lot of trouble—making accusations like that—and that he better have enough facts and enough people to back him up if he was going to go press charges like that—Well, I thought he just might lay off, might just stop the whole thing. I should have known better. With someone like Macdavitt, it would only have the opposite effect. I told him he'd never be able to prove anything, it would never stick. And even if it did . . . what difference did it make?" Lloyd's voice trailed off.

"Between this and all the assassination-conspiracy theories—Oswald, Sirhan, Bremer, Ray—what kind of world are you trying to suggest we live in?" Jim asked.

"Global smoke screen," Tom said. "Of course this is not quite the same thing."

"The ultimate mystery," Nick said.

"Well, you know, Jim, you yourself took those photos on the moon flight," Tom reminded him.

"That's true," Jim admitted.

"Still, it sounds pretty farfetched to me. More like fiction. Pulp, if you ask me," Lloyd said.

The four men remained silent for a few minutes. It was almost dark now, almost night.

"I have some shots I took while in space," Jim said. "Not the official NASA ones. We'll arrange to show them to you."

"In most of the official ones, the UFOs were identified as either solar-axis reflections, Agena ranging lights prior to docking, or, better yet, trash floating out of the spaceship," Tom said.

"Or they were unidentifiable," Jim added. "Misidentification of stars or some other natural phenomenon or a result of weather inversions. There are explanations for everything."

"Except this," Lloyd said.

Tom walked Nick out to his car. "What about Lloyd?" Nick asked. "I can't figure him out."

"Oh, don't worry about him. He's all right. He's just wary."

Nick got into his car. "I'll phone you sometime tomorrow afternoon."

"That should give me enough time." Tom held on to the open door. "There are a number of people I'm going to try to get hold of . . . Philip Wells. I really want you to meet Philip Wells, but I'm not even sure if he's back in the country yet. He's always on a dig somewhere."

"He's in Yucatán," Nick said.

"How did you know?" Tom was taken aback for a moment. "Yes, of course, he was working with Macdavitt up until a few months ago. Well, I'll try both his home and his office. He should be coming back soon, if he isn't already. You know, he was one of the last people to work with Macdavitt. They were on a dig somewhere in Yucatán this last winter and then out in the desert in Arizona and New Mexico this spring. Wells is really onto something. But he won't let on what. He dropped by the lab just before he left with Macdavitt in May. He said he couldn't go into it. But it would be quite a find. He thought they were really onto it, almost had it. Haven't heard anything since then, though. I'll try him tomorrow."

Nick started the car.

Tom stood on the curb at the foot of his lawn on this dark residential street. He waited a few minutes before going back in.

"Is that the baby? Shh. No. listen." Tina Sturgis laughed softly, pretending to be surprised, though she wasn't. "Tom! What are you . . ." Tom opened the drawer of her night table. "Honestly, the things you make me do. Where do you get the energy? I thought you were so tired."

"You better get me while you can, you better take advantage of me while you have the chance."

"Ha! As if that were the problem."

Afterward, he pulled the covers back over them. They lay there silently together, side by side. "Hmm." Tom touched the nape of her neck, still damp. "You know, that's what I dream of. All day, sitting in my office or when I'm right in the middle of something in the lab or in the middle of some profound discussion—a whole day in bed with you. At this point I'd settle for an afternoon, an hour."

"The boys would race in. I can just see it. Traumatized for life . . . They didn't bother you this evening, did they?"

"No, I think they were worn out. Jim had them climbing —racing each other up and down that tree I don't know how many times in the space of fifteen minutes."

"Nick Schrader," Tina said. "Is he going to join the lab?"

"Oh, God, no. Let's hope not, at least. We've got enough problems. No, nothing like that. Besides, he's a sociologist. He's with the Foundation for Contemporary Sciences in Sonora Pines. They're putting together some sort of book on George Macdavitt. And he wants me to write something. And Jim and Lloyd also, of course."

"But you hardly knew him."

"Well, I was at NASA and on the Air Force projects the same time he was."

"That mess." Tina turned on her side, resting on her elbow. She kept staring at Tom's face, even though it was too dark—the only light in the room was from the open curtains—to really see anything. "What does he want you to do—write something about that?"

"More than that. It seems Macdavitt left some papers, citing names. Top people in the government who would corroborate the whole cover-up."

"You're not going to get involved in all that again, are you? Oh, God. You're not going to get involved in all that again. Are you really? Tom? Don't you remember? Those people were hounding us. I couldn't go out the front door to get the mail or the paper without one of them jumping out of his car across the street. Don't you remember? We were under constant surveillance. You're not really going to start it again?"

Tom turned his head toward her. "George Macdavitt was murdered."

Tina didn't respond immediately. She sat up. "I don't want to seem callous. But that has nothing to do with us. We can't do anything about it. I thought you'd already proved that to yourself. Well, Lloyd can't have approved.

And Jim. What about Jim? He couldn't possibly . . . He can't afford any kind of . . ."

"They're both going to help."

"But you're going against the government. It's insane . . . insane. You have no proof. What proof—"

"Schrader has proof."

"And so what? Who's going to believe you? Why can't you just let it drop, Tom?"

"I can't." Tom kept shaking his head. "I thought I could. I almost did. But I don't know. Something . . . It was like I was just pulled right back into it."

"Oh, Tom," was all Tina said. She waited a moment again. "Things are so quiet, so peaceful. I thought you were happy. I thought you liked your work at the lab . . . this house. The whole way of life out here."

"I do." Tom sighed; he rubbed his lip as if he were feeling for a cut. "Believe me, I do. You know I do." He sighed again. "I don't want to drag you into this . . . I promise you I'll get out of it . . . if it gets too . . . I promise you this time." He pulled himself up, put his arms around her. "I just want to hold you. Sitting out there tonight in the dark, under the stars . . . I don't know, suddenly I was terrified. There wasn't any reason . . . maybe I was cold or something. But suddenly I got the chills. I guess it just hit me, what I was getting into. It was like standing at the edge of this abyss—this endless night, nothing but darkness, and these points of flashing lights, these dim messages, signals coming from what extinct worlds or machines . . ."

Nick took the coastal route back. At that time of night there wasn't much traffic. The expanse of freeway stretched out in front of him like a runway. It was more like piloting a plane. It was a perpetual takeoff. He felt as if he could keep driving forever. Even his tiredness was put in suspension; and that sort of automated feeling of distance, as if he had absented himself from his body, took hold of him— yet he felt in total contact. That sort of effortless glide of communion with the road, the invisible dark coast, with the imaginary ocean on one side and the imaginary mountains on the other, and the night on all sides. He felt as if he could just keep driving forever.

Michelle was already in bed, asleep. At least he thought

she was. He tried not to make any noise. He slipped into bed; she groped toward him, warm, groggy for a moment. And then she smiled, completely awake. She drew him down against her. "How was he?" He had told her he was going to hear Ornstein speak at UCLA. "Oh, you know, the same old stuff, same old rehash."

"How was the drive back? Did you get caught in any traffic?"

"Oh, no, fine, no cars. It was like gliding."

She increased the pressure of her hold. She didn't say anything else. She smiled again, widely—and that smile hurt him, because it seemed so open, so trusting, and he, after all, was deceiving her. He wanted to say something. But what? What could he really say? Instead he buried himself in the warm particular smell of her sleepy body.

Report by Agent R. Castle to Security 5A200 Washington. 27 August.

Note: Schrader has no sessions this week with Richardson.

Richardson on vacation with his family on Vancouver Island in British Columbia. Surveillance of Richardson will be maintained.

The next morning, after more than an hour of staring at the alienation transcripts, Nick gave up, got into his car, pulled out of the Foundation driveway, drove down the length of Westview, and headed toward the water. He was at the intersection of San Luis and Monterey when he saw Michelle's car ahead of him. He followed her. Down Tierra del Sol, past Edgewood, down Palm Drive into Verdugo, to the Alhambra Shopping Center. He stopped. She parked, got out of her car, and walked straight across the shopping center, past the drugstore, the Laundromat, Thrifty's, the health-food takeout, the post office. She was walking along nonchalantly, swinging her knit shoulder bag. But he didn't wait to see where she was going. He didn't want to know. He felt like a fool, not trusting her, acting like this, spying on her. It was ridiculous. He drove on, out of the shopping center, back to the Foundation. He'd forgotten all about going down to the water. He didn't remember until he'd pulled into the Foundation parking lot why he'd gone out in the first place.

He left early, a couple of hours later, wanting to surprise Michelle. He thought they could go out for a walk on the beach or to his place for a swim or something—the kids were with Tony. He let himself in. He heard Michelle on the phone in the kitchen. She had her bikini on. She swung around, startled. Then, slowly, she smiled. "I'll speak to you later," she said, and hung up.

"Who was that?"

"Tony." She smiled again and made a vague gesture with her hand. "You know—the kids and all that. Just because he has them for a few days . . . But I sure in hell's name don't have to put up with his flak." She beamed, her eyes resting on the marigolds. Nick handed them over. "I thought we could go for a walk or something." She continued smiling, putting the flowers in water, totally absorbed in arranging them. "Fine, just let me change." She went into the bedroom, closed the door—which he thought was strange. He went out onto the sun deck to bring in the cassette recorder. She must have been lying there in the sun: her pack of Marlboros, a full ashtray, Castaneda's *A Separate Reality*. He thought he heard her on the phone again, but he decided he must be imagining that. Besides, the birds were too noisy for him to really hear anything.

Unedited transcript of meeting with Kip Galveston; Dr. Richard Prebble, flight director at NASA; Sturgis and Schrader. 29 August.

PREBBLE: I agree with Tom, Kip, you're being too suspicious. He probably lost his way . . . these halls. I almost did myself. Well, you know you wouldn't be here, Kip, if you weren't intrigued, credulous. You're not that suspicious as to not have an open mind. After all, where else could he get such information? I mean, the combination of things is too much. He couldn't possibly be with the CIA or, for that matter, any branch of theirs. They wouldn't have access to those names—not that kind of cross-reference— not the combination.

GALVESTON: I know. That's what gets to me, darn it. I just don't know how he got those names. How did he get General Kinnan's and Commnader Sargüis's names? Epsilon in '71? Nobody knows about that. And Zimmer, Whitford, Moore, Garlock. Nobody knows about them. No. Only Macdavitt could have had access to those names.

SECRETARY [*on intercom*]: Dr. Sturgis, Dr. Schrader is here.

STURGIS: Send him in. . . . Hello, Nick. We were beginning to wonder—

SCHRADER: I got off at the wrong exit.

GALVESTON: Well, I wouldn't worry about that. That's a sign you're a real Californian! Take the wrong exit and sometimes you can't get back on for miles. It happened to me once. Had to go around and around. Forty-three miles. Yes, sir, that can be a dangerous thing out here, in the West. The same thing in Texas. You can go for miles and miles without seeing a soul . . . that's untouched land for you. In the high chaparrals. Of course there's a price: You can get lost.

SCHRADER: Well . . . yes.

STURGIS: I guess I don't have to introduce Kip Galveston to you.

GALVESTON: Howdy, Nick, pleased to meet you. How are you?

STURGIS: Dr. Richard Prebble, Dr. Nick Schrader. Richard is still with NASA, as you know. Well, we might as well all sit down.

GALVESTON: This view here, Tom, just gets to me. You don't see anything else like it. The rest of the coast around here is just a high rise in comparison. Hmm. Yes, sir. That's good zoning for you. God darn it, it is just a dream!

STURGIS: Well, Kip, you're not exactly a tourist around here.

GALVESTON: Oh, no. I was almost brought up around these parts, well, farther inland. My old man was and is— as much as he's able to be—a rancher. He used to come for the horse shows, the rodeos around here, Arizona, parts of California. And me and my brother, John, used to ride for him. Well, you know, it's good for the biography. But you're right. I'm not exactly retired. You know I was out at Point Mugu a couple of weeks ago. And then since Jim and POLO . . . Well, I've come out here a number of times to talk at different fund-raising events. It's good for the constituency back home in Palo Pinto County. Looks like we're all going to run. As I say to Jim, you go to the moon and where all can you go after that but into politics? [*Laughs.*] I figure I've been around this country so many times giving speeches—universities, Rotary clubs, Jaycees, you name it—by the end of this decade I'll have logged more than to the moon and back in this country alone . . . and mind you, that's not including Europe and the other continents, no, sir.

SCHRADER: Jim isn't here?

STURGIS: No. He had to go to Chicago to talk to some members of the board. Sound familiar?

SCHRADER: Sure does. But we won't get onto the problems of foundations.

STURGIS: No, we won't. He just found out last night. It was a last-minute thing. He left this morning. But he asked me to tell you that he did try to get out of it. I'll fill him in on everything that we talked about, if we ever get started. And Lloyd also, of course. He has a class this afternoon. Well, Kip, why don't you sit down, you'll be more comfortable.

GALVESTON: I'll just sit right here on the arm of this chair—it is a chair, isn't it? [*Laughs.*] This modern furniture . . .

STURGIS: Nick, if you want to ask any questions of either Kip or Richard, and, of course, if you both want to ask Nick—

SCHRADER: Yes. I'm interested in how . . . Kip . . . well, I'd like him to tell me his version, tell me in his own words what happened—exactly what happened when he and Franklin were on the moon in July 1970.

GALVESTON: Well, well! I didn't expect you to dig up that one.

SCHRADER: To see if my version coincides with yours.

GALVESTON: Well, I don't know if that's what we're all really here for. I don't believe there are more than a handful of men in this whole country—including me and Franklin . . . Let's hear what you know. In detail.

SCHRADER: All right. If you want me to. I'll run through the whole thing for you, if that's what you want. You and Commander Franklin left Drew Johnson in the command module and went into the lunar module. Johnson closed the hatches, installed the drogue and probe, disconnected the electrical umbilical. He rigged the TV cameras to shoot out of one of the windows to show the departure of the LM. He was on the radio constantly, going through the joint checks with you in the lunar module. He threw the switch which released you. You saw his face pressed against the glass of window 2. He fired his thrusters precisely as planned and you began to separate, checking velocities and distances as you went along. The burn was a small one, just to give the LM some breathing room. In other words, everything was going on schedule, as planned.

Now, what was not reported—what was blocked out from the transmissions—was the strange series of sounds that both you and Franklin, and Johnson in the CM, started hearing during this time, and which you would continue to hear throughout your time on the moon, a strange series of—as Franklin described—"eerie *woo-woo*-like sounds." You started hearing these sounds as soon as you separated your two vehicles and you turned on your VHF radios. As Franklin said, "It sounded like wind whipping around the trees." Of course all this was blocked out throughout the live TV and radio coverage. You continued, however, with the flight as planned.

You and Franklin made two separate burns in reaching the lunar surface—the descent orbit insertion took place behind the moon and dropped the LM's perilune to 50,000 feet at a point 16 degrees west of the landing site. You reached this spot over the western edge of the Sea of Tranquillity. The LM's descent engine fired up for the second and last time—power descent initiation—and the LM arced over into a 12-minute computer-controlled descent to some point at which Franklin took over the manual landing.

As you and Franklin in the LM approached PDI, Johnson was peering through his sextant at a minuscule dot—the LM was nearly invisible and not to be differentiated from any of the thousand tiny craters, except that it was moving. Finally, it passed the 100-mile mark, and Johnson lost sight of it. It was during this time that Johnson first noticed some—as he described them—"patches of white haze—almost ghostlike in appearance—in the distance." But at this point Johnson kept quiet as you and Houston discussed power descent initiation, and the final descent began. All this time you were still hearing these strange sounds. At five minutes into the burn, Franklin called out, "Program alarm. It's a 1202"—an executive overflow: The computer had been called upon to do too many things. Houston replied immediately with reassurances. And then, at just 3,000 feet above the surface, the computer again flashed 1201, another overflow condition. Again Houston immediately responded with reassurances. You called out altitude and velocity to Franklin, who had his eyes glued to the window: "300 feet, 200 feet, 4½ down . . . 100 feet, 3½ down, 9 forward . . . 5 percent [fuel remaining] . . . Forty feet, down 2½, kicking up some dust." Houston replied: "30 seconds." "Contact light!" you called out, and then shut down the engine. Franklin made it official: "Houston, Tranquillity Base here." Johnson then reestablished radio contact with Houston, which informed him of the landing.

Johnson, at this point, was about to swing around behind the left edge of the moon when he had a coolant problem. And of course radio contact was cut off the moment he disappeared behind the moon. But when he swung into view of the earth, whatever the problem had been was gone.

Johnson couldn't hear the LM—the preflight agreement had been that all LM transmissions would be automatically relayed to him. Johnson asked Houston if it could enable S-band relay at least one way from the LM to the CM so that he could hear what was going on. Houston replied there wasn't much going on. Johnson said he hadn't heard a word from the LM. At this time it was still two hours from depressurizing the LM. Houston confirmed that Johnson's coolant problem seemed to have solved itself. Johnson disappeared behind the moon again.

You and Franklin were still in the Tranquillity Base collecting rock samples. In other words, everything seemed to be going as scheduled—a routine flight with some unexpected problems that seemed to be under control. Whereas in reality, you were trying to do everything you could to maintain the appearance that everything was going according to schedule. Neither you nor Franklin nor Johnson in the CM had reported to Houston these strange sounds you were receiving. Houston had been systematically blocking them out from the live transmission; but since Houston

made no mention of them to you, you each separately—
you and Franklin, and Johnson in the CM—thought it
might be some transmission difficulty you were experi-
encing, so you said nothing.

The next morning, after lift-off, Johnson locked onto the
LM with his electronic ranging device—part of his VHF
radio. He was still hearing—as he had been all along—
these strange sounds in his headset; as he also described,
"an eerie sort of *woo-woo* sound." Both you and Franklin
confirmed with Johnson in the command module that
neither one of you was making these sounds. You mentioned it—in an offhand manner—in your debriefing
sessions; the radio technicians, predictably, explained it as
interference between the LM's and command module's
VHF radios.

What neither you nor Franklin nor Johnson mentioned
in the debriefing sessions were the visual effects that accompanied these sounds—a strange pattern, "sort of like
patches of cylindrical-shaped haze," which you noticed
throughout at intervals. You revealed this in top-secret
debriefings. You and Franklin, on the lunar surface, saw
these strange nebulous forms in the distance; these forms
were accompanied by these same sort of *woo-woo* sounds.
Johnson, alone on the back side of the moon, also saw
these same nebulous forms and heard the same unexplainable sounds.

Both you and Franklin and Johnson took photographs,
and also were able to film some of these objects. These
photographs and films revealed a number of hazy white
objects, more ghostlike than actual, which appeared at
intervals every few minutes, in the distance—against the
back side of the moon and on the lunar surface—and then
the film was blank again, showing only an empty expanse
of sky, an ordinary lunar surface. As for what these films
and photographs contained, the objects were classified by
NASA as unidentifiable; NASA simply said there had been
transmission trouble perhaps due to weather interference
. . . and of course the Soviet Space Agency also edited the
transmission they had received during the flight. It was
explained to various officials as an adverse reaction . . . a
gravity problem . . . a malfunction in adjusting to the
lunar atmosphere.

GALVESTON: Ha. Well, I can see he's done his homework, Tom.

PREBBLE: Who would have believed it, anyway? It belongs to science fiction. When we first told a few of the top people in the Pentagon, they thought it was a gag—that we were joking. We showed them the films, the photographs. They thought it was a cartoon at first—that we had retouched it. Then the room became pretty quiet.

SCHRADER: What I'd really like to do is talk to Franklin and to Johnson.

STURGIS: Oh, they won't talk to you or anybody else. As far as Franklin's concerned, it's all strictly unidentifiable—radio interference and weather interference. And as for Johnson, you know he's a bigwig executive at TWA; he feels just about the same as Franklin. He dismissed the whole thing, felt it was unworthy of someone of his scientific background—an interpretation more like that of a science-fiction buff. It didn't even merit a mention in the part on the flight in his autobiography.

GALVESTON: Well, if he knows about that—those details —then he must know about Jackson and Redmond.

SCHRADER: And McCracken in Fra Mauro region, Powell in the Hadley-Apennine region, Anderson in the Descartes region, Wilson in the Taurus-Littrow . . .

STURGIS: And on and on. The same unexplainable sounds accompanied by the same unexplainable patches of cyclindrical-shaped haze. I think he's proved his credentials.

GALVESTON: Scott Jordan's your man, Tom. How come you didn't get Scott here?

STURGIS: I spoke to Barbara. He's in Europe—at some convention.

GALVESTON: The mystical astronaut. Well, I guess that's just keeping up with the times. But, you know, he's really sincere. Well, I guess you've read about it.

SCHRADER: I have.

GALVESTON: Underwent some sort of mystical experience—right there in outer space. Cracked up when he got back here . . . the strain was too much. The sight of our puny little world from out there. To me, it was just beautiful, awe-inspiring, what a sight. But Scott's got a religious bent to start with. Not that I'm not a churchman myself, no, but he was really shook up . . . now, of course, he's all into mysticism.

STURGIS: Parapsychology.

GALVESTON: I'm not putting it down. Believe me. Once you're out there you believe anything. You should really introduce Nick to him. I'm sure they'd hit it off. Scott's all involved in that ESP center of his up in San Francisco . . . got all sorts of clairvoyants, tests being conducted . . . the place is getting to be pretty famous. Of course he had a head start, not every mystic's an astronaut. All sorts of tests. I've seen some of them. No gimmicks. Pretty impressive. And who's to say it's not true? No, sir, not after what I've seen.

STURGIS: I'm going to try him again. Barbara said he'd be back the end of the week.

GALVESTON: Some truly amazing people working with him. What about that Israeli fellow?

STURGIS: Barrowsky?

GALVESTON: Yeah, that's right. Barrowsky. Why don't you get Scott to bring him? You'd have food for thought there, Nick. Not that you don't already. No, sir. We all do. There have just been too many such instances to dismiss. I've seen too many things with my own eyes. Believe me. Things I wouldn't want anyone else to see, no sir. I've sat frozen stiff in my seat during training flights, on the two space flights, even in commercial jets. I've seen these things —that's all I'm going to say they are is things—and Richard will tell you the same thing, and so will Jim, and Lloyd, too, and Tom can tell you about when he was with us at NASA, and we can get you dozens and dozens, hundreds of top men in the space program, in government, in the scientific world, to vouch for all this.

PREBBLE: And yet every time we continue to dismiss them at NASA—every time they occur, every month, every week, sometimes every day.

GALVESTON: What are you going to do about it? Get it into the newspapers, put it on TV, over the radio? And then what? What have you got? No. It won't do any good. You'll just scare a lot of people crazy.

SCHRADER: They deserve to know.

GALVESTON: Oh, I agree with you.

PREBBLE: You're an idealist.

GALVESTON: I agree with you wholeheartedly. You just tell me how.

PREBBLE: And we all know where idealism gets us: nowhere.

STURGIS: The solution is obviously with Macdavitt's papers.

PREBBLE: Oh, yes, it's easy. Totally logical: Make the papers public and your problem is solved. We can all assume that Macdavitt had enough evidence to satisfy everyone—how they didn't get his papers, God only knows! Well, the only problem is making the papers public . . . providing they're not found first, "confiscated," for all practical purposes destroyed.

SCHRADER: There's no problem. That won't happen.

PREBBLE: I trust they're in a safe place.

SCHRADER: They won't be found.

PREBBLE: I hope not, for your own sake . . . for all our sakes, now that we've been associated with you.

Synopsis of remainder of preceding unedited transcript.
At 1353 the subject was switched to a general recounting of "censorship," CIA and other, unnamed groups' intervention, the "pressure" for an investigation by the Science and Astronautics Committee in March of 1961. In May of 1961 a UFO investigation was announced (to be carried out by three members of the House Space Committee), but an AF fight against the hearings was started by the then director of legislative liaison. Quoted by Schrader: " 'Hearings would only benefit the sensation seekers and publishers of science fiction.' " Mostly from Schrader's recounting: The conference was set for August 24, but Congressman Brooks (of the House Space Committee) was taken seriously ill and died (much was made of this, as was to be expected). Soon afterward his successor bluntly announced he would not order the hearings (this was also commented on). One case was presented at this time to try to break the "blockade" (this from Schrader and Sturgis), that of Commander James Kent, a navy pilot for ten years, and Admiral Dowson. Commander Kent and Admiral Dowson were aboard a four-engine navy transport flying west over the Atlantic, its altitude 19,000 feet, when there was the predictable occurrence: A huge flying disk

was witnessed and then photographed (the photographs were later confirmed by the AF to be optical illusions). Other examples were given. (Admiral Hillenkoetter's name was dragged through the Kent-Dowson case as well as through most of the other cases, and his integrity as the former director of the CIA was questioned.) Schrader said, "In AF Regulation 11-30, withholding information 'in the public interest' is admitted as official policy. In AF Regulation 11-7, it is stated that sometimes information requested by Congress may not be furnished 'even in confidence.' " (This was also commented upon, at length.)

Synopsis of preceding surveillance log.

At 1656 the meeting was terminated. (Commander Galveston had an appointment with Senator William Pewter prior to speaking at a benefit dinner for the Republican party at 1930 in Los Angeles.) Sturgis walked Dr. Prebble and Schrader out through the grounds to the parking lot. Dr. Prebble got into his car, leaving Sturgis and Schrader alone. The exchange that followed lasted several minutes but was impossible to pick up—the foliage here is too recent, trees and hedges still low, visibility unobstructed. Then Sturgis smiled, shook Schrader's hand. They both seemed satisfied with whatever had transpired. Schrader got into his car, drove straight up to Sonora Pines.

Edited transcript of telephone conversation between Schrader and Sturgis. 30 August.

STURGIS: Hello, Nick? Have you been trying to get through?

SCHRADER: For over an hour. What's wrong with your phones?

STURGIS: Oh, we had some sort of small fire. An accident in one of the labs. Nothing serious. It was put out almost immediately, but some wires were damaged, and all our outside lines were cut off—just as a precautionary measure while the phone company was fixing them.

SCHRADER: I was just about ready to call you at home.

STURGIS: I finally got hold of Scott Jordan. He's been at some parapsychology convention in Utrecht—just got back last night. Just our luck he's coming down to Burbank tonight to be on some TV special and he's going to stay over in LA and drive down here in the morning. Barrowsky's going to be with him on the TV thing, so he's going to bring him over, too. So, around about noon tomorrow. How's that with you?

SCHRADER: Yeah. Fine.

From Security 5A200 Washington. 30 August.

Re Gerald Barrowsky: His association with Jordan has revealed some questionable findings. (His work in electrostatic and electromagnetic fields has gained worldwide attention. And his intriguing hypotheses have been brought to the public eyes by his recent publicity tours and by his vastly popular books—*ESP in Everyday Life, Other Worlds at Your Fingertips,* and *Worlds (Within Worlds) Around Us*—which have been best sellers both in this country and abroad.)

We have refrained, up to now, from intervening in this matter, as we hoped Barrowsky would absent himself of his own accord.

However, it seems that now (in the light of his meeting with Schrader) his presence could only complicate matters even further in regard to Schrader. We suggest that (should this association with Schrader continue) Barrowsky be persuaded of the sensitivity of the issues involved here.

See Barrowsky files for reference.

Nick arrived early, before the others. Tom showed him around the house, his art collection—including some rare stones, meteor fragments, and a small vial of lunar dust. Within fifteen minutes a white Jaguar with the license plate PSI pulled up. Tom went out to meet them. Nick saw from the wall-length living-room window Scott Jordan, with his Vandyke beard, in his check sport jacket, check pants, white patent-leather loafers, get out of the car. Nick recognized him from the photographs, as well as the young man who had been at the wheel. A Beverly Hills–style hippie—jewelry, silk shirt, shredded jeans. Nick pretended to be studying a small Eskimo statue on the marble coffee table. He waited. He heard Jordan—he presumed it was Jordan because of the familiarity and the lack of accent—say, "Did we drive Tina out?"

"Oh, no, you know we don't have that kind of relationship. No, she wanted to get out. You know her parents have a place in La Jolla, and one of her brothers and his family are there for the weekend. They'll probably go sailing." Nick heard their footsteps on the parquet, and then the footsteps were muffled by the thick rug. He turned around to face them. They shook hands.

"Why don't we just sit down here?" Tom pointed to the white sofa and chairs in the all-white living room, which appeared to be even whiter because of the quantity of natural light pouring through the glass walls and sky-lights. "Can I get you something now? We can have lunch in a little while. If you want to eat now, though, of course . . . Tina left some sandwiches."

The consensus was to wait. Tom sat or, rather, slumped in the pliable posture of an athlete, as if he didn't have a bone in his body, his legs wide apart, leaning forward on the white ottoman, the tips of his fingers arched together. "As I tried to explain to you on the phone yesterday, Scott—but I couldn't really get into it, anyway we had a bad connection—Nick has access to some of Macdavitt's papers. Some of the papers he didn't hand over, and now that Macdavitt's dead, well, he wants to make the papers public."

"Terrible thing to have happened. He was seeing some-one, though, wasn't he?" Scott asked. "I mean a psychia-trist."

"No." Barrowsky shook his head. "No, that's not the way it was at all. It wasn't suicide."

Nick caught Tom's eye. "Yes, he was seeing a psychia-trist," Nick said.

"Gerald's putting us on." Scott laughed uncertainly. "He does that once in a while. That way he has the advantage, anything he comes up with after that will seem credible, right, Gerald?"

But Gerald just kept shaking his head.

Tom nodded, smiling blithely as if he was not aware of Gerald. "What I wanted you to do, Scott, is just talk to Nick. He knows everything, all the different incidents— about all of your—what do you want me to call them?— 'encounters' with UFOs. I'll put it to you straight. Nick wants to make the whole thing public. Jim is behind him, so are Lloyd and Kip, Rick Prebble, and I think we can get a lot of other people."

"Just like that, huh?" Scott recrossed his legs. He was seated on the couch, balancing an ashtay on his knee, his cigarette extended from his arm in such a rigid way that it made his arm look like an artificial limb. He tilted his head back into a sardonic laugh; he shook his head. "You know, it has been tried before."

"Nick has the brunt of Macdavitt's research. He left a number of papers. But that's not enough. What we want to do is get enough names, people like you and Jim, Kip, who carry the prestige of NASA . . . enough weight to swing the balance to our side—put enough pressure on the Air Force, force them to reopen the cases, hold public hearings, as they've been threatening to do for years."

"So Macdavitt held out on them. Well, you know how I feel about it."

"I think we can pull it off," Tom went on. "Macdavitt had everybody's name—the top names in the country, in government, the Pentagon, the Air Force, NASA."

"I don't think I have to explain where I stand." Scott crushed out his cigarette, shrugged, making a motion of dismissal with his bony hand, as if it were unnecessary to even explain. "You can count me in."

"I pick up waves . . . a warm field of magnetic . . . liquid." Gerald has his eyes closed; he lowered his voice to an almost inaudible whisper. "Now . . . now . . . yes . . ." And then, as if taking the others in the room into confidence, he clarified what was happening. "The voltage is decreasing in my occipital area. I will be able to influence the temperature of this field soon . . . yes . . . now . . . I am penetrating the superconducting shield . . . the magnetic field is perturbed . . . Dr. Macdavitt is . . . yes . . . Dr. Macdavitt . . ."

"Yes?" Scott leaned forward, anxiously solicitous, eyes almost glazed in anticipation "Yes?"

"It is Dr. Macdavitt . . . yes . . . and he is there surrounded"—Gerald suddenly shivered—"cold . . ."

Nick and Tom looked at each other, not quite certain how to react or not react.

"It is cold," Scott repeated on cue, as if to coax Gerald.

"No . . . I am losing it . . . there is an impediment . . .

a grid of impediments . . . nuclear particles from a magnetic field are affecting the output . . . water . . . a pool . . . night. I can visualize . . . a distant spatial location . . . Macdavitt . . . Macdavitt . . . no, the projection is blocked." Gerald opened his eyes, smiled innocently like a child. "I'm sorry. I will try again later; perhaps the mental resistance in this room will be less then."

"Gerald has seventy-five-percent accuracy in out-of-body experiments," Scott said.

Tom nodded vigorously, as if he were the last one to doubt that.

"But he's been traveling a lot, been distracted—at lot of pressure. You know, very few sensitives can concentrate for extended periods of time."

"Yes, I am trying to cut back my schedule. But there are so many requests . . . it is difficult not to accept. For instance, yesterday . . . three airplane flights. I was on a television program with Scott in the evening in Burbank and then last night I spoke at UC Davis . . . and then there was the usual gathering afterward backstage, a restaurant, the Plaka, right in the heart of a shopping center. Ha! That is America for you, the future. Very good Greek food and then back to someone's house for more tricks—that's what all this is to most people, you know."

Scott nodded. "That's right . . . but how else can you educate them?"

"Yes, of course . . . so I must go through with the boxes, the closed eyes, the roll of film in a dark closet . . . tricks . . . these are magicians' feats to these people."

"That's why I think it would be a good idea to have Gerald at the lab, where we can use equipment. He had some incredible reactions—all scientifically tested beyond doubt—to the UFO films and photographs last year at the Center. Macdavitt was there. Well, you remember, Tom you were there."

"That's what I was hoping we could do again. With Nick," Tom said.

"We have a number of top-secret selected films and photographs at the Center." Scott lit another cigarette. "NASA doesn't even know I have them. And they're all authentic—I should know, since I took most of them on the flight in '71. I duplicated them at NASA—I would never have gotten hold of them otherwise—took them with me when I left. My farewell gesture. We've had some really incredible results. We've done all sorts of tests on them: blown them up out of proportion—fifty feet—projected them onto walls, huge screens, scanned them electromagnetically, and so on. And, of course, we've been working with Gerald on them. I'll bring them to the lab."

"I'd like very much to see them," Nick said.

"Well, why don't we set up a time?"

"Let's make it toward the end of next week," Nick suggested.

"Yes, of course. When's a good time for you, Tom?"

This was discussed for several minutes. Finally, a general agreement was reached, and a date was set—pending last-minute changes in Gerald's hectic schedule—for the following Saturday at the Watkins Laboratory.

Tom suggested they break off for lunch. They went into the kitchen; Gerald wandered off to "open himself up to the house . . . feel the house."

Lunch (sandwiches and coffee—Sanka for Scott and rose-hip tea for Gerald) was taken on trays into the living room. They went over some of the list of names.

Tom brought up Macdavitt's murder. Gerald closed his eyes. He concentrated. Then he nodded. "Yes, I can see it." But all he would say was "There was someone he knew there . . . came into his office. . . ." But no, he said, he couldn't see any more.

They went over some of the names again.

Nick had Johanna for the second half of the Labor Day weekend: At eight o'clock Sunday morning, in order to avoid the traffic, Carole and Mike dropped her off on their way up to San Francisco (Mike was going to record the Company Crackers, a group from England, who were giving a concert in Golden Gate Park).

The 450 SL roared out of Nick's driveway. Johanna ran through all the rooms—her way of refamiliarizing herself. Nick had decided the only way to broach the subject with her was not to say anything, just take her duffel bag, her flight bag, and her laundry bag of stuffed animals and toys over to Michelle's, which he did. Michelle fixed breakfast.

He waited until Johanna was out in the back, playing with Heather and Peter. He explained to Michelle he wanted to have some time alone.

He drove down to the water. He sat parked in his car at the side of the road, on the hill above the beach. He looked down, past the ledge of cypresses and palm trees that framed the scene, out to the turquoise panoramic sweep of ocean. He watched two divers in their black wetsuits clambering out of the water. He could hear in the distance the hypnotic trance of the surf. The car windows were open. The air was warm. The hot sunlight made him feel dizzy. Everything was so still. The silver fronds of the palm trees, the cypress leaves not even moving, the stark primitive pastels of the sky, the water. He felt he was almost in a dream. There was not a sound. He felt so tired, he felt he could almost fall asleep without even closing his eyes. None of this would have happened to me if I hadn't . . . He didn't finish his thought. He was jolted awake. The horn was screeching. His head was down on the steering wheel.

He drove back to Michelle's. She was lying on her unmade bed in her jeans and T-shirt, surrounded by books. She looked up from the book she was reading. Erving Goffman's *The Presentation of Self in Everyday Life;* she smiled. Nick let himself collapse beside her, onto some of the books. She ruffled his hair the way one would a child's. He offered no resistance and let his head rock back and forth; she took his head against her breast and they lay there together for several minutes without moving. Johanna appeared in the doorway. Michelle nudged Nick, who looked up. Johanna giggled and ran away. Sighing, Nick got up. "Let's go down to the beach."

They walked along the beach—the children stayed in front of the house, building a sand castle. Nick went toward the cove, away from the Walkers'. He didn't feel like seeing the Walkers' house-sitter. "I've been trying to tell you for the last couple of weeks. I just don't know how. How can I explain it to you? I shouldn't even be telling you . . . but it's getting between us. You have a right to know, if anyone does." He tried to figure out what would be the best way, but of course there wasn't any. The only way was just to come out and tell her directly, no matter what her reaction was: incredulity, disbelief, laughter. She'd probably think he was putting her on.

She stopped for a moment, studied some footprints in the sand—not theirs. "You don't have to tell me anything," she said. "I mean I don't want you to tell me anything you'll regret."

"No. I want to. I have to tell someone." Then he rephrased it. "I want to tell you."

"It's because Richardson's away. You should be talking to him, not to me."

"What a modern attitude. You tell your psychiatrist."

"No, I mean I don't want you to tell me something you should be telling him."

"It's not that kind of thing. It has to do with George Macdavitt."

Michelle laughed. "And here I thought all this time it had something to do with Carole. Ever since she came up here that day . . . I thought it had triggered off something; you know, that you wanted to get back together with her. Ha!" She laughed again. "You can't imagine the things that were going through my head . . . what I was going through."

"No. It's not Carole. Macdavitt left some papers."

"You don't have to tell me."

"I'm going to."

"Don't. Really . . . it just sounds like you shouldn't."

"Sounds like I shouldn't? What do you mean? What are you talking about?"

"I don't know. I just feel it. I just feel you shouldn't. It'd be better if you didn't."

"That's absurd. If anybody has a right to know, it's you. I mean ever since Macdavitt's death—since they dragged up his body . . ."

"Isn't that Johanna?" Michelle pointed to a small hazy figure in the distance. "She's waving to us."

Nick squinted. "They're playing with the Frisbee."

"Why don't we go back?" It wasn't a question so much as an imploration. There was an edge in her voice; it made him nervous, apprehensive in a vague way. He felt she was trying to tell him something. But what? "What's the matter? What are you trying—"

"Nothing." She laughed lightheartedly. "Nothing." She

pushed back a lock of hair that had fallen down his forehead.

Nick looked away, toward some rocks that jutted out of
the slick sand in the low tide. "Macdavitt left some papers,
the main part of his research. The government thought
they'd gotten hold of everything—they'd forced him to
hand over his papers—but he didn't hand over everything.
He left some of his most important papers with his wife,
with instructions to give them to Osmond in the event of his
death. And then he also left some other papers with Osmond. Osmond felt he couldn't really take on something
like that, couldn't really go through his papers. He was
really shattered, you know, and then, well, he really didn't
know what was in the papers. He thought they were just
notes for the latest volume of *A Scientist's Notebooks*, or
maybe some reminiscences about his life, his work. He was
too upset to even read them. He had the idea of putting
together some sort of collection—some of Macdavitt's
jottings, notes, whatever was in the papers—and then en-
larging the whole thing with some personal recollections by
people who had worked with him. At Los Alamos, NASA,
and so on. He asked me to look them over with that idea in
mind . . . to see what could be used."

Nick heard himself speaking, as if he were reciting lines
in a drugged dream—here on this beach, with this tanned
girl, in the midday sun. It was as if he had no volition of
his own, as if he had no control. "Well, I started reading
late one night—the day you left for Yosemite. I couldn't
believe it. I just read straight through. I was in a state of
shock. I got hold of Osmond. I told him what was in the
papers. And of course he didn't want any part of it—at
first—felt they should be given to the government. Well,
he's concerned about the Foundation's future, feels he has
enough problems; he's worried about getting enough funding for next year. But then he came around. He got in
touch with someone in San Francisco who had worked
with Macdavitt at both Los Alamos and NASA. And
then the strangest thing . . . he suddenly backed off. Someone, some people in the government, must have gotten
hold of him. But I've gone on with it myself. I've gotten
in touch with some people myself, people mentioned in
Macdavitt's papers. He has everyone's name—the top

people in the government, the Pentagon, the Air Force, NASA. So you see, now I find myself in the middle of this insane surrealistic plot—nightmare. I've been wanting to tell you, but I just haven't known how. You see, Macdavitt's papers have to do with unidentified flying objects." Nick paused. He waited, watching Michelle's face for some sign of surprise, disbelief, for some reaction. But she didn't show any. She turned her head and looked away. She looked out at the brilliant expanse of sunlit water. She couldn't have been looking, though. The sun was too bright for her to be able to see clearly.

Nick went on. "I want to tell you . . . about what was in the papers, some of the contents."

"Don't tell me. I don't want to hear. I don't want to know."

He hadn't counted on this; he was taken aback. "You're acting very strangely. What is it?"

She turned away. "You wouldn't understand. Please don't ask."

"All right. I won't. But you're really acting very strangely."

"Let's go back."

They did. They didn't talk. Nick was puzzled. He let it drop, though, for the time being. But he brought it up again later that evening when they were in bed. She said she didn't want to talk about it, really she didn't. Didn't want to know anything about it. And then, when he was inside her, about ready to explode, almost at that moment, waiting for her so that he could go ahead, let go, just at that moment before . . . She was writhing under him, they were both drenched, covered with sweat, locked and straining against each other, her hair thrown back across the sheet, her nails digging deeper into him, he couldn't hold out any longer. Throbbing, his penis beating like a heart, in the wet sliding chamber of her body, lined and slippery with contractions. He was just about to . . . when suddenly she stopped, shook her head, and gently pushed him away, pulled him out. He couldn't believe it. She rolled over and lit a cigarette. His nerves were shot. And then, of all things, she brought up Macdavitt and the papers again. He couldn't believe it. She wanted to talk about it. He was more than puzzled. She wanted to know

everything. He told her it was all about the government
cover-up, how the government had been covering up. He
explained he couldn't really go into details. She smiled.
She didn't push it. He decided she must have really been
upset, shocked by what he had told her. That was the only
explanation. She put out her cigarette, And they started
up again. She wanted to go down on the floor this time.
They went down on the floor. And soon he didn't care,
didn't bother to analyze why she had suddenly stopped
before. He didn't care. He had almost forgotten about it.
They started over again. And then he was spent. Completely spent. And couldn't think of anything beyond her
warm body; he had completely forgotten what had happened. He was asleep.

In the middle of the night Michelle got out of bed. She
had been lying awake for hours, it seemed—actually it had
been only an hour—waiting. She waited until she was certain Nick was asleep. She got out of bed, slipped on the
terrycloth robe she kept on the chair by the bed in case the
children came in, and went out into the living room. The
curtains were open. She went over to the sliding glass door
and stood there, looking out at the night scenery, at the
dark hills below at the foot of the house. There were no
lights anywhere, in the entire valley, it seemed. This might
as well have been some evacuated planet, a deserted space
colony. It was too late. This part of the world was now
inhabited only by sleepers. Everyone was asleep. Or those
few remaining were lying awake in their beds, having long
ago given up on the *Late Late Show* or the all-night disc
jockeys, the programs with the listeners phoning in from
L.A. or San Francisco on the short-wave.

Oh, this is just insane, she thought. Just insane. How
could I have let myself get caught like this? How? Oh, God!
What have I done? Oh, this is just ridiculous. I've got to
stop it. I've got to get out of it . . . got to stop. She pressed
her forehead against the cold pane of glass, jumped back,
startled by the unexpected chill. She picked up a pack of
Marlboros from the dining table, lit one. She went back to
the glass door of the sun deck, smoking, trying to calm
herself. The orange glow at the end of her cigarette was
reflected across the way in the pool of dark glass, in some

trees, or at least she thought it was the cigarette. She looked again. No, it was impossible. The light went out. Now she was imagining things. She kept staring but the light didn't appear again. She finished her cigarette. She lay down on the couch. The house was still. Not a sound. She could imagine the soundless rhythms of sleep: the sleepers in this house, in this valley, in this part of the world. The slow ebb of night—tones of gray were now surfacing in the glass door.

She felt nervous, restless. Annoyed with herself now that she hadn't slept. She lit another cigarette. She went behind the bar counter, into the kitchen, turned on the radio low. But the night disc jockey, on the station she sometimes listened to in L.A. when she couldn't sleep, was already off.

She put out her cigarette. No, this just couldn't go on like this. Just couldn't. It was driving her crazy.

It was almost gray, almost dawn. There was some noise, the rustle of some birds outside in the trees, beginning to panic . . . another day. And then something came over her. She shivered. She didn't know what it was. It was almost a physical fear. She ran back into the bedroom, closed the door behind her, ran into bed, her robe still on. She lay there, the covers over her, barely breathing. Her eyes closed, her heart racing. There was something outside. She'd heard something. Nick turned over, his hand brushing her shoulder accidentally. Her eyes shot open. The sound again. She lay still, stopped breathing. She closed her eyes again. There . . . There it was again. She kept her eyes closed. She didn't want to look—she felt that if she didn't look, it would go away. It was a way of keeping it at bay, whatever was out there, whatever was lurking around outside, beyond this room, somewhere out there in the deserted countryside, in the gray dawn. But it didn't work. The sound was still there. Some branches scraped against one of the windows. She froze, rigid. There it was, it happened again. *There was something out there. . . .*

Edited transcript from Dr. H. I. Richardson's tapes. 3 September.

RICHARDSON: Hello, Nick, how've you been? C'mon in. Enjoy your vacation?

SCHRADER: Right.

RICHARDSON: You've been out in the sun, huh?

SCHRADER: The tan? Oh, that's just from over this last weekend. I had Johanna. There wasn't much to do besides the beach. It kept the kids under control. I stayed over with Johnna at Michelle's.

RICHARDSON: Uh-huh. How did that work out?

SCHRADER: Oh, fine. . . . Fine. Well, you know the kids have their hang-ups . . . they get jealous. But I guess that's to be expected.

RICHARDSON: Uh-huh. How's it working out with Michelle?

SCHRADER: Oh, fine. Fine.

RICHARDSON: Something seems to be troubling you. Am I accurate?

SCHRADER: What makes you think that?

RICHARDSON: You seem—how shall I put it?—not overly communicative. Are you angry that I went away? Is that it?

SCHRADER: [Laughs.] No. No. It isn't that. [Laugh.]

RICHARDSON: Uh-huh. Anything you want to tell me in particular?

SCHRADER: I don't think so. Nothing really new.

RICHARDSON: Uh-huh.

SCHRADER: I had an interesting dream, though.

RICHARDSON: Yes?

SCHRADER: Well, the other night . . . you'll find this interesting, I think. It's a perfect example of symbolization as a dream mechanism—this was just about when I was finishing up the second series of the transcripts. Very strange . . . I can remember only parts of it. I was in a room, a strange sort of room. A room I'd never been in before. I mean it wasn't any room I recognized. In this room there was a bed, a single bed, more like an army cot, a radio on a desk. On this desk there was also a note pad, you know, sort of a stenographer's pad, and—this is the strange thing—there was a very small window, but this window was really a square of night sky, stars. You see, the room was really a prison, and at the window, elevated on some sort of platform, was this gyroscope. And that's all. I mean the room didn't have any other furniture. So in that sense it was symbolic, a metaphor. I guess that's the way I see my life at this moment in time. But the interesting thing is that in the dream I was waiting, waiting for something. I don't know what.

And when I woke up, I knew that was right, that was it, that for the last couple of weeks, maybe months, I've been waiting. I was lying on the bed, the cot in the dream. Suddenly I heard something, something on the other side of the wall. I pressed my ear against the spot where the sound was coming from. I listened. But I didn't hear anything. I went back to bed, lay down again. And there was the sound again. I got up. Again the same thing. There was a sound but I couldn't hear it . . . I hadn't waited long enough. You see, I could do nothing but wait. Then the scene shifted. I was driving . . . driving down these roads. It could have been here, I mean anywhere in southern California. Typical southern California foliage—eucalyptus trees, palms. It was a beautiful day, the car windows were open, music—a Mozart concerto, I think—was on the radio. My eyes were almost closed. I was just driving along . . . effortlessly . . . everything seemed effortless. Then something, I don't know what, but something caught my eye. I looked in the rearview mirror and there was a car following me, the same car—it had been following me for hours, days. I mean I realized that in the dream.

Then another scene: I was lying on the beach. It was night. I was sleeping at the edge of the water—in pajamas. I haven't worn pajamas in years. Several other people were also on the beach, also sleeping. A long line of bodies at the edge of the water . . . and the water moving in and out, closer and closer all the time, the tide coming in. But we kept sleeping. . . . Then there was something involving Michelle. I can't remember. This dream took place between four and five, shortly before I woke up. I was sleeping at her house that night. . . .

Synopsis of remainder of preceding edited transcript.

The rest of the tape involves Schrader's wife, Carole; his daughter, Johanna, etc. The above is of interest as it relates to what Schrader may be picking up on some (subconscious) level—i.e., that he is being followed.

RICHARDSON [*at close of tape*]: I would say on the whole that he has taken my absence very well. But I do note— the dreams especially relate to this—a certain amount of

paranoia, a sense of isolation . . . a deep-rooted insecurity
that is coming more and more to the forefront.

Security 5A200 Washington to R. Castle. 4 September.
Re Richardson session: Schrader surveillance should be
altered, i.e., car changed, etc.

On Wednesday morning, two days after Labor Day,
Michelle dropped her children off at school. Afterward she
drove into town. She pulled into a vacant lot next to a
coffee shop, a run-down place downtown, El Cielito, off
Main Street, in the Mexican section. The shafts of sunlight
on the dirty windowpanes made them even more opaque,
as if they were screens of smoke, impossible to see through.
She got out of her car and went in. It was almost empty
—a Mexican counterman, two men at the counter. Cracked
linoleum floor, flies on the doughnuts, and Mexican pastries
under the bell jars on the colorless old counter, lime-green-
plastic revolving stools, a couple of booths, badly worn,
puncture marks masked with tape. She sat at one of the
booths, ordered a black coffee, smoked several cigarettes.
She was joined by a relatively nondescript, relatively young
businessman in a seersucker suit with a large mole under
his left eye. He ordered an iced tea. They sat and talked
for about fifteen minutes. Then the man got up, paid the
two checks, and left. Michelle waited a few minutes before
she went out into the vacant lot, got into her car, and
drove back to her house.

R. Castle to Security 5A200 Washington. 4 September.
Contact with Worthington was carried out earlier this
morning (detailed report available). Worthington was informed of overall state of present situation. She was also
told of dissatisfaction with her role and progress in this
operation—and it was insinuated that certain pressure
would be brought to bear on her should the present situation continue. She seemed compliant. Yet her involvement
re Schrader has caused us some apprehension. We have
questioned her over the last number of weeks about
whether we had any reason to feel this way—and though
she has repeatedly denied any emotional involvement, we
sense otherwise. We have reason to believe this relationship

may have impaired her ability to carry out certain measures. Of course, on the other hand, if this were so, we
could use this development to our own advantage without
letting her know that we were aware of this involvement.
Suggest, though, at the moment, we still continue to wait
and see how she handles further developments.

Mt. Corona is located some thirty-five miles inland, in
the desolate arid stretches that make up most of the
southern region of California that is not on the coast—the
area that is not part of the tourist's mythology of the
state. What was once all desert, and before that ocean—
valleys, vistas of sand filled with the ghosts of water—
what had once been all ocean, and would be again. In
this interim of sand, trees, buildings, shopping centers, all
the signs of habitation are really no more than apparitions,
as if they had been grafted onto the landscape. Days when
the Santa Ana blows, and the palm trees are drenched in
its tidal gusts, and the shrouds of sand rise up, swirling
through the raw, bare modern streets, and the green
chandeliers of orange and lemon groves are tossed back
and forth in this stormy sea of wind and sand, and the
cars in the used-car lots are sprayed with fresh coats of
dust, and the huge shopping centers are evacuated, it is
as if the land were shaking off these vestiges of civilization
and reasserting itself, a reminder that this was still the
province of the uninhabitable, that this was still desert.
This was the season. And the Santa Ana was blowing
strong. Nick recognized the symptoms: the slow gen-
eralized throb, a pulse in the brain, the third eye opening
wide—a lens letting in all light, all sound—seeing, hearing
for miles—stretching the field of perception—until it was
unbearable.
Nick drove carefully, slowly. He had left early to make
sure he had plenty of time. He'd gotten up in the middle of
the night, had breakfast with Michelle in the dark. She
went out into the driveway with him, barefoot in her terrycloth robe, clung to him as she kissed him. "Be careful,"
she said. Later, on the dark curves around Malibu, it
crossed his mind she wasn't referring to the road or the
traffic or the wind. (He'd told her the night before about
Mt. Corona, about Pickering. "Isn't he getting kind of

old?" was all she'd said.) And then he didn't think about
it again. He had the radio on. A local all-night rock station.
He heard the weather reports. He wasn't surprised. The
soft glare. The slicks of light, the oil deposits of dawn out
on the water, flotilla of flaring foil. The rocks and cliffs
that bordered the road coming out into relief. Beams of
light slitting trees, signs, crashing through the windshield,
fragmenting the scenery. And then inland at Oceanside
and toward Mt. Corona, the wind. The sand lifting up on
all sides of the road—ghostly forms striking out, blowing
at random.

Pickering's secretary, a prim, middle-aged woman with
a corsage, told him Dr. Pickering was still up in the observatory dome. It would probably be only another ten or
fifteen minutes. Nick waited on a bench in the long hallway
outside. The hallway reminded him of a hallway in a
school or in a government building; dozens of people went
by—some in white coats, all ages, kids in jeans—with their
names on badges on their chests. The office door opened
again; Pickering's secretary led him into the inside office—
a jumble of papers, old file cabinets, old office furniture,
clocks, instrument panels everywhere ticking away. An
elderly man—white hair, unfocused gaze, distracted,
matching his photographs, yet somehow, again, as with Jim
Ingels, frailer, Dr. Alfred Pickering—came out of another
door, a closet, Nick thought at first; then he saw it was a
bathroom.

Dr. Pickering put out his hand, but it was more of a
gesture than an intention: He withdrew it (or forgot what
he was going to do) before Nick had a chance to shake it.
"Excuse me for being late. I was going over some old sky
photographs. We had a most interesting formation last
night." He stared questioningly at his secretary.

"Dr. Nicholas Schrader." The Secretary smiled at Nick
and went out, closing the door behind her.

"Ah, yes, Dr. Schrader. Sit down. Thomas Sturgis told
me about you. You're assembling a collection of reminiscences for a book on Dr. Macdavitt." He turned his head,
stared out of the sunlit window a moment, pushed his
rimless glasses back on the bridge of his nose. "Yes. Most
tragic. Most tragic. You know, we knew each other well
. . . the scientific world is a small world. And Macdavitt

was a most brilliant mind, a brilliant colleague. . . .
Thomas tells me you are particularly interested in some
of his projects here with us. Dr. Macdavitt was most in-
strumental in getting a number of things off the ground,
including funding, and so on." Dr. Pickering sat down.
"Now, what is it that you would like to know in particular?"

Nick, seated in a chair across from Pickering's desk,
kept his eyes on a small aluminum replica of the solar
system that was on the desk—a sort of mobile of an
alignment of the planets. "Project Ozymandias," he said.

Pickering blinked—an involuntary spasm of fluttering
white lashes magnified behind his thick lenses. He smiled
awkwardly, more of a twitch. "Dr. Schrader, these are not
matters to joke about."

"Oh, I assure you I'm not joking."

"I am afraid I cannot help you."

"I think you can."

"It's not possible."

"What about Fleming, Koenig, Wells?"

"What is the purpose of bandying these names about?
May I ask you what is the purpose of your visit? Dr.
Sturgis said you were interested in personal recollections
of Dr. Macdavitt."

"Well, he couldn't exactly go over it on the phone,
could he?" Nick asked, smiling deadpan.

Pickering pushed back his chair as if he had suddenly
been monitored into motion by some external power. He
got up and went back to one of the windows. He looked
out a moment, another afterthought. He turned around
again, facing Nick. "Project Ozymandias involved some
very naive scientists who wanted immediate results—something that is simply not possible. It was a dead end, a
waste of funds. There were other priorities for the large
amounts involved. The project was based on theoretical
notions. It was all theory, at best. Nothing ever materialized, could ever be even remotely proven."

"You yourself were there. . . . You were there . . . with
Fleming and Koenig, Macdavitt. The space signals from
Tau Ceti on Project Ozma that were decoded. The repeated space signals in an intelligent code. It was going to
be made public, and then the Pentagon stepped in and said

the signals came from a secret military station. . . . You were on Project Epsilon from its inception. You heard the signals received by Wells—you were witness to them with Macdavitt. And they were later explained as quote reflection from ionized gas scattered around the solar system or magnetic or atmospheric quirks end quote. . . . I can go on."

Pickering's eyes appeared to close bhind his lenses for a moment, as if he were about to get angry, or perhaps he was merely registering delayed surprise. In either case, he had been taunted long enough. "I think if you checked your facts carefully you would find that the official conclusion was that there were always other explanations, other factors involved."

"Yes, the official conclusion. But that's not what General Palmer thought. Nor Commander Garrison," Nick went on, "nor Admiral Larsborough nor General Kinnan nor General Martin, Senator Williams, Senator Lasseter, Senator Sperry. . . . The list goes on, as you know."

"You could just be making these names up."

"You know that's not true."

"I know no such thing. And why should I?"

"Because you worked with Macdavitt."

"That was years ago."

"You worked with Macdavitt last year."

Pickering stared. Then he tilted back his head slightly, breaking into a mocking laugh. "Oh, that," he said, as if he'd just remembered. "That was for a symposium we were going to conduct at UCLA. On the Space Age."

Nick shook his head, the tips of his arched fingers touching his lips. "You see, I have Macdavitt's papers."

"He gave them . . . handed them over to the government."

"No. Not all of them. He left some papers with his wife and with Dr. Osmond. After his death, Dr. Osmond handed them over to me. You see, Dr. Macdavitt did not kill himself. He was murdered. The whole story of the suicide was simply a cover the government created."

Pickering turned to the window again, his eyes closed a moment. "I told him . . ." He shook his head. He sighed, a brief sign of compliance. "Why don't you spend the day here—I can show you the big telescopes tonight. You see all this." He pointed to the file cabinets. "These are some of the photographic plates of Alpha Centauri, a triple-star system close to the sun; Barnard's star, a red dwarf about six light-years away from the sun; Tau Ceti, one of the closest stars thought to have a planetary system; and other nearby stars. This is just one part of our work here. The other involves our telescope charts, which register radio signals." He paused a moment. "Macdavitt," he sighed, shaking his head again. "Yes." He looked at Nick, almost as if he couldn't quite remember what Nick was doing here, in his office.

"Yes. For the last thirty-two years. Every night I've been up there. Thirty-two years," he went on as if, Nick felt, he were in the middle of a monologue with himself. "Our progress is so slow, it may not even be progress. I have to go check last night's plates again. See how they compare over the last thirty two-years. That way there is less possibility of mistaking an actual shift or signal from some interference or an accident. You're welcome to come with me and see. Sometimes we think we've come upon something, it looks conclusive, everything checks out, and then, as often as not it turns out to be just another mistake. . . . Well, why don't I show you around? You might as well have a look."

Nick followed Pickering down the hall into an elevator, out onto a platform, down a narrow steel staircase into a large, bare room. Gray file drawers built into the walls from floor to ceiling like the drawers in a morgue, a procession of soundless computers arranged in symmetrical rows in the middle of the room. Not a sign of anything human. A room of the future, Nick thought. A room of machines.

"This is where all the photographic plates, the records of the graphs, are kept," Pickering said. "The computers here work around the clock breaking down the information they've received from the photographic plates and the graphs. Breaking down radio signals from outer space—signals that may simply turn out to be radio signals from Earth reflected into outer space and transmitted back to us. NASA is working on a similar project." Pickering smiled slightly. "But of course we have a head start of twenty years. On our telescope charts, which register radio signals," Pickering went on, "we very often get strange signals that show up on the graph. But for it to be, tentatively, an artificial sign of intelligence—it will show up as a spike on the broad-band curve graph—it has to show up at least three times the height of the normal noise, or static, spikes. Quite a few number of times when we thought we were getting spikes that were six, seven, eight times larger, something was wrong with the telescope correlator. It's a very slow process. Every move of the telescope is controlled by a computer card— Well, you must know some of this from Macdavitt's papers."

Pickering explained the function of each of the computers, pausing to check the spools of tape inside some of them. "Tape from the stars," he said.

He took several photographic plates out of one of the file drawers. They went into another large sterile room, where there were also a number of computers.

"As you know," Pickering said, stopping in front of a long table covered with graph paper, "current searches for extraterrestrial signals are concentrated on very wide bandwidths—which is what we do here—and not on the narrow bandwidths, because we want to cover a wider part of the universe within a shorter time. Macdavitt and some of the people he worked with on Ozymandias and the other secret projects thought it was—is—the narrow bandwidth that an intelligent civilization would be—is—likely to be using. Everything they found—all the radio signals that were decoded by Macdavitt and the others—was on a narrow bandwidth."

"A simple explanation," Nick said.

"Yes." Pickering sighed. "But after all these years I'm not going to give up here." His expression was almost apologetic. "They had undeniable proof. And then these latest findings—there was no way of proving they were not authentic. . . ."

Nick spent the rest of the morning with Pickering, following him around, being shown different photographic plates, some from the end of the last century, different computer cards for the telescopes, computer printouts, graphs. Pickering suggested Nick come back sometime later in the afternoon, say, around four—he had an appointment in the middle of the afternoon and there were several other things he had to attend to.

Nick went outside, into the hot sunlit wind, past a row of cypresses, into the private parking lot. He stopped, stood still for a moment. But it was only the wind rushing through the trees. He walked on. There it was again. He stopped. But there was no way of telling if it was his footsteps or someone else's. The parked cars glittered in the sun, mute witnesses; the slopes below—the immense pale stone of the different domes across the grounds—inanimate, not a sign of life.

He opened the car door. Something flashed in the outside rearview mirror. He swung around but then realized midmotion it was only his own reflection. He got into the car. Again, there it was. The odd sensation that someone was watching him, following him. He drove out, drove down the road. He'd come to see the observatories, Mt. Corona. What was he doing driving around like this? He passed a lake. Lake Henderson—he looked on the map. He went past some camping sites—semideserted. Summer was over. Bedraggled caravans of kids with their guitars and psychedelic vans and gypsy clothes, and the retired elderly couples, now perpetual tourists, with their hibachis or barbecues, their toy dogs and their supercampers. Nick kept driving though. He knew there was a reason. He kept checking the rearview mirror. There was a blue Plymouth. That was the reason. There was something about that car, the way it kept behind him, never tried to pass (even though he was doing only twenty in a forty zone), waiting for him to make the first move. Warren Springs. He turned back, took the same road back. But the blue Plymouth didn't follow. He felt foolish. His paranoia was getting the better of him. He drove straight back to Mt. Corona, into the parking lot. He got out. And there it was again. He could feel it. He was certain. There was someone there.

He went into the cafeteria. Noisy families with whining kids. He picked at his vegetable plate, at his fruit salad. He wasn't really very hungry anyway. The clash of dishes and silverware ebbed. The place was emptying out, grew quieter. He singled out a man in a denim suit, sunglasses on; a kid in torn jeans; a girl reading a paperback in a corner. He kept his eyes on them. But, one by one, they got up and left. He walked around the grounds, down the gravel paths onto a terraced slope above one of the observatories. The white dome sticking out above the level grass, from his field of vision like a white helmet, a semi-abstract gigantic helmet—an artifact from ancient Greece. The smooth white stone against the glare of blue sky, phallic and eerie, an apparition from another planet, from the future. He stood for several minutes, taking in the view. And then it happened again. The sound was too distinct, intentional. The way some shrubs brushed against each other, twigs cracked underfoot. A padded, steady sort of sound, a procession of sounds: footsteps. And then the wind wiped it all out. He stared, listened. But there was nothing to see, nothing to hear. The light was too harsh, the wind too strong. He went into the rear of the building, toward Pickering's office.

At dusk Pickering took him to the main observatory, where the night's work was starting. There were three tanned kids there, two long-haired boys and a girl seated in front of some of the computers. His assistants. Pickering explained they were working for their doctorates. His other assistants (his regular team) were scattered all around—some in the adjoining towers, some in the other control rooms with the other computer terminals. "They type into the computer terminal to move the telescope and tell it what to do. Almost all of the equipment is controlled by computers. The computers keep the telescopes tracked on a star and record its light data," Pickering went on. "Then we use spectrographs on the starlight, split it up into the colors of the spectrum. That way we can analyze the chemical composition, temperature, and other characteristics."

Nick sat with Pickering in the heated control room waiting for the night to fall. "Thirty-two years," Pickering said. "For thirty-two years I have sat up here night after night. For thirty-two years I have watched, stared, until I could no longer see. Charting these unknown paths, this unknown course. I look upon these telescopes as viewfinders, but what they show is not necessarily what is there. How much do we put into this picture, how much of ourselves? It's like a Rorschach. There is something there, but what? It's open to too many possibilities, too many divergent definitions. Reality. What is there. Yet how badly do we interpret what is there? What is objective reality? How much do we distort, out of some strange subjective need? Night after night . . . And I may never know. No, I will probably never know if it wasn't all a mistake. If we weren't staring at the wrong stars all along. And the stars we wanted were right there, right next to the ones we were studying. A mistake. A slight error, the slightest point off . . . and what we thought we were looking at was not at all what we were looking at."

It was starting to get dark. The gray tones fading out, vision evaporating. It was almost night. Nick felt as if he were slowly being hypnotized, entering some sort of strange, barely lit chamber. Or going underwater. He could almost visualize speeding down in slow motion, down through different levels of depth, of perception; plummeting through the strata of colors into night, the colorless world. Nick stared at one of the computer screens: lines jutting out at odd angles, the splutter of strange lights, sputtering sounds, strange bleeps. A convoy of radio signals ticking, an electronic heartbeat, dispersing into silence; clots of light humming in and out.

"This is all arbitrary," Pickering went on, as if again he were in the middle of some interior monologue. "These are imaginary boundaries. The IAU—the International Astronomical Union—sanctions them. After all, these boundaries separate one constellation from another and how else can we agree on which constellation is which? But you see here, for instance, on this screen." Pickering indicated one of the smaller screens on one of the smaller computers. "The constellations appear as two-dimensional, whereas they are really three-dimensional. Now, this cluster here, Orion, composed of fairly bright stars, is at a considerable distance from the earth, and the closer we get to the earth, the dimmer the stars get. But if we were to shift our point of view—if we were in a space vehicle—our perspective would change—the appearance of the sky would change. We have electronic computers here programmed all around, programmed with information on the three-dimensional positions from the earth to each of the brightest and nearest stars—down to almost fifth magnitude, the limiting brightness that the naked eye can see on a clear night."

"What is that?" Nick pointed to the screen on another computer.

"Alpha Centauri, the triple-star system about 4.3 light-years from here. In terms of the Milky Way galaxy this is such a short distance that our perspectives are almost exactly the same. From *A* Cen the Big Dipper appears just as it does from the earth. Now, over here is Tau Ceti." Pickering moved over to another screen. "In the constellation of Cetus—that is, as seen from here. Tau Ceti and Epsilon Eridani were the first two stars examined on Project Ozma. In 1961. Fleming, Koenig, Wells, Macdavitt, received the first signals. It was an unmistakably intelligent code. I was there myself several times. And then, during Ozymandias, they focused on Tau Ceti and Epsilon Eridani and kept hearing the same intelligent signals. Then there was Project Epsilon, where they focused principally on Epsilon Eridani. And the same thing, the same intelligent signals. And all the other projects . . .

"Project Cetus, they focused on the whole constellation. The same thing." Pickering sighed; he nodded several times, as if trying to remember where he was. "Yes. This computer," he went on, "has drawn the sky as seen from a hypothetical planet of τ Cet. We are now a little more than eleven years away from the sun. In other words, our perspective has changed slightly, the relative orientation of the stars has been altered, and we can invent new constellations. These clusters here jut out into this tiny star, which is barely a point. That faint and uninspiringly positioned star is the sun. Now, over here, when we move"— Pickering pointed to another screen—"to a greater distance from the sun than Tau Ceti, to forty or fifty light-years, the sun diminishes even more until it is invisible to the naked eye. Interstellar voyages—if they ever occur on our part—will not use the sun as any kind of reckoning point. The sun cannot be seen at all from a distance of a few dozen light-years, that is, a thousandth of the distance to the center of our galaxy." Pickering paused for a moment and scrutinized the screen. "Now, you see this batch over here. These stars—we've been getting strange signals from them for the last two years. We can't draw any conclusion yet, of course. We're so near Burbank, it could just be TV intercepting signals echoing back at us from outer space."

Pickering checked his watch, checked the screens of several computers, glanced at the clocks all around. He nodded. "Now, if you just follow me, here." He opened a locker in a corner of the room. He called to one of his assistants—one of the long-haired kids, jeans and sneakers, his glasses bandaged together. "Bill, do we have a jacket for Dr. Schrader?"

Bill puhed back some of the coats that were hanging in the locker. He pulled out a windbreaker. "Here, this should fit you."

Pickering put on a faded suede coat with a worn lining. It looked so old that it was difficult to tell what color it had originally been.

A young man in a tennis sweater, with a scarf around his neck and a trimmed beard, emerged from one of the side doors, carrying a tray. He put the tray down on the bench against the wall, next to the other trays, also bulging with used paper napkins, small torn boxes of corn flakes, open containers of orange juice, milk, empty coffee cups. The team here was on a reverse schedule.

"Frank, this is Dr. Schrader. Dr. Morrow. Dr. Schrader's going to spend the night with us."

Frank Morrow ran his fingers back through his long hair. He yawned. "Sorry, Dr. Pickering. I must have overslept."

"Frank is studying Cassiopeia and its vicinity. He's been examining the photographic plates by microscope. Before each photographic plate is exposed in the telescope, it's baked for five hours in a nitrogen-filled oven to make it highly sensitive. Afterward Frank goes into a darkroom and works with a blink microscope. The microscope gives him glimpses, in rapid succession, of two plates, each one showing the same part of the sky at different times. When a speck of one of the star-filled pictures seems to move against the background of fixed stars on the second plate— well, it's an event. He's been studying Cassiopeia for the last three years."

"A ways to go yet." Frank laughed.

Pickering nodded, smiling perfunctorily. "Well, are we all set?"

Nick followed him up a metal ladder, at the top of which was a small, low steel door. Pickering opened the door.

Nick felt as if he were about to enter a spaceship of sorts. They came out onto a narrow elevated platform that looked down on a huge empty room. Empty, and quiet, the sterile silence of machines: the interior of the dome. A modern church, the cathedral of the future, the huge telescope at one end a nave, and lined on either side by the pews of computers with their whirling spools of tape, their screens. They walked across the narrow platform, which went halfway around the ceiling of the dome, to another ladder and down to another platform, another ladder, and then down across the waxed linoleum floor. Pickering made the rounds of the computers, checking them and glancing at screens, stopping in front of each one in the manner of a doctor making bedside rounds.

Suspended above them, the huge, gleaming telescope, unearthly, mythical—a strange distorted skeleton of a building, a strange inverted mammothsized sculpture from another world. They went up onto the platform, directly under the telescope. Nick looked up, at the opening in the dome, at the night. Pickering pulled back the sleeve of his coat, glanced again at his watch. "Time for the real work." They climbed back up the ladders, back to the small door at the top of the dome, and back out into the control room, where Pickering's four assistants were where they had left them, keeping watch over the computers.

Pickering poured Nick some coffee from a Thermos. He gave him his choice of sandwiches. Nick took a tuna fish on whole wheat; he sat down on the bench and ate. Pickering went off, coffee cup in hand, to make another round. Nick stared at the rows of computers, the soundless whirling of the tapes, the dots of mapped-out lights on the screens. Pickering and his assistants wandered around this crowded museum of machines. Nick felt slightly dazed. Pickering called him over. He was looking through a small telescope. He made Nick look, too. Nick saw only patches of white—nothing very interesting—a sort of white haze. "The glare from Los Angeles affects observations up to forty-five degrees in the north," Pickering explained, "while the glare from San Diego affects the southern horizon to about thirty-five degrees. We're stuck on both sides. Our best low-level observation is done in the eastern horizon." He went on to clarify. "The glare of lights from both L.A. and San Diego blocks out a lot of visibility—that's pollution for you, the effects of increasing population—as a result you get more light from the cities. The only time it's really clear is when there's fog. I mean when the fog is really thick. A good dense natural fog layer cuts out that glare you just saw—the glare from the cities—almost competely, and puts us back to having natural dark conditions. Back to the cavemen. Hmm. Let's see." He looked through another, larger telescope. "Well, tonight it's not too bad—there is some fog. That's what we hope for here. Excuse me, I think . . ." Pickering looked up as if he'd heard something. "I want to check something." He went over to one of the telescopes.

"Some signals are showing up on the graph," Bill explained.

"You can never tell," Frank said. "It can really come in just like that at any moment. Of course if any signals from an unknown source show up on the graph, we look at the star again, over and over. Sometimes we check ten, twenty times. We check through the plates also. So there's hardly any possibility of missing something, no matter how tangential it seems—which it usually is, or sounds. Usually" —he shrugged—"we don't find anything."

"I think we'll run these through." Pickering took out some of the plates and handed them to Frank. Frank took the plates over to another computer. "Here, let me show you something. Look in here." Pickering pointed out one of the screens to Nick. "Recognize it?"

"It's Lyra—the turtle." Nick leaned closer.

"Yes, a small, rather dim constellation but it has one very bright star that makes it stand out; that star is Vega. See how really brilliant it is?" Pickering traced his finger over a group of bright dots. "That's the second-brightest of the stars that can be seen from northern latitude—Sirius is more brilliant. We've had our eye on Vega now for about fifteen years. Every once in a while we get a peculiar signal from Vega. At first we thought it was random, but there was something—for instance, length, duration—that made us have our doubts. In another ten years we'll know if we were right or not. In another twelve thousand years Vega will be the polestar. It will be a marvelous guide for night travelers. If you know your stars you'll know that Vega actually means 'falling vulture' but nobody knows why it has that name. . . . Now, over here you see Epsilon, a system of four stars revolving around a common center of gravity. And over here you have a more complete picture." Pickering bent down to the small screen again. "If you look carefully, you'll probably see a series of lights . . . yes, right over there."

Nick looked at the portion of the screen being indicated.

"You see they're moving around in a swarm, a sort of hazy blotch of light, if you want. Now, you see the way it's moving. That's what's been interesting." Pickering lowered his voice. "It's obviously moving toward Tau Ceti. In that direction. We've been following it for months now. We have absolutely no idea what it is. Not a meteor, doesn't seem to be an asteroid, no . . ."

"I'm going to compare them with last week's." Frank came back with the plates. "I'm going to go in and use the microscope."

"Yes, why don't you?" Pickering turned to Nick. "This will all be much clearer fifty years from now—after we have cable television and communication satellites that relay signals in a narrow beam, the earth will again be relatively quiet at radio wavelengths and we'll be able to detect much more." He picked up a color photograph from the top of one of the computers. He handed it to Nick: a striated pattern of lights, some patches of white with blue smoke trailing in its wake. "It's a comet," Nick said. "Isn't it?"

"Yes, its great perihelion distance is some four astronomical units from the sun. You see that blue—do you notice the blue in there? That's due to emission from ionized molecules such as carbon monoxide, molecular nitrogen, the hydroxyl radical, cyanogen—CN and CH+. And those streaks in the background are really stars; that's because this telescope was following the comet's motion. Yes, these questions will be answered," Pickering continued, as if he had been asked. "NASA is actually considering studying the feasibility of sending space probes to the nucleus of a comet . . . and to the surface of an asteroid. These would be unmanned observatories, much less expensive than some of the planetary probes that have already been tried. The earliest mission under consideration is to Comet Encke in 1980." Pickering looked again into the telescope. He sighed. "Yes, well, until then . . ."

"You can't really see a UFO through a telescope, can you?" Nick asked.

"No, a telescope focuses so far away and has such a small field of view. Even if we did spot a UFO through the beam, it would be off focus." Pickering picked up some black-and-white photographs on top of another computer. "Here, I'll show you something. See"—he showed Nick the photographs—"that's what I pointed out to you before. Our mysterious lights. We used the forty-eight-inch Schmidt telescope. Here they are magnified." He laid out several photographs on top of the computer. "Here you can see them much better, much sharper. This is a composite of five images made from five different photographs ranging in exposure time from four to eight seconds. We used the sixty-one-inch Catalina Observatory reflecting telescope for these. You see that ring, the area of light around it—absolutely no explanation . . . and the shape, too. Everything's all wrong. Nothing fits. Everything's wrong about it. Hmm. Yes." Pickering nodded; he didn't say anything else. Then suddenly he looked up, as if he'd only been waiting; he looked straight up at one of the computers. Nick went over with him. They both stood there, watching the spikes on the graph; the spikes suddenly stopped.

"We get them several times a night . . . oh, during the day, too. Sometimes on the hour. Our mysterious lights moving in the direction of Tau Ceti, hovering in that region. Our friend Macdavitt would have been interested." Pickering went over to another computer. He paused a moment, nodded again, staring vacantly, off focus a moment; his eyes, magnified behind his thick lenses, stopped midway in their course across the huge room, and then he sighed again. His white coat hanging on him, standing there in the middle of the room, with computers, screens, graphs, telescopes on all sides—a forest of machines—he looked shrunken. A sort of befuddled large white bird in his coat, his arms, useless wings. And then he sighed again, his eyes resuming their course across the room, only to rest on one of the computer screens. "Here. This is all we know, all we can see. That darkness up there—empty night—this black field of vision that we cannot extend,

cannot see beyond . . . and those nebulous little points
there—stars. Forty or fifty years, perhaps, we'll have a
more accurate idea, a more accurate blueprint of this
emptiness.

"Sometimes, late at night, I find myself staring for hours,
and I'm not even aware that I am. Almost as if I were in a
trance, staring at this emptiness as if it could tell me something. Even when I close my eyes I can see the patterns, the
networks like grids, this blueprint of lights, of sounds.
Quasars, gases, stars . . . I stand here and stare at these
panels as if I were at the controls of some peculiar spaceship traveling, navigating through this dark emptiness. It's
like a desert. Nothing out there but mirages, apparitions of
light, hazy, nebulous, ghostlike visions on the horizon . . .
And we keep staring, staring . . . until we are convinced
that what we imagine we see is what is there—these apparitions . . . nebulous mirages of light in this dark desert . . .
tenuous clusters, inaudible echoes. The ghosts of hope or
dread? That we are not alone, there is something—other
forms of life—out there. The fantasies of science fiction,
only now they're real. It's as if we're standing at the edge
of this desert—at the edge of the desert of the night. A
poetic notion, but rather maudlin . . . Well, back to work."

Pickering poured some more coffee for himself and
Nick. He sat down in front of one of the computers, his
eyes on the blank screen. It was almost five, almost dawn.
But he hadn't given up yet. There was still time. Often, he
said, some signals, something, would register in the last
few minutes just before the day team came on. Nick sat
with him and waited—this vigil in the night, in silence. It
was almost five-thirty. Pickering finally got up. It was almost light. Gray. Night diluting, mixing with the fog of
dawn. "Well, it looks like the show is over."

Pickering walked him to one of the doors. Why didn't
he come down, Pickering said, sometime—some night—
next week with Thomas Sturgis? He'd set up a time when
he'd be able to talk more privately, without his assistants
around. They'd be able to talk then more about what Nick
wanted to know—what he wanted to find out about. Pickering had lowered his voice even though no one was
around. His assistants were all at the other end of the
huge room.

They shook hands. Pickering suggested that either he or Thomas call him the beginning of next week here at the observatory. They would set up a date then for another meeting.

Nick went outside into the parking lot. It wasn't completely light yet. It was cold. The wind had died down but had been replaced by a sort of unnatural stillness. Nick got into his car. The windows were frosted over with dew. He turned on the windshield wipers, but they didn't really seem to help. The fog was slowly coming in.

Though it was chilly and he was shivering, he left his window open. He kept wiping off the outside rearview mirror with his hand. He drove slowly. There was no one on the road. It was almost six. It was light now, though the fog made it hard to tell. The landscape was gray, enveloped on either side by layers of fog—eerie drifts like clouds. He could have been floating out on a sea of pale dense air. He turned the radio on. The news was on. He felt as if he were flying through an endless empty mass of clouds. The car veered. Strange. He was about to pull over to the side of the road when suddenly the car went out of control. He gripped the wheel, forcing it—pushing it against its will —and pulled over to the side. He got out. He opened the hood, looked. Nothing. He got back into the car, tried to start it, but it was dead. He walked almost two miles to a Texaco station. Only the night attendant was on. He went across the road to a diner and had breakfast.

The day shift came on. He went in the pickup with one of the attendants. The car was pulled back to the station, checked out. But they couldn't find anything. Nick drove straight on through up to Sonora Pines—the car seemed fine—without another incident. He went to his own house and collapsed. He hadn't slept in over twenty-eight hours. Later in the morning he went to the Foundation. He called Michelle. He didn't mention anything about the car. He thought he'd tell her later in the afternoon when he saw her. But then he decided she'd only worry, so he didn't.

Synopsis of surveillance log. 6 September.

Schrader took his car to the Exxon garage off Westview (his regular garage). He told them something was wrong with the transmission valve. He had the car checked over thoroughly—left there for the day. Of course, there was nothing wrong. They found nothing.

Report by Agent R. Castle to Security 5A200 Washington. 6 September.

Routine search of Richardson's office re Schrader file (intact through 3 September) failed to reveal most recent Schrader tape (6 September). Since Schrader saw Richardson today (1730–1825) as usual, search was continued through all other tape files. Conclude tape has been purposefully removed. Presumably by Richardson. We will continue accordingly until further notice.

"Hmm. Yes. That's it," Mike groaned.

"Tell me if I'm pressing too hard," Carole said, pressing down on his lower back. She was kneeling beside him on the bed. All the lights were on. The high windows, with the curtains open, were like some strange abstract black paintings. It was 1:32 on the digital clock on the white night table, next to the Twining's Russian Caravan tea tin of top-quality Colombian red, the small antique gold pipe, the full ashtray. "God! What is in there? It's just a tangle of nerves in there. You're really about as tense as I've ever seen you. I thought Mr. Yoshiko would help."

"I think he's the one that pulled it in the first place."

"How's that? Better?" Carole continued pressing in the same area.

"Hmm, yes. I really think it's that damn Yoshiko who pulled something. I always feel like a battering board afterward—he just pounds away. I just don't think that can really help. Do you think—ow!—it really helps?"

"The art of Oriental massage." Carole laughed.

"Ah! I'll take you any day over him. You have—how shall I say?—a more insinuating touch. Hmm . . . lower. Yes. Ow!"

"Are you all right? Did I pull something?"

"I don't know." Mike sat up slowly, testing his coordination. "Hmm. I think I'll just lie here." He carefully slid back down. "Hmm, that feels better already. I think I pulled something when I was walking on the beach, when we were up at Sonora Pines. My back just hasn't felt . . . .

And then with your claws—I think you left your mark again. I'm just a collection of scars. What am I supposed to say to Mr. Yoshiko? It's embarrassing."

"You'll think of something."

"Thanks." Mike turned to look at her. "You OK?" Then he was staring at the ceiling again. "Something bothering you?"

"No. Why do you ask?"

"I don't know. I just get a feeling. You just seem . . ."

"What?"

"I don't know. Something is bothering you, isn't it?"

"No, not really."

"What is it? C'mon, with that tone of voice, you expect me to believe you?"

"It's Nick." Carole turned to Mike, who was lying there now with his eyes closed. She had the feeling, as she sometimes did, that he wasn't really completely there. As if he were reciting these lines and he was really thinking about something else. "I'm worried about him."

"Nick. Oh, Nick." Mike sighed, in comment. "What's the matter with Nick?"

"I don't know." Carole shrugged, looking away. "He's been acting strangely."

"He seemed fine to me." Mike closed his eyes again. "He's got a girlfriend now, what more do you want? What are you worried about? He proved he could take care of himself. He seems to have survived pretty well. Oh, is that it? I see! You don't approve of her? She doesn't meet your standards?"

"No, she seems very nice."

"That's some endorsement." Mike laughed. "Let me tell you, you'll really get far on that one. I'm really going to believe you."

"Well, she seems strange to me. There's something about her."

"Something about her?" Mike yawned. "She's just a pretty girl. C'mon. Are you kidding? In the old lingo she's a real knockout. And that body! That's some body . . . well, we certainly saw enough of it. C'mon, what's wrong with her? Seems intelligent, sensitive. What more do you want?"

"It's just a feeling I get. . . . There's something about her."

"Why don't we talk about it in the morning?" He yawned again.

"I don't know what it is. I just pick up something. . . . And I get the feeling, too, that Nick doesn't trust her completely."

"Why don't we talk about it—"

"No, you know, like the way they met . . . like that, on the beach . . . and the way she just moved in on him. It's almost predatory. And that ex-husband of hers. No, I just don't like the whole scene. There's something going on there. I just don't trust her. You know, at first I thought it *was* just jealousy. I thought I was just jealous . . . maybe on some level I still had mixed feelings about Nick, well, you know, as a way of protecting myself against you . . . from getting overly involved . . . in case it didn't work out. Of course Nick wasn't involved with anyone in the beginning. She's the first one, so I guess it's been kind of a shock. But I guess that's a natural reaction . . . under the circumstances. There's something false about her. I mean she just seems like such a phony—I guess that's it. The way she took off her bikini top when she was lying in the sun . . . when we were all on the beach that day. Of course it's such an obvious way of drawing attention, you don't even have to mention it. A way of drawing attention to herself. But it's also a way of detracting from what she's really up to . . . whatever that is. She's just very calculating. Oh, I know I sound ridiculous; it must sound like some ridiculous feminine intuition thing or something like that. But it's not that. I'm really serious. There's something up with her. She seems so vague, you know, like you can never get a straight answer from her. I'm not asking her for her past, to be accountable for anything. I'd be the last person to do that. But you know, I mean she's just taken over. . . . And then he's gotten so secretive. He's up to something . . . something . . . it just doesn't strike me as . . . Mike. Mike? Are you asleep? Mike?"

Security 5A200 Washington. 7 September.
Re Pickering: The consequences of his further involve-

ment confirmed. His position will be nullified at the first available opportunity.

Edited transcript of meeting at the Watkins Research Laboratory. Commanders James Ingels, Kip Galveston, Scott Jordan; Lloyd Parker, Richard Prebble, Gerald Barrowsky, Sturgis, and Schrader. 7 September.

INGELS: Here we have one of the first sightings from a manned space flight. Of course we can't really assess what we haven't seen. I mean what the unmanned satellites have filmed. . . . These are from Gemini IV in June of '65. These—remember—are not the official sightings. These again, as in the previous batch, were thought too inconclusive . . . quote ball lightning or reflective lights from the ship unquote. This next one you see is cylindrical and appears to be equipped with some sort of antenna. Here's another shot of it—apparently it followed the crew of Gemini IV quite a while . . . this is against the day sky. You can see that against the daylight it appears to be white or silvery. Here in this one it appears to be moving toward the craft on a collision course. But of course at the last moment it too disappeared, just as it seemed as if it was going to collide . . . suddenly it was lost from view. The crew apparently was pretty shook up.

GALVESTON: I can imagine!

JORDAN: Can we see that last slide again, Jim?

INGELS: Sure. This was taken with a Hasselblad, wasn't it, Kip?

GALVESTON: That's right. That's what those guys had. Gemini IV had a Hasselblad on it, didn't they, Lloyd?

PARKER: Yes.

INGELS: As I said, all the previous ones were taken with a movie camera. But freezing them like this, isolating them, in separate frames. . . . In these slides you get, of course, a much better perspective.

PREBBLE: Don't we have an official air-to-ground transcription of Gemini IV when they sighted the thing?

INGELS: Yeah, we do.

PREBBLE: Why don't we play it? By the way, this is the one that was made public.

INGELS: That's right. Lloyd, you want to turn the lights on? You're closest. . . . Thanks.

BARROWSKY: I definitely . . . yes . . . definitely . . . there is a clear interception. I will be able to pick up . . .

INGELS: I think it's in this file. Yeah. Yes, here we are. OK? [*Sound identified as tape spools winding.*]

29 40 45 C	Hawaii
29 52 09 CC	Gemini IV, Guayamas CAP COM.
29 52 12 C	Go ahead, Guayamas, Gemini IV.
29 52 14 CC	Roger. We've got you green, how are you doing up there?
29 52 17 C	Fine. I just saw something else up here with me, but just as I was getting close enough to it to take a good picture, the sun got in the way and I lost it.
29 52 26 CC	Roger. We got some flight-plan changes for you. Want to stand by to copy?
29 52 29 C	Yes. Stand by and let me see if I can find this thing again.
29 52 45 C	. . . and there are a great number of thunderstorms around at the present time. Lightning is actually lighting up the interior of the spacecraft . . . activity . . . thunderstorms.
29 53 35 C	OK. Go ahead. It doesn't look like I'm going to see him again.
29 57 09 CC	That's affirm—you still looking at that thing up there?
29 57 12 C	No, I've lost it. It had big arms sticking out of it, it looked like. I only had it for just a minute. I got a couple of pictures with a movie camera and one with the Hasselblad; but I was in free drift, and before I could get the control back I drifted and lost it.
29 57 29 CC	Good show.

PARKER: What about Gemini V?

INGELS: Yeah, right here. [*Pause.*] Here we are. This is again on the air-to-ground voice network.

> "Hey, do you guys have anything flying alongside of you?"
> "Wait one." (*Crackling.*)

INGELS: That's the crackling over the airwaves.

> "Negative. Why do you ask?"
> "We have a radar image of a space object going right along with you from two thousand to ten thousand yards away. Their radar return is approximately the same magnitude as Gemini V."

JORDAN: The crew of Gemini V then reconfirmed they couldn't see anything. The next statement in the log read: "A tumbling radar signature was observed. This info is to be withheld pending further investigation."

INGELS: Here, I'm going to play you an excerpt of the conversation between ground and air that day—the Cape tracked this UFO alongside the spacecraft until they both went beyond the curvature of the earth past Ascension Island, the last tracking station in the Atlantic. At the next station, Carnarvon, Australia, the UFO was gone—in other words, the same pattern as in Gemini IV. Here it is. Listen.

03 04 57 21 CC	Gemini V, Gemini V, this is Houston. Over.
03 04 57 26 C	. . . Houston, Gemini V.
03 04 57 29 CC	Roger, Gemini V, this is Houston. Be advised that we tracked another object with you on your pass across the States. Range was two to ten thousand yards from the spacecraft. You might look around and see if you can see anything. Unfortunately, I can't tell you which direction to look.
03 04 57 53 C	What time is this?
03 04 57 57 CC	Did you say what size or what time?
03 04 58 00 C	Time.

03 04 58 02 CC	Well, it seems to be going right along with you. So we're tracking it right with you.
03 04 58 13 C	Roger.
03 04 58 21 CC	We're going to lose you here shortly but if you see anything, why don't you let us know at the next station?
03 04 58 27 C	OK.
03 04 58 31 CC	The radar return was approximately the same as yours as far as magnitude.
03 04 58 38 C	Roger.

INGELS: Gemini VII was in space when quote a bogey at ten o'clock high unquote was described. Houston at first thought it was the booster from the rocket itself but the astronauts had the booster in sight at the same time as the UFO. They watched this object at two o'clock as it slowly tumbled—rotated without control end over end. Again quote: No other explanation for the subject seemed to be conclusive. It remains single quote unknown end quote.

PARKER: You got Apollo XI. Why don't you play that one?

INGELS: Yeah. It should be right here . . . right . . . here it is. This one took place on board the ship—on board the Apollo XI—on its way to the moon—this was, of course, the first moon landing. The ship was one day out when the crew spotted a strange object—it was between their ship and the moon. At first they thought it was the Saturn IV booster rocket; they called Houston for confirmation. Houston informed them the booster in question was some six thousand miles away. Looking through binoculars, it appeared to be an L shape—quote like an open suitcase unquote; I think that's how Neil described it. What impressed them was the object's size and its nearness to their craft. The crew looked again, this time through a sextant. They had the instrument just off-focus; the object appeared a different shape—now it looked cylindrical or, according again to Neil, like quote two hollow cylinders unquote. As it tumbled, when it came around on end, again quote you could look right down in its guts unquote. They refocused the sextant and the object took on the open-book shape again. As Collins summarized it—this incident—quote it was really weird unquote. And so the object remained an unknown.

JORDAN: Why don't you play that tape from the technical debriefing that refers to the object?

INGELS: That's just what I was going to do. This is Neil, Aldrin, and Collins.

BARROWSKY: These men are lying. Their voices are not natural . . . there is strain.

INGELS: OK? Can I play it now?

ALDRIN: The first unusual thing that we saw I guess was one day out or something pretty close to the moon. It had a sizable dimension to it, so we put the monocular on it.

COLLINS: How'd we see this thing? Did we just look out the window and there it was?

ALDRIN: Yes, and we weren't sure but what it might be the S-IVB. We called the ground and were told the S-IVB was six thousand miles away. We had a problem with the high gain about this time, didn't we?

COLLINS: There was something. We felt a bump or maybe I just imagined it.

ARMSTRONG: He was wondering whether the MESA had come off.

COLLINS: I don't guess we felt anything.

ALDRIN: Of course, we were seeing all sorts of little objects going by at the various dumps and we happened to see this one brighter object going by. We couldn't think of anything it could be other than the S-IVB. We looked at it through the monocular and it seemed to have a bit of an L shape to it.

ARMSTRONG: Like an open suitcase.

ALDRIN: We were in PTC at the time, so each of us had a chance to take a look at this and it certainly seemed to be within our vicinity and of a very sizable dimension.

ARMSTRONG: We should say it was right at the limit of the resolution of the eye. It was very difficult to tell just what shape it was. And there was no way to tell the size without knowing the range or the range without knowing the size.

ALDRIN: So then I got down in the LEB and started looking for it in the optics. We were grossly misled because with the sextant off focus what we saw appeared to be a cylinder.

ARMSTRONG: Or really two rings.

ALDRIN: Yes.

ARMSTRONG: Two rings. Two connected rings.

COLLINS: No, it looked like a hollow cylinder to me. It didn't look like two connected rings. You could see this thing tumbling and, when it came around end-on, you could look right down in its guts. It was a hollow cylinder. But then you could change the focus on the sextant and it would be replaced by this open-book shape. It was really weird.

ALDRIN: I guess there's not too much more to say about it other than it wasn't a cylinder.

COLLINS: It was during the period when we thought it was a cylinder that we inquired about the S-IVB and we'd almost convinced ourselves that's what it had to be. But we don't have any more conclusion than that, really. The fact that we didn't see it much past this one period—we really don't have a conclusion as to what it might have been, how big it was, or how far away it was. It was something that wasn't part of the urine dump, we're pretty sure of that.

BARROWSKY: Their voices . . .

PREBBLE: What about Sky Lab? They had their share of UFOs. . . . During Sky Lab II the crew observed a large, star-shaped object, much brighter than any planet or star could possibly be . . . and this object was observed slowly rotating. . . . They observed it for approximately ten minutes. It was about thirty to fifty nautical miles from Sky Lab, by their estimates. . . . But it too remains just another unknown . . . in spite of North American Air Defense Command's and NASA's attempts to identify it.

INGELS: Yeah. [*Deep sigh.*] Here, since we're at it, I might as well show you a couple more slides. Lloyd, do you

mind again? Thanks. [*Slight chuckle.*] Here we are. Sorry
. . . no . . . it's upside down, doesn't quite look that way.
[*General sound of laughter.*] Here, I'll just run through
these—this set here—real quickly—just an overall view,
really, of different shapes, positions, altitudes, distances,
and so on. These are all from NASA's top-classified files—
ha! One of the souvenirs I took with me when I left . . .

Here we are. This is a saucer with the moon in the background—you can see right over there to the left. A saucer
disappearing over the desert—this was out in Arizona. A
saucer, top view. Here, over a city—Chicago. Here's an
enlargement of that same slide. Here's a Klaner saucer. A
saucer in clouds—from a Pan Am jet over the southern
Pacific. Over a housing development, Miami Beach. Pyramid saucer. Wheel saucer, Trent.

And now here's a table—this is all just to convey some
idea of the variety of shapes that have appeared . . . on
record. The images that have most commonly appeared are
either small points, formless blobs, or what look like fuzzy
ellipses—that is, in the night sky—or a more distinct
ellipse—like the one in D9, to the left—against a lighter,
daytime sky. Except for some of the exceptions, such as the
rocket or "cigar"-shaped object with "exhaust trail" that
supposedly was photographed in 1952 over Peru, the more
well-defined objects appear to be some variant, really, of
the common saucer or domed disk.

Now here are some more from the Gemini XII in
space . . . these are also from the top-classified series. This
was shot on November 12, 1966. It's unidentifiable. Notice
the white haze around it like a band of light. . . . They said
it seemed to be speeding back and forth at incredible rates.
Five, seven hundred miles a minute? NASA Photo Evaluation Lab identified it as trash floating out of a spaceship.

Here's more trash . . . another sphere of light . . . blue
with a blurred edge of what appears to be red. . . . This
one's from Gemini XI during the eighteenth revolution,
twenty-seven hours and forty-seven minutes Greenwich
mean time, September 12, 1966—an unidentified object,
as determined again by NASA Photo Evaluation Lab.
Here, take another look at it. And this next one was shot
during Sky Lab III's second manned sky-lab flight, day
263 of '73—1645 Zulu time. Ten shots were taken—four

made public. . . . Here's an enlargement of one of the classified ones you just saw. It's listed as an unidentified object or satellite by the Evaluation Lab. Notice the area of red at the edges again.

And here [sighs] this one is from Apollo XI . . . this one on June 16, 1969 . . . considered unidentifiable . . . You can clearly see—here's another enlargement of it—you can clearly see the blue glow lights, black fuselage. And this one . . . this was shot during Gemini XII's flight of November '66—November 11. Four hours and forty-five minutes after lift-off. Here are several enlargements—the explanation of this one is that it's a solar-axis reflection. . . . And here are some I took myself . . . in space. The next three were on the return from the moon. And this next batch coming up is by Kip. . . . Here's an enlargement of that last one. . . . And here's one of the most incredible— just look at that—Scott took that one . . . unbelievable. No, they couldn't identify that one, either.

Well, that just about wraps it up. Yes . . . Oh, I have some more here. There are a few more, they must have gotten misfiled. I must have put them in the wrong order by mistake. Ha. I don't see how but . . . well, here, this is one from Gemini XII again, November 13, 1966. Here are a number of different shots of it from different angles. Here we are . . . Incredible, huh? I mean you can see the outline of the whole thing. It couldn't be clearer. And NASA identified it, of course, said to be Agena ranging lights prior to docking. . . . And there you have it. . . . Thanks. Why don't we open the curtains, too? Yeah . . . Well, I'll put this stuff away later. . . .

Here are some photos. These are from Air Force top-secret files. They're from the desert. Arizona. Arizona again . . . in the northwest part of the state. They document, ah . . . several . . . actually a number of sightings in the area. These were filed—this whole batch here—as either lenticular clouds or mirages or ball lightning—a sphere-shaped plasma blob usually associated with electrical storms—or atmospheric inversion layers or anomalous propagation of radar signals. It doesn't really matter. They might as well all be interchangeable. You can see for yourself. But the Air Force maintains that our knowledge of these phenomena is so limited that there's no way they can really be identified positively. And here are some more—some others. These are just photos of the sites taken by top security investigators. Rocks, pod marks, burned bushes . . . arroyos . . . tracks in the clay, and so on. Here, take a look at them . . . why don't you just pass them around?

JORDAN: Gerald, why don't you take a look? What do you think?

BARROWSKY: Yes . . . almost . . . I can almost pick it up . . . there . . . my palm is warmer now . . . the tips of my fingers are touching the area. This is in the northwest part of the state . . . thirty-six degrees latitude . . . between Rose Bar Flat and Coyote Canyon . . . the bushes have been burned there . . . oxidation traces.

SCHRADER: Are these from the Blue Book in '69?

INGELS: Let's see. Yes, and that next one, too. But you won't see these anywhere. These are the ones they didn't even dare file—most of these aren't even in the top-secret files.

BARROWSKY: There is a field . . . here . . . right in this range—on this photograph here. This one . . . a magnetic field of energy.

Synopsis of preceding edited transcript.
Barrowsky continued to keep his eyes closed, touching the photographs. At 1255 they stopped for lunch. Ingels sent up for some sandwiches from the cafeteria, as they did not think it would be a good idea to break Barrowsky's concentration. Then the curtains were closed again, the lights switched off. Barrowsky concentrated again on the slides and the photographs—trying to establish contact. But he sensed interference: There was "resistance in the room"; he was not able to "conduct proper communication." He also announced, "This place is wired electronically. It's bugged." An argument followed. Ingels vehemently denied it, said it was impossible. The Watkins Research Laboratory had never been tapped. It was an apolitical institution.

Barrowsky tried to "clear the air"—a last measure to connect—closing his eyes, having everyone else also close theirs, while they all sat in silence, establishing complete silence. As this did not prove successful, either, it was arranged they would try again some other time soon—in the next week—whenever it was convenient to everyone present. Barrowsky explained his "circuits were overloaded." He had been overworked. Jordan corroborated this. The meeting terminated.

At 1448 Sturgis walked Schrader out to the parking lot. There followed a short but wordy exchange, again the visibility—the low bushes and recent trees—made it impossible to observe this area. Schrader got into his car. Sturgis waited a moment, standing beside the car as if he were about to say something else, but then he must have either decided not to or that it wasn't important. He waved good-bye and walked quickly away, back into the building. Schrader pulled out. He drove straight back to Sonora Pines, arriving at 1950.

Unedited transcript of telephone conversation between Schrader and Sturgis. 9 September.

WORTHINGTON: Hello.

STURGIS: Hello?

WORTHINGTON: Yes?

STURGIS: Oh, hello, is Nick . . . ah, there?

WORTHINGTON: Who's this?

STURGIS: Tom Sturgis.

WORTHINGTON: Oh . . . Ah, yeah . . . Nick! Nick [*voice inaudible*].

SCHRADER: Hello. Tom?

STURGIS: I just called Pickering to confirm for Thursday.

SCHRADER: Fine. As I said, anything with me—

STURGIS: He's dead.

SCHRADER: Dead? Are you serious?

STURGIS: He had a massive heart attack Saturday night. I spoke to one of his assistants. In the middle of the night . . . right in the observatory. He was looking through a telescope and . . . just went out. Just like that, sitting right there in a chair. One minute he was looking through the lens and the next . . . They rushed him to the hospital.

SCHRADER: I don't believe it.

STURGIS: Well, you'll see it in the papers tomorrow.

SCHRADER: Did he have a history of—

STURGIS: No. No heart condition.

SCHRADER: What about his family? His wife . . . children.

STURGIS: Wasn't married . . . His whole life was up there. Naw. He had no one. His sister lived with him. A widow. He had some cats. But you know he was hardly ever home. . . . Hello? Are you there?

SCHRADER: [*Low voice.*] No, it's Pickering. . . . He's dead. . . . Yeah. Ah, yeah, I was just telling Michelle.

STURGIS: Yeah. Well . . . I guess that takes care of Thursday.

SCHRADER: Yeah, I guess so. I guess it does, doesn't it? Well, I'll come down, of course, for the services.

STURGIS: Naw, there aren't any. Didn't want it. He's being cremated.

SCHRADER: Hmm. Yeah, well . . . Tom?

STURGIS: Yeah.

SCHRADER: Was it . . . was it . . . an accident?

STURGIS: I don't know, Nick. I don't know.

SCHRADER: Is there going to be an autopsy?

STURGIS: Yeah. There already was. It was a heart attack.

SCHRADER: Well, it could have been . . .

STURGIS: I don't know, Nick. I don't know.

SCHRADER: Hmm. What can you say? There isn't much. Yeah. [*Sighs.*] Well, all right, I'll speak to you.

STURGIS: Yeah, I'll call you.

Agent R. Castle to Security 5A200 Washington. 10 September.

Search of Richardson's office again failed to reveal Schrader file. Schrader was observed arriving and departing. Richardson tapes every session. The intent seems conclusive and deliberate.

Carole went out into the driveway. Another gray day, she thought. Or was it just the pollution? She couldn't tell any longer. She got into the Ford station wagon, the car she'd had last year in Sonora Pines. The pale yellow convertible vintage Jaguar with its rebuilt engine (a birthday present from Mike) remained in the garage. Carole, contrary to what she had assumed about herself for years, really didn't like speed. She didn't like the noise of the engine, the ease with which the car took the sharpest turns, the way it glided on the freeways as if it were an animate spirit just waiting to take off. She didn't like the contact with the road. Nor did she like being so conspicuous. It made her feel unprotected, singled out. The Jaguar stayed in the garage. Mike occasionally took it out, sometimes in the middle of the night when he'd wake up and decide to go to the studio early—at 4 or 5 A.M.—he would race it on the freeways, or when he took it to have it periodically checked over. It had been used so little it was having engine problems.

Carole got into the Ford. She slowly pulled out of the long driveway, carefully checking out either end of the street even though there were hardly ever any cars. Everyone seemed to be either always away or keeping strange hours. Sometimes Carole had the feeling no one really lived there; it was really just a set: the Tudor houses, pseudo *palazzi*, Rollses, Bentleys, Ferraris displayed for show in the driveways, the impeccable lawns, the palm trees fluttering in the mild breeze, incongruously out of place on the sedate sidewalk. Carole drove down the length of Crescent into Santa Monica, down North Rodeo Drive, past the set of town houses—boutiques. The row of Gucci, Hermès, Van Cleef, Aquascutum . . . Nothing was open yet. It was still too early. The streets were empty. Water spilled out from an unattended hose, staining the pavement, growing like a shadow, seeping into the pale stone; the hose was just lying there forgotten. Carole looked into the rearview mirror. The water was still gushing out, the stain steadily spreading.

She turned onto Wilshire, past the Beverly Wilshire, and down toward La Cienega. A car behind her honked. She was driving too slowly. She rolled down her window. It was getting hot again. Her eyes burned. With one hand she opened her bag, slipped on her sunglasses. The car honked again. This time she didn't even look. She took her foot off the gas. Now she would really go slowly. She stopped at a red light. A pregnant Mexican girl, about fourteen, in a dress that looked like a nightgown, lumbered across the street. Carole stared at the huge bulge of her stomach, which seemed to be leading her, as if it were pulling her across the street. The girl's head, tilted backward, enhanced this impression. Then a raggedy couple in shredded dungarees, the guy with a Jesus hairdo, the girl with a flaming orange Afro. They also seemed to be having trouble keep-

ing their balance. . . . An old lady in a dark heavy coat
dragging behind her a shopping cart stuffed with old grocery bags and newspapers . . . Two tanned boys in swimming trunks and a girl in a bikini on speedbikes. The light
changed and the driver in back of Carole sped out, raising
his fist in passing and cursing her—but he was going too
fast for her to hear what he was saying.

She checked the rearview again. Where had she seen
that car before? It was a white Plymouth. She continued
down La Cienega. It was still there. She pressed her foot
down. Thirty, thirty-five. The car was still there. She
pulled into a Texaco station. The car slowed down, stopped,
waited. Oh, it must be a mistake. I must be imagining this.
She pulled out. The white Plymouth followed. Down La
Cienega, into Melrose. It was probably just going in the
same direction. Still, there was something . . . she couldn't
be sure . . . after all, strange things happened out here.
Ridiculous. That's on the news. For the movies. These
things didn't really happen. Still, it was unnerving.

She switched on the radio. KFAC. The classical station.
Bartók. She tried to figure out if it was Bartók or not. That
strain . . . No, it might not be . . . those violins . . . It got
on her nerves. She flicked it off. The white Plymouth was
still there. This was a scene in a movie, she decided. She
was driving down this avenue in Los Angeles. And a car
was following her. She turned the radio back on: the same
music. She flicked it off again. And the Plymouth was still
there. Her heart was pounding now, her whole body
seemed wired for sound, for noise—drilling in the background, a garbage truck, the deafening clatter of a bus. It
was as if she were registering every sound, as if she were
programmed. She was gripping the wheel. She had the
image of incredible strength, she could pull the wheel off,
effortlessly. The thought panicked her. She relaxed her
hold. Her hands were wet and remained glued to the
wheel. She felt sweat trickle down her underarms, spreading down her yellow jersey. Her tan pants were molded to
her body, and her body molded to the car seat. She was
a part of the car . . . and all those other cars out there
. . . they were just cars: No one was really in them. Maybe
she had been mistaken for someone else, maybe her car
had been mistaken for someone else's. She was just

imagining all of this, the white Plymouth following her. She closed her eyes a split second and then quickly looked into the rearview. It was still there. She slowed down. She was now passing the art galleries, the decorator stores, the boutiques . . . the newly developed part of Melrose. She pulled into an alley, the side of a small building where the store—the House of Spirits—was. She ran out of the car, into the store. Lin, her assistant, who opened up for her, was sitting on the counter with her acting-student boyfriend. Carole ran past them, to the front window. She looked out surreptitiously—the car wasn't there.

"What's the matter?" Lin came toward her. "Are you OK?"

Carole didn't answer. She looked again. But the car was gone.

Agent R. Castle to Security 5A200 Washington. 12 September.

In routine surveillance of Schrader's wife, leaving Beverly Hills residence of Michael Gallagher this morning, heading east along Wilshire, La Cienega, to occult shop off Melrose, we spotted white Plymouth license plate traced and confirmed through Tchernilkov as part of Russian network.

We suggest we set up, through Tchernilkov, meeting with the Russians to clarify that they are on the wrong track, we are not keeping anything from them (our surveillance of Schrader's wife is purely routine, merely a precaution on our part); that, after all, in this matter we have nothing to gain by withholding information from them; that we will continue keeping them informed as the situation develops.

"Good to have you with us again." The United Airlines stewardess smiled. Nick almost looked behind him to see whom she was referring to and then, of course, he realized she meant him. He smiled weakly. He went down the aisle, toward the back.

When they landed in San Francisco, the same stewardess smiled again. "Have a pleasant stay." And Nick could have sworn that she winked. He went straight to the Avis counter. One of the same girls was on. He tried to get to the other one, but she was busy. "Hi." The girl smiled. In her Avis outfit, with the little Avis cap, Nick had the image of an office Mouseketeer or cartoon human. "You . . ." She pointed to Nick, pretending to try to place him. "You rented a . . ." She paused, then beamed. "A red Duster, right?"

"No, but close. Green. How do you know?" He went along.

"I have a good memory for faces." She smiled, but she had already started filling out the sheet.

"But you must see hundreds of people a day. Thousands."

Her eyes lowered, she kept filling out the sheet. She smiled insinuatingly. "The same thing?"

"What?" He was looking at a man in plaid suit and sunglasses standing by the doors. He'd seen him somewhere before. "Yeah, fine."

"Here. Just sign here."

Nick felt someone's eyes on him as he went outside. He turned around, squinting in the light. He saw the man in the plaid suit using the phone behind the Avis counter.

He parked a block from the university, got out of the car, and walked slowly up through the grounds. He was early again. Hammond's office door was open. He was sitting at his desk, writing in a steno pad. He almost jumped out of his chair. "God! You scared me." He took out his handkerchief, wiped off his forehead. Nick saw he really was sweating. "I'm a little early."

"Yes. It's only a quarter after."

"There was less traffic than I thought—"

"I don't . . . I thought the whole point was not to meet here. I thought when we spoke the other day . . ." Hammond stopped mid-sentence, went to the door, and closed it. He whispered something.

Nick shook his head. Hammond annoyed him. "Sorry, but I can't hear you. You'll have to speak louder."

"Some other people are following me," Hammond whispered. It was barely audible. "I think Macdavitt was right. I think it's the Russians."

"You're just imagining things."

"No, these people really stick out. These men have nothing to do with Washington. There's some whole other group involved in this. Some sort of front, that's what Macdavitt thought." Hammond's eyes were opened wide, transfixed by fear. "And I think we're just going . . . after we've served . . ." Nick could hardly hear what he was saying. ". . . our purpose . . . expendable."

"You're just getting paranoid."

But Hammond was convinced; he didn't want them to be seen outside together.

Nick went to the Silver Spur, sat at a booth, and waited. Hammond turned up five minutes later. He ordered hamburgers so they wouldn't be bothered. He kept looking at the clock on the wall, pulling back his sleeve and checking his watch. He asked Nick several times what time he had.

A few minutes before four, two men came in together and, without looking around, went straight to the booth where Nick and Hammond were seated. They were both in check jackets, white shirts, narrow ties, black pants, black shoes, sunglasses—almost twins or, rather, look-alike robots—the only difference seemed to be the sunglasses: One had Polaroid sunglasses.

Hammond rose slightly, not quite standing up, not quite seated. "This is Captain Bob Palmer of Pan Am, who used to be with the Pentagon."

"Sshh." Bob Palmer, the one with the Polaroid sunglasses, winced. "Lower your voice."

This was all Hammond needed. "And this, this"—he almost stuttered—"is Vic Wagner, the aerologist I told you about, at Gray Sands . . . who also worked with Macdavitt. Dr. Nicholas Schrader."

Vic put out his hand. Bob looked away. He was chewing his gum rapidly. "OK," Bob said. "OK, let's keep our voices down. Let's not broadcast it. I don't like meeting like this, Warren, I told you. I said a public place. There's nobody in this place. Why didn't you have us meet in some park or something?"

"Oh, I wouldn't say that." Hammond looked hurt. "There are quite a few people here."

"Well, we're here." His jaws dropped a moment, he looked the young waitress over, then his jaws started up again. He ordered a dietetic root beer, Vic an iced tea. Bob waited until the waitress had gone. "OK, well, we're—

here, so it's too late to cry over spilled milk, as they say. Now, what do you want to know?"

Nick looked at Hammond. Hammond swallowed. "He wants to know how to get into the top-secret files at Gray Sands."

"He does, does he?" Bob nodded. "Just like that. What for?"

"He wants to look into the files of Blue Book and the two O projects."

"Why doesn't he go to Washington? Why doesn't he look into the files there?"

"Well, Bob, you know no one can get to the ones in Washington. The security's too tight," Hammond explained, smiling. "But Macdavitt said there were a number of duplicate files kept at Gray Sands. And we can get access to those. He wants to look into them."

"Really? I'm going to tell him right here, huh? You really expect me to discuss it, go into that in this place, huh? You nuts or something?" Bob looked disgusted.

Hammond squirmed. "Well, Bob, you said a public place."

"Maybe we could set up another meeting?" Nick suggested. "I mean if it's amenable to both of you . . . some other time."

"No. We'll talk here. Well, now that we're here, we might as well." Bob sighed.

"Well, I was just hoping you could talk to him," Hammond said. "As I told you, he has Macdavitt's papers."

"Macdavitt never mentioned anything about him." Vic looked dubious.

"I was given the papers after his death."

"Yeah." Bob nodded. "We know all about that. We heard all about it." He glanced at Hammond. "We're here, aren't we?"

"And Osmond gave you the papers?" Vic asked.

"That's right."

"And where are these papers now?" Bob asked.

Nick and Hammond looked at each other.

"Well? Where are they? It's such an unreasonable question? You have the papers, right?"

Nick nodded.

"So everybody in the country'd be after you. Nobody

even knew Macdavitt had kept any papers. I mean on this thing."

"I can only say they're safe."

Bob stopped chewing, pursed his lips, nodded, and studied Nick absentmindedly, as if to say, You don't say. . . . "Well, I hope so. For your sake." And he started chewing again. "OK. Shoot."

"I want to know how to get into the main compound at Gray Sands."

Bob laughed, his head went back slightly, mockingly. "Ha! Here?" he asked sarcastically.

"I want to microfilm some of the papers in the files from the Blue Book and the two O projects—the papers that have been removed from even the top-secret files in the Pentagon."

"The papers that have been removed?" Bob nodded thoughtfully without changing his expression at all. The waitress put down the glasses. "Is this dietetic?" he asked. The glass said Cocoa-Cola on it. The platinum-blond waitress nodded, not overly concerned. "OK. Because it says Coke."

"No, it's dietetic." She checked her pad.

"Gotta watch my waistline." He kept his eyes on her haunches as she walked away. "Well, OK. What do you think, Vic?"

"Well, if he has access to Macdavitt's papers, then he should know about some of the encounters we've had," Vic said. "Let him tell us—in his own words—like, for instance, about Austin in 1969."

"Well, most of that is declassified," Bob said. "He could have just looked it up."

"No, I'm thinking more of what was omitted," Vic said. "Give us some facts. Like I said. Austin."

"Austin, November 16, 1969," Nick said. "You were at an altitude of 35,000 feet. As you were approaching Austin you sighted a huge, round object overhead. Because of its size, you thought at first it might be an unusually large research balloon. Then you realized it was moving with you. What wasn't revealed was the fact that you checked out its speed and that this unknown object was pacing the jet, matching its ground speed: 535 knots, 616 miles an hour.

It was about the size of a DC-8. Your guess: 500 to 600 feet in diameter. There were no protrusions or windows—"

"Oh, look, c'mon, Vic," Bob said. "We're just wasting time. How do we come into the picture?"

Hammond hesitated. "He wants to know, Bob, Vic, if you'd be prepared to back him up if he went public."

"He's going to make it public?" Bob asked incredulously.

"I hope to."

"Good luck! They'll laugh in your face."

"No, I don't think so. I think I have enough material. Macdavitt left enough material."

"Yeah? Well, you keep jabbering away about this material. Well, where is it?"

"I told you it's safe."

"OK, OK, fellow." Bob put out his hand in mock defense. "I'm not disputing you."

Vic cocked his head. "Who's that?" A man in a light blue striped seersucker suit, sunglasses, holding an attaché case, was standing at the window. Bob shrugged, made a face.

"I hope to avoid having to get to the files," Nick said. "I'll do it only if we can't get enough support."

"It's only a precaution." Hammond smiled apologetically.

Bob nodded mechanically without much interest.

"What I really want is to find more about the present security behind the cover-up and the two O projects."

"You do, do you?" Bob nodded, then added, laughing, "Who doesn't? Well, you're not the only one. He can tell you about that just as well as I can." He indicated Hammond.

Hammond blushed. "Well, Bob, you were on the O projects long after I—"

"Why does he want to know the security aspects of the thing anyway?" Bob asked suspiciously.

"Well, Bob, he'd like to know more about who's really behind it."

"I want to know more about the background. To fill me in on what Macdavitt's papers leave out."

Bob snorted sarcastically. "We can only guess. But I'd

say it was some sort of international network, wouldn't you, Vic? Involving the CIA, Russian Intelligence."

"Could be." Vic nodded informatively.

Nick caught Hammond's eye.

"But I wouldn't jump the gun if I were you. Who knows?" Bob laughed. "Could be any combination."

Hammond nodded, intent. "Macdavitt had leads indicating that it was some offshoot of the CIA. Some specially formed group."

Vic seemed taken aback. He frowned, ultrasober. "Well, Bob, it's not as if we ever really got any real leads, is it?"

"No, we sure didn't," Bob said. "But it doesn't sound so farfetched. Some sort of offshoot group of the CIA . . ."

"How does this offshoot group work?" Nick asked.

Bob made a face, shrugged. "The CIA's probably just using it as a front, a cover. In order to deal with the Russians on this thing, in order to find out just how much they know—how much they knew—and how much they know of what we are up to."

"Macdavitt had leads indicating who was involved in this offshoot group. He had leads from a number of government people, including the Pentagon. Macdavitt thought it was a front created to make it look like it was the Russians." Hammond waited for a challenge. There wasn't any. "He was going to confront them directly. That this group was just a cover . . ."

Vic cocked his head again. The man at the window was looking in their direction. "Look, let's get out of here. I don't like this."

"I told you someone was following me," Hammond stuttered.

"Sshh." Bob scowled. "Why don't you quietly go pay the check, Vic?"

Vic got up, took their two checks, and casually went up to the cashier.

"You set up some other time for us to meet." Bob kept his voice low. "In a public place. We'll go over all this in more detail next time. You just phone me or Vic at home. You have the numbers." Bob slipped out of the booth, joined Vic. The man at the window turned the other way, his eyes on the street. Hammond took out his handkerchief and dabbed his forehead. He was breathing so heavily, Nick thought he might pass out.

The man turned toward Bob and Vic for a moment as they came out, then he looked away again, in the opposite direction. Bob and Vic got into a Corvette parked across the street—Bob at the wheel—and roared off. A tanned girl in a flowery dress appeared in the far angle of the window. She was smiling widely, swinging a cloth shoulder bag. The man grinned, put his arm around her.

Hammond ran outside. Nick left a tip, paid the cashier. When he came out, Hammond was still standing in the middle of the street, but the Corvette was gone; the couple with their arms around each other were almost at the corner.

"I'll set up something for next week," Hammond stuttered. "I'll call them both up this evening."

"That was certainly a waste." Nick sighed. "Yeah. Well. All right. Why don't you phone me at that second number I gave you on Sunday morning? You should be able to get hold of them by then."

The police car on its routine nightly patrol went slowly down the dark countryside roads, past the rows of unlit houses and estates along Westview, Eucalyptus Lane, down Mountain Road into Green Acres, past the new condominiums. Everything seemed normal. Then past the Sonora Pines Village—a pseudo Spanish-Colonial complex of stores, boutiques, two banks, a gas station.

The young officer flashed his brights onto the Barclays Bank, onto Frocks & Smocks, onto the dark office of the Exxon station, the Clotheshorse, the Georgian Touch, the Bank of America, the Green Thumb, the Molde of Fashion.

He drove down the length of Westview, into Cold Springs, flashed his brights on the driveway of the Bly estate, past Captain Burke's, the Sheldon place, Los Ríos Vista Ranch, down into Eldorado Hills to New Appian Way. There was a light in the guesthouse of the Richardson place, where Dr. Richardson had his office. He turned back, switched off his lights, and slowly pulled up to the side of the road. He got out of the car. A slight wind covered the sound of his footsteps on the gravel, the fallen eucalyptus bark, the dead leaves, and then the pebbles down the Richardson driveway.

The door to the guesthouse was open, the yellow light cutting across the darkness, the sitting room with its two chairs, banquette, prints on the wallpapered walls, waiting, like a stage set, an invitation. He moved back, took out his gun, and then rushed in, slamming the door against the wall. The door reverberated and swung back and forth. He kicked it back, standing frozen, slumped forward, his gun pointing, a live statue in action. There was no sound. Only the wind flapping the curtains, rubbing against the loose pane of a window, rummaging through the leaves. The door to the office was open. He crossed the dark threshold, kicking the door back, his pointed gun running an arc like a speeded-up beam from a lighthouse. But there was nothing, no one in there in the dark. He pulled out his flashlight and traced a steady thorough path on the desk with the open drawer, the file cabinet with all the drawers open, the open closet with the file cabinets in there open, the leather couch, the modern upright lamp lying on top of the clutter of books on the floor, the open window with its green curtains indicating the presence now only of the night wind.

The officer went back out, into the driveway. He put back his gun, his flashlight. He took out his walkie-talkie. But then, at that moment, some lights came on in a series of upstairs windows. He went to the imposing large oak-paneled front door and rang the bell.

In fumbling for the receiver, Nick pushed the phone off the night table. A split second before, he had still thought that he was dreaming that a phone was ringing. But the jolt of the phone hitting he floor made him open his eyes and notice the room, the receiver in his hand, Michelle lying across from him in the bed. "Hello? . . . Yes."

"Nick?"

Nick tried to place the voice. It was familiar.

"Harold Richardson."

"Oh . . . I didn't recognize your voice."

"I'm sorry to call you this time of the night. Nick?"

"Yeah. I'm here."

"Can you hear me?"

"What? . . . What time is it?"

"Somebody broke into the office. . . . Can you come over here right away?"

"What?" Nick blinked rapidly, shaking his head as if he were drunk and trying to rouse himself. The drunkenness wore off immediately.

"The police are here now. I want you to come over. There are some things I want to talk to you about."

Nick pulled into the Richardson driveway. There were two police cars with their lights whirling away, red white, red white, soundlessly. "Over here," Richardson called to him from the side of the house. Richardson had on pants, his pajama-top collar sticking out from his turtleneck. Two officers were wandering around the lawn with their flashlights, showing brief trails of gray shrubs, garden furniture, buoys, air mattresses, some flowers.

Nick followed Richardson into the brightly lit office, where nothing had been touched. "We're waiting for the photographer," Richardson explained, then he lowered his voice. "They took the last two tapes."

"I thought you said . . ."

"They found them . . . look, I don't know how. I told you I put them in somebody else's file."

"Are you sure?"

"Yes. I've looked everywhere."

"Do they know?" Nick tilted his head, indicating the two policemen.

"No, they just think it's an ordinary burglary—attempted burglary. But I'm not that surprised. I didn't think they'd really do it, though. After Ellsberg you'd think they'd know better. It's a good thing we didn't tape the last two sessions . . . in view of what was discussed . . . what you talked about. You were right. It's a good thing none of that's on tape. But the fact remains, they were here. This wasn't any robbery. Nothing was taken. No, they were looking for those tapes. . . . What are you going to do?"

"I don't know. Ha! I'd like to see their expressions when they realize the tapes are blank."

"You didn't tell, ah . . . anyone you were coming here, did you?"

"No. Of course not. Who am I going to tell at two-thirty

in the morning? I just rushed right over here. Who am I going to tell? I told Michelle. What am I supposed to do—run right out of the house in the middle of the night without telling her?"

R. Castle to Security 5A200 Washington. 13 September.
Someone has broken into Richardson's office. We assume it was the Russians. But we cannot understand why they continue to disregard what we have repeatedly told them—that we have nothing to hide from them in this matter.

Again, if there is anything being withheld from us, we would appreciate being so informed.

Tina Sturgis looked up from the *History of Keyboard Music to 1700*, the book she was reading. The man in the blue blazer staring by the window in the university library almost blushed—or maybe it just looked that way because of the light through the panes, which were tinted—and immediately turned the other way, pretending he was actually looking at something out of the tinted window on the lawn below. Tina went back to her book, but she was distracted again—she had seen that man in the hallway outside the cafeteria at lunch and earlier in the parking lot. She'd seen him standing on the front steps when she came in. He seemed to be waiting for something. He didn't really look at her, gave no indication that he was aware of her. But she knew. She knew he was waiting for her.

For the last three days, four? She couldn't remember. At first it just seemed a coincidence; but then slowly, like a figure in a dream, someone almost symbolic—it seemed that way to her—she slowly became aware of his presence; slowly he came into focus: in the hall, in his white Falcon in the parking lot, in passing, yesterday—or was it the day before?—in the shopping center, outside Vons at dusk, at the intersection of Freemark and Mission, at the bookstore, or outside the club where she played tennis every afternoon, on the stairs, on the lawn, standing there against a pole . . . in the library, seated across from her, pretending to be looking into space, pretending to be reading . . . pretending to look out of a window . . . at a window . . . He slowly rose out of the depth of the sea of unknown faces around her, into her consciousness.

She didn't know how long she'd been reading. She hadn't even been aware that she was reading, but she must have been, because here she was on page 221 and she had been on page 190 when she had come into the library at two o'clock. And then suddenly—this time when she looked up—he looked straight at her, straight into her eyes. And she knew. And she knew she was meant to know. That he wanted her to know. Her eyes opened wide, the pupils dilating as if trying to take in as much as she could, as if she were trying to absorb all the light, all the infinitesimal points of color, all the disparate dots that made up the scene before her. She stared straight back at him. But she didn't really see him, wasn't aware of what she was seeing. It was like being hypnotized. Her heart was pounding. She could hear it in her ears. She was breathing heavily. The room seemed to be very far away. She felt as if she were watching everything, watching herself watching this man, as if from a great distance. The man seemed to be so removed from her, so far away, that it was more like a dream. It was that unreal. And then she heard something, some sound, someone walking by. She heard the steady rhythm of someone's shoes on the parquet. And she came to. Her eyes readjusted to the light, closed slightly. Something almost snapped. She was aware of the man's expression. The slit of his mouth. He was pretending to be smiling. Or was she imagining that, too? She jumped up, grabbed her books, her bag, and ran out of the library, out into the hall, down the stairs, out into the parking lot, into her car. She didn't look back once. She didn't have to. She knew she was being followed. She sped back to the house.

She wouldn't let the baby-sitter go. When Tom came back later that afternoon to change for his squash game, he was surprised to find the front door locked.

After the baby-sitter left, she pulled him into the study, closed the door. "I'm being followed," she said.

He didn't show any reaction. All he said was, "Are you sure?"

She nodded and started to cry. He put his arms around her but he didn't say anything. There wasn't really anything he could say.

* * *

Nick waited all day Sunday. But Hammond never called. Nick figured he probably hadn't been able to set up an appointment with Palmer and Wagner. So there was no point in calling. He'd call him tomorrow at the university.

He waited until after lunchtime. Two-fifteen. He should have been able to set up something by now. He let the phone ring and ring. There was no answer. He waited fifteen minutes. Hammond might have been out. He tried again. He knew Hammond didn't have a class until late in the afternoon, and he was usually in his office using the time for his own work. Still no answer. Nick got the operator, tried another number. The switchboard. Got someone, a woman. No, Dr. Hammond wasn't in. She worked in the office across the way. No, she was quite sure. He hadn't come in today. No, she had no idea why. Perhaps he was sick. Who was this?

Nick tried his home. No answer. He tried later from Michelle's. Still no answer. Hammond had probably gone away with his family for the weekend and stayed away longer. . . . He'd wait a day or two, try him again in the middle of the week.

He lay down on the bed. Where the hell was Michelle, anyway? It was almost seven o'clock. What the hell was she doing? He got up, went into the living room. Of course! The barbecue at the children's school. There was a note Scotch taped to the refrigerator: "Cold salmon and sauces on top shelf. Love and xxxs, M."

He was lying on the bed. He must have been drifting. The ringing didn't stop. He picked up the phone. "Hello? Dr. Hammond?"

"Hello?" It was Tom.

The next morning, Nick got to the Foundation late—Michelle didn't have a class and they'd gone back to bed after the children had left on the school bus. It was close to noon by the time he got to the Foundation. He found a note on his desk: "Could you drop by my office when you get in? R.B.O."—in ornate initials.

Nick was annoyed and then puzzled. Osmond had been avoiding him the last couple of weeks, since he had bowed out. What could he possibly want now?

He knocked and went in. Rodney was standing with his back to the door, at one of the open French windows, looking out onto the garden. One of his habitual poses, Nick thought. Rodney turned around slowly, almost absentmindedly. He looked at Nick or, rather, at a point beyond him, let his eyes rest on some point on the wall beyond Nick. Nick closed the door. Rodney's mouth was pursed, a grim noncommunicative expression. "I just got in." Then Nick added, as if that were the reason, "I overslept."

Rodney went over to his desk, shoved a newspaper across to the side of the desk where Nick was standing. It was the San Francisco *Chronicle*. Nick looked puzzled. Was this some kind of joke? But he read, anyway, his eyes scanning the page, page 3. He read:

UNIVERSITY PROFESSOR DROWNS: APPARENT SUICIDE
The body of Dr. Warren L. Hammond, professor of physics at UC Berkeley, was found by a patrolman yesterday morning washed ashore on the Alameda Memorial Beach. His death was listed as an apparent suicide. Autopsy reports show a high level of barbiturates in his bloodstream. . . . Dr. Hammond left a note to his wife. Mrs. Hammond found the note late Sunday evening and contacted the police. . . . Dr. Hammond is survived by his wife and three children. . . . Dr. Hammond, at the time of his death, had been working on the revised edition of his textbook, *Fundamentals of Modern Physics*, which has been in wide use in colleges and universities since its publication in 1962. He had hoped to finish this revised editon by the end of the year. . . . Dr. Hammond, a figure of controversy durng the McCarthy era . . .

Outside of Malibu, the car was still there behind him, trailing. Nick accelerated. There was no other car in sight, no police car. Sixty, sixty-five, seventy, eighty. The tan Impala with the two men in the front seat was still there, less than a hundred feet back. Nick tried to keep his eyes off the side of the road, where the road suddenly broke off and the white lava of waves erupted, smoldering against the rocks in the blinding sunlight, and beyond that, the turquoise field of water stretched out beneath the endless dome of sheer blue sky. He felt surrounded on all sides—on the

edge of this sunlit abyss of sky and water. Eighty-five,
ninety. He kept his eyes on the road, on the turns, the
curves, as if he were following a grid, doing no more than
sitting in a car, turning the wheel, and the scenery spinning
around him, the road before him speeding under him,
were only superimposed, a superimposed movie background, and he himself simply a character—some irrelevant, fairly expendable character in this movie—in this
chase-scene sequence of some movie. The Impala seemed
to be gaining speed. They were now almost in Malibu.
Nick started to slow down. The boardwalk of flimsy beach
houses cropped away the view of the water. Another half
mile. Nick came to a sudden stop. A kid in flowery trunks,
carrying a surfboard under his arm, was slowly walking
across the road, swaying visibly. There was a yellow light
ahead. A cop was parked in front of the Chevron station.
Nick glanced in the mirror. The Impala was gone.

He took his time the rest of the way down; but the Impala didn't reappear.

R. Castle to Security 5A200 Washington. 18 September.
Schrader was followed down 101 by what we presume
again to be Russian agents, temporarily disrupting our surveillance.

Schrader's security will be increased during the interim,
until this matter is cleared up, as we cannot yet tell what
their intentions are or what consequences may be involved.

Again, we repeat, if there is anything being withheld
from us, we would appreciate being so informed.

Dr. Luis Ruz-Silveiro's office was on the third floor. Nick
went down the sunlit Plexiglas hall. The hall looked unreal: panels of sky and light. He felt as if he were going
down a hall in some mythical dream down which he—
the dreamer—was being inexorably led.

Dr. Ruz's large office overlooked a football field. The
door was open. Nick went in. Tom was standing by one of
the windows with Dr. Ruz. They were both looking out.
"Nick, this is Dr. Ruz. Dr. Ruz, Dr. Schrader."

They shook hands. Dr. Ruz was a frail, dapper elderly
gentleman on whom everything seemed to hang. Not only
his clothes—his ill-fitting off-white, slightly worn-out

three-piece suit, protruding pink striped shirt sleeves, oversized bow tie—but also his skin seemed to be loose, to hang on his emaciated frame. His eyes were like bits of light behind his spectacles. His hand was on his watch chain. "Yes, Dr. Sturgis and I were beginning to wonder . . ." He had a trace of an accent Nick couldn't quite identify. "This place is so big. Very easy to get lost . . . Yes. Why don't we sit down?" He pointed to the modern easy chairs around the glass coffee table. "I understand you have some of Dr. Macdavitt's papers. As you know, Dr. Macdavitt and I were friends of long standing. Since Cambridge. He was teaching at Oxford, I was teaching at Cambridge, 1953." It was the trace of an English accent.

Tom closed the door. They sat down. Dr. Ruz in the middle. "Dr. Ruz, perhaps you could fill Nick in on some of the background."

"Yes." Dr. Ruz sighed. "Of course . . . of course."

Unedited transcript of meeting in Dr. Ruz-Silveiro's office (Room 968, Hancock Building, UCLA). 18 September. Dr. Ruz, Sturgis, and Schrader.

RUZ: Yes. [*Sighs.*] Of course . . . of course. In view of the current cult figures, the pop literature, even my most enlightened students are—how shall I say?—intrigued by such theories as those propagated by such quick-buck theorists as von Däniken and company. Oh, of course I try to keep up. It's intriguing to see just how close science fiction can come to truth, or, as our friend Dr. Macdavitt would have said, science fact. Now, of course we have always had leads. The greatest common denominator of all that speaks to the mass consciousness—I mean, of course, mythology. As Euphemerus said, "Myth is history in disguise." You have folklore, religion—all truth veiled as metaphor.

Last century no one believed the city of Troy had ever existed. And then Schliemann discovered the ruins of many Troys—one built over the other. Yes. Well, for instance, the Dogon of Mali, in Africa, worship a pyramid with steps leading up to a square platform on top of which, according to a legend of theirs, sky gods landed on their visits long ago. Their ancient tradition speaks also of the dark brother of the star Sirius—as you know, Sirius is visible only through the most powerful telescope. And yes. In the Mediterranean basin there are some cave carvings where the Pleiades are depicted as ten stars—only six or seven, as you know, are visible to the naked eye on a clear night. It is only through a telescope that you can see ten or more stars in that constellation. The astronomer-priests of Babylon also had stepped pyramids, which were also used by the sky beings coming down to Earth. The pyramids of Chichén, Itzá and Tikal in Central America—again similar to those of the Dogon and of Babylon.

The Nuba people of the Sudan have passed down a myth in which once the sky was so close, man could actually touch it—there was a rope suspended from the sky by which certain people could ascend to and descend from heaven. And then the priests of ancient Egypt made allusions to "the first time" when gods actually lived on Earth. This was during the Golden Age. The Egyptians built obelisks and dedicated them to the sun-god, Re. These obelisks had gilded tops called *benben*. Now, were these obelisks inspired by space rockets in which the sky gods arrived? Who knows? In the Book of the Dead, there are strange passages: "Those with their knowledge reach the vault of the sky . . . those who live among the stars . . ." Or are we simply reading metaphorical meaning into a straightforward, matter-of-fact statement—simply a longing for the stars, in the sense of aspiration? But then what about Thoth, the great culture bearer of Egypt, who after bringing culture to the people of the Nile returned to the starry heavens? Or then again the legend of Osiris . . .

STURGIS: Yes, that's one Macdavitt was so fascinated by, obsessed with, I should say.

RUZ: Yes, Osiris . . . the legend of Osiris, of Isis . . . the puzzle of Osiris's coffin—parts of it scattered, his body scattered in different places all along the Nile. Fragments of what? Is it an allegory? Or did some cosmic civilizers plant underground treasures in those areas? Heliopolis, Memphis, Dendera, Elephantine—now Aswan—Byblos, where the whole body was found in the coffin the first time; Buto, where is was brought from Lebanon by Isis; the delta towns of Athribis, Bubastis, Busiris, Sais, Balamun . . .

SCHRADER: He had almost conclusive proof that the body was some sort of ultracomputer left thousand of years ago by space travelers.

RUZ: Yes. Yes. [*Sighs.*] And again, across the oceans, you have the same thing. According to Garcilaso de la Vega, God the sun sent one of his sons and one of his daughters—Manco Copac and Mama Ocllo—to teach early mankind how to build cities, raise food plants, and "live as men in reason and comity." Of course, again you could say this is only a simple, logical explanation, the way simple men, primitive men, would explain evolution to themselves . . .

And then in Mexico you have the god Tezcatlipoca, who gave mankind the gift of music and ordered his messengers to go to the High House of the Sun "to bring back to Earth a cluster, the most flowering of those musicians and singers." Quetzalcoatl, the plumed serpent, arrived in a winged ship and brought culture to Mexico—astronomy, mathematics, the most precise calendar in existence—even by today's standards—architecture; the most massive pyramid ever built, as far as the base is concerned, was built by the Mayas. But because of lack of cooperation, Quetzalcoatl departed in a dramatic display of fiery flashes and returned to the sky. Then you have the Cabala. References by Rabbi Simon Ben Jochai in the Book of Zohar concerning the arrival of superior beings from the sky . . . And you have Plutarch of Chaeroneia in *The Visions of Aridaeus* describing swift voyages in space, traveling as effortlessly "as a ship in calm weather." You have the Vedic hymns . . . agents descending from the skies. The northern Buddhists in the Tongshaktchi Sangye Songa: "The kings of light departed." You have . . . whatnot. The list could go on and on. And it does. Still, this is all amateurism—and these are all amateur speculations, theories.

STURGIS: I was hoping you'd go into the background of some of the recent findings, tell Nick about the Caracol, go into some of the work you did last year with Philip and—

RUZ: Yes, Wells. You should arrange a meeting with him when he gets back from Yucatán.

STURGIS: Yes, I'm going to. I thought he'd be back by now.

Ruz: He should be any day now. I was supposed to hear from him a few weeks ago . . . but you know him. Once he gets out there in the field . . . Well, he should be back, certainly by the end of the month. We can set up something then.

Sturgis: I thought you could fill Nick in on the Caracol tower, Callanis, Castle Rigg.

Ruz: Yes, Macdavitt and Wells were—

Schrader: The parts of his papers dealing with the Caracol, Callanis, are rather sketchy.

Ruz: Yes, well, those were not the most important, as you know . . . in the light of what followed . . . still, they led us to certain hypotheses . . . which eventually led us to the findings . . . so we cannot dismiss them outright. Even though they are really more in the interpretive field of astro-archaeology, archaeo-astronomy, or even, if you want, prehistoric astronomy.

Schrader: Macdavitt made a number of trips down to Chichén Itzá.

Ruz: Yes, he was also, of course, at Callanis with us, Castle Rigg . . . the stone slabs erected there thousands of years ago . . . and in other sites in the British Isles . . . in Carnac, France . . . and in this country, too—Cahokia, Illinois—but there was a while ago . . . a number of years ago . . . in the Big Horn Mountains in northern Wyoming, the Rocky Mountains, Fort Smith, Montana, and in Canada, in the provinces of Alberta and Saskatchewan. Yes . . . yes, but to get back to the findings at the Caracol— since that is what led us to where we are now, rather circuitously, I must add, but still undeniably. [*Coughs.*] Well, as you know, until recently it was assumed that knowledge of astronomy belonged only to the Egyptian, Babylonian, Greek, and Chinese civilizations. The Mayas were certainly not included in this group. Now, the Caracol had always held a special fascination for us—more so than any of the other Mayan ruins at Chichén Itzá. There was something about it . . . its multistoried structure of circular rooms built atop rectangular platforms . . . the tower has a spiral passage in its inner core—*caracol* means "snail shell" in Spanish. Yes. [*Sighs.*] Well, there has always been a controversy over the tower's function. Even a hundred years ago, some scientists thought it might have been used as an observation deck—an observatory—while other scientists said it was a sundial or a watchtower. Well, none of that takes into account the peculiarities of its structure. With that in mind, we went down to the Yucatán Peninsula in 1971 . . . of course we'd been down there before, a number of times . . . separately and also together. But in '71 we took with us modern surveying instruments. We made careful sightings across the corners of the rectangular platforms and through the doorways and windows of the circular portions of the Caracol. We found twenty-nine possible alignments, of which twenty coincided exactly with celestial objects, such as the planet Venus or the stars Canopus Castor and Pollux, or celestial events such as solar solstices and equinoxes.

Now, what made these alignments different from so many other alignments in other sites was that we were looking beyond the mere statistical possibility of alignments of doorways and windows with objects and events . . . what we were banking on was that those alignments correlated with written documentation, with documents that served some useful purpose, such as giving the specific date of an event—such as an equinox or the start of an important time of the year—such as, let's say, spring planting. . . . Now, one document that we used was the so-called Dresden Codex, the Mayan parchment that has been laboratory-dated as having been written around the thirteenth century, but is believed to have been copied from a document dating back to the ninth century. As you know, there are only three such known codexes, or manuscripts, which escaped the bonfires of the Inquisition. These three manuscripts surfaced in the eighteenth and nineteenth centuries in Europe. The originals are held in libraries in Dresden, Paris, and Madrid. Now, what made the Dresden Codex particularly interesting to us was the fact that it was written at approximately the same time the Caracol was being built. Investigations, based on architectural styles and motifs, date the start of the construction at A.D. 850 and its completion at about A.D. 1000. Close to five pages of the codex deal with sightings of the planet Venus . . . five pages of a sort of almanac on Venus . . . . . . indicating if the planet would be seen as a morning or an evening star, the limits of its northern and southern risings and its settings on the horizon. You have to have some sort of calendar if you want to know with any precision the synodic periods of an object such as Venus. The Caracol is just that—an edifice that contains in stone a way of calculating where and when Venus will be appearing. Venus, of course, was a major element in the religion and myths of the Mayas. But Venus was just one of the series of alignments we found.

For instance, we also found it was possible, in aligning other features on the structure, to anticipate the day when the sun, at its zenith, passed directly across Chichén Itzá. That day is the beginning of the Mayan New Year. Now, the fact that Venus can be observed from the tower windows and the platforms on so many different occasions is especially interesting when you consider that Venus was thought to be the spirit of Quetzalcoatl, the feathered serpent god. We speculated that the Mayas might have used markers, something like compass bearings, on the sills of the Caracol windows to monitor the daily progress of Venus as it moved through its eight-year cycle. As Venus drifted farther north or south in the sky—this is an optical illusion due to the differences in its and the earth's orbital revolutions—the Mayan astronomer would have to shift his position at the viewing window in order to keep it in sight. And then finally, as the planet reached the extreme limit of its wandering, the astronomer would be standing so far to one side of the six- to seven-foot-long, two-foot-wide window that his field of vision would have been narrowed to a slot . . . and, of course, the narrower the slot, the more precisely the astronomer could fix the date of the planet's declination—that is, angular distance, north or south, of the celestial equator—and be able to compute where and when it would next appear in the sky. It seemed conclusively to us that the windows of the Caracol were deliberately positioned and oriented to yield these alignments.

STURGIS: Like Stonehenge.

RUZ: Yes, like Stonehenge, the mysterious slabs. Have you ever been there at dusk? It is really quite chilling when the light goes out like that, and the monoliths stand vigil there.

STURGIS: But the first find was when you were working on the Caracol.

RUZ: Yes. It was an accident, as you know. . . . But to get back, to bring it into its proper perspective . . . All this, including Caracol, could be dismissed . . . there could be other explanations. . . . No, it had to be samething that could not be interpreted in different contexts. There would have to be only one meaning, one definition, one possibility. It would have to be undeniable. And all these other things were just more mythology, including the Caracol. . . .

No . . . There is only one way, one category, that would be convincing: for instance, if information was contained in a legend that could not possibly have originated in the civilization that created the legends—such as the Dresden Codex, if you want, but obviously on a much more sophisticated level. Let's say if a number transmitted from thousands of years ago as holy were to turn out to be the nuclear fine-structure constant. . . . Also convincing would be a certain class of artifact. An artifact of technology passed on from an ancient civilization. An artifact far beyond the technical capabilities of such a civilization. This would be a prima facie case for an extraterrestrial visitation. An example, say, such as an illuminated manuscript, retrieved from a Celtic monastery, that contains the electronic-circuit diagram for a superheterodyne radio receiver. Yes, and that is exactly what we have—more or less—as you both know. . . .

Macdavitt had come across in, I believe, the late forties some peculiar manuscript in a monastery in Ireland that simply could not be explained: It seemed to contain the theory of universal gravitation—in some sort of code, I should add, that Macdavitt had apparently broken. But, as you know, before it could be completely authenticated and dated, this manuscript disappeared under very mysterious circumstances. In any case, it was never found. But it started Macdavitt off on his search. And he found, over the years, a number of other such unexplainable manuscripts—in the Himalayas, several in hidden passages under the Potale, the Dalai Lama's palace, and in an area around a grotto under the main temple, in subterranean galleries and halls along the ridge of Altyn Tagh, in Angkor Tom.

And then in Egypt—following the chart, the legend of Osiris—where parts of the body had been buried. And in Crete, Bolivia, Peru, Ecuador, Mexico . . . well, you know all this. And though he couldn't really ever prove anything with these first manuscripts, he was convinced . . . convinced that these early manuscripts contained some sort of ultimate proof.

Well, you know all that. You have Macdavitt's papers. And the rest, as you know, was just a pure fluke . . . pure chance. After years of obsession, false clues, false leads, Macdavitt was proven right.

When we were working on the alignments at the Caracol, we also started scanning the area around the Caracol, all of Chichén Itzá—using modern excavating techniques. We came across a number of unknown underground passageways, vaults, chambers—most of them empty, already pillaged; in some we found tomb objects, small statues, cooking utensils, bones. The rest, as I said, was chance. Macdavitt, as was his habit, would roam about, wandering off, finding his way into these underground passages, coming across unknown chambers, finding himself in sealed-off rooms, running his hands along the walls . . .

And then, one day, in one of these rooms, he came upon several parchments, supposedly religious texts. These texts turned out to contain a series of fragments suggesting that light is an electromagnetic wave and implying that there were other electromagnetic waves besides light—from the longest wavelength of radio waves to the shortest wavelengths of X rays and beyond. . . . You know the rest. At first, of course, we thought it was a hoax. But we went through the routine checks anyway. Still, we were not convinced—that is, Wells and I were not convinced. Macdavitt, of course, didn't need any proof . . . more tests . . . this became more difficult to deny. Microscope tests proved conclusively . . . Every possible test was conducted . . . as you both know . . . using chemicals and ultraviolet-and infrared-ray techniques to restore the lost passages in the texts. There was no possible way . . . no possible doubt. . . .

So that is what we are left with—where we are now . . . This first manuscript was found in May of '71. Late in '71

—November—a second such manuscript was found—the one dealing with the postulation of the quantum theory— by pure accident. By Wells in the desert in the Southwest, on the border of Arizona and New Mexico. Macdavitt was, of course, with us in the desert at the time of this second find. Since then, as you know, we have found—should I say retrieved?—several other such manuscripts, and artifacts. As you know, there appears to be a whole network linking these finds together. Yes, a science-fiction blueprint. Except it's turned out to be a nightmare. And of course, as you know, the government is in possession of the finds, even though they dismissed them as fakes. And you can't really blame them, can you? After all, if these things leaked out . . .

STURGIS: Aren't there some people . . . I thought there were some people in Arizona now, in the desert.

SCHRADER: Macdavitt had something about them on the last page of his notebook—scrawled on the side of the page.

RUZ: Yes, a small group, actually—including two archaeologists, an anthropologist, an ethnographer. Macdavitt had gone out to see them only the first week in July. Yes. But I don't know exactly where they are now. Well . . . And it's already a quarter of and I have a class. Well, Tom, why don't we arrange some other meeting, when we can talk again and go into more details?

That next afternoon, after leaving the Foundation, and on his way to Michelle's, Nick stopped off at his house to get some extra blankets—the nights were starting to get colder.

He went to the bedroom closet, took out two blankets wrapped in the cleaner's plastic bags, and was already in the living room, almost on his way out the door, when the phone rang. That was strange. Who would call him here? He'd given everyone Michelle's number. The timing puzzled him.

He went back into the bedroom, the two heavy blankets draped over his arm, to pick up the phone. "Hello?" There didn't seem to be anybody there. "Hello?"

"Hello?" The man's voice sounded uncertain. "Is this Dr. Schrader?"

"Yes. Who is this?"

"Dr. Schrader, we'd like to set up an appointment with you."

"Who is this?"

"I'm afraid we can't go into that."

"Is this some kind of joke? Who the hell are you?"

"Three o'clock tomorrow afternoon. Howard Johnson's, the corner of Fairfax and Del Mar."

"What the hell are you talking about?"

"Three o'clock tomorrow afternoon . . . we'll see you there."

"What—"

But whoever it was had already hung up.

Nick got there early. But they were already there. The three businessmen seated in a booth in the far corner were unmistakable. "Sit down," the one toying with his two scoops of chocolate ice cream said as he motioned; he had an American-flag pin in his lapel. Nick sat down. All three looked about the same: bland, regulation haircuts, button-down shirts, narrow ties—from the same school, variations on the same mold. The one going slightly soft, closing in on middle age, poked with his straw at the lemon in his glass of iced tea; the other, lean athletic, had a cup of coffee and an untouched sandwich on white bread in front of him. "What'll you have?" American-Flag Pin asked.

The place was half filled—kids, older women cultivating the notion of midafternoon tea, various strays. Nothing was said. Apparently they were waiting. The tanned waitress brought over the iced coffee Nick had ordered.

"OK. What's this about?" Nick asked.

"That's what we're here to ask you," American-Flag Pin said.

"Oh, c'mon! This is movie dialogue. Are those your lines?"

American-Flag Pin glanced at the other two. "Dr. Schrader"—he looked at Nick intently—"I think you should understand that your welfare is of the greatest concern to all of us."

"Is that why you tried to get me almost killed outside Malibu the other day?"

"Yes, we know about that," American-Flag Pin said matter-of-factly. "That was certainly not our intention. But you understand you have been making it very difficult for us to guarantee your safety." His tone of voice, his expression, didn't change. "That's all we're concerned about— your safety. If you cooperate, you minimize the chances of these things occurring again."

"What do you want?"

"All right." American-Flag Pin checked with the other two and nodded. "We're not going to beat around. We'll get straight to the point, Dr. Schrader. This is really a matter that has gone far beyond where it should have. We've let you go on like this all this time only because we thought you understood what was at stake. We have no choice now but to intervene. You've been shuffling so many lives back and forth as if they were no more than a deck of playing cards."

"You've made your point. What do you want?"

Lean Athletic narrowed his already narrow hard eyes and glared. "We would like to talk to you some more in Washington." He took out an envelope from his inside breast pocket. "Here's a round-trip ticket to Dulles— tomorrow morning. There'll be a car there waiting for you, take you back, too."

"Why Washington? Why can't we talk here?"

Lean Athletic snorted grimly. "We don't really make this —Howard Johnson's—our headquarters, in spite of what you may think. Some people in Washington want to talk to you. Let's leave it at that."

"May I ask who?"

There was a consultation of glances. "You'll be notified of that soon enough," Lean Athletic said.

"Well, may I ask you how long this visit to Washington is going to be? Or is that also an infringement on your sense of discretion?"

Middle-aged nodded, showing a sign of animation for the first time. "You'll be back in time for dinner Sunday night—that is, dinner Western Standard Time."

"You gotta be kidding." Nick shook his head. He would have laughed if he could have.

The expressions remained the same, grim. The trio didn't react. They were well trained.

"We're sorry to disrupt your schedule like this," American-Flag Pin recited. "We're sure you can find a suitable explanation for Dr. Osmond and, of course, Miss Worthington."

Early the next morning, at dawn, he left his car in the Sonora Pines Airport parking lot. He took the plane down to Los Angeles, waited an hour. Sitting outside his boarding gate, he thought he saw a man standing next to the gift shop watching him. The man was pretending to read a newspaper. He was about to get up and approach him when the man suddenly turned, walked away, into the men's room. He was obviously mistaken again. He took the eight-o'clock flight to Dulles. He looked out his window, down at Los Angeles below. At the monotonous rows of one-story houses, the turquoise geometrical patterns of swimming pools, the convoluted innards of freeways enveloped in a low-grade smog. And beyond that, on one side, the desolate arid topography of dust-colored valleys and hills—a lunar landscape; and on the other side, the indistinct expanse of sunlit ocean. And then that, too, was gone, giving way to clouds and to stretches of rubble. Blank endless vistas: America. An unpopulated quarry and then the sedation of clouds took over once more. He had another gin and tonic. He must have fallen asleep. For a moment he forgot where he was. It was cold. People were wandering up and down the aisles, holding their plastic glasses with drinks. He was cold, almost shivering. He felt drugged, listless. He picked at the children's portions of sample food: the Beef Wellington, unchewable shreds shrouded in thick brown lukewarm glue; frozen rubber string beans; a small neat cup of chopped-up white iceberg with some pink toothpaste on top; for dessert, soft candle wax decorated with shaving cream—Nesselrode pudding, according to the menu. He kept sipping at the coffee, which was vaguely reminiscent of chalk, trying to warm himself.

The stewardesses kept passing, smiling as if they were live commercials for stewardesses: "Is there anything I can do for you?" He could hear them repeating it all the way down the aisle.

The movie came on: *The Seven Thieves of Rome.* Nick

kept his eyes on the narrow cube of window, though there wasn't anything to see.

It was late afternoon when they landed. Nick walked out of the terminal, carrying his overnight bag. The heat was oppressive. A yellow haze permeated the concrete landscape: Nick finally realized it was raining slightly. A man in a dark suit came toward him. Unmistakable. "Dr. Schrader, if you'll just follow me." He didn't wait for Nick to confirm his identity. Another man, who had been standing inside the terminal, in the doorway, reading a newspaper, suddenly came out and joined them. The first man led the way down the curb to a black Cadillac limousine. He opened the back door for Nick and, wordlessly, Nick got in. The two of them sat in front, the man in the dark suit driving. The car's safety locks shot down. The crowds of people, rushing, waiting for cabs, standing in lines, looked almost unreal. Nick felt as if he were watching a movie.

He didn't try to break the silence. It would have been even more unnatural. He kept his eyes on the window, studied the highway, then the outskirts of the city, across the bridge, into Virginia. The two men up front sat like statues. Once in a while, Nick thought he caught the driver's eyes in the rearview mirror. But as the driver had dark glasses on, he couldn't really be sure. The other man had sunglasses on, too. Polaroid ones.

It had stopped raining. Smears of foggy light cut up the monotony of the scenery at intervals. Gray. Gray, more gray. Buildings, streets, another highway.

Toward Langley. The sign loomed ahead: CIA NEXT RIGHT. Like some sort of placard in a surrealistic dream or cartoon, Nick thought. Through the wire gates, down the long driveway. Surrounded by green hills. The bucolic countryside. This was, after all, farmland. Past the parking lots. The man with the Polaroid sunglasses came to life: He slipped a stick of Juicy Fruit gum into his mouth and started to chew rapidly. He pointed out the turns in the driveway to the driver, who just kept his eyes on the road.

They pulled up at a side entrance. The safety locks shot up. The man with the Polaroid sunglasses got out, opened Nick's door. "You can leave that there." He pointed to the bag. "We'll take it to your hotel." Nick didn't ask which hotel.

They went into the cool air-conditioned building. Nick followed the man with the Polaroid sunglasses down a series of long corridors: Human robots scurried up and down. Past the shooting galleries of open doorways: secretaries clicking away at typewriters, snatches of fuzzy conversations, the cacophony of machines, fragments of unidentified sounds. An accelerated procession of multimedia life.

They stopped finally at a large double door. A young mannequin, a guard, nodded. They went in. Past some more mannequins, across a thick-carpeted lobby. Through the mahogany doors of an elevator, up to another floor, out into a waiting room, another guard. Into a large office with a number of windows looking out onto some trees, outlined against the weakening light, and a barely visible field in the distance, an imposing mahogany desk, a U.S. flag mounted on a pole, several low easy chairs. The man with the Polaroid sunglasses went over to one of the windows and, using the open curtain as a cover, looked out for a moment, then remained standing there at the window. Standing guard, Nick thought. He had stopped chewing his gum. The muffled sound of voices, and a side door opened; a three-star army general walked in, accompanied by two other men, indistinguishable products: similar builds, features. One in a striped suit, the other in a gray suit.

The one in the gray suit spoke first, handled the introductions. "General Condon"—in an immaculately pressed outfit, not a crease or sign of wear, sculpted cloth—"Dr. Nicholas Schrader. David Griffin"—in the striped suit—"Dr. Nicholas Schrader." He failed to introduce himself. Apparently his name was not called for. He nodded to the man in the Polaroid sunglasses, who, on cue, walked out, soundlessly closing the door behind him.

The general spoke: "Why don't we sit down?" They moved over to the chairs and sat down.

"Now, I don't think we need go through any preliminary formalities," Gray Suit said. "I think you know why you're here."

"No, I don't, really."

"Schrader." Gray Suit almost closed his eyes, bored beyond weariness. "What in the hell are you up to?"

"All right, Schrader, this has really gone far enough. We've tolerated all this—your shenanigans—until now. The game stops here." The general nodded for emphasis, in case Nick didn't understand. "Now, what's all this crazy business about, hmm? Do you have any idea what you've gotten yourself into? What you're stirring up? Do you have any idea where all this could lead to?" He didn't seem to be interested in an answer. "No, you just go right along, making a mess of everything, without any regard for other people's lives."

Are they putting me on or what? Nick wondered.

"You've been playing amateur games, not knowing what was at stake or, in any case, certainly disregarding what was at stake," Gray Suit said.

They must be using the same speech writers, Nick thought.

"We've let you go on like this, this long, only because we thought you'd eventually comprehend on your own the detrimental effect you were having. But apparently, it seems you haven't," Griffin added sadly.

"Amateur games? Are you serious? Who's been chasing me up and down the freeways? Who's been watching me—keeping tabs on me—following me around like some hick?"

"I'm sorry you don't like our methods, but they're for your own safety," Griffin said.

"Safety from what? You drag me across the country, get me here for a day, practically coerce me."

"I think you came of your own volition. After all, this is in both our interests." Gray Suit tried to smile but grimaced instead.

"All right. We're just going around." The general made a gesture to stop with his hand. "Where are the papers?"

"What papers?"

"Oh, c'mon!" Gray Suit snorted sarcastically.

"You mean Macdavitt's papers?" Nick asked as if he'd just realized what they were talking about.

"Yeah, that's right. You guessed it." Gray Suit wasn't amused. He raised his voice. "Where are they?"

"I don't have them."

"You don't have them," Griffin repeated, as if by repeating it, he could understand it better.

"Then where are they?" Gray Suit asked.

Nick stared out the window for a moment . . . the tops of some trees through the pale sunlit panes. He had a momentary urge to fling himself through the glass, crash down into that green sea. He turned and looked at the three faces without answering.

"Don't make this difficult for us," Gray Suit said. But Nick picked up something in the tone of his voice: He really hoped for the opposite.

"I destroyed them."

There was no response. Gray Suit tapped his fingers on the arm of his leather chair. The general coughed, got up, and went over to one of the windows.

Griffin smiled or, rather, his thin lips took on a sort of pucker and disappeared completely, slipping into his clean-shaven jowls. He motioned with his hand as if to indicate that he was going to say this only as a matter of course; it was already understood and therefore unnecessary to even mention. But he had to, anyway. For the record. "You've memorized them." His tone of voice couldn't have been softer.

Nick nodded once, feeling so uncomfortable he almost smirked. A gleam came into his eyes. "That's right." He shifted in his chair.

The general was looking out the window, his back to the room.

"Dr. Schrader." Griffin paused for emphasis. "You've got to understand this is a matter of the highest national security, not to say international—"

"You know, of course, you're going to have to tell us what was in those papers," Gray Suit interrupted.

"You've put us in the most embarrassing position you can imagine," Griffin said.

"You know Macdavitt was . . ." Gray Suit pointed to his own head. "That was a well-known fact. His theories were crackpot."

"C'mon, Schrader." The general turned around. "You don't really believe all this, do you?"

"Then why are you so interested in his papers?"

"Don't play wise guy with me." Gray Suit looked disgusted.

"C'mon, Schrader." The general was going to try to be more reasonable. "You don't really believe all this, do you? C'mon, this is kid stuff. Some guy makes a quick buck out of this. Look, my eight-year-old kid goes to see this stuff. *Chariots of the Gods* at a Saturday matinee along with the cartoons . . . C'mon, Schrader, you strike me as being a little too intelligent for this." He let out a deep sigh. "OK, Schrader. We'll lay our cards on the table. Macdavitt was nothing but a traitor . . . a Communist traitor . . . slipping information, state secrets, to the enemy for years."

"He was working with them," Griffin explained ultrasoberly, "hand in hand, in this thing. And when they got all the information they wanted from him, they got rid of him." Griffin's eyes widened in an expression of pseudo-naiveté, and he nodded.

"That's your great scientist," the general said. "Your Nobel-prize candidate. One of your founders of the Atomic Age."

"In the wrong hands these ideas can germinate all sorts of doubts," Griffin said, "plant all sorts of ideas—"

"And that's exactly what they've done," Gray Suit said. "Until you've got a whole network, a whole bunch of people, disseminating these cockeyed theories. Bolstering one another up until they convince themselves they've really got proof when what do they really have? At best some intriguing ideas verging more on mythology, astrology. It's just about as relevant."

"Oh, you know I'd be the first not to deny some credence to some of this." The general had on his milder expression. He was going to try another tack. "I mean there are things out there we don't know about. Well, I hope I don't sound like a fool to you, but there are all sorts of things we just don't understand. But to go and concoct these cock-and-bull theories to explain them, to solve the mystery, that's just a lot of you know what. Look, there are all kinds of things we just can't explain. Now, for instance, I've been into Transcendental Meditation for the last year. A lot of people have in the Pentagon, and also here. And I can tell you it sure has helped me. My ulcer's gone, my back trouble . . . oh, I'm not the same man.

Used to be a raw ball of nerves, now I do my TM every morning, noon, and night. Whenever I get a chance. I don't want to sound like some kind of nut, but it's true. So I'd be the first to admit there are some things—a lot of things —we just don't know or begin to understand. And that's the way they should be kept. Now, Schrader, you're an intelligent man, you should be able to assess this situation. The repercussions all this could have. Why, just look at the *War of the Worlds*, that Mars stunt Orson Welles pulled, back in '38. Had the whole country believing him, too. You had total panic. Now, c'mon, you can see, you can understand . . . it's just not that simple. Even if it were true, and believe me it sure in hell's name isn't. But you can understand the position we'd be put in if this thing— such a rumor—leaked out. The position you'd put us in, you scientists . . . These are mysteries . . . should remain mysteries."

He's finished, Nick thought. He's given his speech. It's out of his system now.

Gray Suit sighed dramatically. "Do you realize what the odds are? Do you have any idea?" He paused. "Of course you do. You're an intelligent person, a man of thought. I'm sure you've come across it. In your reading or in discussion, perhaps even at the Foundation. These theories are all hogwash. But because of what they give rise to, the hysteria, and so on, they're of prime concern to us." He paused again, turned around in his chair, and pressed a button on the intercom on the desk in back of him. "Send Dr. Stafford in." He nodded to Nick.

The same side door opened and a boyish middle-aged man, an ex-football-player type, fairly unobtrusive, blending with the mold, came in, closed the door behind him. "Dr. James Stafford, Dr. Nicholas Schrader. Dr. Stafford is with NASA." Gray Suit motioned to Stafford to sit down. Stafford sat down. The general was staring out the window, his back to the room once again. It was now dusk. The trees in the windows were beginning to fade, and it seemed to be raining again.

"OK. Explain it to him." Gray Suit gave the cue.

Dr. Stafford smiled apologetically and kept his eyes on an indeterminate fixed point on the wall. Nick braced himself for a lecture. "All right, we're going to break down the extraterrestrial hypothesis that a number of UFOs are space vehicles coming from planets of other stars. In the last couple of decades we've had rumors of at least a couple a day. So we'll make a more realistic estimate and say that one of these rumors every year is an actual interstellar visitation. All right?

"So let's say that x is the number of extant technical civilizations in the galaxy—that is to say, civilizations that are way ahead of ours and are even able to conduct interstellar space flights. Now we have to specify what determines the number of such extant technical civilizations. First of all, x depends on the mean rate at which stars are formed in the galaxy. We know that pretty well. Then it depends on the number of stars that have planets; we don't know that as well, but there's some available info. Then you've got to have the fraction of such planets that are suitably located in regard to their stars so that the environment is one conducive to life. OK, so that depends on the fraction of extant possible planets on which life does actually exist. Then it depends on the fraction of those planets on which life can originate, life which, after it has supposedly appeared, can evolve into an intelligent form of life. Then, after you have that, well, it depends on the fraction of those planets on which intelligent forms could have evolved into a technically advanced civilization, one that is way ahead of ours. And then, after that, you've got the average lifetime of such a technical civilization. . . .

"As you see, you quickly run out of places. True, you've got a lot of stars, but only one conducive to the origin of life, and only a very limited number—maybe even only one—conducive to an intelligent form that could evolve into a highly technical civilization.

"Of course we readily admit we have no way to judge the mean lifetime of such a civilization. Still, our estimates about these numbers indicate that x equals approximately one tenth the average lifetime of a technical civilization in years. OK, then, say ten million—that is, 10^7 years for the average lifetime of your technically advanced civilization; you've got a number for such technically advanced civilizations in the galaxy of about a million—10^6—that is, a million other stars with planets on which right now—today—such an advanced civilization could exist. . . . Ten million years is probably a little naïve, but we'll give them the benefit of the doubt. OK. Let's see where it gets us. Let's say each of these million technical civilizations launches y interstellar space vehicles a year. So that $10^6 y$ interstellar space vehicles are launched every year. Assume only one contact is made per journey. In this situation you've got $10^6 y$ arrivals someplace or other per year. Let's say there are about 10^{10} places worth visiting in the galaxy—after all, there are several times 10^{11} stars—and an average of $1/10^4$ equals 10^{-4} arrivals at any given place —a planet—per year.

"In other words, if only one UFO is to visit Earth each year, we can figure out what mean launch rate is needed at each of these million worlds. It turns out to be 10,000 launches per year per civilization—or 10 billion launches in the galaxy per year. That's quite a bit of traffic. This civilization so much more advanced than our own launches 10,000 vehicles in order for one to appear here. That somehow seems a little unrealistic—a little too much to expect from them. And of course if we're more realistic— less naive about the life-span of such advanced civiliza- tions—we would have to increase proportionally the launch rate. But then, on the other hand, if the lifetime of such a civilization decreases—which it most likely does—the as- sumption that such a civilization would develop interstellar flight also decreases . . . and then so does the chance of our having any such visitors.

"Now you've got another point . . . and that is if you figure more than one UFO arrives on Earth every year, the total mass of metals during the history of the galaxy—we assume the vehicle has to be large enough—let's say larger than the Apollo capsule—so we calculate how much metal is needed . . . and it turns out to be the total mass of half a million stars has to be processed and all their metals ex- tracted. Or if you continue this argument and say that only the outer few hundred miles or so of stars, such as the sun, could be mined by these advanced civilizations—after all, if it were farther in, it would be too hot—you find that two billion stars would have to be processed—that is, one per- cent of the stars in the galaxy. That somehow doesn't seem really very realistic either, does it?" Stafford asked rhetori- cally.

No one bothered to answer. "All right, so maybe their spaceships are plastic—possible, after all, why not? OK. You've got plastic spaceships . . . that's quite possible—after all, just about anything is, theoretically. But this plastic still has to come from someplace—and plastics as opposed to metals doesn't really substantially change the picture. In other words, this is the magnitude of what's involved when we assume that there are routine interstellar flights to Earth. Then, of course, you've got the other side of the coin. Why would we be the object of such curiosity? OK. That's saying there's something special about us and that's in contradiction to the notion that there are lots of other civilizations around. After all, why would anyone want to come here . . . if it's their one visit? No, why would they want their interstellar tour to stop here? To visit what? No, most likely they'd just bypass this third planet from the sun and continue on to some other, more interesting-looking place. After all, if there are a lot of other civilizations around, then it stands to reason we must be pretty common, so why should we be of interest to anyone? Certainly not to this theoretically advanced civilization. And then OK, again, take the other side of that coin. If we're not pretty common, then there aren't going to be too many visitors from your advanced civilizations flocking here. No. In that case, nobody'll be visiting us because most likely there won't be anybody around to visit us. And so we're just right back where we started."

"Is this what I was brought here for? To get a lecture on nihilism and the stars?"

"There's nothing nihilistic about it at all," Stafford said. "Those are just simply the facts."

"There's only one thing you've omitted."

"Oh? What's that?" Stafford asked, not very interested.

"Macdavitt's papers. The exception that would invalidate everything you've just proposed in your lecture. Legends, myths that would prove to contain a series of numbers or figures that had been passed down as holy through the centuries and turned out to be the fundamentals of nuclear fission or molecular orbital theories or theories of atomic and molecular states. Or if you had artifacts. An illuminated manuscript or a Mayan parchment that contained a table of the properties of atomic weights or a text on electromagnetic waves. Or maybe even some tablet found here in this country, in the desert in Arizona or New Mexico, that pertained to the atom or to nuclear energy. And then, of course, the signals that have been received . . ."

The general turned around. But Nick couldn't see his expression. The room was too dim, almost gray, taking on the tones of the dusk outside in the rows of windows. There was not a sound. The four men looked at one another in the dim light.

"Project Ozymandias," Nick added. The stillness in the room contradicted whatever lingering doubts he had that this was all somehow unreal.

"All right," Gray Suit finally said. "When do you want to start dictating?"

"I'm not going to."

Again, for a moment, there was no reaction. "OK." Gray Suit had on his matter-of-fact voice. "We can't force you . . . and we're not even going to try. You see, we're reasonable people here. We haven't really coerced you . . . up until now. We've let you go your own way. And we're going to continue to."

"But you think I'll eventually come around. What makes you so sure?"

"You're being a fool." The general shook his head.

Without a word, Griffin got up and went over to switch on the top lights. The room was jolted back to life. Nick winced. He felt as if he were in a fishbowl. He watched the shadows of the figures in the room projected against the walls. They reminded him of animated semiabstract cartoons in some nightmare.

"Well." Gray Suit smiled. A smile that bore no resemblance to a smile, that could only be called a smile because it didn't fit into any other category. "Let's just say it's in our mutual interest."

"You don't really believe all that, do you?" The general had on his pained expression, his highly confidential voice. "C'mon, Schrader! Those things were plants. Ancient artifacts, my ass! Your two-bit swindler, forger, finds out about that nut Macdavitt and his team, hears all these rumors— maybe even some scientist. One of those into pranks. This other nut gets hold of some parchment, some stone tablets.

Scribbles them up, doctors them up with all sorts of twentieth-century scientific formulas, theories . . . scruffs them up a bit, gets them chemically treated, and bingo! You've got your ancient artifacts. Now bury them in your strategic places. All the ruins that have been scrutinized—I mean where every stone has been classified. C'mon, you got to be kidding. That Chicken Itsat's been turned inside out. Along comes your cartoon crew—Macdavitt. And he's got his interplanetary artifacts. And as for the radio signals, there were explanations for all of them—mistakes; a number of them were signals from top-secret military bases. Don't you realize, Schrader, the guy was . . ." The general tapped his head.

"That's right." Griffin nodded. "Let's just leave it at that."

"Look, Schrader, you're just wasting your time." The general came toward him. He leaned down, his hands on the back of an empty chair. "Here we've wasted a whole damn afternoon." He gestured toward a window. "All cooped up in here, going around and around. Going nowhere. Circles only keep going, covering the same ground. And that's all you're doing. Look, I'll be straight with you. Here I am in this room when I could have been out shooting a round of golf and instead I'm here with you. And you've got better things to do, too, I'm sure. Now, you live in a nice place. Beautiful out there. I've been out there myself a lot. Not just on duty, but with the family, too—on vacations. Now, why are you fooling around like this? Why do you want to get mixed up in something like this? Look, at first I thought, leave him alone. He'll come around. He'll see the magnitude of this thing. He'll see what's at stake, what's involved . . . and he'll understand we're on his side . . . he'll come around. . . . I've got this kid, my eldest boy. He's at West Point now, just like his old man. Well, last year—two years ago—he was bumming around the country, doing nothing, a good-for-nothing. He was even going to go off to India. One of those. Well, he had some sense left in him and he didn't. But I let him alone. Didn't say a word all that time. Not that I didn't want to. Oh, boy. But I restrained myself. I figured he'd come around. Well, he did. He worked it out of his system.

Going to graduate next year." He nodded briskly for emphasis. "You wonder what I'm leading up to? You're missing the point, hmm? No, Schrader, we're going to let you go on your own way. There maye be certain things at stake here that we can't take even an iota of a chance on. But we're going to give you, as they say, all the time you want. Up to a point," he added.

Gray Suit nodded in turn, his eyes zeroing in on Nick. "We'll be in touch with you. Don't you worry about that. Someone will contact you again very soon."

"You mean I can go now?" It couldn't be that simple. Yet it seemed to be.

He went out. The agent with his Polaroid sunglasses still on was stationed outside, still chewing his gum, and staring blankly into pace. Wordlessly, Nick followed him back out. The limousine was waiting. It was almost dark now, and the rain had long since stopped.

He was driven back into the city, through the traffic. The streetlights were on, store windows, neon signs: Everything was scintillating, the sharp delineation of colors after the rain.

He was dropped off at the Madison Hotel. The agent in the Polaroid sunglasses motioned to him to go in. "We'll pick you up in the morning," he said. "Your flight's at ten. Give yourself a good two hours."

Nick went to the desk. A reservation had been made for him in his name.

He went up to the room. He left the door open. His bag was on the luggage rack. Twin beds, cheap modern furniture. The two windows overlooked an angle of park. He switched on the color TV. Walter Cronkite. He walked around the room, his eyes scanning the walls; he checked behind the mirror, in the closet, in the bathroom, behind the shower curtain; he went back into the room, looked behind the bureau, under the beds. He switched the TV off. He left the room and went down the hall, took the elevator down, went out through the lobby, into the street. He had an egg-salad sandwich in a drugstore across the park. Saturday night, but he had lost all sense of time. It was raining slightly again. He walked back slowly through the park.

He spent the rest of the evening in his room in the hotel, getting up every few minutes to check the door. He felt closed in. Trapped. He would jump up, go check the door. It was almost a game he was playing with himself, but each time he was also half convinced he would try the door and find it locked. He turned the knob, the door opened. He looked out: 1126 was still there on his door. His room was still 1126. He looked down the hall. Nothing. The hall was empty. No one was there. But still he felt trapped, as if someone were watching him; and he kept jumping up, jumping up from the bed every few minutes, rushing to the door, opening the door, looking out. No one was ever there. The hall was always empty. Not a sign of life. Not even a single pair of shoes outside any of the other rooms. He had the eerie feeling that he was alone on the floor, that his was the only occupied room. Finally he fell asleep. On top of the bed with his clothes on.

He was up at dawn. Showered, shaved, changed his underpants, socks, shirt. He held his breath. The moment of reckoning. But the door was still open. He had breakfast downstairs in the hotel coffee shop. The agent with the Polaroid sunglasses was there in the lobby, waiting, when Nick came out. The limousine was in the driveway. Wordlessly, he was taken back out to Dulles. The agent with the Polaroid sunglasses waited until the plane had started moving down the runway. Nick could see him watching from the observation deck. Standing there, inert. Nick imagined him still chewing his gum.

Synopsis of surveillance logs. 22 September.

Schrader called Sturgis at home from Exxon-station phone booth. Sonora Pines (1645). Schrader told Sturgis of his trip to Washington. Arrangements were made for a meeting tomorrow morning at 1100 with Ruz-Silveiro at the Lighthouse Coffee Shop at the marina in San Diego.

Schrader tried all evening to get hold of Palmer and Wagner. There was never any answer. He was finally persuaded by Worthington to go to bed (0100).

Security 5A200 Washington to R. Castle. 23 September. 1015.

Re Richardson blank tapes: Contact Richardson. Proceed accordingly.

Nick pulled off the freeway, into Harbor Drive, to the Shelter Island marina. He got out, walked down toward the water. He looked into the Lighthouse Coffee Shop. Neither Sturgis nor Ruz was there. He continued on down the pier to the wire gate. Tom was waiting on the dock below. "Dr. Ruz is on the boat," he said, letting him in. "He was getting nervous in the coffee shop. Were you followed?"

"No, I don't think so."

"That means you probably were."

They went down the narrow dock, through the crowd of moored boats—most of them empty now that the weekend was over—to the cabin cruiser. Dr. Ruz was inside the cabin. In his three-piece suit, bow tie, watch chain—only the Panama and walking stick were missing; he looked up, startled. Clearly a case of mistaken identity. He had been mistaken for someone else and was now trapped in this plot, not knowing what to expect next.

"Well, I hope you're ready for a little excursion tour of the harbor," Tom said. "He doesn't think it's a good idea to stay here." He motioned in Ruz's direction. He threw off the ropes, started the motor.

They passed the lighthouse. Dr. Ruz finally came out. "Obviously, we can't keep meeting like this." Tom turned off the motor, his arm resting on the steering wheel.

"No." Dr. Ruz nodded vigorously, on cue. He sat down in the other mounted chair, opposite Tom's. "It is very unwise."

"Yes" was all Nick said. He stood between them, in the cabin doorway.

A motorboat pulling a water-skier raced by. The cruiser swayed. Dr. Ruz gripped the back of his seat. The boat sped by again. It was circling them. Tom started the motor and headed farther out, away from the other boats. He turned the motor off again. Silhouettes of boats blurred, ghostly shapes in the distance. The shore had receded to an indistinct line. An occasional gull hovered above them in the deserted blue sky like some sort of strangely animated kite. The only sounds were the monotonous lapping of the water against the hull, the drawn-out creaking rhythm of the boat tilting back and forth, and the mild rush of wind swirling around them, swelling the canopy above their heads.

"I've tried to get hold of Galveston." Tom squinted, not looking at either of them. "Prebble, Lloyd. I can't get through to any of them. Jordan. Not even Barrowsky. None of them returned any of my calls. I called all last night until after two. I kept calling, and then again early this morning. I got Scott at the PSI Center. He hung up. I called back. His secretary must have put me through by mistake. He said it was impossible, there was no way. I tried to get him to explain—find out who was pulling the plug. But he said he couldn't talk anymore. He had to get off. Then, on my way here, I dropped by the lab. I confronted Jim in the hall. He took me into his office. He said he thought it would be a good idea not to make any more mention of or reference to the subject we had been discussing. I asked him to elaborate. He just kept shaking his head, saying he couldn't. So you see, that's where we are now."

"And I haven't been able to get hold of Vic Wagner or Bob Palmer, either."

"Well, you know Macdavitt left directions with Dr. Ruz for getting into Gray Sands."

"I know. He mentioned it in his notebook—if anything happened."

"It doesn't look as if we have much choice."

"Yes, unfortunately." Dr. Ruz sighed. "I am forced to agree."

"I'm going with you," Tom said.

Nick looked puzzled a moment. His mouth twitched slightly as if he had involuntarily bitten his lip. He nodded. "OK."

"There are some papers. Some recent files I myself am most interested in. Project Night Lights—PRO NIL," Dr. Ruz said. "They have been testing with a helium-neon laser transmitting and receiving system. This involves transmission of a television picture through the invisible laser beam. Television transmission sent over a laser is a very visible and quite obvious type of signal. UFOs have responded to light signals in the past. They hope to have more concrete evidence very soon—so I am told, at least. Perhaps they already do._. . . Well, we might as well get on with it."

Dr. Ruz took out a small notebook from an inside pocket of his jacket. He tore out a page and started drawing. A series of lines; then he tore out another page, drew some more lines. "This is just to give you a vague idea of the area," he said, pointing with his ballpoint to a small square across from some lines in the first drawing. "This is right off the main highway. Now, from here you drive five miles down a dirt road. See this line here"—he pointed to another line—"toward Rancho Mirage, an abandoned mining town. You'll veer left at the deserted railroad station there. Then three miles south-southwest on this road"—he pointed to some other lines—"at the foot of the Peregrinos de Pesar Mountains. A quarter of a mile off this unpaved road here . . . in the direction of the Rio Muerto—you'll be able to follow its trail without any difficulty—for another half mile until you reach the Arroyo del Oro. There —here"—he pointed to some more lines—"at the arroyo, you'll cut sharply left on another dirt road until you come to the Cristobal Pass. There will be a sign to that effect. You'll leave your car there, at Cristobal, and continue on foot on this road here for three miles. Continue south-southwest—this road is paved—until you reach the dirt road outside the base. This is only the perimeter of the base. A barbed-wire fence four feet high surrounds it, cutting it off from the rest of the area. There are no guards there. And don't worry, there's hardly ever any cars on the road. You'll pass under the barbed wire.

"However, be careful not to touch it," Dr. Ruz added as an afterthought, "the wire is electrified. But there is enough room—twenty inches, two feet perhaps—to be able to pass underneath. You will remember that reptiles abound in that part of the country. Once inside, you'll stay as low as possible, as close to the ground as you can. There are a number of cacti in the area, and besides, the terrain is far from flat, so you will be well protected. There is really very little possibility that you would be seen. Almost none, really. But this is only a quarter of a mile, anyway, and besides, you'll be going in the direction away from the main entrance, where the guards are stationed. This area is totally unlit. The beam from the main watchtower comes full circle at intervals of five minutes.

"Now, outside the main compound is more barbed wire —over here." Dr. Ruz pointed to another set of lines. "This, too, is electrified. But there is a main switch, an underground alarm right before the barbed wire, next to this flagpole—right here, you see." He marked an X across one of the lines. "You'll unscrew the top, disconnect these wires. The alarm will be deactivated. When you leave the compound, when you are finished, the next morning, you will put the alarm back on, reconnect the wires. You will run across the one hundred yards from where the alarm switch is, into the side entrance of the main building—this building here—directly across the second wire."

Dr. Ruz drew several other diagrams, then went on. "Now listen carefully. The files you want—the duplicates of some of the Ozymandias files—are kept in this building . . . in the basement of this building here." He pointed to a square. "Now, the guards change shifts every two hours on the even hour. The guards patrol regularly. These rounds take about twenty minutes each. If you just wait to make sure you do not hear anything, you should not have any problem . . . you just go straight into the building. Once you're inside, you head straight down the hall. Past a men's room, a storage room—you can't miss it. It's right across from the side entrance you'll be entering. You'll hide in the storage room and wait there for the next guard shift. After you hear the guards passing, you'll head straight down the stairs—again, you won't be able to miss them. They're directly across from the storage room—over here. You'll go down to the floor below—there's only one below. The basement. Go to a door marked 310—right in front of you. This leads down another hallway, past a row of offices. There's never anyone down there at night. Go down this hallway until you come to the main file room. Now, there are a number of cubicle-type offices outside this main file room, but don't worry, as I said, they'll be empty. No one works down there at night. You go past these cubicles to a door marked 10. You'll go in there. And there you are. In there you'll find the Ozymandias files. There is a fuse box on the wall to the right as you come in. It's an alarm system. You'll unscrew the top, again disconnect the wires. This will deactivate the alarms on the locks of all the file cabinets. And there you are . . . Just make sure you have enough film with you . . . and needless to say, whatever you do, as soon as you hear something, any sound, stop. Stop whatever you're doing. But that should not happen. I wouldn't worry about that. Hardly anyone ever goes down there. The files are strictly off limits. And besides, the people who work there don't even know of their existence—they have no idea of the nature of the files. And the floor are concrete, so you'll be abe to hear everything. But as I said, there's no reason for you to worry about that. You'll be wearing rubber-soled shoes, of course. I think that would be best, don't you, Tom?"

Tom nodded. "What do you think?" he asked Nick.

"Couldn't be easier," Nick said. "A cinch. An obstacle course through an electrified maze."

"And when you're finished," Dr. Ruz said, "you'll take the same way out."

"What's that?" Tom pointed to a helicopter in the distance. The helicopter seemed to be coming closer, the faint rotary-motor sound growing louder. The helicopter was coming toward them, the clatter of its choppers dominating the air. The water continued sloshing against the sides of the boat, a gull flapped by, the smoke trail of a jet streaked across the cloudless sky, another speedboat—suddenly appearing out of nowhere—raced by, dashing across the ruptured, rocky water—all soundlessly. The only sound was that of the helicopter.

The helicopter was coming closer to them. The sun was bright and it was difficult to see, but there seemed to be two men inside. Dr. Ruz pointed to the lettering: KNXT, a Los Angeles TV station. The helicopter circled around them once and then headed toward the coast.

Tom turned the motor on. Dr. Ruz tossed the pieces of paper into the water. They started back. As they approached the shore Tom handed Nick a pair of binoculars so he could check out the marina. There were boats now everywhere. Nick focused on the harbor, making an arc down across the pier, past a row of boats, to the dock, a German shepherd wagging its tail, walking behind a tanned kid in swimming trunks lugging a carton of Schlitz beer, and up past a yacht where a young woman was lying on the deck, on her stomach, with her bikini top off, down toward a crate of slick silvery fish on a fishing boat—the *Santa Maria*—up to another dock, to a deeply tanned girl in a white bikini, and up to a man in a seersucker suit staring through a pair of binoculars directly out at them. Nick looked away, reversed his course. Back to the girl in the white bikini, the crate of fish, the yacht, and back, back to the man with the binoculars. And back again. And each time he was still there, still looking out in their direction. Nick didn't say anything, though, to Tom or Dr. Ruz.

Synopsis of surveillance logs. 23 September. 1415.

Schrader and Sturgis met with Dr. Ruz as per directions on Sturgis's boat in the San Diego marina (1100). Sturgis took the boat out a quarter of a mile in the vicinity of the lighthouse. We tried to maintain visual surveillance—using a speedboat and water-skier—but were unable to. Sturgis took the boat farther out—two and a half to three miles. There were no other boats in sight in the immediate area.

We passed above them in a KNXT chopper. Observation was difficult, but we picked up through binoculars Dr. Ruz writing (?) something on a piece of paper—or possibly several pieces of paper. Dr. Ruz then threw this paper or papers into the water.

Observation insubstantial. However, we suggest there may be some link between this and previous meeting with Dr. Ruz, i.e., the O projects.

Security 5A200 Washington. 23 September. 1706.
Remain as posted until further notice.

Report to Security 5A200 Washington. 23 September. 1730.

We approached Richardson as he was leaving his country club. He was getting into his car. Castle and I got in with him. We had him drive around the area for ten minutes. We had him then drop us off in the country-club parking lot, where our car was. Richardson did not prove to be cooperative. Suspect he has more knowledge of what Schrader is involved in than he will admit.

Report to Security 5A200 Washington. 23 September. 2142.
Call from Sturgis (from his home) to Schrader at Worthington's.
Undecipherable. In quotes, meeting arranged. In quotes, conferences on the twenty-fifth—this Wednesday—at UCLA on science and the future does not check out. Invalidated. Note: no such conference.
And from there—Los Angeles—they will, in quotes, fly up to San Francisco for symposium on the twenty-sixth— this Thursday. Check. There is a symposium on the year 2074 at the university there.
Suggest above, though, invalid. Posted as advised. Remain.

Top-secret cable to Security 5A200 Washington. 23 September. 2358.
CONFIRM STOP SUGGEST NOTIFY OF POSSIBLE ATTEMPT STOP ADVISE SECURITY MEASURES

Security 5A200 Washington. 24 September. 0702.
Notified. Advise per security, remain as is.

Security 5A200 Washington. 24 September. 1400.
All persons previously involved re Schrader and Sturgis have been contacted again and advised once more. We do not believe, this time, there will be any more undermining activity on their parts.

Security 5A200 Washington. 24 September. 1430.
It has been projected that Schrader will try to get access to some of the more relevant papers in the O files. Yet, having Schrader exposed to the files would be a good way of assessing his exact knowledge of the projects and perhaps of gauging the content of Macdavitt's papers. The division therefore recommends giving Schrader full leeway in his projected undertaking.
To ensure the Russians do not get wind of this and try to take advantage of the situation, suggest convey through

Tchernilkov that we have the matter fully under control and that they have nothing repeat nothing to gain by intercepting Schrader at any point in this juncture. That it would be ill advised.

We hope, therefore, they will refrain from any such undertaking and will relinquish accordingly their surveillance of Schrader, if not in full, then at least in part for the duration of this phase of the operation.

From Reed, Security 5A200 Washington. 24 September. 1600.

We are sending the attached transcript of a taped conversation between General Condon, Dr. Stafford, Griffin, and myself, to those concerned in the division, for further reference.

We believe this follow-up in regard to our session the other day with Schrader may be of interest to those who have so far participated in this operation.

This tape was made with the knowledge of everyone present, in the security offices at Langley.

REED: I think we should go over this confidential report before we pass it around the division. Now, according to this report, last year, November, to be exact, the Russians, at their radio institute at Gorky—the receiving equipment there, as we know, has been probing round the clock for unusual signals from space—started picking up signals that might be originating from an intelligent extraterrestrial source. I think we should go into the nature of these signals, Dr. Stafford.

STAFFORD: Yes. Well, these signals seem to be occurring in pulses after definite lapses of time and are repeated over a wide range of wavelengths. We simply can't rule out, at this stage, the possibility that these signals are of extraterrestrial origin.

The character of these signals—their consistent pattern and their regular transmissions—leaves us in no doubt that they're of artificial origin—that is to say, they're not natural signals. We just simply can't rule out the possibility that they're being transmitted by extraterrestrials with the most highly sophisticated transmission equipment.

Now, the Russians maintain that these signals are com-

ing from within our own solar system. If these signals are
not produced by some natural radiological phenomenon in
the outer atmosphere, it is quite possible they could be
originating from an artificial source, probably orbiting our
planet—perhaps from a satellite especially programmed to
transmit such signals.

GRIFFIN: We believe the Russians have not yet suc-
ceeded in identifying what this object is—but of course if
they had, they certainly wouldn't have volunteered the information to us.

REED: We've been using our own channels of investigation, though, as you know, and we're going to continue
on that.

STAFFORD: Our first explanation was that perhaps the
signals were being picked up from one of our secret communication satellites launched by the Air Force. But most
of these satellites change position rapidly and would simply
not produce the sort of signal sequences the Russian astro-
physicists claim to have picked up.

The one exception to this would be a satellite that takes
up a position in what is known as a Molniya-type orbit. In
this system, the orbit is highly elliptical and is timed to
take twelve hours to complete—that is, half the rotational
period of the earth. The top end of the ellipse is high over
our northern hemisphere and coincides with, let's say, latitude fifty degrees—which places this satelitte of ours over
the Soviet Union on one orbit and, twelve hours later, on
the second orbit, over the United States. The center of the
Soviet Union roughly corresponds to longitude ninety degrees east, and the center of the United States corresponds
to longitude ninety degrees west.

Also, at the peak of the ellipse, this sort of satellite will
travel extremely slowly, and any signals it transmits will
have very little Doppler shift—that is, the change in frequency caused by objects moving away from or toward a
moving observer.

CONDON: Yes. Well, as you know, this arrangement is
specially chosen for our spy satellites, so that as they pass
over the Soviet Union they can photograph different instal-
lations. They can also pick up any infrared hot spots—
such as rocket launches, gamma radiation, nuclear ex-
plosions—and they can also listen in to the Russian radio

transmission. All this information is stored in the computer memory cells. And when the satellite passes over the United States it will give up, on receipt of a command signal from base, all its coded data.

STAFFORD: Yes, but the thing is, the transmission system employed by the satellite is usually in the form of bursts or trains of radio signals such as those received by the Russians at Gorky.

Yet, if this is the case, why are the Russians receiving these signals when the satellite transmits only over the United States? It's most unlikely that it's some transmission or ionospheric phenomenon because the bulk of the earth would shield the Soviet Union from receiving at the reported frequencies when the satellite is over the United States. It's also unlikely that one of these satellites has gone out of control.

CONDON: No, our military satellites are programmed to self-destruct in such cases.

STAFFORD: Yes. And then, again, it's also highly unlikely that such experienced radio astronomers as those at Gorky would not be able to differentiate signals from an American satellite.

REED: The Russians have carried out a substantial number of experiments to try to separate space signals from atmospherics and noises of a technical origin.

STAFFORD: Now, we know for a fact they started organizing groups of researchers in 1970. They started on the fifty-centimeter wavelength, and further measurements were made at wavelengths of thirty, sixteen, eight, and three centimeters. Simultaneous experiments have been carried out, at different periods of time, for twenty-four hours a day.

REED: And we know that they have picked up all sorts of questionable phenomena.

STAFFORD: Now, we have leads indicating that these signals were heard on all the wavelengths the Russians sampled. We assumed for a while that any initial "call sign" from an alien intelligence would be a powerful one transmitted on a very broad wave band so that it could be easily detected. It would interfere with all global radio traffic on various wavelengths and be just about impossible to tune out. But by doing this, it would be immediately revealing its whereabouts. Which brings us to the signals received on the narrow bandwidths. This, of course, would fit in completely with the findings recorded—the numerous signals received by Macdavitt and the other scientists on Project Ozymandias—of signals received on the narrow bandwidths. Now, from the studies we've conducted, we believe this alien intelligence might be wary of revealing its exact whereabouts and might prefer to remain undetected until it had studied us more closely and was more certain of our reactions. And a solution would be for them to transmit signals on the narrow bandwidths, which could not be that easily detected.

Still, wherever the Russian signals are coming from, the fact remains this is precisely the sort of signal an extraterrestrial civilization would be expected to use as its call sign.

REED: And the Russians, of course, have chosen to remain silent about these mysterious signals. We still haven't been able to establish the motives behind this secrecy. For all we know, they could be receiving new evidence all the time. Evidence they've systematically been keeping hidden.

And then if such a situation were ever to develop, and the Russians were the first to establish contact with these extraterrestrials, where would we be? Where would we stand? We certainly cannot expect the Russians to look out for our interests. Now, surely you must be able to see, given these circumstances, how vital it is for us to be able to progress beyond the Russians. And the element of time enters into this. We have no way of knowing just how much—or how little—time we have.

STAFFORD: Yes, it's not as if we can formulate an exact timetable to indicate when this contact might occur. After all, who's to say it hasn't already . . . or isn't about to? We readily admit we're not really at the stage where we could definitely recognize such an occurrence. Under these circumstances, it's quite feasible that an alien probe has been orbiting our planet for all these years, programmed to begin communications with us only when our technology is sufficiently advanced. And by the same token, it's probably been reconnoitering data on us and our level of technology by monitoring such clues as stray radio and television signals, the detonation of nuclear devices, the amount of energy we use. And as we have said on so many different occasion, the evidence presented by the Project Ozymandias team simply cannot be dismissed—despite all the odds. And then, of course, we have the matter of the artifacts, which we still cannot say are anything but authentic.

Now, as we in this room are all aware, the Russians are preparing to mobilize the largest optical radio telescope in the world for their imminent investigations—a gigantic 236-inch reflector to go alongside a 1,889-foot radio telescope. And whatever's out there should be, eventually, more easily detectable.

CONDON: If it is out there.

SAFFORD: It simply isn't something we can just dismiss, at this stage of the game.

REED: Well, I think that pretty much covers the groundwork.

To Security 5A200 Washington. 24 September. 1900.
Richardson approached again. His position confirmed. We suggest immediate security measures. His knowledge could only be detrimental to us.

Nick went into the bedroom. Michelle was leaning over her dressing table. She stared at him, startled. A frozen expression. She was holding a pair of his shoes. "What are you doing?" he asked. He was more than mildly curious. He was puzzled. She smiled weakly. For some reason, he thought—he didn't really know why—she looked as if she were going to be sick. Her smile was that weak; and she looked pale inasmuch as she could look pale with her deep tan. So that her pallor was more of an impression than anything else.

"I was looking to see what had to be fixed. I'm taking the children's shoes, so I figured I might as well take yours, too." She smiled again. That same kind of smile.

Nick didn't say anything. He was aware of her reflection in the mirror above the dressing table and in the mirror on the open closet door; the dim reflection of the room, his own reflection standing there in the doorway; the reflection of the trees in the windows outside in the dusk. He felt, probably because of the quality of the light, he thought, as if he were in an aquarium. Everything seemed so slow, languorous. Remote. There wasn't a sound. It was as if the room were soundproof. Some leaves brushed against a window. Michelle smiled again, this time more animatedly. She put the shoe down on the chair in front of the dressing table, next to the other shoe. She came toward him, put her arms around him. "How come you're home so early? I thought you said you were going back to the Foundation after Richardson."

Nick inhaled the scent of her hair, of her skin, of sunlight, salt water: the warm heady odors of summer. He pressed her more tightly against him. She was breathing softly down his neck, blowing warm air inside his open shirt collar. He moved back, locked the door, took off his shoes, his shirt, his pants.

Michelle waited until he went to the curtains. She had something in her hand, which she slipped into the back of the open drawer of the dressing table, under some lipstick tubes. She closed the drawer. Nick was turned the other way. He was drawing the curtains. She went over to the bed and lay down. She held out her arms.

Security 5A200 Washington. 24 September. 2215.

Schrader has told Worthington he is going down to Los Angeles for conference. Sturgis has told wife he is also going down to L.A. At least the story is consistent.

Meanwhile, please equip Sturgis boat. We suggest this as the best measure, as we do not wish to involve anyone else. Sturgis goes out in the boat regularly, every Saturday, by himself.

Security 5A200 Washington. 24 September. 2300.

Richardson's position will be nullified at the first opportunity presented.

Report to Security 5A200 Washington. 25 September. 0900.

Schrader has flown down from Sonora Pines (7:10 flight); Sturgis up from San Diego (6:40 flight). They met in terminal (7:46). Rented tan Ford sedan at Hertz desk. Left L.A. airport 8:10. Drove out bypassing city. Conference? To Pasadena Freeway. Onto 10 east. Heading east.

Tom drove the first three hundred miles, Nick the last. They stopped off for something to eat twice (once at a Denny's, the other time at a roadside joint) and for gas. It was hot in the desert; and the air conditioning wasn't working. But they didn't want to overheat the engine anyway; they kept all the windows open, but there still wasn't much of a breeze. They had the radio on. They could get only the local stations. Country and Western. There were hardly any cars on the road. Once, they thought they were being followed. But they were mistaken.

They reached Casa Grande shortly after lunch, crossed over the border in the late afternoon. Around Lordsburg, just outside the city limits, they noticed an army helicopter flying above them. It circled once, twice, and then turned back, in another direction, away from the city.

Synopsis of surveillance logs. 25 September. 1740.
On 10 east. Maintaining speed limit. Keeping within visibility. Outside Lordsburg we intercepted in army chopper.

They reached Gardner in the early dusk and checked into a motel. But they were both too nervous to stay in the motel room or to go sit somewhere and eat dinner. They got back into the car and drove around—away from Gardner, toward the Peregrinos de Pesar Mountains.

Synopsis of surveillance logs. 25 September. 2040.
Schrader and Sturgis arrived Gardner 1823. Checked into small motel off road outside of town (Elk Horn Motel). But did not stay in motel. Driving around area for the last hour and a half. Presently toward mountains.

They drove around in the desert for nearly two hours, stopping every once in a while at the side of the road, with the radio on, waiting. They didn't say much of anything, and except for the raw current of nervousness between them, Nick felt they might as well have been robots propped up, sitting rigidly in a car at night, with the lights off, parked in the middle of nowhere, in the desert. Tom lit cigarette after cigarette, crushing them out before they were even half finished. Nick, at the wheel, kept his eyes on the dark landscape. The roster of diagrams and lines going through his head like a broken record. The desert was quiet. The heat and the glare had long since evaporated and been transformed into cold night wind. The cold wind, in almost visible forms, swept across the night, evacuating and sending on the run stretches of sand, tumbleweed, loose plants—whatever was in its way; plucking the ghostly notes of the telephone-pole wires. No other car, no one went by. It was a clear night. The barely open eyelid of the new moon oozing out a soft metallic glow on the devastated landscape, the arroyos, the mesquites; herds of marble clouds fleeing across the limestone sky.

At eleevn they pulled off the main highway. Five miles down a dirt road. Rancho Mirage, the abandoned mining town. At the railroad station they veered left. Three miles south-southwest. At the foot of the Peregrinos de Pesar Mountains. A quarter of a mile in the direction of the Rio Muerto, a dried-up, wrinkled stream of sand. Half a mile. The Arroyo del Oro. Left. Along another dirt road. A sign. Cristobal Pass. It was eleven-thirty. They got out of the car, took out the knapsack of equipment they had brought with them—screwdrivers, hammer, work gloves, surgical gloves, two drills, flashlights, dozens of packs of film, flashbulbs wrapped in two towels. Each kept a Minox in his pants pocket. Each put on another sweater. They locked the car and headed down the badly paved road at the edge of the desert, taking their time. Three miles. The road was empty, but still they kept to the side, walking in the sand.

A pickup with two drunks passed them, flashing their brights on them. The pickup lurched across the road, slowed down. A Country and Western song was blasting on the radio. The driver yelled out to them, asking them if they wanted a ride, and without waiting for an answer, switched on his brights again; and then both men started whistling, hooting, making catcalls and yelping with laughter, calling out incoherently as they raced off, zigzagging down across the road, the tires screeching in the distance.

They reached the base. It was ten to one. They dragged

themselves under the barbed wire and, staying down, bent over, scuttling from cactus to cactus, they made their way across the unlit gray quarter of a mile to the main compound. They crouched in the shadows across from the main compound. They waited. They waited for two o'clock. The beam of light from the watchtower drifted over them, at painfully slow intervals. A trail of sickly anemic dust lighting up and highlighting the grim landscape of sand. The night was almost soundless—only the occasional twitch or slithering of some animal across the sand, or the otherworldly call of some strange bird, or the low howling echo of some wild dog slitting the silence. But it was all more a part of a distant background. Nick was aware only of the steady vibration of his heart. Pounding out its rhythm in his ear. He had the image of his heart, of his body, as a thin, translucent membrane, almost shining in the dark. Of his body as a hollow socket gorged with blood, of his whole body as a target of skin riddled with bullets. Sweat spread down his back. It was winter now, the heart of the night, as if an invisible sheen of ice had permeated the desert.

Hypnotized by the illuminated dials of their watches, they waited. A group of soldiers with M-16 rifles went by, marching in time. At the exact second, Tom nodded, leaped up, and raced, skidding across the sand, coming to a stop inches away from the barbed wire; he swooped down onto the flagpole. He fumbled around, his hands, in awkward work gloves, digging at the hard clumps of parched weeds, the rough stone-crusted sand under the pole. He struck something hard, some rocks. The alarm. Holding the screwdriver with both hands, his hands shaking, he unscrewed the alarm, disconnected the wires.

Nick, with the knapsack under his arm, scuttled after him under the barbed wire. Cowering, two deformed shapes, they sped across the hundred yards to the main building, into the side entrance. They flung the door open, shut, fled soundlessly, in their rubber-soled shoes, down the hall: empty, jarringly lit; the eerie, alienating gloss of waxed linoleum under the fluorescent lights. No one. The men's room. The storage room. They pounced in. Into the dark storage room, heaving, out of breath.

In the dark. Crouched, rigid against a wall. They waited

in there in the dark for the next guard shift. Four o'clock. Surrounded by strange shapes. Nick thought they could have been in a room full of people and never known it. A strange cold, unfamiliar odor. Unidentifiable. In this unknown darkness. Their breathing finally subsided, and with it the chill of the last few hours. The storage room, though unheated, seemed warm after the night outside in the desert. Their eyes monitored—their whole existence was monitored by—the luminous dials of their watches, which seemed to have almost stopped. As if time had slowed down. And here they were, trapped in here, in this storage room, which reeked. Nick now identified the smell as that of some sort of plastic. They could hear the guards at intervals, passing back and forth, up and down. Just outside the door . . . a few feet away.

Five to four. They listened to the sounds of the steps of the guards, diminishing. They opened the door slowly. Empty. They made their way down the stairs, to the file rooms. The place was empty, not a sound. All the lights were on. It might as well have just been evacuated. The door marked 310, down another hallway, a row of offices. The main file room—empty cubicles of file cabinets. A library of file cabinets. The door: 10. They went in. In the dark. Nick put down the knapsack and, groping in the dark, took out a flashlight. He made an arc with the flashlight: They were surrounded by file cabinets. Tom took out the other flashlight and ran it along the walls. Again, more slowly. Until he came to the fuse box. Nick held the flashlight. Tom took out another, smaller screwdriver from the knapsack and started unscrewing the fuse box. He disconnected the wires: The alarm was deactivated. Nick was aware of his heart racing again as he stared at the blank label slots on the file cabinets. He frowned, made a face, pointed to them. Tom shrugged. He pulled out one of the drills, fitted a muffler on it, and started drilling one of the locks. Nick kept the flashlight on the lock. A flurry of bright yellow sparks ignited the dark, soundlessly. The lock snapped, dropped to the floor. Tom pulled out a drawer. It was empty. Another. Empty. He tried all five drawers. Empty. He motioned to Nick to put the flashlight on another lock. He used the drill again. The lock snapped . . . he pulled open a drawer. Empty. Another drawer. All

the drawers were empty. They tried another file. Tom used
the drill. The drawers were empty. Another file. The drill.
The lock. Empty. Another file, empty. Another, the same
thing. They pulled open another drawer, all the drawers,
empty. All the files were empty. All the drawers. Ten file
cabinets. Empty.

Synopsis of surveillance logs. 26 September. 0750.

From a phone booth on road outside of Gardner, Sturgis
called Dr. Ruz at Pacific Palisades home. Informed Ruz
about files. Ruz told Sturgis to phone him back at the
university in the afternoon.

From R. Castle to Security 5A200 Washington. 26 September. 0900.

Try to clear up this matter for me regarding Schrader
and Sturgis break-in at Gray Sands. It's baffling. I just can't
figure it out. How could the files have been removed like
that? If they were removed. But no one seems to know
anything. They couldn't have just disappeared. If it was
one of our branches, why weren't we told?

The only conclusion is that, once more, we were not
told. We proceeded according to plan. We coordinated and
carried out this operation for no purpose. Why were we
not even informed of the latest development until after it
was all over?

To R. Castle from Security 5A200 Washington. 26 September. 1230.

The memo you sent out to headquarters has come to our
attention. We will try to answer it as best we can to help
you understand the situation.

The files were removed at the last moment, as it was
deemed advisable. We had strong evidence that the Russians were going to try either to intercept Schrader and
Sturgis or to enter Gray Sands with them in the confusion.

Also, as an added factor, at the last hour it was discovered there were some highly sensitive documents among
the files, whose existence we had not previously been aware
of, and therefore the division decided, as a precautionary
measure, it would be best not to have Schrader exposed to

such documents, which might be potentially damaging to the division.

We had no alternative but to let those involved proceed according to plan because of the grave security risk involved.

Security 5A200 Washington. 26 September. 1400.

Perhaps now Schrader will finally assess the situation. The removal of the files should clarify our position. He should have perceived by now that we are anticipating every game plan of his, that he will be intercepted in every move. In any case, regardless of whether he has acknowledged his position or not, we are confident he will soon enough.

Synopsis of surveillance logs. 26 September. 1500.

From a phone booth in a Chevron station outside Indio, Sturgis called Dr. Ruz at UCLA. Ruz told Sturgis that his source had told him that he could only surmise files must have been recently removed—as they had been there only last week—that he, source, would find out where so that, quote, they could assay again, end quote. Ruz to contact source for further info and will contact Sturgis in P.M. Saturday. (This same source is the one we set up for Macdavitt.)

Security 5A200 Washington. 27 September. 1100.

Ruz's removal has been considered; though we are not underestimating the embarrassment his position could cause for us, his usefulness still in question. And his being a continual link in the research aspects of this matter is still necessary to us, for the time being. Suggest therefore suspend such action until further developments.

To Security 5A200 Washington. 27 September. 2000.

Sturgis is taking his boat out tomorrow. (He usually leaves his house before nine, drops his wife off at the university library on the way.) To insure proper results, we will disconnect ship-to-shore radio, remove life jackets and buoys and fire extinguisher. A small bomb will be detonated by remote control at said specified time. The results will be immediate. Using a Coast Guard vessel and

Coast Guard uniforms, we will effect rescue. We will wait, however, keeping close watch through binoculars, until the results are confirmed.

Michelle closed her eyes.

"What's the matter?" Nick asked. "What is it?"

But she couldn't answer. She thought she was going to be sick.

"What is it?"

She thought, My God, what are they going to do to him? I've got to . . . She didn't finish. She didn't want to voice what she felt, even to herself. As if, if she didn't, she could ward it off; it wouldn't take place. I should have known. She stared at the sunlight, through the trees at the window, on the wall, across the table. The backdrop for this scene, this life she was trapped in. I should have known. Tears came into her eyes. How could I have thought . . .

"What?"

Wordlessly, she passed him the newspaper. His eyes raced across the page, there, at the bottom of the page. He read: "DR. HAROLD RICHARDSON DIES IN CAR CRASH. Late last night Dr. Harold Richardson's car overturned at the Westview exit of 101. Dr. Richardson appears to have been driving while inebriated, according to preliminary autopsy reports. . . ."

Tina decided to make a few more egg-salad sandwiches. Tom, in his shorts, was piling the towels, the beach bag, buoys, scuba equipment, fishing poles into the back of the station wagon. The two boys in their swimming trunks were running around the front lawn, in and out of the hedges, across the driveway, into the garage.

Tina finished packing the picnic basket, went out into the driveway, and put it in the car. She went back into the house, went upstairs to check on the baby again: She was still sleeping. The sitter, her UCSD sweat shirt over her bikini, was on the phone in the living room. She waved good-bye to Tina and, with her hand over the mouthpiece, whispered, "I'm going to give her her bottle as soon as she wakes up."

Tina waved back and, smiling, said they'd be home, at

the latest, by six. Tom was already at the wheel, the two boys bouncing around in the back. She got in. It wasn't even eight yet. There wasn't much traffic. Saturday morning, the freeway was quiet. She touched his arm. "I think it was a good idea to go out like this—spend the day on the boat. It's been a long time." Tom didn't say anything. She asked him if anything was the matter. He said there wasn't. He had on his sunglasses, so she couldn't tell at first that he kept looking—much more than was necessary, considering there were hardly any other cars—into the rearview mirror. Finally she looked back herself. Nothing. There was only a blue car behind them, but it was way back. A Ford or a Chevrolet. It was too far away to tell. Tom switched on the radio: "The former President is still in seclusion at San Clemente." He switched it off. Tina noticed that he still kept looking in the mirror. The boys were pretending to punch each other. Tom yelled back at them that he was driving. They stopped. Tina turned around, smiling at them. The blue car was still there. Tom pulled off the freeway at the Harbor Drive exit. Tina looked again: The car was still there. Down into the Shelter Island marina, into the parking lot; the blue car—a Ford —was following them. Tom parked. Oh, I must be imagining this, she thought. They're probably just going to the marina also. She looked back, the car wasn't even there. She almost smiled to herself. She'd been imagining this one.

They got out. Tina took some of the towels, the beach bag. Each of the boys insisted on carrying his own towel and buoy. Tom was loaded down with the scuba equipment, the fishing poles, and the picnic basket. They started down toward the marina. She caught Tom's eye or, rather, the direction of his eye: the blue Ford. It was there— across the way in the parking lot. Two men got out. Tom kept walking. There was no expression on his face. They went down the steps, down to the pier. Tina saw that one of the men was following them. She had to say something. What was this game, anyway? How could he pretend he hadn't noticed? This was just what they'd been talking about—what she'd told him about. "Who is that?" she asked. "Keep walking," he said. He pushed her on lightly with the hand that was gripping the fishing poles. They

stopped at the gate. Tom got out the key. They went in.
One of the boys turned around. "Why is that man wearing
a suit if he's going to go out in a boat?" He pointed to the
man who was following them. He wasn't given an answer.
Tom told him to hurry up.

"What are we going to do?" Tina asked. "What does he
want?"

"Just keep walking." They went down the stone stairs
onto the narrow dock in single file, the boys leading the
procession. Most of the boats were not yet occupied. It was
still too early. Tom got onto the boat first. Tina handed
him the things, and then she got on with the boys, who insisted on jumping over by themselves, without being helped.

The man was standing on the other side of the wire gate
watching them. There was no one else in sight. No one
else he could have been watching. One of the boys said,
"Why is that man watching us, Mommy?" He pointed.
Tina pushed his hand down. She looked at Tom.

"I know," he said. "C'mon, let's get out of here." He unwound the ropes, started the motor, and pulled out, past the
congestion of docked boats, and glided out into the placid
open water, into the brilliant sunlit morning. The weather
forecast had been for the low eighties, winds five to ten
miles an hour.

Nick saw it in the papers two days later:

PROMINENT SCIENTIST AND FAMILY
DROWN IN SAN DIEGO

Dr. Thomas A. Sturgis, 36, of the Watkins Research
Laboratory, and his wife, Christina, 30, and two small
sons drowned here Saturday morning off the bay as
their boat apparently caught fire. It is suspected that a
leak in the fuel tanks caused the fire, which must have
then rapidly spread to the rest of the boat before they
had a chance to extinguish it. A Coast Guard vessel
rushed to the site. One of the Coast Guards described
it as follows: "We spotted this blazing about two miles
out. Suspecting fire, we rushed to the scene. But by the
time we got there, there was no sign of either Dr.
Sturgis or Mrs. Sturgis or their two small sons. We

can only speculate they must have been badly burned and could not manage to stay afloat. The bodies recovered early this morning were severely charred." Dr. Sturgis had been associated with the space program. . . . Their youngest child, a six-month-old baby girl, had been left at home with a sitter. . . . Before joining the Watkins Laboratory three years ago, Dr. Sturgis had been with NASA. . . .

Security 5A200 Washington. 30 September. 1500.
Schrader has arranged to meet with Osmond at 1730 this afternoon. Contact Osmond before this and reiterate consequences should he try to re-ally himself, in even the most minimal way, with Schrader.

Schrader seems to be proving more intractable than we had assessed. Our game plan should be revised for a more direct confrontation. The question of his security, however, remains of first importance. Therefore, perhaps the Russian intervention in this matter has not been overtly enough discouraged. Inform Tchernilkov to relay to the Russians that Schrader's lead did not confirm. This will leave the course free for us to deal with him in a more direct way.

Johanna, in the bottom half of her dark green bikini and a yellow T-shirt, was seated on the floor of her old room. She was surrounded by her toys. There was T. Bear, there was Rags—an appropriate name for a more than raggedy doll—there was T. Bear Jr.—a polar bear—there was Cola, the koala; Leo Lion; the doll that cried—she only cried, so she had no name: She didn't deserve one. Johanna liked to change her clothes, but that was all. She brought her along only because she felt sorry for her. They were all having lunch. But Johanna was bored. Bored. She rolled her favorite truck, a red fire engine that made lots of noise, back and forth, back and forth across the parquet. Something she'd been told not to do. The truck screeched. But no one said anything, so she stopped. Where were they, anyway?

She moved over to some toy cars. She lined them up. There was going to be a race. She made some sounds: This was the motor; she sent a few cars across the room. Then she jumped up. Where was he, anyway? She looked out the window, looked down at the water, at the beach. He had told her to stay in the house, not to go out. He was going to have to go back to his office, but he'd be back in time to take a swim with her before dinner. He had to go back to his office to talk to someone there. He'd be back in a little while. Michelle had gone out to the university. She had to get some books from the library. Heather and Peter had gone with her. But Johanna hadn't wanted to go. She knew what that meant: sitting in the car while Michelle disappeared. She always said she'd be back in a few minutes. And they'd wait and wait; and they weren't allowed out of the car. No, she'd rather stay here, by herself. All right, she could do that. He said you can stay here if you don't go out. You promise? She nodded. Look at me. She said yes, she wouldn't. Wouldn't what? Go out. He said he'd be back in a little while. . . .

She went into his room. Sometimes—when they didn't sleep at Michelle's (which seemed to be all the time now) —she could sleep with him in his bed. She went over to the night table. She studied the clock. It was twenty after five or twenty of . . . She studied it some more—where the hands pointed—but it didn't become any clearer, just more confusing. She went into the guest bedroom, turned on the TV. This was strange color. She tried to fix the dials but only made it worse. She walked away, leaving the TV on. She went into the kitchen. The buns for the hot dogs and hamburgers were on the counter. They were going to have a barbecue dinner on the beach. She opened the refrigerator. She studied the shelves. But she didn't really know what she wanted; she didn't see anything there. She went into the living room, went out onto the sun deck. She stood on her toes, her hands pressing the rail, her chin resting down on her hands. Why couldn't she go outside? She could say she forgot. She ran back into her room, grabbed T. Bear, T. Bear Jr., and Cola, and ran down to the beach.

She sat the animals on the sand facing her. This was much better. Then she ran back into the house, brought out her toy set of plates, cups, and a small pot. She set them up. This was going to be a tea party. She ran down to the water, filled the pot—quickly running away before the surf got to her. She poured tea. First T. Bear . . . She filled each cup. Then her own. This was much better! But there were no cakes. She scooped up some sand onto a plate and served everybody a slice. She asked T. Bear how he liked the party. Wasn't this much better? T. Bear grunted. It sure was. Then T. Bear Jr. They had an animated conversation.

She blushed. It was that man next door in his torn cutoff jeans. He was smiling. He leaned down. He asked if he could join her. She blushed again. She wasn't supposed to talk to strangers, but she'd seen Michelle talking to him, and he lived next door, so he wasn't really a stranger. But she didn't answer. Then he said, "I see you're having a tea party. May I join you?" She nodded. He served himself a cup of tea, a slice of cake. Then she served him. He asked about T. Bear. She introduced them. They all had a conversation. They played with the Frisbee, then with the beach ball. Then he asked if she'd like to run with him. They ran, and she always won; then they had the game with the surf, in and out, playing tag with the surf; then she got her buoy and the inflated raft, and they were going to take a trip, down to where those rocks were. They were going to sail down that way, past the pirates who were all along the shore, watching them, hidden behind the deck chairs. She splashed him, kicking her feet, he splashed back. She splashed his face, he pretended he couldn't see, he was hurt. She was laughing. "This is fun, isn't it?" he asked. She nodded, grinning. Why hadn't they played with him before? She put on her buoy, he held on to the raft, and they waited to set sail—until they were sure the pirates weren't watching. Now. He gave the signal. They crept out into the water with the raft and set sail.

Nick pulled into the driveway. Shit! Michelle had said she'd be back in half an hour. She's been alone all this time. I should have known better. Half an hour! Why did I let her stay by herself? She should have gone with Michelle, or the kids should have all stayed here. He let himself in the house. At least the front door was locked. "Johanna!" he called out in a singsong. "Jo-Jo?" The TV was blaring. He went into the guest room. She wasn't there. He'd told her how many times not to leave the TV on if she wasn't watching it. He switched it off. "Jo-Jo? Where are you? Are you hiding again? Give me a hint? Are you in the bathroom? In the closet? I'm coming . . . closer." He went into her bedroom. Not there. Her toys on the floor. He opened her closet, pushed back the clothes wrapped in the cleaner's plastic bags (her "winter" clothes —mostly sweaters—Carole hadn't picked up yet), looked behind them, behind a number of boxes—Saks, Bloomingdale's, I. Magnin; knocking them down. He went into her bathroom, looked behind the shower curtain. He went into his bedroom. Opened the two closets, looked into his bathroom. "Johanna! Where are you? C'mon!" He went back out into the living room, got down on his hands and knees to look under the dining table, under the cocktail table. "Jo-Jo? Jo-Jo?" He got back up. Stood still for a moment to see if he could hear anything. "Jo-Jo?" He listened. Not a giggle, not a sound. Hmm. Strange. "Jo-Jo?" He looked at the open sliding door. He ran out, ran down the stairs, ran down to the beach.

He almost reeled. He couldn't believe what he was seeing. She was lying there. That kid was on top of her, giving her mouth-to-mouth resuscitation. "What the hell are you . . ." Nick pounced on him.

"I swear! I swear . . . I didn't! I didn't do it! She . . . she . . . the phone rang . . I was only gone a few minutes . . I was playing with her . . . I went to answer the phone." He gestured toward the Walkers' house. "Not even five minutes. She . . . she . . ." The kid was incoherent, on his knees, rocking back and forth.

Nick hovered over her, gingerly holding her, pressing down with his two hands on her small, delicate chest, his mouth glued to hers, trying to force it open more, trying to breathe into her, trying to breathe air back into her, trying to breathe life back into her. His whole body was trembling, shaking, limbs jerking out in reflex. He was shaking so much he was almost in convulsions. Every few seconds, another fit. He was pumping so hard, breathing out, he had no more breath, as if he could breathe out his life into hers. His whole body was palsied, out of control, only his mouth, his hands, were steady, fixed, attached like vises, gripping her mouth, her chest. He kept breathing, pressing, harder and harder, more and more. . . .

To Security 5A200 Washington. 30 September. 1900.
We've had some trouble we didn't anticipate. Hawkins was playing with Schrader's four-year-old daughter on the beach outside Schrader's house. We phoned Hawkins at the Walker house, as we had arranged beforehand, at 1730. Hawkins left the child alone on the beach, with her buoy, at the edge of the water, and ran for the phone. He maintains the windows of the Walker house were open, and that was how he was able to hear the phone. When he came back out, ten minutes later, the child was nowhere in sight. As he came closer he saw her in the water. The child must have lost her buoy and, not knowing how to swim, started to go under. Hawkins ran in for her, pulled her ashore, gave her mouth-to-mouth resuscitation. At this stage Schrader returned (from his meeting with Osmond) and walked in on the previously mentioned scene.

The child was rushed to the hospital, where she is now.

This was a most unfortunate incident, which points only to Hawkins's general carelessness.

Seated on a bench in the hospital hall, outside the room, Mike had his arm around Carole, who was sobbing into his chest. Nick stood in the doorway. Johanna lay dwarfed in the huge bed under the huge oxygen tent. Nurses, orderlies were running around, rolling more equipment in. Two doctors were inside the tent with her, pounding down on her tiny body. Nick turned away. Carole now had her eyes closed and was crying soundlessly. Her head was up, but barely, tears running out from her closed eyes, down her face; then she let her head go down again, against Mike's chest, and his arm tightened around her, to support her. The kid was wandering up and down the hall in a daze, barefoot, in his torn cutoff jeans. Michelle was standing at the other end of the hall. One of the doctors came out. He looked at Nick, a grim expression, and shook his head. Carole, as if by instinct, was calm now and was watching as if from the center of this great calm, at the heart of the storm. "I'm sorry," the young doctor whispered almost inaudibly.

But Carole read his lips instantaneously. She let out a shriek. Michelle ran toward Nick, who remained in the doorway, motionless. For a moment. She put out her arms, he pushed her away, pushed her out of his way, pushed her out of the doorway and went out, down the hall, toward the stairs. Down the stairs and out, into the driveway, into the night.

Part III

INTO THE DESERT

He drove all night. It was almost dawn when he reached Las Vegas. The White Ford still there behind him, the only other car on the road in the last laps—15, a carpet unrolled—across the desert. The yellow headlights smearing in the pale tints of otherworldly dawn. The flat monotony stretching to infinity—tan rubble, gigantic cacti, monolithic sandstones, across the lunar landscape of the desert. Past Hoover Dam, the road became a belt procession, cars coming out of nowhere, like rockets zeroing in toward the colony of lights below, a station in outer space. And the white Ford still there, never losing sight of him. Out of the desert, the mirage of Las Vegas, another set of props, one-dimensional buildings cropping up. The avenues of neons, casinos, driveways filled with cars, limousines. Suntanned call girls in bead dresses stalking along, swinging their bead evening bags. Men in blue tuxedos with their wives in long evening gowns and corsages. Slicks, hicks, kids, liveried doormen, a group of performers in eighteenth-century costumes, white wigs, gold lamé clothes flashing . . . all the assorted types of insomniacs, tourists of the night.

He drove down the Strip. Past the hotels, the twenty-four-hour wedding chapels, the massage parlors, the clubs. Toward some construction sites—what had been all only desert until recently. He drove down to the end of the Strip: 6:10. 82°. The white Ford behind him. To the end of the Strip and the desert once again.

He drove on, drove to Flagstaff, drove around. Down to Phoenix and back up to Show Low, to Snowflake, Holbrook, Sanders, across the border to Gallup, Albuquerque, Santa Fe, back down to Stanley, Encino, and back to Albuquerque. Another night. He pulled in at a seedy motel off the road. Dream Pines. He slept for a few hours, and at the first sign of light was up. The white Ford was parked across the highway outside the Drifter's Paradise Motel. It was cold. He walked across the highway, to an all-night diner. Steamy, filled with truckers. He had a big breakfast. He wiped a space in the foggy pane so he could see the train go by. He counted the cars. Twelve. The Santa Fe, the Southern Pacific, the Western . . .

He got back into the car. Ten of seven. He was on the road again, and he drove, kept driving, drove all around again, up the state to the border and back down to Roswell, just kept driving. The white Ford was there all the time. Late afternoon. He drove up and down the main street of Roswell, pulled in at a rent-a-car. A kid sent him into the back, into the office. Big fat guy. Half Indian, in shirt sleeves, sucking a cigar. Yeah, there was one. The guy looked at him strangely. What was it for? He explained he wanted to go into the desert. He showed his camera. To photograph. He showed his credit cards. A hundred-dollar deposit. Yeah, credit card would be OK. The guy made him sign a number of sheets. He said he'd be back by nightfall. He wanted to photograph the desert at dusk. Would they be open then? Yeah. He looked at Nick strangely again—his beady eyes receding between the slits of fat lids. He pointed to the sign on the wall: OPEN ALL DAY & ALL NIGHT. He got his overnight bag out of his car, left his car in the back, in the yard of the rent-a-car place. He climbed into the Rover, threw his bag on the floor next to him. He pulled into a gas station, had the Rover filled up, had the spare tank filled. The white Ford waited, discreetly, across the street. He drove out of town, the white Ford following.

He drove down to Hagerman. It was dusk now. He pulled off the road, went a quarter of a mile into the desert, across the sand. He watched the white Ford, left behind on the road, diminishing in the rearview mirror. He stopped, took out his bag, pulled out a sweater, tied the arms around his neck. Took off his shoes. He looked at the left one. He hadn't noticed that before. What . . . Those were new heels. The ones Michelle had had put on. He looked at the left heel; there was something different about that one. It looked wider than the right. He held the shoe up. He shook it. A strange sound. There was something attached to the heel. He knocked the shoe against the frame of the Rover, kept knocking it until a part of the heel came off. He picked it up—some sort of radio transmitter—studied it a moment, then flung it out, across the sand. He flung the shoes out, too. Filthy bitch, he said to himself. Filthy fucking bitch! An image of Johanna lying in the tent flashed in his mind a moment. Tears started to well up, came into his eyes. No! I'm not going to think about that. . . . He quickly put on the pair of rubber-soled shoes that were in the bag, hurriedly tied the laces.

He started the Rover up again. He didn't want to lose any time, wanted to do at least twenty, thirty miles while the light was still good. He drove on, rocking, bumping, swerving across this obstacle course—the rubble of gravel and sand of the desert, cacti and the weird shapes of stones, parched vegetation, bushes like batches of cracked bones: a graveyard all around him. The wind at his back. The mountains above, on all sides, were beginning to stand out like cutouts, in relief, against the immense runway of light—the sky. It was now the heart of dusk. There wasn't a moment to lose. Light now seemed to come from everywhere. It was as if the sky had opened up. As if the desert were lit up by floodlights. He heard the sound again. He looked back. A motorcycle had appeared out of nowhere. A surrealistic comic strip, he thought. His solitary quest, his communion with the desert, was at stake. He pressed down on the gas. He wanted to get to where he was going—wherever that was—before it was dark. And he wanted to get there alone. He pressed his foot down more, more. Strapped in his seat in the Rover, he felt as if he were in some sort of contraption in some surrealistic nightmare; as if the Rover had been transformed into a rocket. A car with a rocket engine hurtling across the desert at dusk.

And then he saw something in the distance, in line with

the solid shadow cutouts of the mountains, above him. Some sort of cloud, against the pale cloudless sky. Pulsating with light. Something that shouldn't have been there. Light swarming from it, spreading, diffuse, an imprint of light growing in size on the blotter of dusk. He closed his eyes. He could almost still see it. Vibrating at full speed, trapped in this seat, his hands gripping the wheel. His eyes shot open. And it was still there. This cloud of light. Only it wasn't a cloud, wasn't light. He pressed his foot down, down, as if he couldn't press anymore, striking down on the pedal, which struck only the stereophonic monotone of the wind mingled with the din of the motor, to the crazed machine works of his heart racing itself, exploding in his ears, fragments of lights, bursts of blood cells, fireworks, a network of sputtering colors fizzling out, a convulsion of afterimages against the backdrop of the ice-blue scenery. He could almost make it out. Closer. If only he could get closer. Almost. He could almost see it. A disk of light. And then it faded out again. He kept his eyes fixed. Now, he could see. Yes. Oval-shaped. Elliptical. The disk of light magnified in size. It rose slightly. Lifting above the mountains. It came into focus—a reflector, saucer-shaped, with a charge of light emanating from it. The bottom of the object, he recited to himself, appeared somewhat elliptical. With blunt ends. Its altitude . . . between 100 and 150 feet. The structure and light formations on the object could clearly be seen. Ringed with windows . . . through which appeared . . . steady amber-colored lights . . . Pumping down on the pedal, his foot welded to it, wired in his seat, blasting across the landscape. A mirage of hallucinatory shapes and sounds, the blur of animate, pursuing rocks, cacti, the dye of merging colors whirling by. He kept his eyes fixed on the disk of light, electrocuted by the image, which grew in size as he raced toward it.

His body was never found. But several months later, a group of soldiers on training maneuvers in the desert came across a heap of ashes and some torn bits of clothes, a shoe, a rusted section of the frame of a car, a melted piece of nickel that might have been a key, a smashed Omega watch, and, farther on, some parts of a human skeleton, including the teeth. The dental records were traced. But they were not Nicholas Schrader's. They were identified, tentatively, as belonging to Dr. Philip Wells. Apparently there was some difficulty in ascertaining the authenticity of the records.